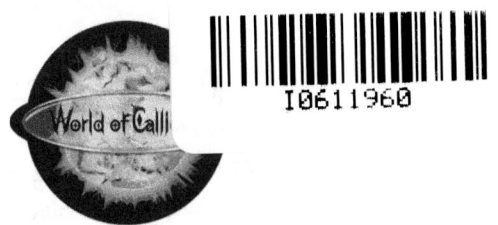

SUMMER OF CROWS

World of Calliome

SUMMER OF CROWS

Hans Cummings

VFF PUBLISHING

Summer of Crows

Hans Cummings

This is a work of fiction. All characters and events portrayed in this book are fictional, and any resemblance to real people or incidents is purely coincidental.

ISBN: 978-1-944999-09-4

Electronic edition available through Amazon.com,

Acknowledgements
For Tink, without whom this would not have been possible.

Special thanks to Bernie Todd, Scott Schwartz, Jeremy Morgan, Sam Halpern, and Craig Majors, and my readers for all their encouragement and feedback.

Edited by Cynthia Shepp
cynthiashepp.wordpress.com/

Cover design by Eric Hubbel
hubbelcreative.deviantart.com/

Cover Art by Nicoleta Georgeta
Stavarache
artstation.com/nicooo

Heraldy by
Axel Löfving

Cartography by Anna B. Meyer
ghmaps.net
and
Brian Patterson
d2omonkey.com

World of Calliome Logo by
Gwyneth Ravenscraft of G-Sharp
Productions
g-sharpproductions.com/

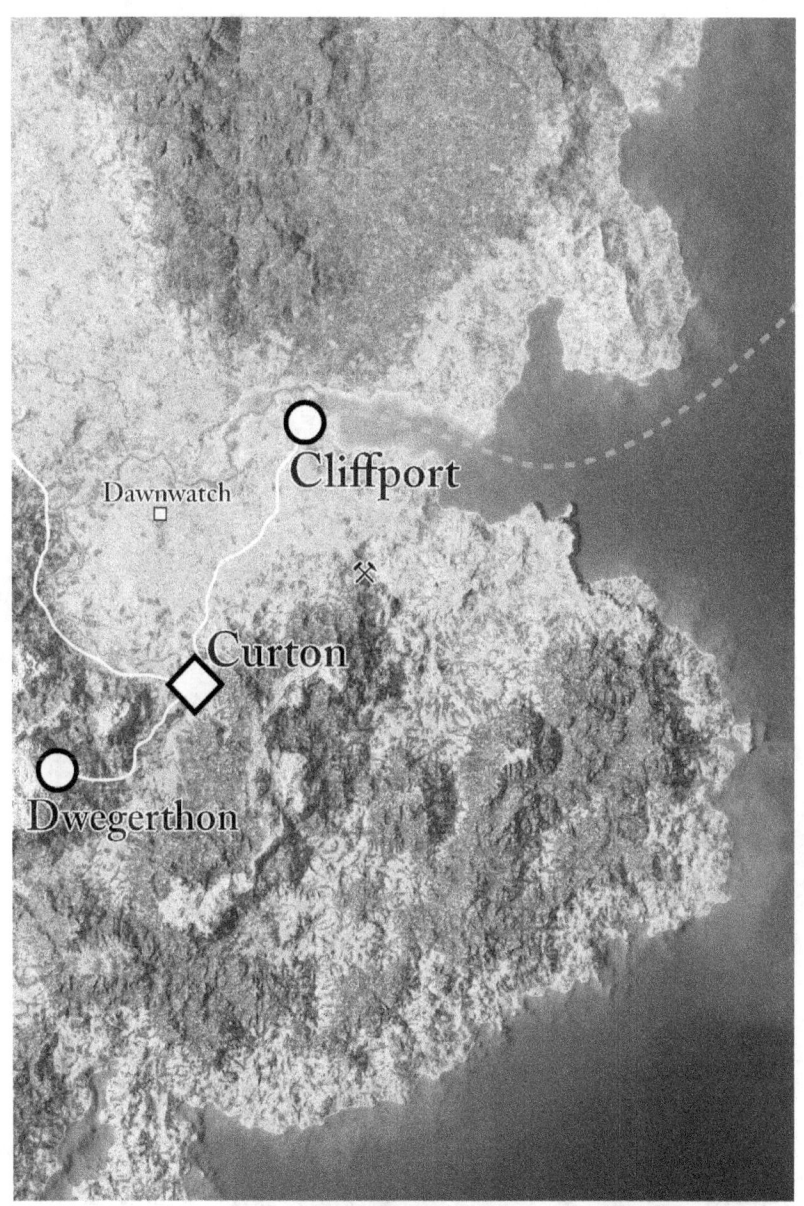

Cliffport

Dawnwatch

Curton

Dwegerthon

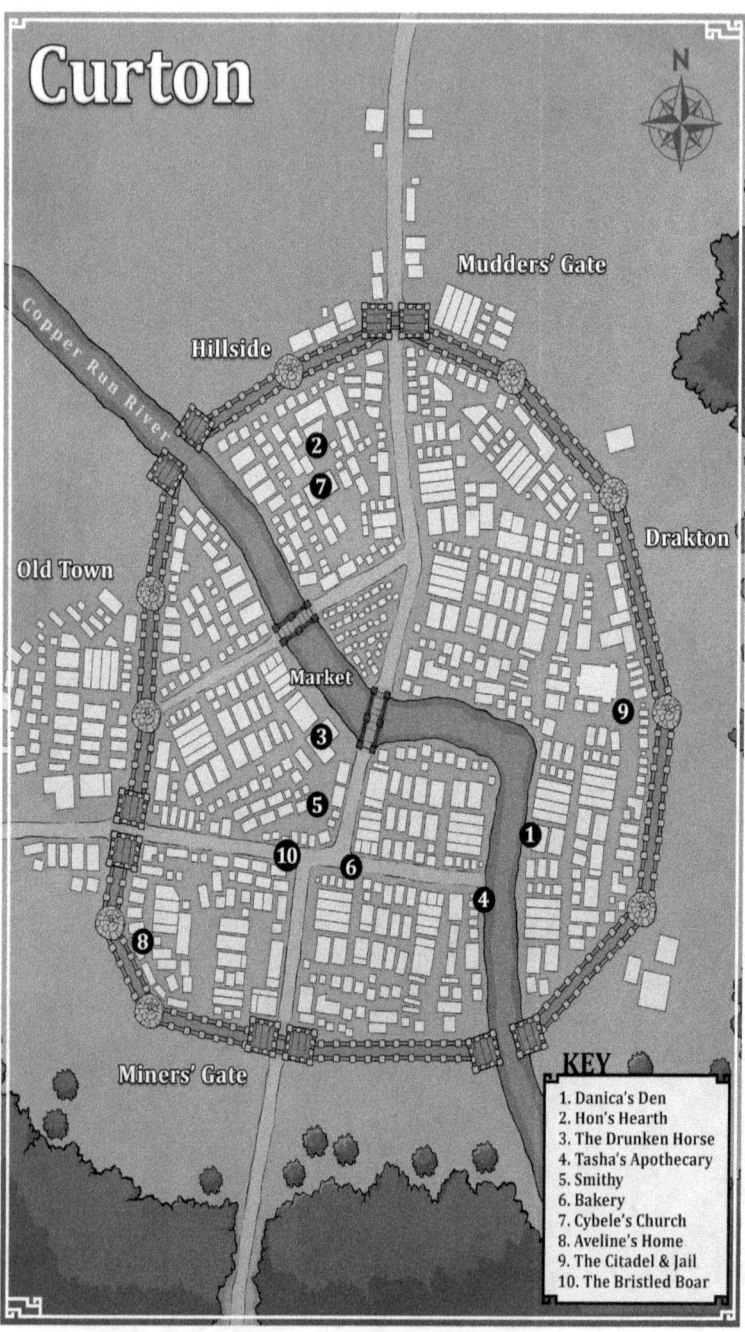

Curton

N

Mudders' Gate

Hillside

Copper Run River

Old Town

Drakton

Market

9

2

7

3

5

10

6

1

4

8

Miners' Gate

Chapter 1

"Look out!" Aveline heard the man's voice moments before she noticed the cart rumbling toward her on the cobblestones of Curton's town square. She leapt to the side as it sped past, witnessing it crash into a vegetable wagon. Spewing from the wreckage in a fountain of food-stuffs, fruits and meats mingled. Aveline groaned as the head of her mace dug into her thigh. *That's going to leave a mark.*

"Terribly sorry, m'lady!" The vendor helped Aveline to her feet. She recognized the one-armed man, but she did not know his name. "The brick I was using as a wheel chock crumbled."

"Time for a new brick." She brushed dirt off her armored skirt, then adjusted her belts.

"I suppose so. Are you hurt?"

"No, I'm fine. See to your goods." Aveline pointed at the tangled mass of destroyed food carts.

The vendor turned away to check on his merchandise. He shooed away scavenging street urchins who already picked at the fruit scattered across the town square. Aveline left him to sort his business on his own. Technically, she could have arrested the children for stealing from the over-turned cart. However, she had no desire to detain hungry orphans for claiming bruised apples and dirt-covered sausages from the street. From her perspective, it was a more grievous crime that so many orphans in town were hungry enough to scavenge for food.

It was a problem best left to those in authority. Knight-Captain Aveline Durant was a keeper of the peace, not the solver of Curton's economic problems. She heard the vendor scolding the children as he attempted to salvage his merchandise, but his admonitions seemed intended toward keeping them out of his path as he righted the cart rather than preventing them from taking the fallen food.

By the time Aveline reached the Temple District, also known as Hillside, the sun shone high in the sky. Its radiance burned away the chilly morning air. Already, she felt uncomfortable in her armor, and the wispy clouds crossing the blazing sun offered no relief from the coming heat. A light breeze carried the aroma of incense.

A shrine to Aurora, goddess of love, proved to be the source of the fragrance, but whoever lit the offering was gone. Aveline approached the shrine, ensuring no open flames persisted before she moved on toward Cybele's church.

Since most of the mines had closed, people turned increasingly to agriculture to sustain them, and, thus, to Cybele. Aveline remembered the church's renovation just over twenty years earlier. Few people claimed to dislike Cybele even before they needed her, but the goddess's message of hope for the future played a big part in the church's growth.

Aveline remained unconvinced Cybele could solve the city's problems. In her experience, the gods did not make a habit of meddling directly in the affairs of mortals. She couldn't honestly say whether any existed in the corporeal sense.

As long as people treated each other well, she supposed it didn't matter. Most people needed—or at least wanted—a guide for their lives, someone to look up to. Whether they found their answers from Cybele, Hon, Tinian, or each other did not matter to her.

She entered the sole large room on the first floor that served as the main worship area. Benches formed two rows of pews leading to the altar in the center of the sanctuary. Rich tapestries hung behind the altar depicted the blessings of Cybele—healthy crops and babies. Atop the altar stood a bronze statue of the sacred cow led by a voluptuous woman wearing a crown of wheat and a simple gown.

Sunlight streamed in from windows high on the walls. A door on the left side opened to a stairway leading to the second level where Mother Anya and her priests lived. A door on the opposite side led to storage rooms below the altar. Aveline noticed Mother Anya seated in a pew, talking with a golden-haired girl.

Mother Anya smiled when she saw Aveline. The priestess's wrinkle-lined face told of a hard life working under the sun, and she had her dull grey hair pulled into a bun. The young girl curtsied as Aveline approached.

"Good day to you, Lady Aveline." Mother Anya remained seated as she greeted the knight-captain. Long ago, they'd established rising was neither necessary nor desired.

"I hope I'm not interrupting anything. I wanted to see how you were getting along." Aveline checked on Mother Anya several times a week. The matriarch had proved to be a good friend during her formative years after Aveline's parents died.

"Not at all, child. I was just advising young Innya here as to the best flowers to gather for her father's naming day."

Innya curtsied to Mother Anya. "Thank you for your help. I'm sure Mother will be happy with what I bring home now." Once again, she curtsied to Aveline.

Aveline watched the girl leave. "Polite young lady."

"Yes." Bowing her head, Mother Anya's eyes glistened. "I wish there were more young people like her here in town. So many have given over to despair."

"Many people have difficulty seeing hope when there are children starving in our streets." All too often, Aveline found herself among the most affected.

"It is true—things are difficult. But there is always hope. We will find a way to prosper again. Perhaps the caravans will bring good news when they return." Upon standing, the old woman limped toward the sanctuary. She beckoned Aveline to follow.

"Perhaps. I've left word at the gate to send for me when the caravans arrive, which should be any day now." Aveline followed Mother Anya to the altar. The matriarch pulled a cloth from within her robes, then dusted the pink granite slab.

"We need them now more than ever, child. The crop outlook is grim this year, and I keep hearing of stillbirths." Mother Anya shook her head as she scrubbed at a blemish on the altar. During her rounds, Aveline heard speculation about the increase in infant deaths, as well as low crop yields. The rumors seemed to increase from year to year.

Slapping at it with her cloth, Mother Anya abandoned the blemish. "Would you do a favor for me, Lady Aveline?"

"Of course, Mother. What would you ask of me?"

After returning the dusting cloth to her pocket, Mother Anya took Aveline's hands and searched the knight-captain's eyes. "I would like the city to help me expand this church. Not for more worshippers, but to give those homeless children food and shelter. Surely the Lord Mayor can support such an endeavor?"

"An orphanage of sorts?" It sounded like a promising idea to Aveline. One of the best she'd heard in years. Unfortunately, the Lord Mayor might not perceive it as such. "I think the Lord Mayor would see his approval of such an endeavor as an acknowledgment on his part that there is a problem."

"He does so little to help…"

Smiling, Aveline squeezed Mother Anya's hands. "I will talk to him. Did you have a location in mind? There's so little space around here."

"There is an abandoned building just behind the church—Alina's old fabric shop."

The knight-captain scratched her head. The ability to recall every abandoned building in Curton since the end of the mining boom eluded her.

"Oh, but that was when you were a little girl. The building has a strong foundation. Alina left it to the church when Aita took her, but we've never had the funds to do anything with it."

"Well, there is no harm in broaching the subject with him. Perhaps I'll bring Tasha along. Together, we may be more persuasive."

One of Aveline's closest friends, and an Etrunian sorceress, Tasha had arrived in town about a dozen years earlier. Folk around Curton, fearful and mistrusting of sorcerers and their ilk, treated her with suspicion bordering on malice. Tasha's sullen and dour attitude at the time helped little in the matter. Aveline recalled separating more than one mob intent on lynching Tasha for some perceived insult or threat amounting, in reality, to little more than the sorceress being antisocial.

Aveline appreciated Tasha's no-nonsense approach to problems. Once Aveline broke through the woman's shell, she'd found an intelligent, strong friend.

Mother Anya nodded. "The sorceress? The Lord Mayor fancies her, doesn't he?"

"Is there any woman he doesn't fancy? Fortunately for him, she doesn't care much for him. He couldn't handle a woman like her." The Lord Mayor liked his women beautiful, compliant, and uneducated. Tasha, although attractive enough for him, did not fit anyone's definition of meek.

"I appreciate anything you can do."

Aveline bowed. "It's my pleasure to help."

* * *

Tasha sat hunched over her writing desk, copying Dwarvish runes. When the caravan passed through Curton the previous year, Darrock Granitebinder paid her a thousand talons to transcribe into one codex the bundle of scrolls he carried. It proved to be painstaking work, but she understood his desire to preserve the words of his ancestors.

Mounted above either side of her desk, two sconces ensorcelled with a spell of perpetual light illuminated her writing area. The magical candlesticks cast a warm yellow glow to her otherwise pale tawny pallor. She'd purchased them from a traveling elf enchanter when she first opened shop in Curton, and they were well worth the expense. Books and scrolls shoved into bookshelves and scattered on the floor surrounded her. A clear path through the mess led from one doorway to the other, connecting the front room to her bedroom through a veritable sea of paper.

The bell attached to her door tinkled as someone entered. After adjusting the beaded choker covering the scar across her throat, she put her quill down and stretched. Though faded with time, the scar still made her feel self-conscious. After several years, she grew tired of telling the story of how she acquired it. Telling the tale certainly didn't pay as well as copying words, but even that didn't provide a daily living. Serving the town as an alchemist and herbalist did. Tasha pushed away from her desk, making her way into the front room. Hopefully, it was the order from the meadery for which she had been waiting.

A low counter divided the room in half. Jars and vials of her alchemical concoctions, which contained mostly salves and ointments, were stashed underneath. Behind the counter, against the wall, stood an apothecary cabinet with scores of drawers in which she stored herbs, roots, powders, and dried flowers. The fragrances of dozens of different florae mingled in the air.

The old woman on the other side of the counter regarded Tasha with rheumy eyes. She was not from the meadery.

"Ah, Dobrila. What can I do for you today?"

The woman withdrew a small leather bag from her belt, then placed it on the counter. "I need some more of that tea you mixed for me, dear." Sniffling, she wiped her nose on her sleeve.

Holding the sack, Tasha faced her cabinet and scanned the labels on the drawers. "Did it work for your husband?"

"Oh yes, but now I have what he had!"

Dobrila's husband worked as a mudder, pulling clay from the banks of the river so potters could work it. Last week, he complained of a runny nose and trouble breathing. Tasha could not identify the cause, of course, but she prepared a combination of herbs and minerals that usually alleviated the symptoms.

After finding the appropriate drawer, Tasha opened it. Using a small scoop, she measured the contents into the bag. She learned a great deal about herbalism from an elf lover she'd lived with in Celtangate long ago. When she arrived in Curton a few years following her lover's death, Tasha put that knowledge to use. Now, years of experience made her the most knowledgeable herbalist in the area.

She tied the bag shut before handing it to the woman. "Do you need me to repeat the instructions again? It's the same as you did for your husband."

"I remember." Dobrila smiled. "I'm not that old. Now then, two pennies, yes?"

Tasha nodded. "Yes, that's right."

The old woman pulled two copper coins from her pocket. She placed them on the counter. "When will you find yourself a husband? You've been here over ten years, Tasha. It's time you settled down and started having children."

Blushing, Tasha shook her head. The old women in town often tried to marry her off. Yet, the time didn't feel right to her. "I don't think it's for me."

"Nonsense. If my rough-and-tumble daughter can land a husband, you certainly can. There are plenty of fine young men in town. What about that potter's boy? What's his name? Bela?"

Tasha suppressed a shudder. She didn't know Bela well, but something about him unsettled her. He tended to stare at pretty girls with narrowed eyes and a grin that suggested salacious thoughts.

"I don't think he's quite right for me."

"Oh, well. What about Bolek? Oh, now he's a nice boy. People think he's dumb just because he's big and doesn't talk much, but, you know, he's always willing to help with anything you need done."

"The baker's apprentice?" Jaromil was one of the most well-regarded bakers in town.

Dobrila nodded. "That's him. He's a sweet boy. What about him? He'd make a good husband. He's a fine hunter too."

Tasha stepped around the counter, ushering the older woman out of the shop. She had met Bolek. Jaromil often sent him to buy herbs to put in his breads and sweet pastries. Although the baker's apprentice didn't speak much, Tasha noticed intelligence behind his eyes.

"I appreciate your concern, but I'm fine with things the way they are. I've never needed a matchmaker to make me a match. Now, go home, rest, and drink your tea."

Shaking her head, she closed the door behind her customer. *It's bad enough the Lord Mayor makes crude attempts to woo me. If I had a talon for every time these old women tried to match me with a young man, I wouldn't need to sell herbs.*

* * *

Aveline sighed, listening to the redsmith and his customer bicker. The patron contended the redsmith tried to cheat him, and the redsmith argued the buyer placed a deposit for a copper pot, but not for the specific one he sold to another. He offered the customer a similar vessel for the same price, one functionally identical but possessing a slightly different handle. The patron insisted the curly-haired redsmith craft a new pot with a handle like the one he'd wanted in the first place.

Placing her hand on the hilt of her mace, Aveline cleared her throat. When that didn't stop their bickering, she rapped her armored knuckles against the side of a copper urn.

"Gentlemen! This is not a matter worthy of my attention. I am hearing miscommunication, not malfeasance. I suggest you resolve this in a manner befitting adults of your stations instead of with this childish squabbling."

Aveline reserved little patience for petty arguments. She suspected none of the other members of the city watch wanted to deal with the situation, so they referred the matter to her.

"So, you're going to do nothing while this robber steals from me?" The irate customer poked the redsmith in the chest.

"I'll arrest you for creating a public disturbance. Imrus is a well-regarded craftsman who is known to be fair and reasonable. What difference does the handle design make, anyway?"

Crossing his arms, Imrus stared at the man with his one good eye. The patron shrugged. "I like the other style better."

"Do you have a written contract specifying the pot your deposit was paid on?"

The customer shook his head. "No, it was a verbal agreement."

"Yes, you paid a deposit for one of my copper hearth pots. You did not say which one."

"Well, I obviously meant the one you were working on when I made the deposit."

Aveline shook her head. "It was obviously not clear to Imrus. You have two choices—pay the remainder due to purchase the pot Imrus has offered, or request a refund of your deposit so you can buy from someone else."

"I do not offer refunds on deposits," Imrus huffed, glaring daggers at Aveline.

She met his glower with a stare. "In this circumstance, it might be better for all if you were flexible with that policy this once."

Behind them, a vendor shouted the virtues of his freshly roasted squab. The aroma took Aveline back to her youth when her family lived in Vlorey, far to the north, where street vendors sold grilled chickens and ducks. There, squabs—known as pigeons—infested the city like pests. In Curton, people ate them.

Both men appeared ready to debate the issue with her. Aveline rose to her full height. While neither man stood short, she loomed over them, cutting an imposing figure. Her warm sepia skin contrasted against her gleaming, steel-plate armor. She made a show of adjusting the grip on her mace in case she needed to draw it. Aveline rarely carried a sword, but she found the heavy cudgel a better deterrent, as well as a reminder of her youth. She'd trained with one when she was young, awkward, and clumsy—with feet that couldn't get out of their own way. Swordplay required a level of finesse of which she was not capable then. By the time she grew into her feet and handled a sword well, she had become accustomed to, and preferred, the mace.

The customer backed down first. He withdrew several silver talons from his money purse, thrusting them at Imrus.

"Should've known you northerners would stick together. I'll take the pot."

Aveline ignored the jibe about her and the redsmith's common origins. Leaving the men to complete their transaction, she strode across the plaza. Standing before the statue of Jayne Hammerfist, she regarded the stern-looking dwarf warrior.

"I think today I would rather face your oroq horde than have to suffer yet another fool squabbling over money."

The statue offered neither advice nor support. As always, Jayne Hammerfist gazed across the rooftops of the city from her vantage point atop the central plaza on the highest hill of Curton. As they passed, city dwellers nodded at Aveline. Her appearance marked her as a foreigner even though she'd lived in Curton most of her life. Over the years, the townsfolk had come to accept her as one of their own. Just as well since she considered Curton her home.

Adjusting the strap that kept her shield secure against her back, she proceeded to check in with the guards at the city gates. With luck, one of the trade caravans would return today. She wanted to greet them herself.

Chapter 2

After the day waned and the light of the setting sun cast a rosy glow across town, Aveline met Tasha at the Drunken Horse. Notably Curton's finest inn, it boasted as the largest tavern. Located near the town square, it served as the most popular gathering place for all but the most destitute townsfolk.

The hearth room seated over one hundred around its central fireplace. Hustling from table to table, attendants served mugs of ale and steaming platters of roasted capon, legs of lamb, stews, root vegetables, and even fish pulled from the river by local fishermen.

In one corner, a group of old people sat around a table complaining about young people. In the opposite corner, a group of young men sat hoisting their mugs and singing bawdy songs. Dozens of other townsfolk clumped together in groups. From a table near the door, a dusky-haired man with dark eyes stared at the two women entering. The fine cut of his silver cord-trimmed ebony robe marked him as a man of means. Although a bladed staff leaned against the table within easy reach, the patron seemed more concerned with his drink and the generous spread covering his table.

The man lifted his mug in a salute as Aveline and Tasha sat at a nearby unoccupied table. "Perhaps you two lovely ladies would care to join me? As you can see, I have plenty to share."

The armored knight-captain's face was a stony mask. "I don't think so, stranger."

"I am Vasco Dragonblade, formerly of Maritropa. I am new in town. If you would grace me with your name, we will no longer be strangers. Perhaps then you will accept my hospitality?"

Scowling, Aveline leaned closer to him, keeping her voice low. "Stranger, I don't know what you're selling. I don't know what your game is. If you want companionship, there is a brothel down by Miners' Gate." Turning away from him, she beckoned one of the barmaids.

Tasha stifled a snort, covering her mouth. "What kind of name is 'Dragonblade' anyway? Seems rather pretentious to me."

The man smiled. "Ah, yes, well, it's a self-inflicted moniker." He stroked the haft of his bladed staff. "From the wing bone of a dragon. Light, strong, exotic. Due to the circumstances under which I left Maritropa, I felt it was best to abandon my family name."

A barmaid approached the ladies' table, then handed them each an ale. When they opted to share a capon, the stranger leaned closer. "Excuse me, perhaps my ignorance is showing. I have, after all, just arrived in town. I don't wish to step on any toes, but maybe I have misinterpreted your relationship to each other."

Aveline snapped her head toward him, narrowing her eyes. "What are you getting at?"

"He thinks we're lovers." Tasha giggled. Watching Aveline take down boorish men remained one of the few pleasures in her life.

Sighing, the armored knight-captain pinched the bridge of her nose. "Because we're sharing a meal?"

"Forgive me if I have given offense. It is common in some cultures. Though, I admit, I am surprised to find it in eastern Etrunia. This region does not have a reputation for being tolerant of certain… choices."

The armored woman regarded her companion. "Tasha…"

"We're just friends. We share because there's no point in wasting food. Now, if you don't mind?" Tasha gestured toward Aveline. "My friend is becoming annoyed, and she's had a hard day. You don't want to be on the bad side of a grumpy city watch captain."

"Indeed not." Bowing his head, he raised his mug toward them once more before draining it. He tossed a few talons on the table for the barmaid before pushing himself away from the table. Taking his staff, he nodded at Tasha and Aveline as he headed toward the stairs leading to the rooms on the second floor.

"He probably thinks he's charming." Aveline shook her head.

Tasha shrugged. "Maybe. He's a sorcerer. I'd bet money on it."

Aveline watched him ascend the stairs. "The staff?"

"It's probably his focus. If he is from Maritropa, as he claims, that would explain it. Most sorcerers from the Maritropa Arcane University train in staff combat. It makes for a good show when they're preening for all the nobles, young ladies, and each other. I trained for a bit, but I never got the hang of it."

Sniffing, Aveline returned attention to her mug of ale. "That blade looks deadly enough." She shifted in her seat, tugging at her armor. "Remind me to take the time to remove this armor before we come here next time."

Tasha nodded. "We should keep an eye on him. Maybe he's just passing through."

The barmaid brought their capon, its skin roasted crisp and golden brown. The aroma of herbs wafted from it. Alongside it, she set a tub of butter and a loaf of bread on the table. Tasha tore a hunk off the loaf, then handed it to Aveline before taking a piece for herself.

"Smells like trouble to me." Aveline spoke around the bread in her mouth, "I didn't like how he just assumed we were lovers."

Tasha smiled. "What's wrong with that?" She liked to tease the knight-captain. Tasha enjoyed the company of both men and women, but none filled the longing in her heart like Lorelei. The elf, unlike so many others, had entered her life at the right time. They had planned a future together, a future to which Tasha had looked forward until Lorelei was killed.

Aveline sighed. "I didn't mean it that way. You know…" She shook her head, taking a long drink of her ale.

Slamming the door of the inn open, a group of draks singing a bawdy song entered. The rowdy group approached a large round table. Banging on the tabletop, their singing stopped only long to get a barmaid's attention.

Tasha changed the topic. "You want to talk about your day?"

"Gods, no. But I suppose it might help. You always have good ideas." Aveline removed one of the capon legs. Grease dripped on the table as she bit into it.

While Tasha waited for Aveline to continue, she carved a hunk of the capon breast for herself.

"First, I was summoned to break up an argument between a merchant and his customer. I don't know why anyone thought it was my job to arbitrate petty disputes. I was nearly run over by a runaway vegetable cart. Next, the dwarf caravan failed to show up today, and the Lord Mayor is breathing down my neck about the missing people. He wants to see you, by the way."

Several of Tasha's customers gossiped about the disappearances of several brothel workers, and they warned her to be careful. While not unusual for workers to leave the brothel without warning from time to time, recently, several had left and never returned. High brothel turnover rates were not abnormal, especially if the proprietor was known to be cruel. However, Madam Danica was kind, if strict.

"What's the count up to?" The last Tasha heard, three or four individuals had vanished. "And what does the Lord Mayor want me for?"

"Seven. Two this week alone, plus a beggar from Old Town. The Lord Mayor? Well, he doesn't share all his plans with me. No doubt he wants to try to entice you to his bed again."

Sighing, Tasha shook her head. "I should never have let him know I can't actually turn him into a frog." Tasha commanded powerful magics of destruction; however, ever since she revealed to the Lord Mayor her repertoire did not include transmutation sorcery, he'd become more aggressive in his pursuit of her.

"Threaten to burn down his damned house."

Tasha laughed. "That I could do. He's harmless, though, the sniveling little weasel."

"Mostly harmless." Aveline wiped the grease off her chin. "Anyway, you should turn the tables on him. I'll bet if you come on strong enough, he'll run away and never bother you again. Honestly, you're too much woman for him."

Tasha blushed. Candid talk was rare from Aveline. "Thank you. I think I'll just continue to ignore him. What do you think is going on at the brothel? Runaways?"

Shaking her head, Aveline swallowed the hunk of meat in her mouth. "No, I don't think so. Danica can be harsh, but she treats her workers quite well. I don't think she's involved at all, but her damned integrity is getting in the way of our investigation. She won't give up the names of any of her clients."

"Have you thought of assigning any constables to watch her place?" Tasha figured her friend tried that first, but it couldn't hurt to ask.

Aveline confirmed her suspicions. "That didn't work out. They... took advantage of her hospitality. I don't have time to watch it myself." She focused her attention on the capon's other leg.

"You need more women in the city watch."

"I already have three, not counting myself. You want a job?"

Tasha shook her head. Helping herself to another hunk of bread, she slathered butter on it. "No, but thank you. I'm busy enough in my little shop, and things are about to get busier."

Aveline cocked an eyebrow. "What's going on?"

"The Flametenders have about a dozen eggs ready to hatch." The most prominent local clan of draks, the Flametenders and the other drak clans relied on her for medicinal herbs and advice. Tasha always set aside extra time to help with the hatchlings.

"You've done more for drak acceptance in this town—"

A constable burst through the door. Gasping for breath, he raced to their table. "Lady Aveline! There's…another…" Sweat poured down his beet-red face as he struggled to speak. Upon rising, Aveline gripped his shoulders to steady him.

"Slow down, breathe, and tell me what's happened." All eyes in the inn focused on them.

"There's another missing girl. Not one of Danica's worker ladies. Innya Myasnik."

* * *

"Myasnik?" Aveline waved to gain the attention of a barmaid. *Wasn't that the girl talking to Mother Anya?* "The butcher's daughter?"

Gulping, the constable nodded. Aveline pulled out a chair, then nudged him into it. Once he sat, she passed her mug to him. Tasha furrowed her brow.

The constable drank the rest of Aveline's ale. "Her mother came to the jail in tears. She said Innya went out in the morning to gather flowers for her father's naming-day celebration and never came back."

"When was this?"

"Just this morning."

Aveline reclined in her chair. "How do they know she's missing? It hasn't even been a day yet."

"That's what we asked. Her mother said she found her basket outside their home, filled with flowers and a note." He produced a scrap of parchment from within his tunic.

Aveline unfolded it. The words were written with a shaky hand.

You have a pretty girl, butcher.
Thanks for keeping her pure.
She is just what we need.

"Pure? What are they on about?" Sighing, Aveline handed the note to Tasha.

Tasha shrugged. "If they are related, maybe whoever's behind the disappearances think they needed a virgin. If the workers are being used in a blood-magic ritual, it wouldn't be unheard of, though any guild mage will tell you arbitrary standards of purity are a load of horse dung. It doesn't explain the missing men, though."

"Maybe they're slavers." The constable took a piece of bread. Aveline frowned. "I hear some pay more for virgins."

"Why leave a note, especially if they're not asking for a ransom?" Tasha returned the parchment to Aveline.

Rubbing her eyes, the knight-captain studied it. "This makes no sense. The note taunts him. Us."

Tasha shrugged. "Maybe the kidnappers want to be found. Perhaps they want to force a confrontation."

"To what end? Maybe they're just arrogant." Aveline considered the possibilities. *If Innya's disappearance is related to the others, why leave a note now? If it is not related, why leave one without asking for ransom? Why draw our attention?*

"What's your name again?" Narrowing her eyes, Aveline scratched the nape of her neck.

"Javor, m'lady." Wisps of sandy hair peeked from under his helmet.

"First"—she took the bread from his hands—"stop eating our food." He shrank in his chair, lowering his head. "Second, find Lieutenant Valon. Have him meet me at the citadel."

Rising, Constable Javor saluted Aveline, placing his fist over his heart, then exited the inn. The patrons murmured to each other. Aveline knew word of Innya's disappearance would spread quickly now.

Sighing, Aveline put her head in her hands. When she glanced up, she caught Tasha smiling at her.

"Don't you love it when the constables make a scene?"

Chapter 3

At Aveline's behest, Tasha proceeded to the Lord Mayor's residence to inform him of the disappearance of the butcher's daughter. He liked to be kept apprised of the city watch's activities. *He'd be more informed if he'd live in the citadel like the previous Lord Mayor.* Scattered clouds blew past Calliome's moons, the King and Queen. Like a crown, the summer constellation of Tinian, king of the gods, hung over them.

Built near the western edge of town, in the sprawl outside of the wall at the edge of Old Town, the Lord Mayor's modest, two-story home was constructed from bricks made with local clay. A brick wall topped with a short, wrought-iron fence surrounded the estate. A lit torch in a lone sconce provided more shadow than light at the gate. The property was not dissimilar in size or style from the traditional manor in which all the previous Lord Mayor's had lived, but because Koloman came from old money and already owned a home, he insisted on remaining on his own estate. Tasha speculated, as many townsfolk did, that rather than it being a gesture of generosity or fiscal responsibility, he did not want to shoulder the expense of maintaining the old manor house and preferred to use town funds for that purpose as the property grew more decrepit each year.

Through the iron-bar-clad windows, Tasha observed flickering candles. Yawning, a man with heavy eyelids, wearing dingy chain mail stood guard. As Tasha approached, he angled his spear across the gate to bar her entrance.

"Who goes there?" The guard's stern tone demanded an answer.

"Tasha Galperin. I bring a message to His Lordship from Lady Aveline." In the dim torchlight, Tasha recognized him.

"Oh, you. He's been asking about you. Go on up." The guard opened the gate for Tasha. As she passed, he cleared his throat. "That salve you gave me helped. Thanks."

I thought that was Rickon. She remembered him clearly now. He came to her during the past week for help with an itchy rash he claimed he contracted from a tumble in some weeds. Tasha suspected it arose from a tumble in the brothel, but she nodded, remaining silent.

Flower gardens lined the river rock path from the gate to the house. Despite her personal feelings about the Lord Mayor, Tasha admired his home's potential. *Pity it's so dark.*

A single crow cawed from atop a broken lamppost at the bottom of the porch stairs. Cocking its head, it cawed once more before flapping away. Shaking her head, Tasha tromped up the creaky steps, approaching the aged, weathered oak door that showed signs of too much exposure and too little care. She rapped the tarnished brass knocker against it.

"It is late, herbalist. I would have thought you'd have more sense than to answer one of milord's summons at this time of night." The Lord Mayor's seneschal, an older man, Alik, opened the door just enough to peer out. The balding man wore a perpetual frown, conveying the impression he disapproved of everyone and their lives in general.

Tasha pursed her lips, biting back a rude remark. "I bear a most urgent message from Lady Aveline."

"Indeed? Very well. Enter. You may wait in the parlor. Take care, he's in a mood tonight." Upon opening the door wide enough for her to enter, Alik stepped aside. After shutting it behind Tasha, he then led her into the parlor. The Lord Mayor liked to pretend he was an influential nobleman of Etrunia, but his salon belied his true station.

The room, barely larger than the business area of Tasha's home, featured two plush armchairs arranged around a table before a fireplace. A bearskin rug sprawled on the floor, a trophy the Lord Mayor told admirers he felled with a single arrow on a hunting trip. Tasha knew the truth—he'd acquired it by paying a hunter.

Fire crackled in the hearth. Tasha examined the various tapestries hanging on the walls. They depicted scenes from Etrunia's history, most of which the Lord Mayor was ignorant, no doubt.

Striding in a manner that reminded Tasha of a proud rooster she encountered as a child, Lord Mayor Koloman Dubvric entered the room. The wiry, lanky man with short, greased-back hair swirled wine in a goblet he cupped in his hand. He smiled when he saw Tasha, his thin mustache riding his upper lip like a smudge of dirt on a little boy's face.

"Ah, my lovely sorceress. So, you have finally deigned to grant me the pleasure of your company!"

"Hardly." Tasha sighed. "I'm here at the behest of Lady Aveline."

Koloman sat in one of the chairs, gesturing for Tasha to do the same. "Are you, indeed? Why would she send you instead of coming herself?" His eyes narrowed. "Are you a belated present for my naming day?"

Unaware it had come and gone, Tasha barely cared she missed the Lord Mayor's naming day. Especially after his suggestion. "Certainly not! There has been a development in the disappearances."

"Pity." He moved to brush her hand. Tasha removed it from his reach, running it through her hair to conceal her avoidance.

"A butcher's daughter has been taken. Innya Myasnik. This time, a note was left with the family. We believe it is related to the other disappearances."

Seemingly unfazed by the news, he sipped his wine. "On what grounds?"

"The note mentioned her purity and how it was just what they needed. All previous abductees we're aware of were prostitutes, beggars, and passing travelers, hardly people the note writer would consider pure. It's circumstantial, to be sure. At any rate, her parents are making a lot of noise. You and Aveline can no longer continue this investigation in secret."

The knight-captain and the Lord Mayor decided after the second abduction to keep things quiet. They felt announcing the disappearances to the townsfolk would cause unrest. Tasha disagreed, but she conceded there was no need to shout the events on the street corners.

Groaning, Koloman drained his goblet. "The public can scream all they want, but the City Council will want answers. You're a sorceress. Can't you just wave a wand and divine where they went? Or summon them to your side?"

Tasha shook her head. "It doesn't work that way. Besides, I'm not some sort of seer or soothsayer." Divination magic, notoriously imprecise, was more the purview of tricksters and charlatans. If she were able to perform some divining ritual, it would probably just indicate the missing people were fraught with danger in a dark, secret place.

"Pity. I'm sure a lady of your many talents could help us." The sly smile returned. Koloman leaned closer. "It's late. Why don't you stay tonight, and we'll discuss this over breakfast?"

Rising, Tasha smoothed her robes. "I should go."

"So soon? You've only just arrived." Setting his goblet on the table, Koloman stood. He approached Tasha, gathering her in his arms.

"Not soon enough." Tasha pushed him away. To his credit, Koloman didn't try to hold on to her or embrace her a second time. He never did.

"Pity."

"I disagree." Tasha exited the parlor. She opened the front door before Koloman had the chance to make further advances. "I'm sure Lady Aveline will have an update in the morning. I suggest you discuss things with the City Council at the earliest opportunity."

Tasha left, shutting the door behind her without waiting for his response. She shivered, although the night was not cold. Something about being alone with Koloman always made her skin crawl. Aveline owed her for this night.

* * *

"I want to know what's being done to find my daughter!" Butcher Myasnik pounded his fist on the table for emphasis. A burly man, he dressed in an oft-mended brown jerkin and wrinkled dark breeches. Myasnik's puffy eyes betrayed the late hour and his lack of sleep, and his dark, stringy hair protruded at odd angles from beneath his dingy cap. Sitting alongside him and attired in her nightclothes, his wife wept into a handkerchief. A guard handed her a long jacket to cover herself.

Aveline despised when people hit objects for emphasis. She tried to remain calm. "I have Watch Sergeant Anton checking with the gate guards who were on duty yesterday morning. Watch Lieutenant Valon is leading the rest of the guards in a citywide search for her. I'm bringing in all the city watch; they're waking the rest now. If she's in Curton, we'll find her."

"And if she's not in Curton?"

It was a possibility Aveline did not care to address at the moment, but it was the most likely one. "We haven't the resources to search the city and the countryside at the same time. I've chosen to concentrate on the city search for now."

"Unacceptable!" Butcher Myasnik snatched his hat off his head. Flinging it, he appeared ready to leap across the table.

"Papa, please." The butcher's wife tugged at her husband's sleeve.

"What would you have me do? Send riders out in all directions in the night? Hoping they spot one person in the vast wilderness that surrounds us? I've already sent constables with torches and dogs into the flower fields east of town. There are myriad ways to confound hounds. Even our best hunters and trackers have difficulty seeing in the dark."

"Papa, please. Let's leave Lady Aveline to her work."

Butcher Myasnik first scowled at his wife, then at Aveline. He rose, his wife clutching at his arm. Brushing her off, he stormed out of the jail.

"Thank you for everything you're doing." The butcher's wife curtsied, then followed her husband.

Aveline pinched the bridge of her nose. Pain blossomed behind her eyes—like some unseen force pushed on them from within her head. The night promised to be as long as the day had been, and she wanted more than anything to rest. She waved the guard over.

"M'lady?"

"Stand watch outside. I'm going to try to get some sleep. Alert me if there's any news of the missing girl."

The guard saluted. "Yes, m'lady. Cybele watch over you."

After the guard exited, Aveline pushed herself away from the table, then headed toward the barracks. Unused since Koloman was appointed, offices for town magistrates and the Lord Mayor were located on the upper floor of the citadel. When he made it clear he wanted nothing to do with the old building, Aveline turned the former Lord Mayor's office into a private sanctuary for herself. Even though she owned a home adjacent to the town's southern wall, Aveline occasionally slept at the citadel to spare herself the walk.

The room she occupied lacked amenities, but it featured a simple cot, a dresser, and a basin with a water pitcher. She didn't bother removing her armor, preferring not to be caught in her smallclothes if the guard returned to wake her. The wooden cot groaned as she lowered herself into it, complaining at the extra weight of her plate mail.

She closed her eyes, thankful for a relatively quiet jail. A few rowdies slept off their ales in the common cell. The stone walls and thick oaken doors of the citadel, along with several furniture-filled offices, deadened noise between the jail and the living quarters. Aveline shifted on the cot, attempting to find a comfortable position. Her armor always pinched sensitive areas if she didn't take care to avoid pressure points, reminding her once again that sleeping in armor ensured an unsatisfactory rest, at best.

From downstairs, a shout for assistance jolted Aveline awake. She turned her head, wincing as her gorget dug into her neck. Rubbing the spot, she eased herself off the cot. She stumbled down the staircase, then headed for the cellblock. Watch Lieutenant Valon wrangled a large hairless man. The prisoner snarled, resisting with foot and fist as the lieutenant maneuvered him toward the common cell.

Upon unlocking it, Aveline opened the door for him. She seized the man's collar, noticing only then the prisoner was a female oroq. Hairless, grey-skinned, and often believed to worship solely Maris, the goddess of war, oroqs were often regarded as the bane of mountain communities. This oroq's red eyes and tattoo that barely covered the gnarled scar circling her left ear and traveled the length of her face and neck before disappearing inside her tunic suggested a dangerous and violent past.

"What's going on?" Aveline pushed the oroq into the cell, then slammed the iron-bar door behind her. The din caused the sleeping drunks to stir, but neither woke. Snarling, the oroq leapt at the cell gate. Wrapping her fingers around the bars, she pressed her face against the barrier near Aveline. Blackened tusks protruded from her bottom lip, and her breath stank of ale and blood. Aveline noticed red flecks on her lips.

"I didn't start that fight."

Aveline stepped backward. She faced Lieutenant Valon. "What fight? I thought you were searching for the butcher's daughter."

Lieutenant Valon shook his head. "Constables are still combing the city. A fight broke out in the Bristled Boar just as I was walking by." A tavern near Miners' Gate, the Bristled Boar enjoyed a reputation as an establishment catering to people of questionable tastes.

He unhooked an axe from his belt before placing it on the spare rack reserved for confiscated weapons. He removed his helmet, revealing matted, brown shoulder-length hair. "One of the mudders came tumbling out the door with this one on top of him. She bit off his ear."

"Where's the mudder?" Aveline locked the cell door. Realizing the opportunity for escape expired, the oroq growled.

"He ran off. Probably home."

"I tried to give him back his ear, but I guess he didn't hear me." The oroq grinned.

Lieutenant Valon huffed. "You threw it at him whilst yelling obscenities as he ran."

Aveline turned to the oroq. "I'm surprised you made it as far into the city as the Bristled Boar. We're not exactly friendly with the local oroq communities."

The prisoner spat on the floor. "I'm not local. Besides, my partner vouched for me."

"I'll bet he's feeling foolish now, isn't he?" Lieutenant Valon passed in front of Aveline, rapping the oroq's fingers with his cudgel. Yanking them off the bars, she snarled at him.

"You said you didn't start the fight?" Aveline eyed Lieutenant Valon. "Where is her partner?"

The lieutenant shrugged, brushing hair off his face. "No one stepped forward. I assumed she was alone, though I was curious how an oroq got into town."

"My partner and I were minding our business, drinking our ale while enjoying a nice meat shank when that mudder came up and called me all manner of unfriendly things." The oroq rubbed her knuckles. "Aerik stood up for me, but when that mudder threw his drink in our faces, I decided to show him what I thought of his hospitality."

"Aerik?" Aveline wondered what manner of man would willingly team up with an oroq.

"Aerik Devilhand, my partner."

Aveline nodded at Lieutenant Valon. "Go back to the Bristled Boar to find this 'Aerik Devilhand.' I want to talk to him."

Lieutenant Valon saluted, then left.

"I assume you have a name, or shall I just call you Oroq?"

"Therkla Fire-Eyes."

Sighing, Aveline paced before the cell door. "As I mentioned, we're not on speaking terms with the local oroqs. Granted, I was just a little girl when Jayne Hammerfist held the pass against the invading oroq army."

Therkla narrowed her eyes. "As I said, I'm not from the mountain communities."

Aveline stopped pacing, peering into Therkla's flame-colored eyes. "Where are you from then, and why are you here?"

"I'm from a place that no longer exists in the Four Watches. Aerik and I are just passing through."

Both hardy folk and dangerous beasts lived in the vast frigid area beyond the southern mountains known as the Four Watches. Traders from the Northern Watch, usually burly, hairy humans dressed in bulky furs and carrying large axes and hammers, sometimes traveled as far north as Curton. Aveline knew little of the land outside the southern border of Etrunia.

"I've heard Watchfolk get along with oroqs better than folks up here do. Harsh climes and dangerous beasts encourage more cooperation, I suppose."

Aveline and Therkla stared at each other. Determined not to look away first, Aveline sighed when the opening door interrupted her. Lieutenant Valon entered, followed by a large man.

"Aerik!"

Where the man's furs stopped and his beard started, Aveline could not determine. His red-rimmed, glassy eyes betrayed the bottle of whiskey, or several, he had consumed.

She turned to the man. "You're Aerik Devilhand?"

Stifling a belch, he nodded, dropping his left hand to the hilt of his broadsword.

"I found him stumbling toward the jail. He looked like he would never find it on his own." Gripping the man's arm, Lieutenant Valon pulled him toward the cell. Aveline stopped him.

"You and your oroq friend will be here until you sober up. You'll have to relinquish your sword."

"Best do it, Aerik. We've done nothing wrong." Therkla stepped away from the cell door.

"Blarg." Aerik collapsed. Aveline jerked his sword out of its scabbard, then placed it on the weapon rack beside the axe. Lieutenant Valon opened the cell door and dragged Aerik inside, dumping his limp body at Therkla's feet.

"Keep him on his side. If he empties his stomach, it won't drown him." Aveline rubbed her neck.

Lieutenant Valon grinned. "Unless you don't care about that."

Therkla curled her lip at him. "I'll watch him. So what? You'll let us out in the morning?"

Aveline shrugged. "If you behave and the mudder doesn't come around wanting us to keep you longer."

The lock of the door clicked into place as Lieutenant Valon turned the key. "He probably won't. Most of these mudders view bar fighting as a hobby. He'll probably tell everyone in the morning how he bested you despite losing his ear. It'll be a badge of honor for him."

Aveline shook her head as Therkla tended to Aerik. *Mudders have a strange sense of honor.*

Chapter 4

The ringing of the shopkeeper's bell at the top of her door interrupted Tasha's translations. With a sigh, she returned her quill to its holder. Rubbing her eyes, she stepped to the front of her store. She never slept well after dealing with Koloman, and retiring late contributed to her fatigue.

Aveline smiled as Tasha approach the counter. "Good morning!"

Tasha nodded, stifling a yawn. "You're cheerful. Did you find the girl?"

Aveline's smile faded, and deep lines grew on her brow. "No. We've started combing the fields around the city. How did it go with our beloved Lord Koloman last night?"

"He was more interested in seducing me than hearing about the girl's disappearance. I advised him to talk to the town council about it, to consider letting people know what was going on." She stifled another yawn.

"Did you stay with him?"

Tasha gasped. "What? No!" She then caught the teasing smile on Aveline's lips and the twinkle in her eyes. "You owe me for that."

Aveline laughed. "Everyone knows you're too good for him."

Approaching her apothecary cabinet, Tasha waved her hand. "There are days I wish I could turn him into a toad." She searched the drawers for a remedy to stave off sleep.

"You've been around oroqs, right?"

Tasha shut the drawer, eyeing Aveline. Her friend's mouth became a tight line, a sign she was no longer joking.

"Only in battle, why?"

"Oh, we jailed one last night for drunken brawling. I've only heard stories, you know, the tales of Jayne Hammerfist. She was well spoken. Better than any of the mudders."

Tasha never conversed with any oroqs she'd fought and had never encountered a female. "I suppose there could be eloquent, relatively peaceful oroqs in the world. I mean, until I traveled to Drak-Anor, I knew nothing good about draks and minotaurs." Tasha tried not to think about those days much.

"That's the city near Ironkrag, right? The minotaur and drak city?"

Tasha grunted an affirmation. Her mind returned to that day. She and Lorelei defended the city against an army of oroqs led by a cathar warlock. The tattered and ugly bird-like creature from the Western Wastes wielded foul blood magic in the battle that took her elf lover, Lorelei, from Tasha. Her hand drifted toward her choker.

Feeling Aveline's hand on her shoulder, Tasha shook her head to clear the dark pictures from her mind.

"I'm sorry, Tasha. I didn't mean to bring back bad memories."

"They..." The words caught in Tasha's throat. She coughed and tried again. "They made a nice monument to her, I'm told. I never went back. I hear the city is quite prosperous now. It enjoys good trade with Ironkrag and Celtangate."

Aveline nodded. She had heard similar stories from traders. Other accounts told of a demonic man ruling over the city with a snake-haired woman at his side, but even the people telling those tales extolled the quality of contraptions they purchased from the draks there.

"Do you want me to talk with her?"

"No, I just wanted to hear your take. Once her companion sleeps off his drink, we're going to release them. She's traveling with a man. Claims they're from the Northern Watch. I'm inclined to believe them. There are a lot of oroqs living there in relative peace with the Watchfolk, I hear."

Tasha smiled. "If the anecdotes I've heard are to be believed, men, oroqs, and ice are about all the Four Watches have to offer."

"You look tired. Why don't you close up and get some sleep?"

Shaking her head, Tasha turned again to her apothecary cabinet. "No, no. I have to finish this translation before Darrock Granitebinder returns. The caravans haven't arrived yet, have they?"

"No, but I'm expecting them any day now."

"All the more reason to finish as soon as possible."

"I'll leave you to it, then. Sorry, Tasha."

With her back toward Aveline, the sorceress waved as the knight-captain exited her shop. She discovered a packet of herbs she often sold to customers who complained of fatigue. After brewing them into a tea, she consumed the drink while it was still hot. She hoped to complete this translation today; it taught her more about dwarven trade agreements than she ever wanted to know.

* * *

Watching one of the constables carry a bucket of water to the cellblock, Aveline applied a coat of oil to the steel shaft of her mace. Most of the drunks had awakened with headaches, albeit sober, shortly before dawn, so she let them leave. Aerik and Therkla remained the jail's only residents.

As a new shift arrived to assume their duties at the Citadel, she sent Lieutenant Valon home to sleep. Reports from most of the guards in the city came in after the lieutenant left—no sign of the girl anywhere in town. Although Aveline developed a plan to search the fields around Curton, her confidence they would find Innya waned. Many hours had passed between when she left home and when she was declared missing. The abductors likely moved her many leagues away from town in that time.

Aveline entered the cellblock just as a constable chucked a full water bucket onto the hefty man snoring fitfully on the cell floor.

"Arrrrgggh!" Aerik coughed and sputtered. Aveline watched the oroq, with a sour expression on her tusked face, roll off her cot. As far as Aveline could tell, Aerik weathered his drunken evening without incident, although, at the moment, he resembled a wild man in from the wilderness for the first time in decades.

"Fiery demon balls, boy!" Helping Aerik to his feet, Therkla glared at the officer. Water streamed from the man's beard and hair.

"Where in the hells—" Aerik's body wracked as he coughed. "Where in the hells am I?" He shook his head like a soggy dog as his eyes darted around the prison. Aveline barely understood the words through his thick southern accent.

Sheathing her sword, Aveline approached the cell. "The citadel, Curton's jail."

"What the hell for?"

"Disturbing the peace. Public drunkenness. I'm sure we can think of a few other things, but mostly because your friend there bit a mudder's ear off."

Aerik rubbed his face, squinting at Therkla.

Shrugging, she grinned, her pointed teeth glistening. "The one who threw his drink in our face, remember?"

Shaking his head, Aerik wrung the water from his beard and approached the bar separating him from Aveline. "How long must we stay here?"

Aveline jingled the keys in her hand before unlocking the cell. "The mudder hasn't come forward yet. I doubt he will, and, even if he does, it sounds like you were provoked. Lieutenant Valon confirmed with the barkeep that you two had not caused any trouble before the incident."

The two exited the cell. Aveline directed them to the rack to claim their weapons. "A hint of advice—find a nicer place to stay. The mudders are the lifeblood of Curton, but they're rough-and-tumble folk. Stay out of trouble."

Aerik nodded as he belted his sheathed sword around his waist. "Glory can be found at the bottom of the deepest cave or in the depths of the murkiest swamp. There is no glory to be found at the bottom of a mug."

Chuckling, the oroq woman picked up her axe. "Oh, like the cave near Haefstaad? The one—"

"We agreed to never speak of that!"

Grinning, Therkla bared her tusks. "My apologies." She bowed. "You are right. There are fine things to be found at the bottom of a mug, but glory is not one of them. I had an idea, Aerik, while you were sleeping. Let's find something to eat, and I'll tell you about it."

Aerik bowed his head as he passed Aveline. She watched them leave before turning to the constable. "I'm off to do my rounds. If anyone returns with news about the missing girl, send them to see Tasha at the apothecary. She can get word to me more quickly than anyone wandering around to find me."

Lieutenant Valon saluted.

The magic Tasha used to send messages fascinated Aveline. While that type of spell was technically outside the sorceress's area of expertise, she explained it proved too useful to fall by the wayside. Useful enough, in fact, that when she gave herself over to the study of Gaia and mysticism, she continued to hone her skill using magical messengers. Aveline often ordered her constables to go to Tasha when they needed to contact her with immediate concerns, and she trusted her friend not to contact her frivolously.

Before slipping her mace through the ring on her belt, Aveline checked the straps on her armor. She then stepped out into the cool morning air. A fine mist hung low over the streets. She heard the creaking of wheels and clanking of crude bells as farmers and merchants wheeled carts laden with their wares into place.

Market day. She shook her head. Unbidden, she felt a pang in her conscience. *It took the abduction of an affluent citizen's child to spur me into real action. The other missing folk were no less deserving of my attention. Yet, because of their chosen profession, I did not give them the treatment they deserved.* Pushing through the gathering crowds of shoppers, she proceeded toward Cybele's Church. Inside, Mother Anya swept the floor in front of the altar. The matron glanced up as Aveline strode down the aisle.

"Two days in a row, Lady Constable? To what do I owe this pleasure?"

"I feel I have been negligent of late. I have placed the value of one life over another's based on social status." Aveline approached the front row of benches and sat. The wood creaked in protest under the weight of her armor.

"Why do so many wait until they feel the burden of guilt before they seek me out?"

Aveline rubbed the bridge of her nose. She did not intend to enter a religious debate with Mother Anya. Aveline was not a devout follower of Cybele, but she appreciated the sense of community the followers of the goddess of harvest brought to the town. "I came here seeking your advice because I know you have sense, Mother Anya. That is all. I do not wish to convert. I will never be a farmer, not a good one, anyway."

"You would probably do better speaking to one of the priests of Hon… or perhaps Adranus. It's unfortunate there's no Temple of Anetha here. Perhaps you could rebuild the shrine to her in the citadel. It is a house of justice, after all." Mother Anya handed her broom to Aveline. Using one of the cloths from her apron, she dusted the statue of Cybele that stood on the altar.

Aveline sighed. She'd once tried to engage the priests of Adranus, god of smiths, and Hon, god of the hearth and family. "They still view me as an outsider, I think. They're less than welcoming toward me, or maybe they're just grumpy bastards. Besides, I wouldn't know where to begin rebuilding the shrine. I don't even know what room it was in. I guess I could have one of the craftsfolk sculpt me an owl for Anetha." None of the gods were as favored in Curton as Cybele these days.

"You are an outsider. It is why you are as popular with the common folk as their constable." Mother Anya chuckled, stuffing her dust rag into her apron before retrieving her broom and sitting beside Aveline. "When you do something unpopular, they can blame the untrustworthy outsider."

"But I was raised here."

Mother Anya nodded. "And when you do something they like, they can praise you as one of their own. The masses are nothing if not fickle."

"Well, I'm not here to be popular, but I am here to see that the laws are followed and justice is served. They're good people, for the most part, but I sometimes have difficulty remembering those with whom I do not agree have the same rights and deserve the same justice as everyone else."

The priestess patted Aveline's knee. "It is a struggle we all have, child."

Chapter 5

Tasha sprinkled sand over the parchment to dry the ink. Completing the translation of the final Dwarvish scroll lifted a weight from her shoulders. She straightened, stretching her arms over her head. The townsfolk who were not crafters had little to trade with the dwarves, and, indeed, never saw them. However, because dwarves were rare visitors to Curton since the mines closed, mudders gossiped about their arrival.

She brushed the sand off the page before flipping through the codex. *There are still a few blank pages. I suppose there's room for more.* After latching the cover, she carried the book into her front room to wrap it in paper. When she finished, she sighed and placed it under the counter. Her sleeve snagged on a splinter, ripping the fabric as she pulled her arm away.

"Damn!"

Tasha clenched her jaw, examining her torn sleeve. *Why do these things always happen when Aveline needs me to make public appearances with her?* The constable returned earlier to tell Tasha of the dwarves' impending arrival and to invite her along to the tavern later to drink and swap stories with them. Tasha stepped into her workroom, then rummaged through a box until she found a planer.

Running her hand along the edge of the counter, she felt a few more rough spots. She ran the planer over it, scraping away burrs and splinters. *Is this what my life is going to be now? Selling herbs, scraping wood, and dealing with busybody matchmakers and lecherous men?* The bell above her door jingled. She glanced, recognizing the big man, whose tousled, mousy-brown hair poked out underneath his pointed, fur-trimmed hat. Flour dusted his clothes and apron. Smiling, he bowed his head at Tasha.

"Good day, m'lady."

"What can I do for you, Bolek?"

"Master Jaromil sent me to see Natalia, but you're closer and pret—" He blushed. "I need, um, that lady herb, and um…" He withdrew a crumpled piece of paper from his pocket. Flattening it on the counter, he squinted at it, as though willing it to reveal its secrets.

"Lady herb?" Tasha giggled. "Rosemary?"

"Yeah. I always forget." He pushed the paper toward her.

Tasha took the list. "Rosemary. Poppy seeds. Rose petals. Sweetleaf. Dried fireberries. Butter. Cream." Nodding, she turned to her apothecary cabinet. Scanning the labels, she opened each drawer to find what she needed, then retrieved several bowls from beneath the counter.

"Um, salt. He said he needed salt too. Twice as much as everything else."

Tasha spooned poppy seeds into a bowl, careful not to spill any. She still remembered when she first started selling herbs. She'd accidentally pulled the drawer out too far, spilling her entire stock of poppy seeds all over the floor. Even years later, she still found poppy seeds between the floorboards and ground into the planks. "I have a little, but if he needs that much, you might need to go to the market."

"Butter and cream too. We're baking."

"I see that." Placing the bowl of poppy seeds on the counter, she smiled at the man. "I love your breads. I may stop by later today to buy some."

She finished pulling together Bolek's order, then tallied the purchases. "Rosemary, poppy seeds, rose petals, sweetleaf, and dried fireberries. That comes to a half-talon and two pennies."

Bolek reached into his pocket. After withdrawing a fistful of change, he picked through the coins. He placed a talon—silver coins of the realm minted with a deep score down the middle—and two pennies on the counter. Tasha snapped the talon in half before returning a piece to Bolek. He stuffed it into his pocket before gathering the bundles Tasha had prepared. He thanked her as he stumbled out the door.

Entering the back room, she loosened her robes, pulling her arm out of the sleeve to examine it more closely. Her shopkeeper's bell jingled again. With an exasperated sigh, Tasha dressed herself and straightened her robes before returning to the front of the store. A dark-haired man wearing a worn leather jack with no sleeves stood at the counter. A round shield slung over his shoulder, he carried a brace of axes on his belt as well as a heavy-looking sword and a fancy dagger that appeared more ornamental than functional. His clothing and manner identified him as one of the Watchfolk. She noticed bandages wrapped around his right arm, covering it from wrist to just above the elbow.

He cleared his throat. "Ah, you are the alchemist, yes?"

"This is Tasha's apothecary." Tasha bowed her head. "Herbs, alchemy, teas... what malady do you have?"

He held out his bandaged arm. "I was forging in the forest west of here. I"—he chuckled—"took a spill into a bramble patch, cut my arm up. There was some sort of plant there. It caused a rash that itches like fire. I wrapped it because I know scratching will make it spread."

"Let me see." Tasha took the man's hand, unwrapping his bandage. Deep scratches covered the skin underneath with patches of raised red blotches. She could not determine if the swelling originated from the scratches, the rash, or both.

"Do you know what the plant looked like? Was it an ivy? A nettle?"

The man shook his head. "No, sorry. I leapt up quickly, and I was too busy nursing my arm to pay attention."

Tasha patted his hand. "I have something that will help. Go ahead and cover it up."

As he did so, she turned to her cabinet. She located a bunch of jewelweed leaves and dumped them into her biggest mortar, then pulped them with the pestle.

"You're from the Four Watches?" She glanced over her shoulder at him as she worked.

"Haefstaad, originally. Well, a village in that hold, near Haefstaad." He wound the bandages around his arm.

"You're a long way from home. What brings you north?"

"Spent a few years in Muncifer. Things didn't work out, so I headed back this way." He secured the bandage, then rested his hands on the counter as he waited. "Still not sure if I'm going to head to Cliffport and take a ship somewhere or go back across the mountains. Neither is particularly appealing right now."

"No family to go home to?"

"None to speak of. Cousins, but I hardly know them."

Tasha finished, scraping the paste onto a sheet of waxed paper. She then tied the package into a bundle.

"After you bathe, take about a fourth of this, mix it with some mud, and spread it over the affected area. Then wrap it." She passed the packet across the counter. "It should alleviate the itching and reduce the rash. I recommend reapplying it daily."

"Mud?" He peered at the packet.

"The mudders will be happy to part with it. Any potter in town will have some as well, though they'll charge you more."

"Very well." He took the packet. "How much?"

"Two talons." His malady required a sizable quantity of her jewelweed, so it demanded a high price. She had no more if someone else needed it.

He fished two silver coins out of his pouch, handed them over, and bowed. "Thank you."

Tasha watched him leave before returning to the back room. She rummaged in a trunk for needle and thread to repair her sleeve. She found a needle, but the spool of thread had barely a finger's length remaining. Tasha sighed. *I guess I need to change clothes.*

* * *

By the time Aveline's morning rounds brought her to Miners' Gate, she noticed the dwarf caravan had already arrived. Guards stationed at the gate progressed down the line of donkeys and oxen, nodding as they verified the dwarves' goods.

Assuming this visit resembled past ones, Aveline guessed at their cargo: metals to be worked in Curton's forges in trade for textiles and what grains Curton could spare. They would probably leave with some new pottery too. Clay mud was one resource Curton possessed in abundance.

Aveline searched the assembled dwarves for a familiar face. Passing through the city gate, she returned the guard's salute. Near the end of the line she located the dwarf she sought. Grey streaked his black beard, and travel rendered the elaborate braid work in his beard unkempt. His cheeks seemed even rosier than the previous year, although Aveline could not tell if age, drink, or exposure affected his complexion. Frowning, he crossed his arms, watching closely as Curton's guards inspected his caravan.

"Hail, Mighty Caravan Master. Welcome back to Curton, Kingdom of Mud and Pots." With one hand on the head of her mace and the other crossing her chest, Aveline bowed deeply.

The dwarf squinted, his green eyes flashing, before roaring a great laugh from his belly. "Lass, I was hoping you'd greet us!" He clapped her on the shoulder.

Aveline smiled. "It is good to see you again, Dwennon." Standing straight, Aveline towered over the dwarf. She always slouched a bit in his presence so he did not have to crane his neck to meet her eye. "I've been looking forward to your visit."

He waved at his caravan and to the guards inspecting it. "Yet, not enough to let us pass without this harassment, eh?"

"The Lord Mayor must collect his taxes."

"I'll bet he takes them coming and going."

Nodding, Aveline accompanied Dwennon toward the end of the caravan. "I'm certain he does. Were these men knights or soldiers of the realm, I would enact some changes. But they are the city's garrison, and my ability to countermand the Lord Mayor is somewhat limited where tax collection is concerned."

"Bah, I wasn't blaming you, lass." Dwennon sighed. "It was a long journey is all."

Aveline looked toward the southern mountains. Dark clouds obscured the tallest peaks, and it appeared as though rain clouds were blowing inland from the eastern shore. Over Curton, however, the cool morning mist gave way to clear blue skies broken only by a few lonely, puffy clouds. "Bad weather or dangers on the road?"

Stopping, Dwennon gestured to the south, down the road by which he had arrived. Aveline spotted a few carts loaded with the stuff Curton's potters used to make their wares traveling from the mudders' shacks by the river toward the gate. "Mostly bad luck. Broken wheels, thrown shoes, that sort of thing. Pacha's balls, you'd think the drivers would check their gear before we come down out of the mountains." He lowered his voice. "You might want to watch out, though. During our last stop, my scouts said a sizeable force of draks was about a day behind us."

"Draks?" Squinting, Aveline shielded her eyes with her hand. The road disappeared into the foothills of the Iron Gate Mountains. Curton's guards would not spot anyone traveling it until they crested the nearby hills, only a few hours away. "A battle force?" Aveline knew little of the diminutive dragon kin, aside from those who lived in town; however, she disbelieved they would mount an assault on Curton.

"A battle force? Of draks? That I'd like to see." The dwarf shook his head. "I don't think so. My scouts said they looked more like refugees. Females, hatchlings, carts full of whatever junk they value. Something's driving them out of their warrens. I'm only glad they didn't head our way."

Refugees. Just what we need. "Thanks."

A constable jogged toward Aveline and Dwennon, stopping in front of them. He saluted. "M'lady, I have a report from Jolan."

"Jolan?"

"One of the men searching the west fields for that girl."

Aveline nodded. Although she often could not recall their names, members of the garrison addressed her as though she knew each part-time constable personally. "Yes?"

"A bit away from town, he found tracks from a cart or wagon near the field where the girl was picking flowers. He said it looked like it came from the west perhaps, toward town, but only came to the fields before turning around and going back."

"Hey, we spotted a cart or wagon or something in the distance on our way here." Dwennon nudged Aveline's arm. "I thought it odd because it wasn't using the road, but I figured it was just some farmer or something. Don't you have mines out that way?"

"Mm… a few. They're abandoned now. Thank you, Constable. Please find Lieutenant Valon and have him meet me here."

Jolan saluted. "Yes, m'lady." Turning, he raced into the city.

"Trouble?" Dwennon glanced over at her as he fiddled with a donkey's bridle.

"Disappearing people. This may be a clue. I hope it is." Aveline's shoulders sagged.

"I'm sure you're doing as much as you can, lass. Maybe the cart is just going to the mines?"

The rock Aveline kicked skittered across the dirt. "The mines that dried up years ago? If that is its destination, it's for no good purpose." She stared at the horizon, wondering if the tracks Jolan found would amount to anything and how many other townspeople would disappear before she finally put a stop to it. *If I'd done something about it when the first reports of missing prostitutes came in, this would never—*

"Master Stonehelm, you're cleared to enter the city now." A guard approached Aveline and Dwennon.

"At last!"

Aveline shook herself away from her thoughts, following the dwarf to the head of the caravan. "Dwennon, what news from Dwegarthon?" The only dwarven city between Curton and the Four Watches, Dwegarthon lay on the far side of the Iron Gate Mountains.

"There's much, lass. Meet me for an ale after I get this caravan secured, and I'll tell you everything."

Watching the caravan move through the entrance to the city, Aveline paced as she considered the new information about Innya's disappearance. By the time the last of the dwarves passed through the gate, Lieutenant Valon arrived. He brushed his fine, dark hair out of his eyes before he saluted.

"M'lady?"

"Constable Jolan found tracks outside of town in the field Innya went to collect flowers. He says they headed west. Assemble a scouting party to investigate. They are not to take any action unless they feel there is an immediate danger. I want them to follow the tracks, then report back to me where they lead. It could be nothing…"

Lieutenant Valon nodded. "Yes, m'lady. I'll put Jolan and Brana on it. They're our best trackers."

Aveline cocked a brow. "Who is Brana?"

"She's the daughter of Milos and Vica. The farmers with all the goats and sheep in the western hills."

Nodding, Aveline returned with Valon to town. She knew of Milos and Vica, although she had never met them. Their farm provided much of the mutton and cheeses sold in Curton's taverns. *I hope this is more than nothing.*

Chapter 6

"That dress is a little formal, isn't it?" Aveline pointed at the sorceress. Tasha wore a gold-trimmed green gown. It fit snugly around her upper body, but hung loosely from the waist, allowing her to move freely. Skipping around a pile of horse dung in the street, the sorceress adjusted the bulky package she carried.

"I tore my sleeve in the shop, but I ran out of thread and didn't have enough time to get more."

Aveline brushed lint from Tasha's shoulder. "People are going to think you're trying to look pretty for someone."

Blushing, the sorceress stared at her feet. "I'm not. I just didn't want to wear ripped clothing."

"Let's go. They're probably halfway through a keg by now."

Aveline and Tasha walked abreast. People passed them on both sides, rushing to and from the market as the sun set in the west, finishing their business before shops closed for the night.

"Where are we going?"

"Hon's Hearth." Aveline liked the tavern, appreciating the dwarves preferred it over rowdier inns like the Drunken Horse. Although she did not know the owner well, she found him respectful and well-spoken every time she dealt with him. The establishment was located on the far side of town, near Miners' Gate.

"I didn't have time to tell you earlier, but we had some news about the girl." Aveline tugged on Tasha's sleeve, moving her to allow a cart to pass. "Well, I hope it's about the girl."

"Oh?"

"A scout found wagon tracks leading away from the fields where Innya supposedly picked flowers the day she disappeared. They led up to the field and then turned away.

I sent some people out to track the wagon. Perhaps we'll have some answers soon."

They meandered through the market, ignoring calls by vendors to purchase their goods at end-of-day discounted prices. The street angled downward as it headed toward the river. During the wet season, rain made the cobblestones treacherous and slick, but on this mild day, walking down the hill only made Aveline's ankles ache. She wished she had dressed more comfortably, although not quite as formally as Tasha. With the recent troubles, Aveline felt ditching her armor would be irresponsible.

Caravan Bridge, so named for the convoys that used to carry their ore loads to the smelteries, arched over the river. Although those establishments were mostly gone, the bridge's name stuck. When she allowed herself the time to stop and listen, she found the babbling of the river running under it mesmerizing. As a little girl, she sat on the parapet with her legs dangling over the side, watching fishermen and imagining her vision extended all the way down the river to the sea. Despite rushing to meet the dwarves, she paused on the bridge to gaze downriver and enjoy the sound she so loved.

Smiling, she recalled one evening during their courtship when her late husband had found her there watching the sunset. *Dorian. I haven't thought about you for a long time.* Feeling a twinge of guilt, she shook herself free of the memories. Tasha nodded at her, and they continued their trek. The streets on the other side of the bridge in the Market District twisted and wound through the terrain more than in Old Town, and Aveline often wondered if the builders suffered from an aversion to straight lines.

By the time they reached Hon's Hearth, the sun disappeared behind the buildings of Curton. Deep shadows cut across the road, and dampness chilled the air. One of the barmaids, the owner's eldest daughter, stood on a ladder, lighting lanterns to illuminate the entrance from the outside. When she noticed Aveline and Tasha approaching, she descended, then held the door for them as they entered.

She curtsied. "Good evening, m'ladies. Welcome to Hon's Hearth."

Aveline nodded a curt acknowledgment before leading Tasha into the main hall of the inn. A singing minstrel strummed a mandolin near the fireplace.

There once was a villain named Vilnas the Bold,
He died in his bed because he was so old.
He burned down the villages and killed all the folk.
Slaughtered the cows and the gods did provoke.

The table of dwarves across the room jeered, booing. "Don't you know any good songs? Sing something about Jayne Hammerfist, you fool!"

Chuckling, Aveline approached the dwarves. Pulling over two chairs from a nearby vacant table, she placed them near Dwennon. After setting her package on the table in front of her, Tasha sat in one, Aveline in the other.

"Ah, good to see you, lass! I see you've brought your friend."

Tasha bowed her head. "Dwennon, I have that transcription Darrock Granitebinder wanted. Is he here?" She scanned the faces at the table, but she did not see him.

Dwennon's expression darkened. "He died this past winter, lass. I suppose I'll have to pay for that, so I can take it back to his family now."

"Died?" Sucking in a breath, Tasha furrowed her brow. Aveline placed her hand on Tasha's shoulder.

"He's gone to the Soul Forge now." Dwennon raised his mug of ale. "To Darrock! May Hon's Hall keep his fantasy of swimming in ale forever."

Whooping, the assembled dwarves raised their mugs in tribute.

Tasha slumped in her chair. "He seemed so young." Dwennon nodded. "Vanity, lass. Black dubbin in his beard. He never left his room unless his beard was as black as his boots, even when his skin started to turn grey and crack. I called him a fool for it, and he thumped me on the head."

A barmaid brought a platter of roasted pork and vegetables to the table. A dozen dwarf hands pawed at it like pigs at a slop pile. Shaking her head, Aveline ordered drinks for Tasha and herself.

"Speaking of libations, lass, I have something for you." Dwennon ducked and rifled in his pack, then withdrew a bottle, which he handed to Aveline.

Recognizing it instantly, she squealed. When it was bottled, melted red wax cascaded over the top, sealing the cork and coating one side of the brown bottle, which bore a familiar emblem: that of Honnigbrow Meadery from across the southern mountains in the Northern Watch city of Vornstaad. Grinning, she tore the paraffin off the bottle of her favorite mead, allowing the pieces to fall to the floor like rain. Clenching the cork in her teeth, Aveline yanked.

Just then, the barmaid returned with their drinks. Aveline emptied the contents of the mugs into the fire, causing the flames to sputter and hiss. She poured mead into the now-empty vessels, then handed one to Tasha. Witnessing the scene, the barmaid's mouth hung agape. Huffing, she stomped away.

"This is the good stuff." Aveline swigged from her mug, letting the honey-sweet liquid slosh around her mouth. Honnigbrow's mead achieved a balance of wildflowers and sweet, peppery spices that lingered after swallowing. "Ah, mud-free mead. Darrock can keep his ale; I'll swim in this when I die!"

"I brought a whole case for you, lass." Dwennon winked at Aveline. Upon draining his mug, he called the barmaid to bring a replacement.

Laughing, Aveline hugged the dwarf. "I owe you for this!"

"Aye, two crowns, you do."

Digging in her money purse, Aveline nodded. "It's worth five." She pressed the coins into his hand, then felt Tasha tug at her sleeve.

The sorceress narrowed her eyes. "Five? That's a lot."

Aveline shrugged. "There are enough supplies to get me through to my next stipend from our esteemed Lord Mayor. It's only a few days."

Seeming unconvinced, Tasha insisted on paying for the rabbit stew. Dining and drinking, they listened to the dwarves heckle the bard. His songs seemed improvised. When one of his mandolin strings broke, the dwarves cheered their good fortune.

"No matter, good people. I don't need my mandolin to regale you with tales of derring-do! Allow me to tell you the story of a man from the south:

Jürgen Fairhair!
His stance was bold, and his sword was old.
He fought the wyrms, wooed the ladies,
And drank deep from his horn.
He came from the Southern Watch to fair Vornstaad,
And he endured the Jarl's scorn.

Aveline took a long draught of mead, put her mug down, and stifled a belch. She leaned closer to Dwennon. "So, what news have you from Dwegarthon?"

Dwennon wiped his mouth with the back of his hand. He motioned Aveline and Tasha closer so they could hear him over the minstrel's oration. "Deep Road is open again."

Aveline glanced at Tasha whose face showed no sign of recognizing the name. She returned her gaze to Dwennon. "Deep Road?"

"It runs under the mountains. For the first time since The Sundering, we have an underground route to our kinfolk in Ironkrag. They contacted us this past winter, a whole caravan!" Chuckling, he placed a meaty hand around Aveline's wrist. "They were aided by a dragon. By Adranus's anvil, I swear it's true!"

"A dragon?" Leaning back in her chair, she regarded Tasha, Dwennon's grip still firm around her wrist. Aveline had heard of dragons returning to the world, of course, but she never knew anyone who claimed to have seen one.

"Aye, a dragon. Could move through earth and stone as easily as the air."

"Terrakaptis. The Earth Dragon. Firstborne of Rannos and Gaia." The sorceress nodded, her jaw clenched.

Aveline and Dwennon stared at Tasha.

Releasing Aveline's arm, Dwennon sat back. "How did you know that?"

The sorceress fidgeted in her seat, gazing into her mug. "I… I encountered him ten… twelve years ago, when I was involved in that business out by Drak-Anor."

Aveline recalled the stories Tasha told of the battle that drove the oroqs out of the city situated in the caldera, paving the way for the residents to open relations with Ironkrag and Celtangate. She did not speak often of the battle during which her lover died, so rarely, in fact, this was the first time Aveline heard a dragon played a part.

"Well, anyway." Dwennon jabbed his fork into a potato. "It's good to reconnect with our kin." Upon biting the end off the tuber, he chewed, shaking his head. "The frost wyrms are stirring again. I can feel it in my bones."

"Frost wyrms? I hope they stay in the Watches." Aveline refilled her mug. Sinuous, reptile-like creatures, frost wyrms lived under the snow and ice of the Four Watches. Mostly dormant in the warmer months, they occasionally emerged en masse in winter to spawn. They were dangerously aggressive. Many scholars thought they might have descended from dragons. They viewed the wyrm as a divergent life form that was not nearly as easy to negotiate with as draks. The wyrms could not speak, and they only concerned themselves with people insofar as considering them a food source.

Dwennon nodded. "I'm glad we don't go into the Four Watches once the snows fall. We hear some of the Jarls are stirring up trouble with the oroq holds, as well, so enjoy that mead, lass. It might be the last of it for a while."

Raising her cup, Aveline nodded. "I shall, indeed!" *As long as the Jarls don't drive the oroqs this way.*

* * *

The next morning, Tasha struggled to focus on cataloging the herbs and reagents in her apothecary cabinet. Try as she might, she still could not keep up with Aveline and the dwarves when they drank and swapped stories. Her best efforts rewarded her with a pounding headache. Tasha searched through the drawers. She did not have any dog hair, but she found willow bark and meadowsweet leaves.

Barely.

What little she had, she wrapped into a bundle, tied it with string, and carried it into the back room. After dropping it into a tankard, she set a kettle on top of her iron stove to heat. Sitting on the edge of her bed, she rubbed her temples. Tasha caught herself dozing as the kettle came to a boil. She shook herself awake to pour the scalding liquid over the herbs.

Steam from the pungent, bitter brew rose from the mug. Feeling guilty for using the last of her willow bark, she muttered a quick prayer that the customer jingling her shop-keeper's bell did not come in search of a headache remedy.

Upon entering the front of her shop, Tasha scanned the room but saw no customer. A raspy voice coughed, making her jump, but then a clawed hand bearing ashen black scales tapped the top of the counter. Leaning forward, she recognized the old drak potter, Toviah.

"Good morrow, good lady." Toviah cleared his throat, then coughed again. "Perhaps you could help me?"

Smiling, Tasha leaned on the counter. "What do you need, Toviah?"

Pounding his chest, he coughed yet again. "I seem to have picked up a chill from somewhere. My throat is also sore. Your herbal remedies are well known. Might you have something to stave off this affliction before it puts this drak in the ground? I don't want to end up like old Abarron."

The old drak's name brought pain to her heart. Abarron had taught her much about Gaia and Cybele, how they connected to the world, and how she could commune with them. The strain of the cough and fever that found him last week proved too much. It had claimed the old drak's life, despite her best efforts to help.

She nodded. "I have just the thing." Searching through her apothecary cabinet, she located the leaves of the velvet plant. She measured out enough for several servings.

"Steep these in boiling water and mix in some honey. Drink the brew, and it should help. I have given you enough for three or four days at two mugs per day. Do you need honey?" She placed the bundle on the counter.

Toviah took it. "Yes, please, if you have some. It will save me a trip to the market." He coughed again.

Nodding, Tasha took a jar from beneath the counter. Upon opening it, she transferred some of the honey into an empty smaller jar, then handed it to Toviah. "That comes to four pennies."

"That's all?" He placed a half-talon on the counter. "You can keep the extra penny, good lady. For your trouble." Bowing, his head disappeared below the surface of the counter.

Tasha beamed. "Why, thank you. If you don't notice any improvement in the next few days, try steeping an onion in honey overnight, then take two spoonfuls of the syrup."

"Indeed? Onion honey?" Toviah squinted at Tasha. Chuckling, he shook his head and waved as he left the shop.

She returned to the back room to pack a bag. It was time to gather more herbs. She hoped to hold out a few more days, but she hadn't realized she had so little willow bark. After stuffing a variety of empty bags and tools into her pack, she extinguished the fire in her stove and double-checked all her candles were snuffed too. No sense going out to gather herbs if her shop would be a smoldering pile of sticks upon her return.

As she closed and locked the door behind her, she became aware of someone quickly approaching her shop. She recognized the wandering mage who recently arrived in town. Her mead-muddled mind tried in vain to remember his name. He'd replaced his ebony robe for a forest green affair with gold trim. "I don't have time right now, Dragonbone." She pushed past him.

"Blade." Spreading his arms, he spun mid-step and followed her. "It's Vasco Dragonblade. I was hoping to gain some insight from you. It won't take long."

"Insight? From me?" Tasha shook her head. No one in town came to her for advice unless they had questions about herbs. She kept a brisk pace toward the market.

"I haven't had an opportunity to meet many people in town, and I find you more approachable than your knightly friend, as wonderful as she may be. Frankly, she's a bit intimidating…"

Tasha narrowed her eyes at Vasco, wondering if he planned to ask her to help him find some angle from which to approach Aveline.

"It's irrelevant. What I was hoping to find out from you, or, rather, what I would like, is some advice in regard to what I can do here in this town." He stumbled alongside Tasha, trying to keep up as she continued on.

Tasha stopped in her tracks. Vasco passed her before he realized she'd halted. *He's asking me for job advice?* She eyed him. The clothes he wore would not be out of place at a party at the Lord Mayor's residence. His gold-trimmed navy tunic and his boots, though flecked with mud, showed signs of a high polish. Only his cloak, a heavy, green woolen cape trimmed in fur, appeared to have come from a local merchant.

"Well, what can you do?"

Vasco shook his head. "Not much. I'm a fairly skilled enchanter, and illusions are my specialty, but I don't think there's much call for that sort of thing among potters and farmers. I can write, of course, but I don't think this town needs a scribe."

"You're well-prepared to be the wizarding son of a noble family, am I right?" Tasha resumed walking, albeit at a slower pace so Vasco could keep up.

"Indeed."

"Then what are you doing in a place like Curton?" To Tasha, Vasco seemed like the exact opposite type of person than one who would visit Curton, let alone make a home here.

"It's… a long story."

Tasha detected sadness and perhaps a bit of frustration in Vasco's hesitation. "Look, I have to leave town for a bit, but I do sympathize with your plight. I'm an outsider, too, and finding a niche for myself was wholly due to luck. Both apothecaries in town were run by old men and women who didn't want to do the work anymore. I helped them gather herbs for a year or so, then took over for the whole town. When I return, perhaps we can discuss your options."

Tasha turned the corner into the market, searching for the preserved food stalls. She relied on hard cheeses, breads, and cured sausages to sustain her when going into the wilderness for several days. Vasco still stood by her side.

"Leaving town? Is it something I can help with?"

Resisting the urge to sigh, Tasha managed a huff and faced Vasco, shaking her head. "I'm just going to gather more reagents; my stocks are running low."

Smiling, Vasco nodded. "I can help with that. I was never good at mixing potions, but I do know the beneficial plants from the toxic ones."

"I always go alone." Tasha found the solitude on her gathering trips to be relaxing. She looked forward to organizing her thoughts and planning for the rest of the year, or until the next time she needed to restock.

"I have a horse. Pepper and I can carry far more than you can alone."

That gave Tasha pause. *A horse would make things easier, but it would mean spending several days alone in the wilderness with this strange man.* Tasha fingered the talisman around her throat, which allowed her to focus on arcane energies and bend them to her will. Despite turning more toward the mysticism of Gaia and Cybele these days, she still found use for her arcane focus now and again.

"We can carry more, and two of us would be more formidable should any bandits decide to prey upon us. If we cannot defeat them, then Pepper can spirit us away much more quickly than we could run."

Tasha held up her hand. "Fine, fine. Get your horse. I will buy provisions, then inform Lady Aveline where we're going. Meet me at Miners' Gate in two hours."

Cocking his head, Vasco narrowed his eyes. "Do you always tell your lady knight your whereabouts?"

"Only when I'm leaving town with a strange man."

Chapter 7

"I'm not comfortable with you letting him tag along. Are you sure this is a good idea?" Aveline looked past Tasha at Vasco. Leaning on his staff, he watched people shop in the market square, his head swiveling to follow every young woman who passed. His horse, a blue roan mare Tasha said was called Pepper, stomped and snorted, yanking at the reins Vasco held.

"No." Tasha tucked a stray lock of hair behind her ear. "Want to come with? Help me keep an eye on him?"

Aveline continued eyeing Vasco. To his credit, he kept a respectful distance as the women spoke. "As much as I would love to leave the city to pick flowers with you, I have a city watch to run. Which way are you headed?"

Murmuring greetings to Tasha and Aveline, a family passed them. The sorceress bowed her head in acknowledgment before returning her attention to Aveline. "I was thinking of following the river south a bit, into the hills."

"What about that drak clan? The Flametenders? Aren't they hatching a brood soon?"

"Mmm." Tasha nodded. "I'm running low on herbs I'll need for them too. I should be back in time."

"All right. Mind keeping to the west bank, away from the mountains? Dwennon says there was a band of draks about a day behind them. Maybe see what they're up to? They might be refugees, traders, I don't know… maybe not." Aveline trusted Tasha would not take unnecessary risks if the draks proved unfriendly. Otherwise, Tasha would point them in the right direction for whatever they sought.

"Sure, anything I can do to help." She put her hand on Aveline's shoulder. "Plus, it keeps me away from the area you think the girl was taken, right?"

Aveline nodded. "You know me well." She clasped Tasha's hand. "Be careful. I know you can take care of yourself, but we know nothing about this man."

"If he tries anything, I'll leave him in a ditch." Tasha glanced over her shoulder at him. "Until then, he's offered to help haul reagents. I should be able to gather enough to last through the summer, maybe more. I've been depleting my stocks more rapidly lately."

"Things getting worse?" Aveline sought to corroborate Mother Anya's report.

"More sickness, and the midwives have been buying all my crampbark, skullcap, and chamomile." Tasha sighed. "I can't keep up."

"Hard times are good for business, eh?"

"That's one way to look at it." Tasha pulled Aveline into a hug. "I'll be back in a few days."

"If you run into trouble, you know how to reach me."

Nodding, Tasha gripped the talisman around her neck. Aveline watched as Tasha joined Vasco and the pair left together. Once they were out of sight, Aveline approached the watch sergeant in charge of Miners' Gate. The woman snapped to attention, saluting when Aveline caught her eye.

"Knight-Captain Aveline." The sergeant held her salute until her commander returned it. "Nothing to report, m'lady."

"That's fine, Sergeant…?"

"Borodin. Niska Borodin, m'lady."

Beneath her city-watch tunic, Sergeant Borodin's ill-fitting mail showed signs of rust and repeated repair, a sure sign the young woman hailed from one of Curton's less affluent families. Aveline noted the cracked wooden hilt of the guard's sword.

"Any news from the farms or other travelers?" Aveline found folk passing through and complaining to the watch as they entered the city a reliable source of news from the surrounding countryside.

"Nothing out of the ordinary, m'lady. They'd just been complaining about taxes, the weather, and the mudders."

Despite the overcast sky, the temperature remained comfortable. Aveline glanced at passersby. "What's to complain about? It's not raining. What of the mudders? Causing trouble?"

Shaking her head, Sergeant Borodin laughed. "Nah, they're complaining about how mudders are too cheap to buy anything good. And some folk always complain about the weather: too hot, too cold, too sunny, too rainy, too dry, too windy. The usual."

"I see. Carry on, then." Aveline turned away from Miners' Gate, resuming her morning rounds. Waiting for the patrols searching the countryside for Innya taxed her patience, and throwing herself into her normal routine did little to stave off frustration. Aveline paused for a moment outside a bakery, inhaling the aroma of freshly baked pastries and bread. A grin crept onto her face as she remembered her mother's baking, a daily ritual until her father dragged them all on that fateful journey south that ended with Aveline orphaned, alone on the streets of Curton. Her smile faded.

"Is there something you need, Lady Aveline?"

Upon the voice shaking the knight-captain from her memory, she opened her eyes. Widow Marya stood before her, cradling a basket of loaves wrapped in blankets. Her stringy blonde hair fluttered in the cool morning breeze. She stared at Aveline with narrowed, brown eyes.

"Just enjoying the smell of fresh-baked bread." Seeing Marya always pained Aveline's heart. "I'll be on my way."

Several years prior, Aveline executed Marya's husband after Piotr smothered his mother. The woman suffered an ailment from which a traveling bonelord had been unable to release her, so Piotr the Smith took it upon himself to ease her suffering. Unfortunately, the law did not recognize his act as one of mercy, and Aveline had been bound by law to administer his sentence. She never put much stock in the abilities of bonelords to enter a spiritual realm with those on death's door to ease their passing. The situation with Piotr did not improve her opinion on the matter.

After bowing to Marya, she resumed her patrol, ignoring the sound of the woman spitting on her footsteps as she departed. She didn't blame the widow for her attitude. Meting the execution was Aveline's duty, rightfully ordered by the magistrate after Piotr's trial. After that day, she favored the mace she had trained on. Something about that blade no longer sat right with her, particularly since Piotr had forged the sword for her in honor of her appointment to Captain of the City Watch.

Aveline's route followed Zeman's Road, just inside the city wall. Save for the section running through the affluent homes of Hillside, the road bore ruts and mudholes, evidence of the noble council's lack of interest in maintaining the parts of the city they neither lived in, nor frequented. A foul stench, exacerbated by the lack of cleansing rain during the past few weeks, wafted from gutters running alongside the street. Wrinkling her nose at the odor, she scanned the sky in vain for the relief dark clouds would bring.

With only wisps of white tracking across the blue sky, the promise of rain in the near future proved a fleeting hope. Zeman's Road followed the curve of the city wall, winding to Drakton, the northern hill. While they were not founders of Curton, drak clans that had emigrated to the city shortly after the mines depleted settled peacefully and caused far less trouble than unhappy mudders.

Giggling drak hatchlings darted across the street, splashing through puddles. Aveline stopped to watch them play, offering a smile and a nod to the parents who beckoned their children to come in off the street. As she resumed her patrol, a husky voice called after her.

A drak with scales the color of summer grain hobbled up to her. The dull sheen of her scales and her bent posture marked the drak as an elder of her clan. She carried a bundle of scrolls under her arm. "Lady Aveline, have you seen the herbalist?"

"Tasha?"

"She's not at her shop. Do you know where she is?"

"Her stocks were running low." Aveline eyed a pair of humans staggering past, their clothes covered in dried mud and filth. She kept her gaze fixed on them as they stumbled down the street. "She went out to gather more herbs."

The drak shifted the bundle she carried. "She'll be back soon?"

"A few days, I think. Maybe a week."

The humans Aveline had been watching approached a building abutting the city wall. After conferring among themselves, they knocked on the door. They entered the building after someone opened the door, and she returned her attention to the drak.

"Well, that won't do at all…"

"There are other herbalists in town. What about Tal… Tar…" Chewing her lip. Aveline failed to recall the man's name.

"No, no. These papers"—the drak held up her scrolls— "they've been bequeathed to Tasha. We leave on the morrow…"

"Bequeathed? By whom?"

"My mate, Abarron. He'd been meaning to talk to her, but he died last week."

"Oh, I'm sorry for your loss." Aveline put her hand on the drak's shoulder. Tasha knew more of the draks in town than she did, but Aveline appreciated the lack of real trouble-makers among their population compared to the rough-and-tumble mudders. That most of drak holidays and observances involved introspection rather than drinking helped.

The drak held the scrolls toward Aveline. "Can you take them and give them to Tasha for me? My family can't delay, and I know you're her friend."

Aveline took the parchment rolls from the drak. "What are they... and who are you? I'm sorry, but I don't know your name."

"I am Orah. Dunscale clan." Pressing her hand against her chest, she bowed. "Abarron promised to teach her all he knew about the mysticism of Gaia and Cybele. When he fell ill and couldn't meet with her as often as he liked, he wrote it down."

Aveline nodded, aware of Tasha's interest in learning more on the subject, a way of honoring her fallen lover and distancing herself from the arcane studies of her youth. Only within the past three or four years had Tasha spoken openly of wanting to move on and change the focus of her life.

"I will see to it she gets these just as soon as she returns, Orah. You have my word."

The drak widow bowed, her tail stretching behind her for balance. "Thank you, Lady Aveline. May you find bounty in this life."

After steadying herself upon rising from her bow, Orah hobbled up the street. Aveline tucked the bundle under her arm. Clasping the hilt of her mace for security, she resumed her patrol.

* * *

"Would you really leave me in a ditch?" Vasco chuckled as he led Pepper off the road. Tasha hoped he hadn't eaves-dropped and would have waited longer than the first few minutes after leaving town before striking up a conversation.

She gripped the talisman at her neck. "I don't know you. If you intend to harm me while we're out here, it will not go well for you."

"No? I'm a university-trained enchanter. You are... an herbalist?" Vasco's voice betrayed his mirth, although Tasha could not see his expression. "I seek only to assist you; I would never harm you. I left Maritropa to see the world and expand my experiences, not to profit from others' misfortunes."

"I was not always so." Stopping, Tasha faced Vasco. "I trained in evocation with the Arcane University before I settled here."

"Did you?" Furrowing his brow, Vasco cocked his head.

Tasha ignored his incredulous tone, stopping to examine some brown, ear-shaped mushrooms growing on a rotting stump. She gathered them, stowing them in one of her pouches. Dual-purpose mushrooms, usable both for remedies and dinner recipes, were among her favorite finds in the wilderness.

Throughout the day, Tasha scanned the underbrush for medicinal plants while deflecting Vasco's personal questions. After a few hours, he restricted his conversation to questions germane to their herb gathering. Between the road and the river, few suitable plants grew, but Tasha managed to fill one of her pouches by the time the midday sun burned away the morning dew.

Afternoon gathering, as they worked their way south along the west bank of the Copper Run River, proved more fruitful. Tasha filled half the sacks she brought by the time the sun dipped below the horizon. Before they were left with only the light of the waxing Queen and waning King, Tasha led Vasco and Pepper to a grotto on the riverbank she had used as a shelter during previous excursions.

"We can make camp here." Tasha helped Vasco secure the mare to a tree before removing her saddle.

"How much longer will we be out here?" Vasco fished a handful of oats from one of his saddlebags, then held out his hand to Pepper. The dappled mare slobbered on him, scarfing the tasty treat.

"A few more days, I think. There's a spot not far from here where dozens of herbs grow. I used to think it was someone's garden, long abandoned, but I haven't found any evidence of a home."

"Have you an axe? We'll need wood for a fire." Vasco tugged at a branch on the nearby tree.

"I should be able to find enough deadwood. I'll gather some while you finish setting up camp, if that's all right."

To Tasha's relief, Vasco agreed. Backtracking from the grotto, she then climbed an incline to the area above their camp. Many branches and twigs littered the area, just as they had the last time she camped here. She dropped an armload off the edge overlooking the grotto, away from the tree where Pepper stood.

Vasco shouted in alarm.

"Oh, sorry. I'm used to being here by myself." Crouching, Tasha glanced over the edge. "Do you know how to build a fire?"

The mage frowned. "Not as such, no. My family had servants to build the fire in our hearth."

"How did you travel from Maritropa to Curton without once building a fire? There aren't enough inns between here and there for you to rent a bed every night."

"The weather has been pleasantly warm, and I had plenty of hardy vegetables and preserved meat in my pack." After he rummaged through one of his saddle bags, he withdrew a plank of dried meat. "I still have some we can eat tonight, and I have a few bottles of wine I picked up in my travels, as well."

"I appreciate that." Grimacing, Tasha drew away from the edge. "I'll be back shortly." Months-old dried meat ranked low on the list of food items she enjoyed while out of town gathering herbs, and she never left town unprepared.

Vasco can keep his jerky. If he's nice, maybe I'll share my sausage, bread and cheese.

Tasha entered a nearby pine grove. She scanned the rocky surface, picking up loose stones where they peeked through the layer of pine needles carpeting the earth. Once she had an armful, she arranged the stones in a circle. She removed her boots, placing them outside the circle, then stood within it. The needles pinched her toes, but she flexed her feet, forcing herself to ignore the pricking sensations until she felt the cool earth beneath. Closing her eyes, Tasha focused on the aroma of pine, birdsong, and the sounds of the forest, allowing a connection to form between her and the Earth Mother.

She felt life all around her. The trees, the birds, the bugs, and the worms. Deer grazed in the forest, not too far from her circle, obscured by the thick foliage. Connecting with the Earth Mother in this way let Tasha feel the world in a way others could not, and it took her years to learn how to do it. Lorelei, Tasha's elf lover from over a decade ago, could have taught her over the course of one season, but given her absence, she stumbled through blindly until Abarron showed her the way.

Her first taste of arcane power, over twenty years ago, now felt electric. Power coursed through her body as she learned to shape it into a flame and light a fire. After training, Tasha found she possessed a talent for bolts of lightning and other directed-energy effects. With each, an intoxicating tingle coursed through her body. Upon connecting with Gaia and Cybele, the mystic power that flowed through all living things reminded her of being wrapped in a thick blanket in front of a warm fire on a cold winter night. It was comfort. It was safety. It was fulfilling.

Connecting to the world granted her no visions, no great insight into the future. Instead, it made her feel satisfied and alive. She allowed her thoughts to stray, her spirit flowing with the eddies and current of the world. The Copper Run rushed toward the sea not too far away, and the Iron Gate Mountains stood strong, a wall separating Andelosia from the Four Watches. Amidst it all, Tasha sensed a creeping darkness, a sickness of the land, rivulets of pus creeping like vines through the fields surrounding Curton and even into the edges of the forest.

Tasha gasped, her eyes snapping open. Twilight consumed the pine grove, a dim glow from the King and Queen illuminating the crows that now surrounded her. Birds alighted on each of the rocks on the perimeter of the circle. A few cocked their heads, and all followed her motions with their tiny black eyes as she rose to her feet. Cawing in unison, they fluttered off, leaving her alone in the ring. She turned in place, scanning the area for any other forest denizens who might be watching her.

After determining she stood alone, Tasha retrieved her boots carrying them with her to the campsite. Vasco crouched near the center of the flattest area, piling up sticks in a manner that suggested he learned fire building from hearing drunken rumors in bars. Tasha tossed her boots toward her bedroll before taking the sticks from him.

"Allow me. I appreciate your efforts, but that's going to be a disaster."

"I was trying to help out and get a head start. I wasn't sure how long you'd be." Vasco brushed off his breeches. Pepper nickered, tossing her head.

Tasha showed Vasco the proper way to build a fire, steeling herself for a night of small talk. His unmistakable flirting kept her mind off the disconcerting sight of crows encircling her while she communed with the Earth Mother.

Chapter 8

Without Tasha to keep her company, Aveline purchased meat, cheese, and bread at the market to bring home for her evening meal. She lived in Old Town, in a building that abutted the southern city wall, not too far from Miners' Gate. Her father, seeing it as an investment opportunity, lucked into the purchase shortly after they arrived in Curton. Tragically, neither of her parents survived that first winter. A plague had ravaged the city while one of the worst blizzards anyone could remember gripped the city.

As she did every evening when she dined at home, Aveline lit candles in front of small shrines for each of her parents and her patron. Sir Agnar, a great bear of a man from the Four Watches, took her in after her parents died. He served Curton as knight-commander of the local Etrunian garrison at Dawnwatch Keep until Etrunia's noble rulers abandoned the outpost. When the soldiers left, he stayed behind as head of the city watch and the sole knightly representative of the town's supposed Etrunian rulers. With his blessing and sponsorship, Aveline followed in his footsteps.

While she ate, Aveline rested her feet on the case of Honnigbrow Mead Dwennon brought her. She raised a mug in thanks to her dwarf friend. When she finished supping, she doused the candles and threw one final log on the fire before turning in for the night.

Rattling her windows, the peal of thunder woke her. Aveline threw off her covers, rolling out of bed. Nothing remained of her fire except for smoldering embers. The dim grey light filtering through her windows put the hour at just past dawn. Torrents of rain pelted the street, falling faster than the thirsty earth absorbed it. Aveline donned a tunic and breeches, then yanked on her boots before wrapping herself in a cloak. Sighing, she glanced at the rack containing her armor. As much as she believed it was better to have something and not need it than need it and not have it, she decided leaving her armor behind would save her back-breaking work later.

As soon as Aveline unlatched her door, a gust of wind blew it open, flooding the doorway. Fighting against the gale, she pulled her door shut and left. Sane people stayed inside in such weather—reasonable people and those without a duty to safety and security of the public. Of course, that meant Lord Mayor Koloman would be deep in his cups, snuggled under warm blankets, while lamenting the tragedy of a life disrupted by something as uncaring as the weather.

Aveline snorted. *Koloman should be out here, making sure everyone is free from harm. People wouldn't joke so much about tragic accidents taking his life.*

As if on cue, she passed a hooded couple struggling against the torrent, complaining about Koloman, "Do you think he's praying for everyone?"

"Don't be stupid." The woman held onto her partner's arm for stability. "He's praying we all drown so he can loot our homes."

Aveline shouted over the storm, "Do you need help getting inside?"

"No, love." The woman shook her head. "We was caught out making our morning deliveries when this all started. We're just a few doors away."

Continuing toward Caravan Bridge, Aveline left the two behind. Already, the Copper Run River ran well above its normal level. Each wind gust blew water over the west bank. Fighting the wind and stinging rain, she made her way to the jail. Shutters protected the windows from the driving rain; the duty officer remembered to shut them this time.

Who is it today? Valon? Aveline pounded on the oak door, since the constable on duty would have barred the door when they closed the shutters. Lieutenant Valon ushered her in, securing the door behind her.

"Nethun's pissing on us today, eh? Or do you think this one is Tinian?" Valon took her cloak, shaking the water from it before hanging it on a peg on the wall.

"I think Nethuns only gets the blame for storms out at sea, so this has to be Tinian's wrath." Another peal of thunder shook the jail. Aveline glanced at the sky. "I mean, blessing. Tinian's blessing us with this wonderful rain."

"I've mulled some wine." Valon lifted two mugs off a rack near the stove, then filled them from a kettle.

"I'm sure the farmers whose fields are getting washed out won't be too thankful for this. The gods need to work in moderation." She took the steaming tankard from Valon. "Thanks."

"At least we don't have anyone staying with us right now. I didn't have a chance to restock the larder yet."

Aveline seated herself behind her desk. Noticing the caked mud on her boots, she resisted the urge to put her feet up. "Maybe it'll let up before it gets too late. Thunder woke me. Do you know how long it's been storming?"

Sudden downpours, strangers to inland towns like Curton, ravaged Vlorey and many coastal towns on a regular basis.

"I'd been dozing, myself." Valon yawned. "I figure it rolled in just before dawn."

"As soon as it lets up, rouse as many others as you can. We'll need all hands to make sure people are safe." Aveline sipped her wine. "You know how they get when unexpected things happen around here. People will act like it's punishment for some nonsense."

"We still have several patrols out searching for those missing people." Valon sipped from his mug as he double-checked each of the storm shutters. "Hopefully, they found some shelter. I sure wouldn't want to be caught out in open fields in all this."

A crash of thunder rattled the windows. Aveline let the warm liquid trickle down her throat, warming her from the inside out. "They'll be all right." *It's Tasha I'm worried about.*

* * *

The grotto provided Tasha and Vasco some protection from the early morning downpour. Pepper received the worst of it in her unprotected spot near the tree. Hearing her whinnies, Vasco rose early. He untied her reins, leading her into the small cave. Hugging her knees close to her chest, Tasha watched the torrent of water cascading over the top edge of the mouth of the cave. While Vasco put the last of their dry wood on the fire, she breathed deeply. The odor of burning wood mingling with wet earth triggered childhood memories of her parents' farm.

Whispering to his horse as the storm raged outside, Vasco stroked Pepper's neck. His attention calmed the mare, and Tasha found herself dozing. When she awoke again, she found a snoring Vasco slumped against the cave wall. Morning light struggled to penetrate the dark clouds emptying their burden of rain. Casting a pall of twilight over the riverbank, the deluge exhibited no sign of relenting. Tasha stretched before tending to the fire. Coaxing higher flames from the smoldering embers smothered by wind-blown water proved impossible. Sighing, she kicked the charred remains of their fire farther out of the cave.

"How long do you think it'll last?"

Tasha started, surprised by Vasco's voice cutting through the constant howling wind. She pulled her cloak tight around her. "Hard to say. Strong storms like these often let up after a few hours, but I've seen one last the better part of a day."

"A whole day?" Vasco peered out into the squall.

"That's unlikely this time of year." She continued watching the rain, aware of Vasco stepping closer to her. He moved to put his arm around her shoulder. Turning, Tasha held a finger in his face. "I did not give you leave to touch me."

"Apologies." Bowing, he backed away.

"Is that what passes for acceptable behavior in Maritropa? I thought you fancied Aveline?" She resumed her observation of the falling rain, keeping Vasco in the periphery of her vision.

"Well, I"—he pointed at the river—"is… is it supposed to rise that quickly?"

Regarding the river spill over its banks creeping toward the remains of their fire, Tasha's eyes widened. She dashed over to her pack to gather her things. "We have to get out. Now!"

They scrambled to break camp as the water first seeped, then gushed, over the bank, lapping at their boots while they snatched their packs off the floor of the cave. The water rose to Pepper's knees by the time Vasco gathered his gear. Upon tossing the saddle over her back, he led her deeper into the flood toward dry land up the hill. Tasha waded behind them, holding her pack above her head. Rushing water tugged at her, ever rising, as she struggled to push her way to shore.

Vasco secured Pepper to a tree branch, then returned to the advancing edge of the river. He reached for Tasha. "Take my hand!"

Tasha threw the bag of herbs at him, slipping on the rocks below the water's surface. She saw the satchel hit him in the chest just before her head plunged underwater. The current swept her downstream. Clawing to keep her head above the surge, she heard Vasco call to her until the river muffled all sounds but the rush of the flood.

Coughing, Tasha kicked to propel herself toward the bank. She reached for an overhanging branch, only catching it at the last moment. The bark dug into her palms as the swift current threatened to drag her downstream. After catching her breath, she hauled herself along the branch and toward the bank.

Losing her grip as soggy bark peeled off the limb, Tasha fell back into the water. She spun toward the center of the eddy, slamming into a boulder before sinking underwater. As the river swept her away, her vision darkened.

Chapter 9

"What a mess." Aveline surveyed the ruts in the earthen streets carved by rushing water during the storm. People busied themselves clearing away debris from the front of their homes and businesses during what surely promised to be a temporary lull in the weather. She helped a farmer right his market stall.

Valon watched a dark cloud slide past overhead. "I hope the next one isn't as bad. Remember when it rained for a week straight a few years back?"

"That was the worst." Aveline shook her head at the memory. The river ran through town within a deep gully, capable of carrying twice the water volume as it did during the dry months. That year when the Copper Run overflowed its banks, every home within a block of the river flooded.

Aveline pointed down the street. "Work your way past the church. See if you can find any of the lads to help with cleanup. Don't take them away from their families if they're needed, though. I'm going across the river, and I'll work my way toward Miners' Gate."

Though the gate lay almost due south from the river, Aveline intended to circle past Tasha's apothecary. She worried the flood waters had spilled over and affected adjacent homes, like Tasha's.

Tromping through the street splattered mud onto her boots and breeches, accumulating a thick layer by the time she crossed the bridge above the Copper Run. On good days, the river ran brown. After the storm, however, broken branches and other detritus flowed downstream, collecting against the bridge pylons. Upriver, she observed a group of draks forming a chain as they waded in to retrieve an approaching object. To her horror, Aveline witnessed them pulling a limp drakling out of the river. Laying it ashore, they gathered around the tiny figure to mourn.

Clenching her jaw, Aveline hurried across the bridge. She knew better than to expect no casualties from such a storm and flash flood; nevertheless, it pained her heart to see proof of the cost in lives. When she came to the Drunken Horse, she made a cursory examination. The tavern appeared to be none the worse for the wear. She observed the owner clearing away storm debris from the side of the building. Calling to him, the smith jogged next door to lend a hand. Aveline ducked down a side street, avoiding mud-filled puddles on the way.

When she reached Tasha's apothecary, she found a group of dark-scaled draks clustered around the door. One stepped away from the group, bowing as Aveline approached.

"Captain Aveline."

"What's going on here?" Aveline assumed they did not know of Tasha's herb-gathering expedition.

"We're in need of some medicines, but Tasha isn't answering her door."

Glancing over their heads at the building, Aveline noted the dark stain that rose halfway up the walls. The hills of Curton afforded some parts of town more protection from rising waters than others, but, unfortunately, Tasha's home was only a few feet above the riverbank.

"Tasha left yesterday to gather more herbs and reagents." Aveline pushed her way through the crowd of diminutive draks. "I'm sure she wouldn't mind if I help you. Do you know what you need?"

Aveline tried the door handle as the draks conferred among themselves, but the lock held firm.

"We've had some sprains and twisted ankles trying to make it through this storm. She usually gives us poultices or teas of white willow bark and turmeric for those kinds of pains. If we could just get the ingredients, we can make the teas and poultices ourselves."

Cupping her hands around her eyes, Aveline peered through the cloudy windows at the interior, the devastation obvious even from her limited view. "Do you know what they look like?"

"Yes."

Aveline rubbed her shoulder. *I wish I had my armor for this.* "All right, step back." She ushered the draks away before throwing her weight against the door. The jamb, softened from the flood water, burst. Aveline, unprepared for the timber to give way, tumbled into Tasha's shop. The shopkeeper's bell at the top of the door flew across the room, landing in a pile of leaves with a jingle and a plop.

The stink of wet, moldy herbs permeated the air. Objects on high shelves remained dry, but as far as Aveline could tell, the water ruined at least half of Tasha's inventory. A drak stuck his head through the doorway.

"She kept them in that cabinet behind the counter." The drak picked his way through the rubble.

Although it bore a high-water stain, Tasha's apothecary cabinet stood unmoved by the flood. Aveline helped the drak through the debris surrounding the counter, then looked for the packets Tasha used for reagents. The drak searched through the lower drawers of the cabinet.

Every stash of packets and pouches Aveline found dripped with fetid water. The drak showed her handfuls of herbs. "I think we'll be all right without the packets. How much money should we leave?"

"That's a good question." Upon rubbing the nape of her neck, Aveline found her fingers clammy. "Look, just tell me who you are and where you live. I'll make sure Tasha settles up with you when she returns, all right?"

"Oh, thank you, Captain." The drak bowed, struggling to keep hold of the herbs in his hands. "May Hon keep your hearth warm and comforting. I am Zadok of the Ashenscale clan. My kin and I live across the river, in Drakton, at the base of the tower."

Aveline nodded. "I know the area." Situated near the guard towers, stone and timber buildings gave way to hovels and lean-tos in the shantytown in which less affluent draks lived. "All right. I'll let her know. I'm going to lock up now, so you best be on your way."

"Yes, Captain. Thank you again." The drak bowed as he backed away, stumbling over bits of wreckage until he exited the shop.

The watch captain locked Tasha's shop by securing the remains of the door with an armchair. Aveline stepped through the opening, then leaned loose boards against the gap. Returning to her rounds and surveying storm damage, she searched for a member of the city watch.

Trotting toward her, a pair of officers saluted. Aveline pointed over her shoulder toward Tasha's shop. "The door is smashed on the apothecary. You there"—she gestured at the short-bearded guard.

"Constable Boboc, Captain." He stood at attention.

"Find Lieutenant Valon and let him know about the apothecary. Have him assign rotating shifts."

Boboc saluted and left the area. His comrade remained at attention. "Captain, the Lord Mayor is looking for you. He's in the market."

Aveline clenched her jaw. *What does that petulant man-child want now?* "Very well, Constable…"

"Grecu."

"Thank you, Constable Grecu." Dropping her hand to the haft of her mace, she squeezed the unyielding wood in lieu of Lord Mayor Koloman's neck. "See to the apothecary until you're relieved."

"Right away, Captain." He saluted, then headed toward the shop.

Once more, rain fell from the sky, a light drizzle at first. However, Aveline observed from the advancing clouds another imminent downpour. Shutting her eyes, she offered a prayer to whichever god listened that Koloman's demands would be reasonable.

* * *

Tasha awoke lying on a rocky embankment, her soggy clothes clinging to her body. Albeit rain no longer fell, but dark clouds continued casting a gloom across the sky. Shivering accompanied the pounding in her head as she rolled over and retched. She pulled herself through the mud, away from the river. A glance backward showed the water level already lower than when it first swept her away.

After crawling a few minutes, Tasha rose to her feet. Her water-laden, mud-coated robes weighed her down, heightening the icy feeling in her bones. Groping at her neck, she breathed a sigh of relief when her fingers closed around her amulet. She anticipated using much of her old magic to get through the rest of the day.

Despite grey skies, the heat of summer pushed through the dank air. Tasha shrugged off her robes, deciding to carry them. With the warm breeze against her skin, Tasha felt the chill dissipate. Traveling in her smallclothes, she decided to search for Vasco by following the river south. Depending on how far it had carried her, she might find him as much as half a day away, assuming he followed the river downstream. Tasha recognized the terrain from their journey to the grotto together, but as the day dragged on, she feared they might have missed each other.

She paused at the base of an uprooted tree. Water collected in the gash by its base, pointing to the storm as the cause of the tree's demise. Cawing, a bird alighted on a nearby root.

The crow stared with beady, black eyes, cocking its head at Tasha. She stepped away from it. Cawing, it hopped once. It blinked, then turned its head to its right. She studied the bird for a moment before pivoting in the same direction. From her position at the base of the uprooted tree, she noticed nothing out of the ordinary, just more forest. Tasha returned her attention to the bird.

"Caw!"

"Well, you're a lot of help."

"Caw! Caw!" Hopping, it fluttered its wings.

Tasha dropped her robes on the ground, then removed her soggy boots. She flexed her toes, digging them into the blanket of moss and pine needles covering the forest floor. Closing her eyes, she reached out with her mind, feeling the life of the forest around her.

"Caw!"

Opening one eye, she stared at the bird. "It's hard to concentrate when you keep doing that."

"Caw!" The crow flew past Tasha to alight on another tree. She gathered up her robes and boots. *Am I seriously going to follow this bird? I must have cracked my head pretty hard.* The throbbing in her head had subsided slightly, especially before the crow interrupted her attempt to connect to the forest. Each time she caught up to the crow, it flew off again, leading her from tree to tree.

By the time they reached the road, Tasha's robes had dried. Encrusted mud broke off as she shook the garment and pulled it over her head. Before crossing the road, she paused to search for signs of Vasco. Lacking tracking experience, she could not determine which of the myriad hoof marks and footprints were freshest. Likewise, she found it impossible to ascertain if any belonged to her companion or his mount. The crow watched her until she finished assessing the tracks before it flapped away again.

Farther away from the river, the terrain became rocky. As the day progressed, the dark overcast sky gave way to scattered clouds. Droning insects and birds serenaded her trek with the crow. Tasha followed the bird until the waning light of dusk fell over the forest. When she realized the crow no longer accompanied her, she stood motionless. Trees surrounded her. Tasha focused solely on following the bird, she failed to keep track of her location with regard to the road.

This is ridiculous. I've wandered these woods for years. I can't be lost.

As the sun set and twilight gave way to night, Tasha admitted she was, in fact, lost. Upon removing her amulet from around her neck, she held it aloft. "*Fos.*"

Light bloomed from the stone within the amulet, illuminating the area around her. She pivoted in a slow circle, scanning the canopy for any sign of the crow she'd been following.

Nothing.

Cursing her foolishness, Tasha extinguished the amulet. She dropped her boots on the ground, closing her eyes. The forest came alive in her mind. She felt life all around her: an ant carrying a scrap of leaf to its colony, a mother sparrow keeping guard over her nest, a fox some distance away on the prowl, and an overwhelming sense of death just ahead of her.

Shivering, her eyes snapped open. The sensation of death brought memories of Lorelei's battered, bloodied, and crushed body back to her. The feeling left as quickly as it arrived. Despite the cold pall of death, she detected no malice. Instead, feelings of grief tinged with anger washed over her. She picked up her boots, then strode in the direction she decided was the right one.

Tightening the grip on her amulet, she prepared to unleash her arcane power on any threat that lay before her.

Tasha passed through a thick cluster of spruce trees into a small clearing. Two structures jutted from the earth in the center of the space, their stark white color prominent against the blackness of night in the deep forest. Covered with moss, the weathered pillars were irregular in shape, unlike stone columns. Running her hand along one of them, she discovered they were bones, enormous leg bones. Beyond them, she noticed a partially collapsed structure at the far edge of the clearing. In the distance, a wolf howled, sending a chill down her spine.

Tasha illuminated her amulet. Ahead, the collapsed building appeared to be a hut. The roof appeared flat, while one of the sides sloped up steeply from the forest floor. Tilting her head, Tasha examined the toppled dwelling. Upon inspection of the flora growing out of its windows and climbing up its sides, she determined the building had been abandoned for years.

Holding her light aloft, Tasha approached the cottage. A glint of light near the gable caught her eye. A crow.

Is that the same one?

It watched her creep toward the hut. Another crow flew by and landed alongside it, then another and another, until the birds lined the edge of the roof. They all stared at her with unblinking black eyes, watching in unison as she continued her approach.

Rotten planks dangled from the doorframe, a curtain of wood obscuring her view of the interior. She pushed one piece of timber aside. Snapping, it fell to the ground. A cloud of white spores swirled from the impact. She pulled the neckline of her robes over her nose and mouth, then proceeded through the door.

Unsurprisingly, the interior of the structure resembled an overgrown garden. Shrubs and creepers covered every surface, despite large furniture, such as the bed and a table, poking through in places. She noted the wooden floor, now occupying the place where the wall should've been, remained intact and in good repair. A stump with a hollowed-out core dominated the center of it.

She recoiled from shards of broken pots and jugs scattered in the area. Crouching, she discovered the pieces appeared to be from standard pottery one might use for water or wine. Wrought-iron utensils intertwined with the grasses.

A flash of light from outside illuminated the interior with more intensity than the glow from her amulet, and the rumble of thunder identified the source. As she blinked away spots in her vision, she noticed what appeared to be an upended shrine.

Tasha let her glowing amulet dangle at her neck while she righted the overturned altar. Carvings on the sides depicted symbols of harvest and fertility. A bow-wielding maiden and a deer flanked the relief of a tree on the top surface of the altar.

Running her fingers over the figures, Tasha identified the goddesses associated with the iconography. "Cybele, Artume, Gaia."

The wolf howled again, sounding as if it stood just outside the clearing. Another flash of light and rumble of thunder shook the hut, followed by a downpour. Despite its ramshackle appearance, little water seeped in. Extinguishing her amulet and folding her legs beneath her, Tasha prepared to wait out the storm.

Chapter 10

To Aveline's dismay, Lord Mayor Koloman awaited her in the market, in spite of the storm. Rivulets of water streamed down the drooping corners of the tarp his servants held for him to stand under. The watch sergeant near him snapped to attention as she approached.

"Now, Lord Mayor"—Aveline drew nearer—"what could possibly be so important you're out here in this foul weather rather than safe in your warm, dry home?"

"My home"—Koloman crossed his arms—"is nothing of the sort! Tree limbs have smashed my windows, and this cursed storm has wreaked havoc with my parlor."

Aveline clenched her jaw. "And what would you like me to do about that? Look around." She gestured to the buildings behind her. "Many homes and businesses are damaged. No one can complete repairs until the storm lets up."

"Have your men round up some vagabonds from Drakton, then send them to my estate immediately." He sniffed, scowling at the servant behind him as the tarp drooped. "I'll put them to work repairing my home."

"In the rain?" Aveline pinched the bridge of her nose.

"Did you not hear me, woman? The rain is coming into my house. This must be rectified at once!"

Closing her eyes, Aveline counted to three before replying. "Yes, very well. I'll get some guards right on that. In the meantime, you can stay dry at the jail until they've finished. There are only a couple of drunks in there today. Hopefully, someone has cleaned up the vomit by now."

Even in the dim, overcast light, Aveline noticed the color drain from Koloman's face. He shook his head. "No. I believe I shall return to my estate now. My bed is warm and dry, at least." Raising an eyebrow, he smiled. "Care to indulge with me, Lady Aveline? Down comforters? Mulled wine? I am quite—"

Aveline held up her hand. "I have duties to attend. I was on my way to help clear debris when I received your summons."

"Hm. Pity." Shrugging, he laughed. "Well, you know where I live if you grow tired of being cold."

Turning, she strode away without further acknowledgment. The sergeant followed her. "Lady Aveline? Who shall I send to round up the draks?"

"Send no one. Let that slimy git pay a fair wage if he wants laborers to fix his house." She put her hand on the sergeant's shoulder, facing him. "Go home to your family. Get out of this damned rain."

The sergeant saluted. "Yes, m'lady. Thank you."

Aveline, noting the river was lower than it had been during the flood, crossed the bridge over the Copper Run. Although she worried more flooding would follow the current downpour, she put those dark thoughts out of her head as she passed the Drunken Horse—open for business by the look of it—and proceeded south toward Mudders' Gate. Smoke rose from the chimneys of the bakery. Even in a storm, the city's artisans worked their trades as long as the weather didn't intrude.

A man, holding the reins of his horse, pounded on the livery door. His once fine clothes, now sodden with mud, clung to his body. "Don't you know it's pouring out here? I can't leave Pepper out in this!"

She recognized Vasco's distinctive Maritropan accent, noticing he stood alone. Dropping her hand to the haft of her mace, she approached him. "Where's Tasha?"

Pausing mid-knock, Vasco turned. "Ah! Lady Aveline… a beautiful sight on such a horrid afternoon."

"You left with Tasha. I didn't expect to see either of you back so soon. Where is she?"

The tall man fell to his knees before her. "Please forgive me. We were caught by the flood, and she was swept away. There was nothing I could do."

"What?" Aveline staggered backward. *Tasha?*

"She threw me the pack of herbs we'd gathered, then was gone." He glanced at his horse. "I kept them safe and dry, but I was unable to locate her after. The river was swift, and I had to seek higher ground lest it swept Pepper and me to our doom."

Aveline pushed the groveling mage aside. Unbidden tears blinded her as she raced toward Miners' Gate. Sliding in the mud, she stopped just outside the gatehouse. She pounded on the door until someone answered.

"Lady Aveline!" A bearded man wearing the livery of a watch sergeant opened the door. "Best come in out of the rain."

She stomped the mud off her boots as he closed the door behind her. "How many can you spare to search for someone?"

The city watch sergeant scratched his wiry beard. "A handful, no more. Once the rain stops, that is."

"Have them search the banks of the river, both sides. Up from Miners' Gate and down from Mudders' Gate."

"What are they looking for?" He shuffled to the stove to tend a bubbling pot, serving Aveline a steaming mug of mulled wine before helping himself.

"Tasha, my frie… the herbalist. The apothecary." Cupping the steaming mug, Aveline blew across the top of the liquid.

"If she was swept away—"

"Just do it!" Unwilling to hear talk of there being no hope, Aveline glared at the watch sergeant. Upon returning the mug to him, she exited, slamming the door behind her. Following a nearby alley toward the city wall, she headed toward Curton's south gate. Her home, a few blocks south of the gate, stood secure and undamaged in its protected location. She threw open the door, immediately slamming it behind herself.

After doffing her sodden clothes, she picked up the open bottle of mead from her table and poured herself a drink. The liquid burned its way into her empty stomach.

Steadying herself on the table, she wiped her eyes. "Dammit."

* * *

Tasha awoke, uncertain for how long she'd slept. A wan smile spread across her face when she realized she maintained a seated, meditative position the entire time she slumbered. However, as she uncrossed her legs from beneath her, tingling pains spread through her feet and her pride faded. Filtered by the forest canopy, dappled light streamed through the windows of the hut. Chirping their morning songs, birds heralded a new day. After emerging from the upended structure, the cawing of crows drew her attention to the surrounding tree branches. Rows of black birds watched her.

She regarded the crows. "So, do you think Vasco actually got my herbs back to town, or is he lost in the wilderness somewhere?"

"Caw!"

"That's what I thought." Tasha turned away from the hut to find her bearings in the forest. Unfamiliar with the area, she decided to head toward the rising sun until she found a landmark.

Tasha figured walking toward the sun would lead her to either the Copper Run or into the eastern mountains, depending on which side of the river she had awakened. As she hiked through the forest, she cursed herself for not paying attention to that detail when she dragged herself ashore. *I suppose, with all the twists and bends in the river, the distinction between left and right bank is meaningless.*

As she traveled, she noticed a crow flying from tree to tree to keep pace with her. "Left, right, east, west. As long as I get my bearings soon, I don't much care, right?"

"Caw! Caw!"

Tasha, hands on her hips, faced the crow. "Why are you following me?"

The bird fluttered away. When it failed to return, she resumed her hike. By the time the sun reached the midpoint to its zenith, the terrain grew rockier and sloped noticeably upward. Tasha adjusted her course to head north, by her reckoning. She should have encountered the river by now, unless she'd awakened on the eastern bank. In the distance, she heard the rapid tapping of a woodpecker searching for grubs in a nearby tree.

A snapping branch and the rustle of underbrush alerted her to a frightened deer bounding away. Breathing deeply, Tasha took in the sounds of the forest around her. The forest after a heavy rain smelled different, a mix of pine and earth combined with an unpleasant undercurrent of natural dank and decay. Again, she recalled the farm her parents owned.

Tasha chuckled. The farm, and her parents, may as well have been on the other side of the world, so far removed were they from her. Her existence there seemed a lifetime ago. In some respects, it was. As a young woman, she left to attend the Arcane University, and, even after Lorelei's death, she had never returned. For all Tasha knew, Cedar Ridge, the village near her parents' farm, no longer existed.

Resigning herself to foraging, Tasha munched on the leaves of familiar plants as she traveled, but they did little to stave off her growing hunger. By the time she emerged from the forest and recognized Curton before her, her stomach, knotted and churning, demanded to be fed.

The Copper Run lay between her and Miners' Gate, with no bridges to allow crossing save for those behind the city walls. Tasha resigned herself to a long hike around the eastern side to Mudders' Gate. Viewing the town from the hills, Tasha noticed the river had overflowed its banks, but she was still too far away from Curton to see any damage.

She examined her boots, muddy and misshapen from their extended stay in the river, before discarding them. Hearing the flutter of wings behind her, Tasha turned to see a crow alight on one of her boots. Pecking at one of the laces, it looked up at her and then pecked at it again.

Kneeling, Tasha reached for her discarded footwear. The crow perched on the other boot as she loosened the string, finally pulling it free. She offered it toward the crow. It snatched it up in its black beak before flying away.

Once it soared out of sight, Tasha resumed her trek to Curton. Traveling to Mudders' Gate took most of the rest of the day. She squinted against the sun, low in the western sky.

To her dismay, the gate stood closed as she approached, despite the lingering light of the late-afternoon sun. She heard members of the city watch chatting from behind the massive oaken doors, which lay to rest her concerns about an imminent threat to the city. Tasha banged a fist against the doors until a guard peeked over the wall.

"Hey there, what's this ruckus about?"

"It's me, Tasha. The herbalist." She gestured at the giant doors. "Why is the gate closed this early?"

"Captain Aveline's orders. We're keeping things locked up until we get a handle on the damage caused by the flood." Ducking behind the wall, the guard called down to comrades at street level. "Here, it's the herbalist. Let her in!"

Heavy metal latches released, and wood groaned in protest as one of the gate doors swung open just enough to admit Tasha entry. Puddles of mud covered the road, squishing between her toes. She took deliberate steps to avoid falling

"Your shop's over by Drakton, right?" A guard offered her a hand as one of her feet slid out from under her.

Tasha steadied herself with his help. "Across the river from Danica's Den, actually."

The raucous customers of Curton's main gambling house rarely intruded upon Tasha's meditations, even when games played long into the night.

"Things were bad down by the river. Hope your shop's all right."

Tasha's stomach knotted at the thought of losing her home. "Me too."

Chapter 11

"All right, pull yourself together." Aveline rolled out of bed, barely getting her feet under her before hitting the floor. Her tongue felt fuzz covered, and her head pounded. An empty mead bottle rolled away as she shuffled toward the wardrobe.

Aveline looked toward the heavens. "I got myself drunk for you, Tasha."

The room spun when she tilted her head, and she clutched at a chair to keep her balance. Closing her eyes, she waited for the spinning to stop. While remaining silent, Aveline noticed rain no longer pelted her roof.

With deliberate motions, she changed into clean clothes and then donned her armor. She secured her mace on her belt, threw her shield over her shoulder, and opened the door. Aveline heard the sounds of the city beyond nearby buildings. After locking the door to her home, she made her way through the alleys and backstreets until she reached Miners' Gate.

The city watch sergeant in charge saluted as she approached. "Nothing to report, Lady Aveline. No trouble."

"Cleanup going all right?" She shielded her eyes from the harsh sunlight streaming from above, the bane of hangovers. "What about those men I ordered to search up and down the river?"

"They left at first light. Haven't heard anything yet." He waved at a pair of robed draks proceeding through the gate. "Haven't heard anything from Mudders' Gate for a while, though. Lieutenant Valon was by earlier. He said he was going to check things there."

"Very well, Sergeant. Thank you." Aveline stepped aside to let a horse and cart through. Its wheels gouged deep ruts in the mud as the driver attempted to guide it in a straight line. She followed the cart on its course through the center of town, straddling one of the ruts as she stepped.

Despite the mud and storm damage, farmers and craftsfolk set up their stalls in Curton's market square, churning up more muck than usual. *Everyone still has to eat, I suppose.*

By the time Aveline crossed to the far side, mud coated her legs up to her knees. She paused at the steps leading into Cybele's Church to knock dried clay off her boots. Mother Anya watched from the open doors of her church.

"The rain is a gift and a curse, is it not?" The old woman nodded to a farmer who bowed his head as he passed.

"Why do all things good for life make such a mess?" Aveline leaned against the stoop as she pried a hardening ball of mud from under her greaves.

Smiling, Anya raised her hands as she glanced skyward. "Ah, child. That is a question for the Keeper of Mysteries." Lowering her hands, she laughed. "Truth be told, I could use a bit less mess myself."

Satisfied she'd cleaned the worst of the muck from her boots, Aveline bowed her head to the matriarchal cleric. "I'm off to check on the missing girl."

"May today bring good news of Innya and the others." Mother Anya placed her hand on her chest. "Blessings of Cybele be with you, Lady Aveline."

Despite the old woman's blessing, Aveline held out little hope. She continued on her way, following the road through Hillside toward Mudders' Gate. Behind the Church of Cybele stood Hon's Hearth, temple of the god of pacts. A small crowd gathered around Hearth Master Marko as he pontificated the virtues of opening one's home to the unfortunate during times of need such as this. Aveline observed long enough to ensure no pickpockets worked the crowd, then left the hearth master to his preaching.

At Mudders' Gate, several guards inspected a covered wagon seeking entry into the city. Aveline allowed them to work unfettered. Instead, she sought out Lieutenant Valon. The officer leaned against the gatehouse, watching his subordinates perform their inspection. Bags under his eyes revealed the lack of sleep from which they'd all suffered since the storm rolled through.

"Anything to report?" Aveline returned his salute as she approached.

"The patrols out searching for that girl returned. They had a rough time out there during the storm. I wasn't sure where you'd be, so I told them to meet you at the jail." Valon tensed as the wagon driver argued with the guard, but he relaxed again when both laughed.

That the guards seemed to have returned without any of the missing people did nothing to alleviate Aveline's anxiety. "Very well. I'll head that way now. Are they all back?"

"They are. They'll probably be waiting for you now." Pushing himself away from the wall, he clapped his hands as a group of farmers approached carrying baskets of produce. "Here, let these folks by."

Aveline left Valon to his duties, making her way to the market. She purchased a wheel of cheese, a rope of cured sausages, and a loaf of bread for the jail's larder. A couple of brightly colored blouses sold by a merchant she didn't recognize caught her eye. Aveline made a mental note to return and peruse his wares before the market closed.

The spartan stone construction of the jail proved a boon during storms like the one Curton experienced. Apart from debris clustered around the walls, it appeared much as it had prior to the storm. Sweeping twigs and leaves away from the door of the adjacent home, the midwife, Petra, nodded in greeting to Aveline.

"Do you need help with that?"

Aveline regarded the bundles of provisions in her arms. "If you could get the door for me, I would greatly appreciate it."

"Of course, Lady Aveline." Petra strode toward her.

"Cybele bless you, Petra."

"I'll be needing that." The midwife bowed her head. "Three babies on the way, any day now."

"Not the same mother, I hope."

Petra laughed. "Oh, that'd be a sight. No, no. One to Ilsa and Nicolae up in Old Town, another to Elena and Andrei at Black Goat Farm, and the last to Adela and Mihai at Fairstone Mill. Do you know them?"

Aveline shook her head. "No. The mill? Is that the one downriver or upriver?"

"Down."

"I wish them all Dolios's luck." Offering a smile of thanks to the midwife, Aveline turned to close the door with her foot.

"Aveline, there you are!"

Her heart skipped a beat when she heard Tasha's voice. The bundles she carried fell from her arms upon seeing her friend rise from the chair behind the desk.

"You're alive!" Aveline leapt over a cheese wheel and hugged the sorceress, spinning her as she laughed.

"All right, all right." Giggling, Tasha patted Aveline's shoulders until she set the sorceress down. Tasha's hair, knotted and tangled with twigs, hung in disarray, and her robes cracked where dried mud stiffened the cloth. "Should I not be?"

"I ran into Vasco last night. He said you were swept away in the river." Aveline retrieved the supplies she had dropped. "The storms didn't give me much reason to hope."

Taking the cheese and bread from Aveline, Tasha accompanied her to the larder. "No, I suppose not."

"Still, you look better than I expected for someone washed downstream during a storm. It's a wonder the current didn't carry you here." After prying open the larder door, Aveline stocked the shelves. When she finished, she picked up one of the older sausages and tore into it. "Hungry?"

Nodding, the sorceress sliced a piece of cheese. Tears welled in her eyes as she chewed. "It's all gone, Aveline."

"Your shop?" Aveline rubbed her friend's arm. "I saw. Don't worry. I'll help you get it sorted."

"Everything in there is ruined. It'll be like starting over." Tasha leaned against the shelf. "The water got everywhere. My reagents. My clothes. My bed. Everything stinks of mold, my door is completely shattered, and there are already rats infesting the place."

Aveline cleared her throat, studying a knot in the shelf. "Yeah, I broke the door. Sorry about that."

"You did?"

The watch captain nodded. "Some draks needed medicine, and there wasn't another way in. We scavenged what we could; they promised to settle up with you when you returned. That was before I spoke to Vasco."

Tasha wiped her eyes. "Which draks?"

"Ashenscale clan. Zodok?"

"Zadok." Tasha nodded. "They're honest. They'll pay if they can find me."

Aveline pulled her friend into a hug. "You can stay with me for as long as you need. It'll be cramped, but we can make do. Or, if you prefer, stay here. We can fix up one of the back cells."

"Thanks."

Stomping accompanied by swearing in the front room of the jail drew their attention. Aveline gestured for Tasha to follow her. "That'll be the patrols returning from the search. Late, as usual."

* * *

Aveline and Tasha found a dozen constables stowing their weapons and armor in racks around the room. They snapped to attention upon noticing Aveline's presence.

After she gestured for them to proceed, one of the men, a grizzled fellow with sandy-brown hair and eyes narrowed from a lifetime of squinting at the sun, stepped forward.

"What news, Lieutenant?"

The man shook his head. "We found tracks in a field east of Mudders' Gate. We followed them as far as we could"—he gestured upward—"but the sky opened up. After that…"

"No use?" Crossing her arms, Aveline sat on the edge of her desk.

"Not after that storm. They looked to be heading toward the old copper mines."

Long since depleted, so little of value remained in the mines that no one ventured there. Tasha expected if one went exploring, they'd find nothing but vermin.

Several guards ducked into the larder. A few minutes later, they returned with a tray filled with meat, bread, and cheese. The grizzled scout selected a sausage before continuing. Aveline motioned for them to offer the tray to Tasha. The sorceress tore off a hunk of bread to accompany the cheese she held.

"I had the lads here"—the scout, Jolen, glanced over his shoulder—"hunker down as best they could, and I headed toward the mines alone." He winked. "Move faster alone, you see. Quieter too."

Jolen breathed deeply. "There's something there now, Lady Aveline. I couldn't make it out in the dark, but I saw fires and folks moving about. There was a sinister feeling in the air… and it wasn't from the storm, if you take my meaning. Seemed too dangerous to move closer during the downpour, so I went back to our camp. When the weather cleared a bit, we headed back here."

"Very well." Aveline clapped her hands to gain everyone's attention. "Get yourselves cleaned up. Go home. Rest. Hopefully, the storm spared your homes. Report for duty when you're able. I'll handle the search from here."

The guards saluted, heading off one by one as they finished eating. Aveline paced the room, chewing her lip.

Tasha regarded her friend. "It could just be draks."

"Draks." Nodding, Aveline raised her eyebrows. "Or oroqs. Maybe even worse."

Running her finger through her hair in a futile attempt to work out a knot, Tasha frowned. "Assuming that is where the girl was taken, and perhaps the rest of the missing folk, what would oroqs want with them?"

"Food? Pleasure?" Aveline opened the storm shutters. "I'm just speculating. Perhaps that oroq I had here with her Watchman friend might provide some insight."

Tasha glanced at her mud-infused clothes. "I think I'll try to find something clean to wear."

"Oh, wait." Aveline withdrew a key from her pouch. She tossed it to Tasha. "Let yourself into my place when you've finished. By the way, Vasco has your pack of herbs. I don't remember where he's staying."

"If he's even still in town." Tasha brushed several strands of hair from her face. "Well, there aren't that many inns. If he's here, I'll find him, or someone who knows where he is. He was staying at the Drunken Horse the other night, right?"

"I think so. He also keeps his horse at the livery by Miners' Gate."

"Good to know, thank you." Leaving her friend to her work, Tasha exited the jail.

As she proceeded down the street, a flutter of motion in the periphery of her vision drew her attention. A crow flew from rooftop to rooftop, shadowing her steps. Squinting at it, Tasha stopped.

The crow stared back.

Chapter 12

After eating her fill from the larder, Aveline noted the returning scouts had almost emptied the food stores of the jail. Sighing, she resigned herself to purchasing more provisions while she scoured the inns and taverns for the oroq woman traveling with the Watchman, Aerik.

When her searches at Hon's Hearth, the Bristled Boar, and the Drunken Horse proved fruitless, Aveline decided to check Danica's Den. The gambling house remained her only hope of finding the pair, assuming they had not yet left town to seek their fortunes elsewhere.

With the sun high in the sky, most of Danica's clientele would be away earning coin at their jobs. Still, Aveline knew from experience that a few dedicated gamblers would have games running. If she found no one else, the game masters would know something.

Danica, herself a stout dwarf woman, held the door open for Aveline. A smoky haze covered the room.

"Can I help you with something, Lady Aveline?" The matron raised her chin to look down her nose at the watch captain, no small feat for one who only stood as tall as Aveline's stomach.

"I'm looking for someone, a…"

"Edric again?" One of Danica's employees, the dwarf worked to pay off gambling debt. When Edric's indentured servitude began, he spent almost as much time in the jail as he had at work. "He's kept his nose clean. He might be sweet on me after all this time."

Aveline held up her hand. "Not Edric. A Watchman and an oroq woman. Aerik Devilhead… or something like that. I don't remember her name, but she had eyes like scorching embers and a tattoo on her head."

"Therkla Fire-Eyes and Aerik Devilhand." Sniffing, Danica rolled a coin over her knuckles. "I know them well. What have they done this time?"

"I just want to talk to them." Squinting, Aveline gazed at the table of gamblers seated at the far side of the room. The fog obscured their identities, but none appeared to be oroqs.

"Then it's unfortunate I seem to be having memory problems." Danica scratched the scruff growing in her cheeks, holding out her other hand expectantly.

Smiling, Aveline squeezed the proprietor's hand. "And isn't it unfortunate I haven't been having my men check the drainage gate by the river that leads into that old cistern under here?"

The dwarf woman, gritting her teeth, snatched her hand from the watch captain's grip. "Yeah, I guess it is too bad." She cleared her throat. "They're upstairs, room three. Don't run them out, eh? Profits have been down lately, and they're paying good coin for that room. Plus, what they lose at the tables helps too."

Pressing a clenched fist to her chest, Aveline bowed. "My primary concern is always for *your* financial well-being, Danica."

"*Kragga nok.*"

Aveline ignored the Dwarvish insult as she headed toward the stairs. A wrought-iron spiral column led both up and down. Climbing, she took shallow breaths as she passed through the haze laced with the odor of pipeweed and burning meat. The roof pitch of the building provided space in the upper level for a few rooms, the one she sought being the farthest from the stairs.

When she reached the door with a crooked numeral three on it, she paused to listen. Echoing laughter from downstairs drowned out any noises that might escape from the rooms in the hallway where she stood, so she knocked.

Thumping and a crash from inside indicated she'd caught someone unawares. Biting her lip, Aveline maintained a neutral expression as the door jerked open.

Therkla's red eyes narrowed. "What do you want? We haven't done anything. Even if we did, you can't prove it."

"I was hoping you could give me information." Aveline interposed her foot between the door and the jamb. "Help out your fellow citizens? Especially if you plan on staying in town much longer."

Therkla stepped backward, allowing the door to swing open. "Talk is free, I guess."

Aveline noted Aerik's absence as she scanned the spartan room. Apart from the tied-log bed that occupied most of the chamber, a small table featuring a wooden washbasin and cracked water pitcher served as the only other furniture in the room. Therkla flopped onto the mattress. Sitting with her back against the headboard, she regarded the watch captain. Lacing her fingers behind her head, she flashed a jagged-toothed smile. "Start asking your questions."

Clasping her hands behind her back, Aveline paced. "You travel a lot, you and your friend, yes? Came up from the Four Watches through the Iron Gate mountains?"

"What of it? It's not illegal." Therkla cleared her throat. "The watches aren't at war with… whatever nation this mudhole town belongs to."

"People have been vanishing. Abducted." Aveline stopped at the foot of the bed. "Loners at first, folk without families and the like. But the villains are getting bolder. Our scouts have evidence they're being taken into the hills southeast of town, where the old abandoned mines are. Are you familiar with that area?"

The oroq woman shrugged. "Yeah, I heard about the runaway whores. Me and Aerik came through there last year, but those old mines got nothing but a bunch of rotting timber, rocks, and vermin."

"Everyone has a right to earn a living however they see fit. If it's not hurting someone, what does it matter? They're not runaways." Aveline scowled. The oldest abduction took place less than a year ago. "You haven't been out that way since last year?"

"What for? The gambling's good here, and when things get too hot"—raising her brow, Therkla stared at Aveline—"Dwegerthon's not too far in the other direction."

"Hey, what's this? A party?" Aerik pushed his way past Aveline, arms laden with bread and cured meats. Dumping the load on the bed, he faced Aveline. His mane and beard appeared only slightly tamer than the night of his drunken say in Curton's jail. "Hey, you're the watch captain. What we done now?"

Therkla picked up a boule of dark bread, then tore it in half. "Relax, she's just asking about those missing whores." She pointed at Aerik's pouch. "Ale? Wine?"

"Missing *people*." Ignoring Aveline's emphasis, Therkla and Aerik continued their banter.

Grunting, Aerik withdrew a bottle from his pouch and tossed it to Therkla. She pulled out the stopper with her teeth, then spat it at Aerik. The cork bounced off his chest.

"Shame, those missing whores—"

"People. Women and men." Aveline growled, the sound emanating from deep within her chest.

"That one was my favorite. Oh, what was her name? Rose? Violet?" He snapped his fingers. "Iris!"

Therkla washed down a hunk of bread with the ale. "Your favorite was whoever was cheapest. Which is stupid since you can have me for free."

Aveline held up her hands. "Look, I really don't care—"

"Free's good"—Aerik retrieved a sausage from the bed—"but you won't wear a wig." He winked at Aveline. "I like them with flowing locks, like mine." He flicked his hair before tearing into the sausage.

"I don't suppose you know anything?" Pinching the bridge of her nose, Aveline shut her eyes.

"About the missing whores? Nah." A mouthful of cured meat muffled Aerik's reply.

"The captain there said they think the abductees may have been brought to those old mines we explored last year. Remember those?"

"Oh yeah." Aerik laughed. "Remember the mine that smelled like a tribe of sick draks had been using it as a shithole?" He tossed the nub end of the sausage at Aveline. It momentarily clung to her breastplate, leaving a perfect circle of grease behind, before it fell to the floor. "Hey, is there a reward for finding them? We're almost out of gambling money."

Aveline bit her tongue to keep a nasty retort from spilling forth, then shook her head. "That's up to the families. Most of the missing were alone in town. I'm heading out that way tomorrow to check it out, but I don't pay mercenaries. You want money, then go talk to the Lord Mayor at his estate outside of town." A crooked smile crept across Aveline's face. "He's looking for help clearing out storm debris from his parlor. Ask for money upfront from him, though."

Leaving the pair to argue over the merits of paid labor, she returned to the jail. Several members of the city watch chatted inside, and Aveline noticed two people occupying cells. One of the sergeants assured her that they were just would-be looters—not worthy of the personal attention of the watch captain. Accepting their word, Aveline left coin for them to restock the larder before she headed out.

* * *

The crow followed Tasha from the jail all the way to the market. It fluttered from stall to stall as she replaced her ruined clothes. Stopping first to peruse the cobbler's wares, she then studied her mud-caked feet. Shoes, a luxury not all in Curton enjoyed, protected her for many years from rocks, sharp sticks, and other trail hazards. Her thoughts turned to communing with the nature spirit of Gaia, and how much easier the connection came when she touched the earth with her bare skin. Satisfied she'd purchased all she needed, she left the cobbler's stall. She headed for Aveline's home, still accompanied by the crow. To her relief, the bird didn't enter the watch captain's house.

Tasha stoked a fire in the stove to warm a water-filled kettle while she sought a washbasin. After locating a hammered copper one in a cabinet near the watch captain's bed, Tasha stripped off her mud-caked garments and contemplated having them laundered. Shaking her head, Tasha opened the stove and shoved them inside, letting them burn with the wood. The basin accepted two full kettles of hot water before she had enough to clean herself. Next, she unwrapped the new jade-trimmed chestnut tunic and pleated wrap purchased in the market. The clothing fit her well. By the time she finished, Tasha felt refreshed.

After dressing, Tasha used the embers from the stove to start a fire in Aveline's hearth. While Summer in Curton enjoyed warm temperatures, her friend's home stood in the shadows of the old city wall. Surrounded by stone and other buildings, the watch captain's dwelling remained cooler throughout the year than Tasha's house near the river. Once a fire crackled in the hearth, she sat in the lone armchair and shut her eyes.

She dozed in front of the fire, her dreams leading her on a flight over Curton. Wheeling and diving, she soared through the sky. Spotting the rotting carcass of a deer just at the edge of the woods, she dove, joining a flock of crows pecking at it. A bit of flesh dangled from her beak. Before she could react, she was airborne again.

Deep in her mind, Tasha wondered why she dreamed of flying with crows—indeed, of being one—but those thoughts buried themselves beneath the exhilaration of unfettered flight. High in the air, she flew southward, seeing beyond the forested hills into the Four Watches. In the summer, shrubs and grasses grew on the gentle hills. She dove again, disappearing within a thicket.

Her vision darkened. Within the blackness, Tasha perceived a dark shape flapping toward her. It enveloped her like a cloak. When her sight cleared, she saw a duplicate of herself, wearing an iridescent black mantle of feathers. Tasha's doppelgänger smiled, pointing at her, then everything vanished.

Tasha awoke with a start when the door opened. From the dimming light, she deduced she'd slept the day away in front of the now-dying fire. Aveline tromped inside, kicking the door shut behind herself. "Can you explain why my house is covered with birds?"

Chapter 13

The sorceress nearly fell out of the armchair at Aveline's entrance. The watch captain dashed forward to catch her friend.

"Sorry, I didn't mean to startle you."

Tasha held onto Aveline's arm as she dug her knuckles into her eyes. "I must have been dozing. I didn't intend to sleep all afternoon."

"I imagine you're exhausted." Aveline released Tasha once she ascertained her friend was steady on her feet. "Do you know anything about the birds?"

"I was dreaming…" Shaking her head, Tasha approached the door. She pulled it open, craning her neck toward the roof before stepping into the street. Aveline followed.

A mass of black-feathered crows covered the roof, all watching the two women as they stared in slack-jawed wonder.

"I have no problem with birds, but that's a little creepy, Tasha."

The sorceress's eyes widened. Shaking her head, Tasha took Aveline's hand. "I… I had a dream about them, but I don't know what this means."

"Are they going to attack?" Aveline had never heard of crows being aggressive toward people, but she'd also never encountered such a massive congregation in a single place like this before. "Maybe we should go in."

Once inside, Aveline locked the door and shuttered the windows while Tasha coaxed the fire in the hearth back to life. The watch captain peeled off her armor, tossing it on the bed, before lighting an oil lamp. She moved a chair from the table, placing it alongside the armchair Tasha had napped in.

"What was this dream about? Birds?" Aveline sat, gesturing for Tasha to take the armchair.

"I was flying with them. Maybe I was one, I'm not sure." After taking her seat, the sorceress rubbed her eyes. "Crows—maybe it's just one, I can't tell. They've been following me the last couple of days." Chuckling, she relaxed in the chair. "It sounds crazy, but I think one led me to the abandoned hut I spent the night in after the storm."

Clenching her jaw, Aveline crossed her arms. "I'd heard they were smart, but that seems… unusual." Tasha's story reminded Aveline of a tale she'd heard as a child, but she couldn't quite place it.

"You've been here longer than me."

The watch captain nodded. "Since I was a little girl."

"Did you ever hear about the Crow Queen?"

Aveline snapped her fingers. "Yes. Yes, that's it. She was a witch, lived in the woods. She'd help people who managed to find her, unless they insulted her, then she'd kill and eat them or feed them to her crows. Or something like that."

Tasha leaned forward. "They said she was connected to the land, like an elf mystic would be. Obviously, she wasn't an elf, though. She had a hut that walked on bird legs."

"Right." Aveline's memories of the stories returned. "A hut shaped like a bird. Probably a crow if she was called the Crow Queen."

"I heard it just had legs like a bird." Gasping, Tasha covered her mouth. "Bones. I found two huge bones stuck in the ground near the hut, like… like legs. The hut was on its side, like it fell over or off the legs."

"Maris take me…" Aveline regarded her friend. "That story was true… and you found the Crow Queen's hut? She disappeared years ago, long before my parents and I arrived in Curton."

"Is there anyone left in town who remembers a time when the Crow Queen was alive?" Tasha tucked a lock of hair behind her ear.

"We can ask around, I guess." Aveline gazed toward the ceiling. "Assuming those birds let us. Are they a warning or what?"

Tasha paced before the hearth. "I feel like they want something from me, but it's not malicious. I don't know how I know that. It's just a feeling I have."

"You've been trying to commune with Gaia, right? Move away from sorcery and Selene, to honor your fallen friend?" Aveline's grasp of the intricacies of deific practices and rituals remained limited, despite attempts by her guardian to instill in her some measure of piety after her parents died.

"I've had moderate success"—Tasha stopped pacing, proceeding to wring her hands—"but I don't know that it has anything to do with all these crows. Lorelei had no particular affinity for animals"—she chuckled—"no matter what people around here think about elves."

Aveline retrieved a bottle of mead from the crate near her table. She removed the stopper, then poured mugs for herself and Tasha. "That reminds me… Abarron's mate gave me some scrolls for you. Seems he bequeathed them to you." She handed Tasha the mug of mead before she retrieved the drak's documents for her friend.

"He must have written all this out while he was sick." Smiling, Tasha examined the parchments. "Even on his deathbed, he found a way to help me reach Gaia. There's nothing in here about crows stalking people, though."

Aveline laughed. "Well, I'd love to help you get to the bottom of this, but I need to head out in the morning. The scouts returned with some useful information about the whereabouts of young Innya, and I'm heading for the old mines tomorrow."

Tasha rolled the scrolls, then sipped her mead. "You're not expecting to find her alive, are you?"

"Look, there's nothing in those mines to dig up. After this much time, I can't imagine they're keeping anyone they're taking there alive for long." Aveline drained her mug. "Cybele's tits, it's probably just a clan of draks making it their home. The weather was too poor for the scouts to see clearly, but I have to check it out."

Tasha chewed her bottom lip. "I'll go with you."

"Are you sure? We'll be out there for three or four days, no bed, no shelter." Although her friend traveled extensively before settling in Curton, Aveline wouldn't blame Tasha for wanting to sleep in a proper bed for weeks before venturing out again after her recent dunk in the river.

"Yes." Tasha took a long drink of mead. "Yes, I'm sure. If there are draks, I can help. If there's trouble, well"—she smiled—"it's been a long time since I blasted evil doers with lightning."

Aveline stoppered the bottle of mead, then clapped Tasha's shoulder. "Let's see what the Bristled Boar has cooking, have a good, hot meal, and head out first thing in the morning."

* * *

Aveline's bed, cramped for two friends not used to sleeping intimately, nevertheless provided a good night's sleep. Tasha awoke refreshed, in spite of having spent too much time reading Abarron's scrolls by candlelight. The weariness in her bones from her misadventure gathering herbs lingered but a little, and the sorceress prepared to help her friend locate the missing girl. *Hopefully, we'll find them, and they'll be alive.*

To her relief, only one bird remained from the previous evening's flock. As before, it shadowed their journey, flying from rooftop to rooftop.

"Birds have been following you for a couple of days now." Aveline pointed at their feathered friend as they rounded the corner onto Market Street.

Tasha regarded their feathered follower. "I first noticed them the night you sent me to speak to Koloman."

"Do you think he's behind it?"

A farmer tipped his hat to the two women as he passed. A drak carrying a sack of leafy greens ran behind him, his short legs pumping to keep up.

"I doubt it." Tasha chuckled, adjusting her pack. "Koloman would wet himself if presented with magic powerful enough to compel a bird to follow me around, let alone the scores that perched on your roof last night."

"Compelling a bird to follow someone doesn't sound like it should take a particularly powerful charm." Aveline's rudimentary knowledge of magic, gained from tutors her guardian hired, did not provide an explanation for the strange crow-related goings-on.

"It doesn't." Tasha held up her pinky finger. "But what Koloman knows about magic couldn't fill a thimble."

Aveline snapped her fingers. "I figured out why he's so enamored of you. He thinks you can enhance his prowess in bed."

Tasha laughed. "I could give him some herbs, maybe sea oak, but none of that stuff really works. He'd be better off talking to a woodcarver or sculptor."

"Woodcarver?" Aveline shuddered. "Ouch. Watch out for splinters."

"It doesn't matter. He's not my type. I prefer my lovers to be intelligent and kind."

The two friends agreed Koloman possessed neither attribute. They entered the northside livery located outside of Mudders' Gate. As they saddled their mounts, Tasha spied Vasco's horse, Pepper, in an adjacent stall. "Damn. I fell asleep yesterday, and I forgot to go look for him."

Aveline peered over her horse's withers as she untangled a knot in the stallion's mane. "I'll take care of getting the horses ready. Why don't you go look for him? It's early enough he probably hasn't broken his fast yet."

"Good idea." Tasha fished in her pouch for a talon, then offered a gold crown to Aveline. "For my portion of the expenses."

Aveline shooed her away. "We'll settle up when we get back. Go find that annoying man. If I finish before you return, I'll take the horses and wait at Fairstone Mill."

Tasha squinted. "Is that the one upriver or down?"

"Down, just by the river. I need to pick up some grain for the horses."

"See you there." Tasha returned to the city proper. She made her way past the temples in Hillside, through the market, and over the bridge into Old Town, intending to check the obvious place first: the Drunken Horse Inn.

Few people patronized the inn this early—mostly only those who'd stayed there the night before or who possessed no means of cooking or storing perishables in their own homes. After a few moments, Tasha's eyes acclimated to the dim light provided by the hearth in a room whose windows were not yet touched by the morning sun.

The sorceress recognized none of the patrons dining in the common room. She approached the bar, where the proprietor, Radu, eyed her with a raised, bushy eyebrow that reminded Tasha of a caterpillar stuck to an old leather glove.

"Don't normally see you in here breaking your fast." His voice resembled the sound of gravel grinding beneath wagon wheels.

"I'm looking for the mage from Maritropa. Vasco Dragonblade? He was staying here, last I heard."

Frowning, Radu nodded. "Still is. Right proper lad, though I think he's a bit touched in the head."

Tasha glanced around again. "Is he upstairs? Or did he leave for the day already?"

"I ain't seen him. It's early yet. He might be up there." Radu leaned in close. "What you want with him, Tasha? Making a delivery?"

Tasha recoiled from Radu's fetid breath, despite her best efforts not to. "He has something of mine. I'm leaving with Lady Aveline, and I want to get it back. If you don't want to tell me what room he's in, maybe you could go fetch him for me?"

"Hrm." Radu scratched under his stringy beard. "Got any more witch hazel? I got me a fierce rash."

"There may be some in the satchel of mine he has." Tasha shook her head. "Most of my supplies were wiped out in the flood, though." *If you'd bathe regularly, your itch would probably disappear.*

"Hrm." Tossing his rag on the counter, Radu stomped his way around the bar and up the stairs of the tavern. After a few moments, Tasha heard him banging on a door, shouting for Vasco to awaken and go to the common room. Tromping down the stairs, the proprietor nodded at her before ducking into the kitchen. "That should rouse him."

To Radu's credit, his coarse wake-up call did indeed stir Vasco, and the tall man stumbled downstairs in his night-clothes. His eyes widened when he saw Tasha at the bar. He ran to her, gathered her in his arms, and lifted her into the air.

"I thought I'd lost you! The river was so swift and fierce. There was nothing I could do."

Tasha slapped him on the shoulders. "Put me down."

Bowing his head, Vasco lowered her to the floor. "My apologies, I couldn't contain my enthusiasm."

"Aveline says you have my satchel with the herbs we gathered?"

"Oh, yes!" Vasco's eyes brightened. "I'll fetch it straight-away!" Turning, he raced upstairs before she could utter another word. When he didn't return after several minutes, she considered following him, but she decided against it. She feared he might forget himself again if she interrupted him.

After an excruciating wait, sunlight began to stream in through the windows. Finally, Vasco returned, wearing a fine loose-cut shirt atop black leather breeches. Tasha's satchel swung from one arm, and he cradled his bladed staff in the other.

"I needed to make myself presentable, and I am prepared to assist you in whatever you need today." Bowing, he held the bag toward her.

Tasha retrieved the satchel from him. She dug through the pack, noting the herbs and flowers had wilted. *No witch hazel, but if there had been, it'd probably be ruined now.* "Thank you, but that won't be necessary. Aveline and I have business out of town. We won't be back for several days."

Vasco snapped to attention, crossing his arm over his chest before bowing again. "Then permit me to accompany you. I would be honored to be your protector."

Biting back an unkind retort and fighting to keep from rolling her eyes, Tasha forced a smile. "We don't need protection."

Radu stomped in from the kitchen, carrying a steaming bowl of porridge. He shoveled bites into his mouth as he approached. "So? Got any witch hazel?"

"No. Try bathing." Hurrying out of the Drunken Horse, Tasha left the two men behind. She hoped to finish with Vasco well before Aveline completed saddling the horses, but, by now, the watch captain surely waited for her at the mill.

Vasco called to her from the steps of the tavern, continuing to do so as she crossed the bridge into the market square. Sighing, Tasha stopped at the far end of the bridge and waited for him to catch up.

"You're not going to take no for an answer, are you?" She crossed her arms over her chest.

Grinning, the Maritropan man planted the butt of his staff in the dirt. "In Maritropa, the first 'no' is simply a challenge to make a better offer."

"This is not Maritropa, and neither Aveline nor I want anything you have." From the corner of her eye, Tasha saw a crow alight on the roof of a nearby stall. It cocked its head, regarding Vasco.

"I would not be so sure. You've already told me the two of you aren't lovers, and you have not seen what I have to offer."

"Aveline has armor and a heavy mace. My magic has been tested in battle." Tasha clasped her hands behind her, leaning forward. "Do we understand each other?"

Vasco placed his hand on his chest, then stepped backward. "My intentions are wholly honorable. I truly only wish to assist you in whatever task you're undertaking. I feel I owe it to you. That is all. I swear on the graves of my ancestors to keep to myself otherwise."

Tasha pointed at the crow on the roof of the stall. "See that? They'll be watching, and they like to pluck eyes."

As if on command, the crow cawed at Vasco, flapped its wings, and hopped closer. He jumped with a start as she struggled not to smirk at the crow's excellent timing. "Since you're not going to stay here in spite of what I say, hurry ahead and saddle your horse. We're meeting Aveline at Fairstone Mill."

"I am your humble servant, Lady Tasha."

He raced away, leaving her no opportunity to correct him. Chuckling, Tasha followed him.

Chapter 14

When Tasha finally caught up to her, Aveline had finished her business with the miller. She found her friend sitting on a stone wall near the waterwheel of the mill watching the river rush over and around nearby rocks. Her chestnut stallion—named Socks for the white coloration of his legs—nuzzled the horse the livery had provided Tasha, a dapple-grey gelding.

Aveline crossed her arms. "So, you've got crows following you, and now an annoying man as well?"

Vasco rubbed Pepper's neck, whispering in his horse's ear as they slowed to let the women greet one another.

Tasha bit her lip to keep from laughing. "He insisted on repaying his debt to me. You know, for not saving me from a flash flood. Besides"—she pointed at the weapon on Aveline's saddle—"you brought your sword, so I'm not worried."

"I keep meaning to take it home. Put it above my mantle or something." She patted the hilt, noticing a pair of crows landing on the far end of the wall. The watch captain narrowed her eyes. "There are two now?"

"Are there?" Tasha scratched her head. "Huh. I didn't notice that."

"Ah, Lady Aveline, your radiance outshines even that of the morning sun." Vasco swept his arm as he bowed.

"Oh, please," Muttering under her breath, she hopped off the wall. She handed the gelding's reins to Tasha. The horse whinnied, stamping his feet at the sorceress's hesitant hand. Aveline motioned to her companions. "Let's get moving. We have a lot of ground to cover today."

Spurring Socks forward, Aveline galloped away from the mill, trusting Tasha would keep up. She directed Socks to cross the road, heading overland toward the mines. Rolling hills covered the land east of town, ranging from meadows and fields of flowers toward the north, to ever-thickening forests toward the south and mountains. Few hostile or predatory beasts called these lands home. Wolves and bears that lived in the area tended to avoid people and campfires.

The road, now far behind them, vanished behind hills. Aveline slowed their pace to give the horses a breather. Adjusting her seat, she reflected on the last time she'd taken Socks out for a run. "It's been too long, my friend." Leaning forward, she rubbed his muscular neck.

Tasha trotted to catch up, then slowed her horse to a walk alongside her. "Nice choice, by the way." Tasha tousled her horse's mane. "I assume he has a name?"

"Silvermane. Nice choice on the clothes too. I noticed them last night. Ditching the robes, huh? Where are your boots?"

Tasha regarded her loose-fitting blouse. "It was time for a change. I feel closer to the Earth Mother without boots, although I'll probably regret not buying some for riding." Her eyes searched the sky, and she pointed upward. "They're still up there, following us."

"Has he noticed?" Aveline glanced over her shoulder at Vasco. He lagged behind, either unable to keep up or deliberately giving them space. "Do you have any ideas about them yet?"

"If Vasco has taken note of the crows, he's been quiet about it. And no, I don't have any ideas." Tasha watched the birds wheel overhead. "I've been having more success connecting with Gaia lately. Maybe they're watching for her."

"Divine emissaries?" Aveline doubted the Earth Mother bothered sending creatures on reconnaissance missions, considering she was literally the world upon which they lived, or so the stories told.

"Maybe they're spies for someone else." Tasha flicked the mane of her steed.

The two women rode ahead of Vasco for several hours before Aveline, feeling a twinge guilty, slowed Socks until the man caught up. When the sun reached its zenith, she motioned for the group to stop before dismounting and stretching her legs. The heat of midsummer made riding in armor a sweaty proposition at best. It was downright uncomfortable on the worst of days. Aveline drained the first of her waterskins as they traveled on foot. A journey without armor, while more comfortable, risked danger if the abductors of Innya and the other people still occupied the mines.

A tributary of the Copper Run River cut across their path, flowing down from the mountains and toward the coast. Letting their mounts cool down, they refilled their waterskins.

Leaning on his staff, Vasco watched Pepper drink. "I don't want to alarm you, but I think someone is following us."

Aveline stiffened. Her hand dropped unbidden to the haft of her mace. "Where?"

The mage looked over his shoulder in the direction from which they'd ridden. "Should be about a hill back. You won't be able to see them from here, but when we get underway, if we wait at the crest of the next hill, we should be able to watch them cross the creek."

Tasha rested her head on Aveline's shoulder. "Probably just travelers, heading to Cliffport."

"Hrm, maybe." Aveline retrieved her stallion's reins. "But why didn't they take the road? It's much easier and more direct."

Crows landed on a boulder across the stream. Aveline narrowed her eyes.

"They're the same ones. In fact"—Tasha pointed at the crow on the right—"that one's been following me for several days. I'm a little scared I'm starting to recognize them."

"They are not your familiars?" Vasco knelt at edge of the stream. Clicking his tongue, he held out his hand toward the crows.

"I guess you *did* notice." Tasha glanced at the watch captain. "I don't know why they're following me."

"We've been over this already." Checking the position of the sun in the sky, Aveline shaded her eyes. "We'll never reach the mines if we hang around talking to crows all day."

"Caw!" As if insulted, the crows took to the air.

Aveline led Socks across the stream before mounting. "With any luck, we'll cover more than half the remaining distance by nightfall."

* * *

Tasha's thighs and lower back ached from gripping the saddle and sitting in an unfamiliar position. She didn't own a horse for good reason—the height at which a rider sat made her head spin. As their horses trotted, the sun now sinking at their backs, Tasha rubbed her sore thighs. Vasco babbled to Aveline about his lengthy journey from Maritropa, being chased out of Raven's Forest by xenophobic elves, then traveling through Almeria and Muncifer before finally arriving in Curton. The knight-captain's slumped posture, angled away from the oblivious man, conveyed her opinion of his conversation.

As Vasco regaled Aveline with stories of his travels, Tasha noted he used more formal language than he had with her, as if he were a noble courting a lady. *If he gets grabby with her like he tried with me, he'll see just how receptive she is.* The thought of Aveline laying him out brought a smile to her lips, even as she chastised herself for finding amusement in violence.

Their shadows still trailed a few hours behind them. Aveline declined to stop at the crest of each hill, insisting their first priority remained covering as much distance between Curton and their destination as possible. When the sun dipped below the western horizon, they set up camp for the evening.

"If they're simply heading the same way we are, they'll catch up while we're stopped." Aveline unbuckled the saddle, then removed it from her horse. She carried it to a spot near the pile of wood Vasco assembled.

"And if they're following us, they'll keep their distance tonight." Tasha nodded, fumbling with the straps on Silvermane's saddle. Taking over for her, Aveline removed his saddle, then filled a feed bag for each horse.

"We should keep watch, in case they do intend to stop us from reaching the mines." Aveline's lip curled. "I hate sleeping in armor."

"Not to fear." Vasco rose as the fire took hold of the kindling. "I can enchant the perimeter of camp to notify us of anyone approaching. We can all sleep soundly."

Raising an eyebrow, Aveline glanced at Tasha.

The sorceress learned of such magic in classes at the Arcane University, but she demonstrated little proficiency with it. She nodded at the watch captain. "Those sorts of enchantments are quite effective, I hear."

"With your permission?" Bowing to Aveline, Vasco awaited her response.

"Very well. I suppose it beats missing out on sleep." She nudged Tasha. "I'm still sleeping in my armor, though."

While Vasco secured the camp with enchantments, Tasha and Aveline set bread to warm on the rocks near the crackling fire, and they distributed portions of the meat and cheese they brought along. Owls called in the distance as nocturnal insects sang their evening songs.

Aveline cradled a bottle of mead she'd withdrawn from her pack. "I brought this for us, but I guess I should share with him too."

"That's up to you. He brought wine when we were out gathering herbs." Reclining against a tree trunk, Tasha inhaled deeply, taking in the splendor of the forest around her. The scent of pine undercut the earthy aroma of the still-damp earth. Her feet ached from resting them in her stirrups; riding without boots proved more difficult than she expected. The sorceress drew her knees to her chest. Planting the soles of her feet on the ground, she curled her toes and dug into the bed of pine needles and leaves covering the earth. The ache faded, as if Gaia drew the pain away.

"All finished." Vasco strode into camp, cradling his bladed staff. "I created several layers of protection in the direction we came, in case our shadows have a mage among them. One enchantment they might look for and dispel, maybe even two? But I doubt they'll look for four."

Aveline gestured for him to join them by the fire. "We've meat, cheese, and bread. Eat." She held up a bottle. "There's mead too."

"Ah, that is most generous of you, my lady." Vasco rummaged in his pack, producing a bulbous bottle. "I have wine from Muncifer. Perhaps we can share and indulge a bit, eh?"

The trio ate and laughed around the fire, sharing first the wine, then the mead. As Tasha enjoyed her third swig of mead, she noticed none of the exhilaration she normally experienced while drinking, just a slight tingling in her fingers.

"All right." Aveline, slurring her words, belched. "You're well-dressed and well-spoken, Vasco Dragonbone. You've been to the Arcane University, and that horse you're riding isn't a mangy nag. Why did you leave Maritropa? What are you running from?"

Tasha stifled a grin. Well-off folk did not travel to Curton lightly, and she had wondered how long it would take Aveline before she interrogated the man who insisted on traveling with them.

"Running? Nonsense." He spread his arms. "Can't a man simply wish to see the world?"

A log cracked in the fire, showering the air with sparks. Aveline shook her head. "Men like you don't elect the hardship of the open road. Only fools go to Raven's Forest, but then onto Almeria, all the way across Etrunia? Then down to Muncifer where there's naught but draks and minotaurs before coming here. Here? Curton? We have all the mud you want but no money. No more copper, no more silver, just mud. We're so remote the princess in Almeria forgets we're part of her realm."

"Ah, it's all politics." Vasco waved his hand before drinking of the wine. He held the bottle toward Tasha. "Maritropan politics."

Tasha took the wine from Vasco, then, without drinking, she passed it to Aveline. The knight-captain peered into the bottle before swigging. "Tell us about Maritropan politics."

Slumping, Vasco reached for his staff, flailing fruitlessly. Finding it nearly beyond reach, he grabbed hold of it, but he tipped over. Righting himself, he brushed leaves off his face. "I was betrothed to be married. She was a beautiful young woman, one of the finest in the city. Her house, perhaps, was not as influential as mine. Marrying me was more a step up for her than it would have been for me."

"I knew it involved a woman." Nodding, Aveline frowned at Tasha.

Marriages for political and economic alliances were foreign to the small farming community in which Tasha grew up, although during her studies at the Arcane University in Maritropa, she'd met others in similar situations.

"So, you fled from an arranged marriage, despite the beauty of your bride-to-be?" Tasha gathered her cloak around her as a cool breeze blew through.

Closing his eyes, Vasco sighed. "That's not how it was. A rival family saw the wedding as an opportunity. They decided to take advantage of her entire family and mine, all gathered at our estate—"

From the trees on the west side of camp, flashes of green light preceded a whooping clamor. Seizing his staff, Vasco leapt to his feet. Tasha helped Aveline up, straining against the weight of her armor-bedecked friend.

"Dammit, Aerik!" The trio heard a gruff, yet feminine, voice followed by a meaty thud.

Green, smoky tendrils coalesced around Vasco's staff as he glanced over his shoulder at the two women. Aveline dropped her hand away from her mace.

"Therkla Fire-Eyes and Aerik Devil... head"—Aveline enunciated each word with deliberate effort to keep from slurring—"approach the fire and be seen." Shaking her head, she stepped toward Vasco.

"You know them?" The emerald wisps around Vasco's staff vanished. Relaxing his stance, he circled the fire, joining Tasha and Aveline on the far side of the camp. To Tasha's surprise, an oroq woman emerged from the woods. She led a southern, wild-haired man who wore the fur-lined armor indicative of a Watchman.

Aveline rubbed her eyes. "Why did you follow us? What do you want?" Tipping her head toward Tasha, she lowered her voice. "I drank too much to put up with these two tonight."

The sorceress squeezed her friend's arm. As she pondered why she didn't feel the effects of the libations as much as Aveline, despite having drunk just as much and never having shared her friend's tolerance in the past, she noticed two crows on a branch near Therkla and Aerik. Firelight reflected in the birds' beady black eyes as, cocking their heads, they observed the conversation.

"We didn't think much of your suggestion to help the Lord Mayor." Therkla narrowed her eyes. "Kalamar?"

"Koloman." Tasha almost laughed at the thought of Aveline sending an oroq and a Watchman to help the Lord Mayor with any endeavor.

"That's him." Using his toe, Aerik prodded a protruding stick, until it dislodged a log, spitting embers over the perimeter of the campfire. "The way people talk around town, he's a right bastard, so we came looking for you."

Aveline stepped backward to lean against a tree. "Why? Why do you seek me?"

Vasco knelt by the fire, keeping his staff in one hand as he stoked the flames. "Following two wizards at night is not very smart."

Therkla pushed Aerik aside. "If we wait for him to get to the point, we'll be here all night. Our gambling money is gone. We figure, we help you find this missing girl, maybe her father gives us a reward. Whoever took her is bound to have some valuables, too, probably more than you can confiscate yourself, right? We'll lend you our swords for no money out of your pocket."

Visions of the warlock-led oroq army responsible for Lorelei's death flooded Tasha's vision. She clenched her fists. "Why should we trust you? Either of you?"

Nearby branches twisted and groaned. Vines burst from the earth, showering the group with soil and decaying leaves as they snaked toward Therkla and Aerik. Screeching, the crows launched themselves at the pair. The Watchman and oroq ducked, lunging out of the crows' path. Therkla's foot caught on a root. She fell toward the fire, jerking to a stop only when vines coiled around her legs. Swearing, Aerik swatted at assaulting branches. They wrapped around him, pinning him against a tree.

"Tasha!" Aveline gripped her friend's shoulders. "Stop it! What are you doing?"

Hordes of grey-skinned warriors covered in blood fleeing from a cloud of black crows filled the sorceress's vision.

They swatted in vain as the birds drove them to a cliff. The caw-cry of crows filled the air as they fell to their death.

Tasha smiled.

Chapter 15

"Tasha!" Aveline recoiled at the azure glow in her friend's eyes. A quick glance revealed the amulet around Tasha's neck lay dormant. Aveline slapped the sorceress across the face. "Stop it!"

Freeing herself from Aveline's grip, she held her reddening cheek. The vines and branches holding Therkla and Aerik relaxed, releasing the two before returning to the earth. Trembling, Tasha kept her eyes fixed on the oroq and her companion. She stepped backward until her heel caught on her pack and she fell.

"Aita's bones, woman! Has your witch gone mad?" Aerik picked himself up, removing leaves and pine needles stuck in his beard and hair.

Snarling, Therkla drew her sword. She swung her weapon in an overhead arc toward Tasha, lunging forward. Vasco leapt to his feet, thrusting his staff. He caught the oroq woman's blade, managing to spin it safely away. He then rammed the butt of his staff into her gut. She doubled over, coughing.

"Everyone, stop!" Aveline jumped between Tasha and the newcomers. Her head pounded from the combination of libations and the rush of adrenaline caused by Tasha's unexpected attack. "Just stop."

Raising her hands before her, Aveline glared at the oroq woman. "Tasha isn't going to hurt anyone, are you?" She glanced over her shoulder at her friend.

Tears streaming, she shook her head. "I don't know what just happened."

"Caw! Caw!" The crows fluttered through camp before alighting on a branch above Tasha's head.

"Tinian's lance…" Pointing at Tasha, his mouth agape, Aerik took Therkla's arm. "Are… are you the Crow Queen?"

"What?" Tasha, wiping her face, swallowed. "No. No.

I'm just… I'm sorry. I had a bad run-in with oroqs years ago, and I thought"—lowering her head, she suppressed a sob—"I thought I was over that by now."

Aveline squeezed her eyes shut, but doing so did not ease the throbbing at the back of her skull. She then knelt alongside her friend. Putting her hand on Tasha's shoulder, she felt her balance falter, so she sat on the ground next to her. "I've never seen you do that kind of magic before."

"That's not arcane power." Vasco regarded the crows above Tasha's head. "I've only heard of mystics of Gaia controlling the trees and animals like that."

"Blood and rust, Aerik." Therkla spat into the fire. "We should've stayed in town and helped that arrogant bastard clean his house."

"I swear to you, that wasn't me."

Aveline searched Tasha's red-rimmed eyes. She stroked the amulet around Tasha's neck. "Your amulet wasn't glowing, but your eyes were." She searched for words to describe what she saw. "It was—"

"It was you, Tasha." Vasco approached, then knelt next to the two women. "I don't know how, but the forest was under your command. What happened to you after the river swept you away?"

"All right, we're done." Therkla smacked Aerik on the shoulder. "Let's get moving. We're going back to Curton. With luck, we'll get there before dawn."

"Wait." Aveline held out her hands to steady herself before approaching the oroq and the human, noting Therkla had not yet sheathed her sword. "I don't know exactly what's going on here, but I'll take your help if you're still willing. I'll even throw in some compensation when we return to Curton. I don't know—maybe pay for your room for a week or just pay you outright." She glanced down at her friend. Tasha buried her head in her knees. Vasco rubbed her shoulder.

Aerik picked leaves from his hair, while Therkla returned her sword to its sheath. She stood toe to toe with Aveline. The oroq woman drew herself up to her full height, a head above Aveline. Crossing her arms, she looked down upon the knight-captain. "All right. But I'm keeping an eye on your witch. If she sends those birds after me again or commands the forest to try to take me on, you won't be able to kill me fast enough to stop me from putting my blade through her heart."

"It won't come to that." Clenching her jaw, Aveline offered her hand to Therkla. The oroq regarded the knight-captain for a moment. Upon spitting in her hand, she grasped Aveline's.

"Fine."

Aveline suppressed a cringe at the sensation of spittle oozing between her fingers. She waited until Therkla turned away to address Aerik before wiping her palm on the seat of her breeches. Resolution of the potential conflict only slightly lessened the throbbing in her head, and she regretted overindulging around the campfire. She returned to her pack to drain the entirety of one of her waterskins.

After drinking her fill, Aveline sat next to Tasha and put her arm around the still-trembling sorceress. Vasco hovered nearby for a few minutes before reclining against his saddle. After Therkla and Aerik settled in for the night on the opposite side of the fire, Aveline allowed herself to relax enough to fall asleep.

* * *

Tasha awoke to the sound of Therkla and Aerik bickering over breaking their fast. Aveline helped Vasco tend to the horses. The sorceress realized the others had been stirring for quite some time. She stretched, working out the kinks from her neck and back muscles before using the nearby tree to pull herself to her feet.

"Why didn't anyone wake me? I thought we were in a hurry."

"I tried. You were out cold." Aveline left Vasco to finish saddling the horses, bringing her friend a piece of bread.

Aerik held up a jar. "Honey for the bread? From my family's hives."

"Thank you." Tasha accepted the honey, in spite of Therkla's snarl at her approach. Ignoring the oroq, she drizzled the viscous amber liquid on her bread. Honey from the Four Watches tasted floral and sweet minus the pungent, urine-tinged flavor local buckwheat honey often possessed. Nearby meaderies cultivated wildflowers for their bees, but, unfortunately, they refused to sell the honey.

"Now we're all awake, I want to talk about the plan." Aveline's puffy eyes betrayed her hangover. Tasha lamented the loss of her stockpile of herbs. A tea made from chamomile, fennel, and rosemary would ease the watch-captain's symptoms.

"Once we're closer to the mine, Vasco will ride ahead and determine how far we need to go on foot, if at all." Aveline stowed gear in her saddlebags. "It's possible we'll find nothing but cobwebs and vermin, but if someone is occupying the mine, I don't want to charge in there and spook them."

"You realize there may be so many there'll be no way for us to sneak into the mine?" Therkla tore the loaf of bread Aerik held in half. "What then?"

"No plan survives contact with the enemy." Aveline secured her shield to her saddle. "We'll make the rest up as we go. Just remember—we're here to find and return the abducted people. We're not doing this for glory or loot."

"Excellent." Therkla drew her blade edge across a whetstone. "I'm sure absolutely nothing will go wrong."

"Frankly, I'm counting on everything to go wrong. I tarried too long in investigating this matter seriously." Aveline approached Tasha. "How much time do you need to get ready?"

Tasha licked the honey from her fingers. "I just need a few minutes of privacy. Is Silvermane saddled?"

"I took care of that for you, lovely lady." Vasco, sweeping his arm as he bowed, gestured to Tasha's steed.

The sorceress smiled her thanks before ducking into the underbrush. When she finished relieving herself of last night's libations, she leaned against a beech tree. Tasha closed her eyes to center herself, taking in the morning scents and sounds of the forest. Insects buzzed, and birds sang their morning songs. The energy of life surrounded her. She felt the rough bark of the tree, the soft layer of leaves beneath her feet, and the warmth of the dying embers in their campfire.

Aveline spoke to the rest of the group, but Tasha found distinguishing between Aerik and Vasco difficult. She focused on the oroq. Therkla's energy reminded her of stone, cold and unyielding, but with an underlying chaos that spoke of her volatile temperament. The ire she felt toward the oroqs who laid siege to Drak-Anor all those years ago still dwelt in her heart. Tasha embraced it, feeling it fill her with rage and grief. A tear fell down her cheek as she aimed her attention at the oroq's aura.

"She wasn't there. The cathar killed Lorelei. It's past. It's done. She's with Gaia now." Tasha whispered the words over and over to herself, like a mantra, until the rage subsided. Two new forms entered the camp from above.

The crows.

Tasha wiped her face, focusing on the crows. For a brief moment, she saw the camp through their eyes, but then a cold hand touched hers.

With a start, her eyes snapped open. She stood alone against the tree. Tasha examined her hand where she'd felt the icy touch.

Nothing.

After taking a deep breath, Tasha released it slowly and returned to camp.

Therkla slammed her blade into its sheath. "All done?"

"Yes." Tasha approached her horse, then mounted. "Let's get going."

Aveline kept their pace slow, so Aerik and Therkla could keep up on foot. Tasha swayed in her saddle with Silvermane's lazy gait, feeling her eyelids grow heavy. After the second time her head fell forward, she pulled her horse to a halt and dismounted.

After assuring the group she felt fine and preferred walking, they continued. The sun rose across the sky, burning off the morning dew and mist. Seeming close enough to touch, the Iron Gate Mountains rose from the hills to greet them as they exited the grove.

"Not long to the mine now." Aveline twisted in her saddle to address those who followed her.

"Is there just the one?" Vasco removed the stopper from his waterskin before taking a drink. "Surely the town operated more than just one."

"Most are little more than flooded holes now." Aveline rose in her saddle to gain a better view of the area ahead. "The one we're going to connects to an extensive network of caves. If anyone is running a nefarious operation, that'll be the mine they're using."

"How deep do the caves go?" A rock Aerik kicked skittered into the underbrush.

Aveline regarded the Watchman. "I've never been in them, mind you, but I hear they go all the way through. Into the Four Watches."

"We might see some action after all, Aerik." Therkla, licking a tusk, shoved her human companion.

"Yeah, frost wyrms and dread wolves live all through the range in that area. Those caves might make a nice hidey hole for them."

"Bah, we should be so lucky to find dread wolves." Therkla spat at a beetle crawling along the ground. "Their pelts fetch a good price. With our luck, we'll find a nasty clan of ettins."

In disgust, Tasha curled her lip. Brutish, two-headed giants, ettins existed as living proof that two heads were not better than one. They fought with each other, and they enjoyed nothing more than smashing almost every other living creature into a pulp before devouring it. Most people viewed them as only barely intelligent, for they lived only to eat, destroy, and make little ettins.

"I heard stories of such beasts at the Arcane University." Vasco patted the shaft of his bladed staff. "I'm certain we can handle them, the Lady Tasha and I."

"Please, that pig-sticker of yours would only piss them off." Laughing, Therkla smacked Aerik on the shoulder. "Devilhand here likes to run between their legs, then gut them from the ground up."

Aerik shoved Therkla away. "Ugh, remember the one that decided to attack that village north of Haefstaad?" He drew his sword, then waved it above his head. "I split him right between the legs. I think everything inside of that beast fell out. Took a bath in entrails and worse."

The oroq burst out laughing. "We had to burn all your clothes. You met Jarl Freydis naked and covered in blood and guts. I thought she was going to add her lunch to your gore."

"Ah, good times, yeah?" Chuckling, Aerik shook his head. "Bitch could have at least given me some new clothes. Instead, she ranted at me for daring to appear before her naked. It's not my fault she didn't wait for me to make myself presentable before charging out to meet us."

Tasha found herself smiling, despite her disgust. *They're certainly not like that last bunch I traveled with. If Lorelei and I had abandoned them before that winter, things would be much different.*

She led her horse alongside Therkla. "I want to apologize for last night. I lost control over something from my past I didn't expect to feel again, and I don't hold you responsible for those events. I try to be better than that."

Therkla grunted in response.

Tasha continued. "You're the first oroq I've ever encountered who didn't try to kill me, and, well, I'm sorry I've misjudged your people for so long."

The oroq turned her blazing eyes on Tasha. "Well, that makes me feel all better now." Turning her back to Tasha, she strode away. "Stay away from me, witch."

Chapter 16

After Therkla's declaration, Aveline encouraged Tasha to ride close to her. To her credit, Therkla kept her distance as well, bantering with Aerik while Vasco rode between the two pairs. Focusing on the mission at hand, Aveline crammed her concerns about Tasha's reaction to Therkla and the oroq's subsequent, justifiable anger into a deep pit within her stomach. Repercussions to the campsite incident would wait until after they investigated the mine.

By her best guess, they would reach the mine around dusk. When she was a squire, her guardian brought her out this way on patrol, during the days before Curton's constabulary was run by a knight of Etrunia. She tried to remember whether groves stood near the mine, but those days seemed so long ago, and her recollection failed her.

"Aerik, Therkla." Aveline gestured for Tasha to keep moving as she slowed Socks to pace alongside the Watchman and oroq. "You said you explored some of the mines around here. In this area?"

"Farther east." Aerik sauntered along, gnawing a stick of dried meat. He offered some to Therkla. "Closer to the coast."

"That whole area is a maze of box canyons and dead-end valleys." Therkla slapped away the meat Aerik waved under her nose. "We spent too many weeks lost, and we returned to the river when our food started to run low. Plus, winter was coming. Those mountains are no place to be when the snow comes."

Snapping the reins, Aveline urged her mount forward to catch up with Tasha and Silvermane. Socks snorted and tossed his head in protest. The area of which Aerik and Therkla spoke, southeast of Curton, provided protection from icy, southern sea storms but little else. The terrain, too harsh for easy travel, rebuked all attempts to mine its hills or harvest its forests.

"Are we there yet?" Tasha rubbed her thighs, wincing, as her friend approached.

"You need to spend more time on horseback." Aveline glanced at Vasco, who tried to engage Aerik and Therkla in conversation. The pair seemed uninterested.

"I prefer walking to riding, honestly. This little trip reminds me why."

Looking ahead, Aveline pointed toward a stand of trees in a small valley. "We should be drawing close now. We'll stop in those trees, and I'll ride ahead a bit to see how close."

"I've been thinking about that." Tasha rubbed her talisman. "This morning, when I went off alone, I took a moment to... well, to connect with Gaia again. To see if I could force those feelings from last night back to the surface, so I could figure out what that was all about."

"That seems unwise." Aveline regarded the sorceress. Experimenting with power she didn't understand after unconsciously lashing out at Therkla seemed the height of foolishness.

"It's fine. Since I wasn't taken off guard this time, I controlled it. But for a few moments, I was able to see you all in the camp"—Tasha touched Aveline's arm—"through the crows' eyes."

"What?" Furrowing her brow, Aveline shook her head. "Is that... how is that possible?"

"Abarron told me some mystics could communicate with beasts. See the world through their eyes. I don't know how they did it, but that is what happened this morning. When we stop, I could try again, maybe see if I could get them to fly ahead and scout the mine. It'll be a lot safer than one of us going ahead alone to see if anyone is there."

Aveline considered Tasha's suggestion. She liked the idea of a safer approach. "It's worth trying, I suppose. We'll have to make sure you don't try to flay the oroq with the trees again, even unconsciously."

"I don't think that will happen again, but I understand you wanting to take precautions. I feel really bad about that, Aveline." Tasha stole a glance over her shoulder. "I'm supposed to be better than that."

"You are." Aveline rubbed the stallion's neck. "Everybody has bad days now and again."

"A bad day like that could get someone killed."

"I can't argue with that. Let's try to have good days from now on, right?" Aveline nudged Socks forward. She wanted to let him run, but she compelled herself to pace with Aerik and Therkla.

The valley, densely forested with beech and poplar trees, seemed the perfect place to hunker down while Tasha communed with Gaia to attempt to connect with the crows. All day, the birds followed the group, disappearing from sight now and again, but always returning within minutes. The sun sank toward the western horizon.

Aveline guided them around the edge of the forest until she judged they neared its eastern tip. After dismounting, she led Socks into the woods on foot. "We'll stop here for now and scout ahead. We must be close to the mine."

Therkla sat on a fallen beech. "Who's going on ahead? Hopefully, one of you who haven't been walking all day." She yanked off her boots, then rubbed her feet.

Aerik sat next to her. "Will you rub mine next?"

"Maris take you!" Therkla shoved Aerik, causing him to tumble off the log. "Rub your own damned feet."

"I'm doing it." Tasha secured Silvermane's reins near Socks. "At least, I'm going to try."

After smoothing her tunic, she collected a handful of oats from her saddlebag to feed Silvermane.

"What do you want me to do?" Vasco leaned on his staff.

"Nothing. Watch my stuff while I'm gone."

Aveline took hold of Tasha's arm as she walked past. "Do you want me to go with you? Keep an eye out?"

Tipping her head toward Therkla and Aerik, Tasha shook her head. "Keep an eye on them."

* * *

As Tasha proceeded into the woods, she heard Therkla and Aerik arguing with Aveline about sending a witch to do a warrior's job. Ignoring them, she pressed onward, eventually finding an area clear of underbrush. Tasha knelt on the mossy earth, shifting her knees to avoid hidden rocks in the loam, and closed her eyes.

Leaning forward, she placed her palms on the dirt, opening her mind to the life-energy flowing all around her. Abarron's scrolls provided valuable insight to facilitate the connection. Within moments, Tasha perceived her group of friends. Her consciousness expanded, encompassing them before she searched for the crows. The wind blowing through the branches flowed around Tasha, like water coursing over her body and around her bones.

On a branch overlooking the camp, the crows groomed themselves. Tasha nudged one of the birds with her mind, a slight caress. It took to the sky in a flash, bursting through the canopy and gliding in a gentle circle. The spinning of the forest below and mountains on the horizon dizzied Tasha until the crow gained its bearings.

Mine. Find the mine. Tasha didn't know if the crow understood her. Her intention must have been clear enough because it turned toward the mountains southeast of the forest valley. Seeing through its eyes, a surreal experience, showed her a world of colors she'd never before experienced.

Ahead, motes of light shone against a dark hole in the side of a hill. As the crow flew closer, she saw timber braces around the hole, the sign of a mine entrance. Scattered tents, two or three, erected just outside of the entrance, sheltered several humanoids. Before she noted more detail, the crow caught an updraft and tilted back, climbing toward the sky. A massive pinwheel filled her vision, the Great Whirlpool of Nethuns, a common sight in the summer skies, rendered in brilliant sapphire detail.

Back, back to the mine. I need to see more. Get closer. The crow obeyed, circling and angling downward. Two humanoid creatures with sinuous tails carried a barrel between them as three smaller figures, draks, pointed toward the mine entrance. One of the draks wielded a whip, cracking it at the two carrying the barrel. A tall figure fell, and the barrel crashed to the ground. It rolled away as the other chased after it.

A drak stared straight at Tasha, or, rather, the crow. Shouting, he pointed just before a ray of flame shot from his finger toward the bird.

Tasha's eyes snapped open. Briefly, she confused the lack of sensation from the crow for blindness and deafness. The real world seemed muted. She sat up, digging the palms of her hands into her eyes. Smoothing her skirt, she returned to the group.

Aveline brushed her stallion's mane while Vasco relaxed against the same fallen beech where Therkla and Aerik sat. She glanced up as Tasha approached. "Anything?"

"They're draks and at least two other creatures I'm not familiar with. Human-sized, with tails." She retrieved the waterskin from her saddle, then took a drink. "There's at least one wizard among them."

"Either they're so close they can hear us talking, or you're lying. There's no way you could have gone all that way and back in that time." Leaning forward, Therkla sneered. "Unless you can fly."

"Crows can fly." Tasha glanced at the sky, noticing only one crow circling over the camp.

Clapping his hands, Aerik nudged Therkla. "You see? She is the Crow Queen!"

"Nonsense." Tasha took another drink. "It's something I decided to try after what happened last night. I'm just a sorceress. I trained at the Arcane University in Maritropa. Old Abarron in Curton taught me a few mystic tricks, that's all."

Aveline took Tasha aside, keeping her voice low. "Are you going to be all right if these draks are the culprit? You have such a good rapport with the draks in town."

Tasha shuffled her feet. "I'll be fine. If these draks are hurting people, they need to be stopped, just like anyone else. They looked like they were beating the tall ones, the ones with tails. I didn't get a good enough look to see who they were."

Just then, the other crow flew into camp. Tasha stiffened when it landed on her shoulder. Aveline stepped away. "New friend?"

"I don't..." Tasha regarded the bird on her shoulder. *Revan.* "His name is Revan." She pointed at the crow still on the overhanging branch. "That one is Korbin. I don't know how I know that."

"Cybele's tits..." Aerik pointed. "They speak to you."

Therkla scoffed. Aerik glared at her. "Stop telling me I'm mad, woman. I know the stories. The Crow Queen can speak to the birds, make them do her bidding. She is one with the land, and the land is one with her."

"Caw-caw, caw!" The birds called in unison, bobbing. Korbin landed alongside Revan.

A bead of sweat rolled down Tasha's spine.

Vasco used his staff to push himself up. "I've not heard of this before. Tell me the stories, Aerik."

"Pacha's balls, it's not bedtime." Therkla smacked Aerik on the hip, glaring at Tasha. "Save the stories for when we're piss-drunk and finished with this business. Are we going to go to these mines or not?"

Therkla's crude rejoinder notwithstanding, her point about the mine resonated with Tasha. Aveline agreed. "Yes. We'll solve Tasha's bird problem later. We'll tie the horses up here, then proceed to the mine on foot."

Pepper whickered at Vasco's approach. The wizard stroked the mare's nose. "Should we leave them unguarded? Aren't there wolves about?"

"Bird girl can watch them." Therkla pushed Aerik out of her way. "I don't want that witch around when we start whacking drak's heads from their necks. She might not remember I'm on your side."

Her words stung Tasha like an angry wasp. Balling her fists, Aveline approached the oroq, but Tasha lunged between them. "She's right. I'm not sure we should trust my magic right now. I'll look after the horses, and I'll keep watch over you with one of the crows. If you need me, Vasco can send a messenger." She nodded at the wizard. "They taught you that spell in Maritropa, yes?"

"Yes, of course." Vasco scowled.

Tasha leaned toward Aveline, lowering her voice. "It'll be all right. It's better this way. Therkla won't be constantly peering over her shoulder if I'm not around, and she looks like she's good in a fight. Just watch out for the tall ones with tails. I don't think they're willing participants."

Aveline gritted her teeth. "All right. I don't feel good about leaving you behind, but forcing the issue right now will cause problems. Damn it." She put her hand on Tasha's shoulder. "Watch our backs and be careful."

Tasha watched the group depart. "You too."

Chapter 17

"All right, let's stay close." Aveline crept forward as the mine came into view over the top of the hill. She lowered herself, wincing each time her plate mail clanked.

Upon crawling next to her, Therkla put her hand on Aveline's arm. "I appreciate heavy steel armor, but there's no point being sneaky with all that noise you're making."

Ignoring her, Aveline peered at the makeshift camp in front of the mine. She did not see the draks Tasha mentioned, but she noted flickering lights coming from within the tents. The lack of cover between the top of the hill and the mine entrance concerned her; leaving her armor behind to enter a potentially dangerous confrontation seemed unwise.

Aerik belly crawled next to Therkla. "Are the kidnapped women there?"

"They won't be keeping them outside," Therkla hissed. Vasco joined them at the top of the hill. Dropping to his belly, he crept forward, stopping when he reached Aveline.

"How do we even know they're the ones we seek?" Vasco regarded the other three. "Has anyone seen any of the missing people?"

"Tasha said it looked like a drak was whipping one of the others." Aveline watched for any trace of movement within the camp. "That doesn't sound very friendly to me."

"You're going to trust the word of that witch?" Therkla spat on the ground.

Aveline glared. "I trust her with my life. The draks she described sounded like slavers to me, and her word is all I require."

"Odd, isn't it?" Vasco scratched his stubble. "That draks would keep slaves?"

"Payback, maybe?" Keeping his eyes on the camp, Aerik held his voice low. "Many draks are kept as slaves in the north, I hear. If I'd been a slave, I'd want to turn the tables on my captors."

After pushing herself backward until the camp was no longer visible, Aveline sat upright. Clouds intermittently obscured the light from the King and Queen, adding to the gloom of early evening. "The princess may not acknowledge it, but this is still Etrunia. Slavery is not permitted here."

She rose, mace in hand. "Let's go."

Therkla wrapped a meaty hand around her ankle. "You're going to wake everyone down there, Clanker."

Vasco held up a finger as green wisps swirled around him. "Not so. *Siopi.*" He touched Aveline. For a brief moment, a green glow surrounded her.

"What's that?" Aveline's eyes widened when she could not hear herself speak.

"I can do the rest of us, if you like."

Aveline nodded in response. Therkla scooted backward. "We're quite enough. Besides, lady knight here can't squawk at us now."

Bitch. After offering Therkla a rude gesture in response, Aveline leapt to her feet and sprinted down the hill. *They can catch up if they want to help.*

Halfway down the hill, Aveline realized Vasco didn't mention how long the spell would last. She hoped it didn't wear off before she'd subdued the first of the tent-dwellers. Without waiting for the others to catch up, Aveline angled toward the tent closest to the mine entrance. Ridge tents such as these often possessed no means of securing their access flaps. As she drew close, Aveline viewed a drak with his back to her hunkered over a pack. Slowing her descent, she crept up behind him.

Stealing a glance behind her, she observed Therkla, Aerik, and Vasco approaching. After securing her mace to her belt, Aveline gestured toward the others. Smiling, Therkla drew her blade, crouching as she moved forward.

When the oroq reached the front of the tent, Aveline dashed forward, clamping her fingers around the drak's snout and wrapping an arm around his neck.

After dragging the wriggling drak out of the tent, she slammed him onto the dirt, maintaining her grip around his mouth. Therkla emerged from the other tent, her blade dripping blood.

Grimacing, Aveline gestured for Vasco. She pointed at her mouth. While Therkla cleaned her blade, Aerik rummaged through the tent from which she'd emerged.

Vasco touched Aveline's arm. "*Ichos*."

"Handy enchantment, that." Aveline struggled to keep hold of the writhing drak.

"Very popular among Maritropa's less savory populace."

"All right, Drak." Aveline forced the prisoner's head toward Therkla. "My oroq companion there just gutted your friend." *By Anetha's shield, these better not be innocent draks.* "I've a mind to let her have her way with you unless you start talking. Quiet now, understand?"

Leaning into his throat as he nodded, she released his jaws. "Master will not like you cutting his fingers. He'll feed us your men. Maybe you women will serve."

Oh good, they're not just a wandering family in search of a new home. "What are you talking about? Who is your master?"

"Fantastic. Cultists." Therkla smacked Aerik's protruding behind with the flat of her blade. "Get out here. We'll loot their crap later."

"Master was a man, like you," the drak hissed. He licked his lips. "Now he is Master Under the Mountain. We fingers find what he needs, and he needs those who can mother."

Aveline regarded the oroq. "I don't suppose either of you have rope. I don't make a habit of traveling with shackles."

"Sure, we have rope." She stopped Aerik from digging through his pack. "I'm not cutting it for him, though. Just stick him and be done with it. This is obviously the place we're looking for."

"That's not necessary." Vasco laid the blade of his staff across the drak's chest. "Step away, please, Lady Aveline."

She released the drak.

Emerald tendrils danced down Vasco's staff, enveloping the drak. "*Syndesi somatos. Siopi.* That should hold him for several hours. Until dawn at least."

The drak's eyes widened, darting back and forth, yet he lay motionless on the ground. Aveline yanked him to his feet. The drak remained rigid, unable to plant his feet to remain upright.

"He can make no voluntary movements nor make a sound." Vasco took the drak from Aveline. He then laid him in the tent. Removing the candle from inside, he extinguished it.

Therkla grunted. "I wouldn't trust that not to wear off. I still say we should stick a blade in him. He won't come after us then for sure."

"Later." Holding up her hand, Aveline pointed at Therkla. "You said 'cultists.' Do you know what he's talking about? The Master Under the Mountain. His fingers? What nonsense is this?"

Therkla peered into the tent where Vasco had placed the drak. "No idea. Most cults are full of nonsense. This one sounds barking mad. They probably found a bunch of bad mushrooms underground, and now they are carving up your townsfolk searching for the answer to their fever dreams."

Great. Insane cultists. Aveline regarded Vasco. "Got an enchantment that will let us see in the dark?"

"Besides fos? No, though that would be useful, wouldn't it? I'll have to do some research when this is over."

"I see fine in the dark." The oroq nudged her companion. "Aerik's blind as a newborn kitten, though."

"Fine, you take point then. Vasco, give us some light." Aveline gripped her mace. "Let's see how deep this mine goes."

* * *

Fighting the urge to connect with the crows again, Tasha brushed Silvermane while she waited. She wanted to allow enough time for Aveline and the others to reach the mine before using the birds to observe them. Socks nudged her while she brushed her own steed, nosing around her waist and free hand searching for treats. Using the flat of her hand, she pushed him away.

Once she finished grooming Silvermane, Tasha fed all three horses. In the distance, an owl hooted. She heard a creature crunching through leaves. Closing her eyes, she cleared her mind. Connecting with Gaia became easier each time she attempted it. Almost immediately, she felt the deer picking through underbrush as they searched for a place to bed down for the night.

She felt the crows take flight. Tasha decided to give Revan a break. Instead, she sought out Korbin. In an instant, she saw through his eyes as he ascended through the trees and over the forest. After guiding him toward the mines, she viewed her friends at the top of a ridge overlooking the camp, conversing. Rather than try to listen in through Korbin, she let him fly free, reveling at the sights of the world through his eyes. The clarity with which he perceived the Great Whirl-pool of Nethuns mesmerized her. By the time Tasha remembered her appointed task, Aveline and the others had already charged down the hill into the camp.

With horror, Tasha witnessed Therkla murder a drak in the far tent while Aveline, dragging the drak from the other tent, pinned him. *Dear Earth Mother, please let these draks be the villains we seek.* Visions of draks she had killed in ignorance came unsolicited to her mind, the ichor of their eggs dripping off boots and lightning from her amulet striking down those who fled.

Korbin landed on the ridge of the first tent in time for Tasha to observe Vasco magically bind and silence the drak Aveline subdued. The knight-captain rose. After a brief discussion, they pushed their prisoner into the other tent and proceeded into the mine.

Releasing Korbin, she lowered herself to the ground, maintaining her connection with Gaia. Tasha felt the massive beating hearts of the horses as they circled her.

Tasha reached out with her mind across the hills toward the mines. Korbin remained on top of the tent, grooming himself. From within the mine, she felt a cold presence and a source of power unlike anything she'd experienced. Colors and shapes flashed in her mind, smells came unbidden, and she felt first the sensation of heat, then cold. The fleeting assault on her senses threatened to overwhelm her. Tasha recoiled from the mine.

Motes of color and sound danced in her mind, even as she fought to clear her vision. She focused on nearby familiarity: the horses, the trees, Revan gliding through the air to join Korbin in the mine camp. Letting him guide her, Tasha viewed the mine again, avoiding the strange, chaotic power within. Instead, she tried to feel the life within the mine. She sensed her friends, but with no eyes to see, she couldn't determine the nature of their activity. Her fears about the draks' innocence vanished when she felt malevolence emanating from them. In the background, she perceived another aura.

A familiar one.

Her consciousness brushed against the presence just before an approaching cloud of screeching crows overwhelmed her. Shrieking, Tasha fell backward. Her eyes snapped open, severing her connection with the world.

Darkness took her.

Chapter 18

Aveline fought the urge to rush ahead, mindful that the oroq's night vision, superior to that of humans, gave Therkla an advantage. She led Vasco and Aerik forward, squinting to see past the glaring light provided by the wizard's staff. A shape appeared out of the darkness ahead. Therkla.

The oroq approached them, shading her eyes with her hand. "Everyone and their brother are going to know we're here with that thing blazing like the sun."

Vasco covered the glowing tip of his staff with his cloak. "My apologies, but we cannot stumble around in the dark."

"It won't matter soon." Therkla pointed back the way she came. "They've got lanterns set up on the deeper levels. There's a fork in the passage a dozen paces or so. To the left is an abandoned shaft. It looks like there was a lift, but it's broken now. Just a frayed rope remains."

"And to the right?" Aveline adjusted the grip on her shield.

"It gets pretty deep. You can see the lanterns from the top. I figure the miners came in using the steep shafts, then used the lift to get the ore out."

"Makes sense." Aveline nodded. "Who'd want to haul ore out on their backs?"

Aerik thumped his chest. "I could do it."

Therkla smacked his shoulder. "All day, every day? You can't even keep up with me for one night."

"All right, let's go." Aveline desired not to hear how Therkla and Aerik entertained themselves after sunset. "Can you lead us through the dark until we get to the lighted area? Vasco will extinguish his staff."

"Put your hand on my shoulder. Staff-man can follow you, and Aerik will bring up the rear." Grinning, she licked a protruding tusk. "He's good at that."

After securing her shield across her back, Aveline put her hand on Therkla's shoulder. She gestured for Vasco to get behind her. When she felt his fingers brush her shoulder, she clasped his hand, securing his grip. Once they moved into position, he extinguished his light, plunging the corridor into utter darkness. Noticing her heart racing, she forced herself to take measured breaths. The combination of darkness so black she couldn't view her own hand in front of her and the weight of the hillside all around them threatened to send her into a panic.

In and out. Just take it slow. This shouldn't bother me like this. Therkla led them at a gradual pace, whispering warnings at low ceilings and protruding rocks. She winced at the creak of leather from her companions' attire. Each rattle of her own armor sounded like warning bells clanging in the dark.

Each step seemed like ten. By the time they reached the downward sloping passage, perspiration dripped down Aveline's face. Dim points of light at the bottom shone like beacons.

Vasco sniffed the air. "That's foul. Do you smell it?"

Aveline wrinkled her nose as a whiff of decay wafted past. "Ugh, I can almost taste it. Something is dead down there."

"Whatever those draks are cooking, it's ripe." Therkla sneered, baring her teeth. "Wait here, I'll check it out."

Crouching, she motioned for Aerik to follow her. Their shadowy forms intermittently blocked the lantern light—the only hint of their motion down the mine shaft. While they waited, Aveline raised her shield, brushing Vasco's hand off her shoulder. He tapped his foot with nervous energy.

Aveline tried not to think of how far underground they were, and how far they'd yet to go. *These mines have been abandoned since I was a girl. It wouldn't take much to bring the ceiling... stop it!* Biting the inside of her cheek, she distracted herself from thoughts of being buried alive.

"How long has it been since these mines were in use?" Vasco prodded the ceiling with the tip of his bladed staff.

Seizing the shaft, Aveline yanked it down. "Stop that. Too long. We don't need to tempt fate."

He pulled his staff from her grip, then tapped the blade against a wooden support. "These supports are in excellent shape for their age. Despite what you say, I'd wager someone's been shoring it up."

The knight-captain removed her glove with her teeth. She reached up to feel the beam. The wood, dry and hard, possessed none of the signs that decades of neglect and moisture damage would cause. "They've been here a while."

"Indeed."

Aveline donned her glove again as Therkla and Aerik returned. The oroq wrinkled her nose, grimacing. "The smell gets worse, but we didn't see the source. That's an antechamber down there. Looks like the miners might have used it to check in for their shifts and whatnot. There's some broken furniture, and a couple of side tunnels."

"We think we heard voices down one of the shafts." Aerik spat. "Maybe draks, maybe those other creatures the witch saw. It's hard to tell without getting closer."

Chewing on her lip, Aveline considered their options. "They still have lanterns down there? Past the antechamber?"

"As far as I could tell." Therkla frowned as Aerik pulled a stick of jerky from his pouch. He tore into it, offering it to each in turn.

Aveline refused with a wave of her hand. *Food now, really?* She gestured for the three to follow. "Let's keep moving."

They crept down the mine shaft into the antechamber. The remains of an oaken desk, probably belonging to the mine foreman, cluttered one corner of the rectangular room. Growing stronger, the odor of decay filled Aveline's nose.

She choked back bile. "All right." She pinched her nose. "That's about the worst thing I've ever smelled."

Aerik pushed past her. "Not as bad as getting an ettin's guts spilled all over you."

While she agreed the Watchman probably had a point, Aveline felt no desire to experience an odor worse than the one currently permeating the air.

"Well, boss, which way?" Therkla pointed to the three exits. "We heard the talking down the middle one."

Aveline sniffed the air at each exit. None smelled significantly fresher than the others. Pinching her nose shut again, she hissed through clenched teeth. "You'd think at least one would smell better."

The oroq grimaced. "Whatever's causing that stink isn't natural. Bet you a case of ale on it."

"No bets." Aveline pointed down the center shaft. "Let's go say 'hello.'"

* * *

Groaning, Tasha rolled onto her side. "That was unpleasant." She squeezed her eyes. "At least there's no hangover."

While remaining in their circle, the horses stood watch over her, each having clearly finished eating. Tasha pulled herself to her feet using Silvermane's reins, then detached each feedbag.

"Sorry, I didn't think I'd pass out on you."

She knelt, smoothing her skirt before pressing her hands against the earth. "Let's see what we can see."

Her thoughts encompassed the grove, then the valley, and finally the land around the mine. Noticing Revan and Korbin no longer guarded the tents, she found them enjoying a freshly killed mouse some distance away. A wave of nausea washed over her upon briefly learning how raw mouse tasted. Revan pecked at Korbin. He hopped away from the mouse and took to the air, flying Tasha's senses back to the mine.

She guided him into the tent with the bound and silent drak, confirming he lived. She then directed the bird to enter the mine.

Revan refused.

No? Won't go underground, huh? Well, I don't blame you. I had to ask.

She let him wander the camp, pecking at scurrying beetles, but she drew the line when he wanted to inspect the dead body in the other tent. Upon finding no shiny baubles, Revan perched on top of the captive drak's tent and treated Tasha to a view of the mine entrance. After a few minutes of viewing nothing of importance, Revan fluttered as Korbin landed alongside him.

I don't suppose there's any way you can notify me if they need help or emerge in distress? They could be hours. The birds bobbed in response. After releasing Revan from her control, Tasha continued meditating. She took care not to encompass the mine again, mindful of the strange presence and abundance of chaos energy.

Momentarily, she considered unrolling Abarron's scrolls and creating light by which to study them. She wasn't sure whether the birds would be able to contact her if she weren't connected to the world in this fashion, though. Forcing them to fly back to her in the event the group needed her would waste valuable time. *I really need more time to experiment with this. I wonder if Lorelei communed with animals in this way. Is it just the crows?*

The horses, a comforting presence surrounding her, seemed a good place to start answering questions. She sought out each in turn. Even though she did not see their physical form in her mind's eye, each presented as an individual to her. Silvermane's calm demeanor stood in contrast to the stallion's eagerness to gallop across open fields, leaving Pepper as the third by default.

She heard Silvermane whicker at her mental touch. Shifting its stance, the horse tossed its head. While she felt the gelding's awareness of her attempt, she remained unable to utilize the horse's senses as she had with the crows.

Perhaps a horse is just too big. Seeking a smaller creature, Tasha found a rabbit in a nearby burrow. Its heart raced as she reached out to it, and it shrank deeper into its nest. Still, she could not connect with it.

Tasha sighed. *Maybe there's something to Aerik's talk of a Crow Queen. That's crazy, though. She's gone off to some other part of the world... or dead.* The sorceress returned to her crows, still standing vigil over the mine. Although she did not see through their eyes, Tasha detected a shape standing in the shadows of the mine entrance.

Curious, Tasha focused on the shape. Its presence felt familiar, like what she'd felt earlier. It called to her, beckoning her closer. As Tasha's mind touched the figure's, clouds of crows filled her vision. When the birds cleared, she observed two women conversing in an underground tunnel near a gaping hole—a mine shaft. A broken winch dangled from the ceiling with its rope trailing into the darkness. Casting dancing shadows on the walls, a burning torch sputtered on the ground at their feet.

One woman, bent, wizened, wearing a black cloak over coarse-woven linen robes trimmed with vines and scarlet autumn leaves, backed toward the hole. "Don't do this, Nika, I beg you."

The other woman, younger and with muscles like knotted rope, held a blade at the older woman's chest. Tasha recognized a familial resemblance in their appearance. "You let him die!"

"You're wrong. I did everything I could." The old woman held up her trembling hands. "Some people cannot be saved."

"You never liked him. You never loved him." Nika swung her sword at the old woman, forcing her backward until her feet teetered at the edge of the shaft. "You took a child from him, then you tossed him aside."

Is this happening now? Is this the past? Tasha tried expanding the view in her mind to encompass her surroundings, to bring the world into focus, but a force fixed her attention on the scene transpiring before her.

"That's not true. The mantle demanded a sacrifice. Gaia, Cybele… they all demanded a sacrifice. I had to give up our love, our baby, my youth, all to save the town." The old woman forced herself to stand upright. "Magic like that has a price. I saved as many as I could. I never asked for anything in return. I saved you and returned to tending my garden, bereft of love and my beauty. The only thing I gained was my sister's hatred."

"Liar! Dimas was mine. You were always jealous he turned to me after you rejected him." She advanced, clenching her jaw. "You murdered him." Nika drew her arm back, preparing to strike.

Roots burst from the earthen walls, seizing her arm and wresting the blade free. Clattering to the ground, it skidded toward the pit.

Nika swiped with her foot, catching the old woman in the chest.

Losing her balance, the old woman clutched at the air. She pitched backward into the shaft. Following the old woman, Tasha's head spun as she plunged into the darkness. The woman's body smashed against a pile of broken rocks, cracking her skull and shattering her bones.

The old woman lifted her head toward the dim, flickering light of her sister's torch. Blood streamed from her nose and mouth. *"Ehfasha uh beed uh coida uhn grey'dioh eych cruad…"*

As the old woman sighed her last breath, Nika, cursed.

Preceded by the hacking of steel against wood and earth, roots and clumps of dirt cascaded upon the woman's body.

With the torch gone, darkness once again fell over Tasha. Feeling a slimy, wet sensation upon her face, she touched her cheek.

Ducking his head, Silvermane lipped her face. When she opened her eyes, he nudged her with his nose.

She pushed him away. "All right, all right. I'm back. I'm up. Everything is fine."

Tasha wiped the slobber from her face with a sleeve before kneeling again. Placing her hands on the mossy earth, she sought out Revan's mind. He and Korbin dozed on their perch at the tent, keeping a furtive watch on the mine.

Chapter 19

As Aveline led Aerik and Therkla down the central passage, the glimmering light from the lanterns gave way to brighter dancing flames of a campfire. Low voices muttered, seemingly arguing, in an unknown language.

From within the shadows, Aveline observed three figures huddled around the fire. Two were covered in black-striped white fur. Leaning on each other, they sat side by side conversing with the third, a lanky, black-furred creature possessing an elongated face and curling horns. Their appearances matched nothing Aveline had ever seen, although the two striped figures appeared vaguely feline.

Vasco bumped into her, causing her to lose her footing. The ears of the two cat-like figures twitched, rotating at the sound of Aveline's pauldron scraping against the wall. Huddling closer, they whispered to their companion, who stared into the darkness. She noticed shackles chaining their legs and arms together, but she observed no weapons near them.

The tall, horned figure shouted. Aveline tightened her grip on her mace, striding into the light. "What... manner of creatures are you?" She kept her voice low, so it would not carry, hoping at least one would understand her.

"I don't think she's with our captors, Yun." One of the seated feline creatures said a few words to the horned one. Aveline had difficulty understanding his words through his thick accent.

"Please, you must help us." He pressed his hand to his chest, bowing his head. "I am Ra-Jareez. This is my sister, Jazeera." The other striped one bowed too. "Our bodyguard is Yun. Have you come to free us?"

He displayed his shackled wrists. After securing her mace to her belt, Aveline gestured for Aerik and Therkla to join her. She knelt by them. Upon closer inspection, she discovered signs of bruising, even through their fur.

"They're not from around here." Therkla examined their makeshift camp. Apart from the fire and a waste bucket, the three had only ratty furs on which to sleep. Their clothes, perhaps once well maintained, now clung to their bodies, torn and dirty.

"We are traders from Gaer Griffon." Ra-Jareez took his sister's hand. "We were on our way to Reorvik to trade."

"From across the Sea of Lost Hopes." Gasping, Vasco leaned on his staff.

"Our ship crashed in a storm. We came ashore, what few of us survived, and were lost in the hills." Jazeera coughed. "A great wyrm—a nasty, white beast—chased us into caves. We were starving, wounded, only three by then. We did not have strength enough to fight the draks when they found us and put these"—she jangled her shackles—"on us."

"Reorvik? In the Southern Watch?" Aveline glanced at Aerik. "Gaer Griffon is in Nakambe. What manner of creatures are you?"

Ra-Jareez bowed his head. "We are faelixes. Yun is caprikin. Apologies, he does not speak your language."

Rising, Aveline regarded the caprikin. His countenance reminded her of a goat, complete with horizontal pupils in his bloodshot eyes. His steely gaze sent a shiver down her spine. "He's your bodyguard?"

"The last who remains." Jazeera placed a hand across her chest. "The wyrm took the rest—may the Radiant Singer always shine down on them."

"Probably a trade caravan." Aerik toed a smoldering log in the fire. "Ships dock in Reorvik, offload caravans, which then make their way across the Four Watches, up the Western Passage. Dangerous journey, but I hear there's good money to be had if you survive it. There's another port up that way, I don't remember what it's called."

"We were planning on going north from Reorvik to Haefstaad, then across the mountains." Ra-Jareez flicked his ear.

Jazeera smiled. "Raj had an idea that perhaps folk beyond the Gods' Wall would have new things to trade with us."

Aveline scratched her head. "Gods' Wall? What's that?"

Grimacing, Ra Jareez stretched his legs. "The mountains that surround the northeast lands of this continent, you call it Andelosia, yes? It is the Gods' Wall…"

"Because it walls us off from the Western Wastes and the Four Watches." Aveline pondered the name. She learned from her tutors that the Iron Gate Mountains ran east to west in the south and the Dragon Spine Mountains ran north to south, joining near Muncifer, thus creating a natural sort of wall.

"And the great plains beyond the badlands." Ra-Jareez arched his back, hauling his sister to her feet as he did so. "We are told terrible faerie queens rule the lands beyond the Gods' Wall, devouring all those who trespass. But I don't believe it."

"I'm sure this is all fascinating, but I didn't come down here for a geography lesson." Using Yun's wrist shackles, Therkla pulled the caprikin to his feet. Glaring at her, he uttered several words Aveline assumed were profanity. "If we're going to free them, let's get on with it. Otherwise, we have to figure out how to shut them up so we can find your missing folk."

"Indeed." Aveline cursed herself for allowing her attention to drift. "Who has the keys to these shackles?"

"Fifth?" Jezeera faced her brother.

He shrugged. "I thought Third had them."

"Those are draks?" Aveline furrowed her brow.

"They're below, except the two guarding the mine entrance."

"We took care of them." Chuckling, Therkla examined Yun's shackles. "I don't suppose one was Fifth or Third?"

Raj posed the question to Yun. The caprikin snorted, shaking his head.

"No." Raj pulled at his shackles. "Just leave us here. Deal with the draks, find the keys, then free us. We swear we will keep quiet."

"Have the wizard bind and silence them." Therkla moved Yun to stand next to Raj and Jazeera.

The faelixes' eyes widened. Aveline held up her hand. "I'm not sure that's necessary. Aerik, take these three back to the camp and turn them over to Tasha. Vasco, Therkla, and I should be more than enough for these draks."

"What? Why me? Send the wizard."

"I beg your pardon." Vasco puffed out his chest. "I may be useful. Two sword arms are enough. We can spare yours."

Therkla snarled. "It pains me, but the fancy man is right, Aerik, even if he can't tell the difference between a sword and a mace. You're strong enough to handle these three if they give you trouble, and the lady knight and I are more than a match for some draks."

"Draks can be wily." Aerik kicked a log in the fire, embers scattering.

"You're not afraid of these northerners, are you?" Therkla licked a tusk.

"Frost Queen freeze you all." Aerik sighed, gesturing to the ascending corridor. "Let's go, you three. Maybe the crows can pick those locks."

As Aerik led the three prisoners away, Therkla scouted the other passages leading deeper in the mine.

Vasco prodded the fire with his blade. "You were wise to keep me. There's some power down here. I can't place it, but a wizard such as myself will prove more useful against it than that brutish man."

"Tasha said there's a wizard in the cave system somewhere." Aveline double-checked all her buckles and straps. "We'll deal with him first."

Therkla returned. "I found the way down. The smell gets worse, if you can believe that. Follow me."

* * *

Tasha perceived Aerik bringing three people out of the mine before her crows saw him. She watched through Revan's eyes as the Watchman led them out, marveling at the sight of the black-and-white-striped feline creatures and their goat-like companion. Through her connection with Gaia, she felt fae magic about them.

Could they have come through a fae nexus? She'd encountered an unlikely fae creature when she and Lorelei first visited Drak-Anor. He appeared to be demonic, but had, in fact, come from the fae realm. Sarvesh later claimed to be a variety of fire faerie. After Lorelei's death, Tasha felt no desire to remain and learn more.

Aerik paused at the tents outside the mine, eyeing Korbin and Revan. "The guard captain said I should bring these prisoners to the Crow Queen. I don't suppose either of you can pick locks?"

The crows remained silent. Tasha found Korbin's mind, suggesting he lead Aerik and the prisoners to her. Korbin complied. After checking with Revan to see if anything else noteworthy required her attention, Tasha released him and prepared for Aerik's impending arrival.

She secured the horses to trees, then built a small fire. Waiting near their mounts, she hoped her presence would soothe the animals should they find the strange creatures objectionable.

"Crow Queen," Aerik called as he approached. Korbin flew past Tasha, landing on a nearby branch overlooking the camp.

Tasha gritted her teeth. "Come ahead and stop calling me that. I'm just Tasha."

With eyes darting to and fro, the lanky goat-like creature followed Aerik, as if surveilling for danger. The two cat-like creatures followed him, hand in hand. All three hobbled, bound by shackles.

She held out her hand. "Why didn't you free them?"

Shrugging, Aerik dug through his pack for a stick of jerky. "No key. I will guard you, Crow Queen."

Tasha bowed her head to the newcomers. "I am Tasha, a sorceress and follower of the Earth Mother. No matter what this one says"—she glanced at Aerik—"I am not a queen. I'm just an herbalist."

The pair holding hands bowed. "I am Ra-Jareez. This is my sister Jazeera. The other is Yun. He does not speak your language." After he spoke to Yun, the tall, goat-like person bowed his head.

"Please, warm yourself by the fire. I'm sorry I have no means to loose your shackles."

"Crows are smart." Aerik pointed at Korbin. "Have him find a twig to pick the locks."

"Why don't you go back to the mine? Aveline... Therkla might need your help. There's a powerful evil down there."

"Bah." Aerik waved his hand. "They sent me here because they think that fancy wizard is enough."

Tasha held out her hand to Yun. In the firelight, she observed lacerations and bruising on all three. "Let me have a look at you. I can help with your wounds."

Ra-Jareez relayed the request to Yun. Nodding, he lowered himself to the ground. His shackles dug into his wrists, leaving crusty, dried blood caked in what wiry fur remained. His eyes followed her movements as she examined similar wounds on his ankles. After prying a jagged rock from between his cloven hoofs, she tossed it away.

"He is caprikin." Jazeera coughed. "Our bodyguard."

"They're traders. Shipwrecked." Aerik spoke around the jerky.

"I've not met anyone from Nakambe before." Tasha looked into his eyes. Despite their bestial appearance, she saw the intelligence behind them. "Are you fae? I sense fae magic around you all."

Ra-Jareez sucked in his breath. "You sense that?" Our people—faelixes, caprikins, and cathar too—we were created ages ago by elf magic from the beasts."

"In the Age of Dreams before The Sundering." Jazeera spoke in a reverent whisper.

"The elves created your people?" Her studies at the Arcane University told nothing of the people across the sea.

"They were inspired by Adranus's creation of oroqs and dwarves." Ra-Jareez rubbed his hands together. "Lacking the ability to create life from nothing, they looked to their animal companions. Cats, goats, and birds."

Dwarves and oroqs are related? Tasha returned to Silvermane's side, retrieving some herbs from her bag as well as a mortar and pestle.

"Oh, Raj. Stop filling her head with nonsense." Jazeera pinched her brother. "Maris created the oroqs. She stole away into the Celestial Forge in the dark of night to create them. Adranus merely gave them the spark of life she could not."

As she cleaned their wounds, Tasha listened to the faelixes debate various creation stories. Although Tasha recognized some, many of the tales related by the siblings bore little resemblance to the fables she heard as a child or to the ones she read while attending the Arcane University. She hoped she would have time to ask them more about their traditions later, when everyone was safely home again.

Chapter 20

Eyes watering, Aveline choked back bile as a wave of nausea engulfed her. Keeping to the shadows, she and Vasco crept behind Therkla.

Rounding a corner, Aveline discovered the stench originated from the pile of mutilated bodies festering in the center of the room. With a quick glance, the knight-captain could not identify any of the rotting corpses as the missing people from town. So decayed were they few discernable features remained. Three draks poked and prodded the pile, humming to themselves.

Screaming with rage, Aveline charged into the room with her mace held high. Bringing it down upon the head of the nearest drak, she caved in his skull.

Kicking his body out of the way when he crumpled to the floor, she lowered her shield. Ramming the next drak, she pinned him to the wall. Snapping his teeth in her face, he snarled.

She felt a tingling sensation as Vasco cast a binding charm on the one she held. Once her prisoner stopped moving, she released him, letting him fall.

Therkla stood over the third drak. Her blade dripped with his blood. "Five down. Do you think there are ten, like fingers?"

"That would make too much sense." Aveline held no hope of any events in this mine working in their favor. "Check their pouches. Maybe one was Fifth or Third."

Vasco checked the still-living drak crumpled against the wall while Therkla and Aveline checked the dead ones. Aveline's drak carried only polished rocks and a few pieces of dried meat in his pouch. Likewise, Therkla's search came up empty.

"Ah-ha! The luck of Dolios is with me." Vasco held up a key.

Aveline wiped bits of flesh and skull from her mace using the edge of her cloak. "Hang on to that. It resembles the key we use for shackles at the jail. Let's find the rest of those draks and this master of theirs."

Vasco held his bladed staff to the throat of the magically bound drak. "What shall we do with this one? Leave him?"

Therkla pushed past Aveline, then plunged her blade into his chest. "No need. We have one captive already."

Blood pooling around the slumped drak, the life-light in his eyes dimmed. Aveline considered confronting Therkla, but she turned her gaze to the pile of bodies instead. *He got off easy.*

"Far be it from me to be the voice of reason." Therkla sheathed her sword. After lifting the drak by his neck, she tossed him on the pile. "We should return to the surface to figure out what is going on here. This"—she gestured toward the rotting corpses—"is not just random killings."

"I'm not leaving here without the butcher's daughter." Aveline pointed at the pile with her mace. "Now, we can dig through that and see if she's in there, or we can go deeper."

Placing her hands on her hips, Therkla approached Aveline. The knight-captain's head barely reached the oroq's chin. "We need to interrogate those prisoners. Find out what they know."

"Fine." Aveline gritted her teeth. "You and Vasco head back to camp. I'll keep searching for the girl."

"Now that's just stupid." Therkla poked Aveline in the chest. "You run in here with only half-assed reconnaissance, and now you want to go deeper and confront a wizard with gods know how many minions by yourself? Do you have a death wish? I thought knights had more sense than that."

Clenching her fists, Aveline felt her face grow hot. The urge to pummel the oroq woman threatened to overwhelm her.

Vasco touched her arm. "Though I would not have said it quite that way, I agree with Therkla. We should regroup and consider our options."

Options? We leave… and Innya dies. If we keep going, we might be able to save her.

"We don't even know if this whore you're looking for is still alive." Therkla seized Aveline's arm.

Backhanding the oroq, Aveline shoved her. "She's a young girl! She doesn't deserve to rot at the bottom of a pile of corpses!"

Stumbling, Therkla spat blood. She lunged, snarling, at Aveline.

"Oh dear…" Backpedaling, Vasco gasped. The oroq slammed into the knight-captain's midsection. The two crashed to the floor.

Pinned under Therkla and gasping for breath, Aveline slammed a mailed fist into the side of the oroq's head.

"K'teep'ma tis astrapis!" An unfamiliar voice shouted the words just before Aveline felt the burning sting of electricity coursing through her body. Therkla convulsed, spewing bloody spittle in Aveline's face.

"Look, First. Two new ones for us to try."

Another voice, guttural and raspy, joined in. "Indeed, Master. *Syndesi somatos.*"

Aveline felt a crushing weight on top of her as the oroq's spasms stopped. Aveline saw fear in Therkla's eyes. Grunting, she pushed at Therkla's unmoving bulk.

"Pity about the rest. We'll deal with them later. *Syndesi somatos.*"

Aveline's muscles froze, and Therkla's body pressed down upon her once again, forcing the air from her lungs. From its hood, the gnarled face of a man peered down at her, half of it drooping like the wax of a melted candle. A steel-colored eye peeked out from beneath folds of skin, while the other remained cloaked in the shadows of his hood.

The gnarled man pulled Therkla off Aveline. "Get your brothers. Take this oroq below. She is strong. She may prove useful."

He wiped blood off Aveline's face with a shaking, claw-like hand. "Oh, this one... beautiful. Strong. Pure of heart. She may be the one for whom we've searched, First. Tell the others."

Aveline strained to move against the enchantment holding her in place. The man pressed his palm against her forehead. "Did you get my note, I wonder? I heard Curton has a stunning lady knight as guard captain." He chuckled. "Sleep now. We'll make you presentable."

Despite fighting against it, her eyes closed. Aveline heard the man cackling in glee before she lost consciousness.

* * *

By the time Tasha finished cleaning the wounds around the prisoners' shackles, fatigue from a long day threatened to overwhelm her. That Aerik snored as he leaned against the base of a tree did little to stave off her own growing desire for sleep.

"I'm sorry I can't do more until these irons come off." She wadded the bloody rag she'd used to blot their wounds. "They've been gone longer than I expected."

She stretched. After centering herself, Tasha summoned Revan. The crow alerted her that Vasco fled the mine and headed for her, alone.

Alone? Feeling her breath quicken, she stopped herself from dashing toward the mine. She risked passing Vasco and missing him in the dark, and she needed to know what happened before she decided what action to take.

Tasha nudged Aerik's feet until he awoke. "Something's gone wrong. Vasco's running back. Alone."

Aerik leapt to his feet, stumbling as he yanked his sword

from its scabbard. "I'll go to them."

"No, wait!" Tasha took his arm. "We don't know what happened down there. We'll wait for Vasco."

"Master…" Snuggling against his arm, Jazeera glanced at her brother. "Master came for them."

Tasha knelt in front of the siblings. "Tell me about this Master. Who is he? What does he want?"

"He is… twisted and sagging, like warm wax." Raj's lips curled exposing his pointed teeth. "He seeks the power within the people he steals. I never saw what was below."

"It is magic we are unfamiliar with, but there is some… *thing* down there." Jazeera shuddered. "I saw it once when I brought him food. So many colors. It was bright, then dark, and swirled with vapors…"

Raj spoked to Yun in the caprikin's rapid language. Yun's reply, a curt flood of syllables, sounded like a curse.

"He says it looked like a tear." Raj furrowed his brow. "A tear in… the air. It just hung there like… a doorway to another realm."

Tasha chewed her lip. "A fae nexus, perhaps?"

Raj posed the question to Yun. Grunting, the caprikin shook his head.

"Yun has seen a fae nexus, in Yoake. He thinks this was not like that."

Vasco burst into the camp. Leaning on his staff, he gasped for breath. Aerik approached him, his sword held at the ready. "Coward! You abandoned them to death."

Vasco shook his head. He panted to utter the words, "No. No."

Tasha pushed Aerik's sword arm down. "Just tell us what happened."

Vasco described the room containing the pile of bodies, Aveline's charge, and her subsequent argument with Therkla. "Then a wizard attacked them. He was… misshapen. I'm not certain he was even human. I was behind the pile of bodies, out of his sight, I think. He subdued them so quickly… I didn't think it was wise to confront him alone. Oh, I have the key to their shackles, I think."

He passed the key to Tasha.

"Master." Raj's voice quivered.

Tasha knelt before the siblings. Using the key Vasco provided, she unlocked their bindings. "What can you tell us about him? Do you know the room Vasco described?"

"He threw all the failures there." Jazeera hissed, curling her lip. "Sometimes, they were dead. Other times, just close to death. Occasionally, the draks would eat from the pile, if the bodies were fresh."

Raj hugged his sister close. "Everyone ended up on the pile. They all failed his tests."

Aerik's eyes widened. "What tests? Why does he test them?"

"We don't know. He only wanted humans, though." Raj rubbed his wrists, shivering.

Tasha took Aerik and Vasco aside. "I'm not going back to Curton without Aveline. We have to go back for her and Therkla."

Aerik gripped her shoulder. "I'm with you."

"As am I." Vasco tapped the earth with the butt of his staff.

"Give us blades." The three former prisoners held out their hands. "We'll help."

Tasha rubbed her amulet as visions of her last expedition into an unknown underground lair with a group of stalwart companions flashed through her mind. She hoped to live the rest of her days without replicating that experience.

Chapter 21

Awakening with a shiver, Aveline groaned. She squinted against the coruscating light that flickered in her vision. To her surprise, chains rattled when she moved to sit up, and she remained pinned against the hard stone table. Restraints bound her arms and legs. Slowly, the room came into focus. Numerous candles illuminated the small space, which appeared to be a ritual chamber of some sort. Whoever bound her had stripped her naked.

Jerking the chain, she labored to free herself. The metal bindings cut into her wrist. "Maris's bloody spear!" Aveline yanked again.

Nothing.

Lying motionless, she closed her eyes, breathing deeply to calm herself. Somewhere in the distance, she heard angry shouting. Rhythmic pounding of metal against stone echoed through the corridor.

Clink.

Clink.

Clink.

Synchronizing her effort with the digging, Aveline heaved against the chain. She hoped to draw no attention as she broke her bonds. The cracking of stone greeted her latest attempt. Despite remaining secure, the fastener loosened, and the chain slackened. She yanked again. And again. Finally, the chain broke free.

Whipping around her, it bashed her head. Stars exploded in her vision. She squeezed her eyes shut against unbidden tears. Manipulating the chain with her free hand, she gathered it to her side. As she willed the pain in her head to subside, Aveline heard the padding of feet approaching.

Returning her free hand to its bound position, Aveline blinked back her tears. Her head throbbed worse than her last hangover. A drak shuffled into the room, mumbling as he approached her.

Which are you? Do any of you have names? She saw a set of keys on his belt.

Aveline waited until he reached her side. Swinging the chain still attached to her wrist, she whipped her arm at him.

"I see you're… what? Urk!" The chain wrapped around his throat. Aveline pulled him closer. His claws scrabbled at the earth as he attempted to make purchase, but her strength more than matched his. Lifting the drak off the ground, she pulled him across her body.

With a sickening crack, she twisted his head with her still-bound hand, breaking his neck. She tried all the keys on his belt until she found the one to unlock the shackles on her wrists. She shoved his limp body to the floor. After unlocking the irons restraining her legs, she rolled off. As her feet hit the floor, she felt an unwelcome, yet familiar, tightening in her lower back and abdomen. *Seriously? Now? This can't wait for a few days?*

A cursory glance around the room confirmed neither her clothes, nor her weapons and armor, lay nearby. Other than the table where she had been held prisoner, the room contained only a rag and bucket. A lone passageway appeared to be the only exit. *Damn it. I don't want to wander down here naked, especially if I'm about to bleed. Damn you, Cybele, can't I pay your price at a more convenient time?* She inspected her wounds. Her ribs ached where Therkla tackled her. Otherwise, Aveline found no signs of further injury. She retrieved one of her shackles and chain, keeping it handy as a makeshift weapon.

From the exit, she peered around the corner. Up ahead, the passageway split—the left branch descending and the right branch continuing level as far as she could see in the dim light. The sound of digging continued, echoing off the earthen walls. Heading deeper led to more danger thus far. She chose the right branch.

Keeping low and close to the wall, she proceeded forward. Ahead, flickering light cast dancing shadows on the walls, although she could not determine who or what made them. As she drew closer to the light source, she heard humming.

"Master says you're not pure, but strong. Strongest we've had, but still not pure. Not like the other lady." The raspy voice hummed between words, half mumbling, half singing. Aveline continued forward, taking care to remain shrouded in darkness.

Peeking around the corner, she viewed a robed, green-scaled drak rubbing a naked, grey-skinned body with a wet cloth. The figure wrung out the cloth on the floor before dipping it into a nearby bucket and repeating the process. Therkla lay on a stone table, similar to the one upon which Aveline awoke, her arms and legs shackled.

Groaning, the oroq's eyes fluttered open. The bones in her neck cracked as she rolled her head. When she moved to rise, her shackles prevented almost all movement. "Where... Maris's bloody spear, what are you doing?" Writhing in an effort to avoid the drak's ministrations, her efforts proved futile.

"Must be clean. Yes, yes. Master says they must all be clean. No filth in the rituals, even for impure souls."

Therkla snarled as the drak scrubbed her thigh. "I'm going to eat your heart to Maris's glory, Drak."

Aveline ran her hand along her arm. *Did they bathe me too?* Putting the thought aside, she weighed the iron shackle in her hand. Doubting the restraint alone could quickly render the drak unconscious, Aveline gripped it in one hand and held the length of chain in the other.

She waited until the drak bent over his bucket. Leaping forward, she brought the chain over his head and around his neck. His squeal of surprise became a strangled gurgle as she lifted him into the air.

His clawed hands scrabbled at his neck, trying to wedge between the chain and his throat. Twisting, Aveline slammed him into the floor. She rammed her knee into the side of his head while continuing to tighten the chain.

With a crunch, the drak's neck snapped. Holding him until his body stopped twitching, Aveline dropped the chain. Upon finding no keys in his pockets, she tried the one she obtained from the other drak.

Therkla regarded her wide-eyed as Aveline unlocked her shackles. "I'm impressed." Sitting up, the oroq's eyes wandered over Aveline's body. "You throw a pretty good punch too. Too bad circumstances are different. I'd take you…"

"Later." Putting the thought of the oroq's lust out of her mind, Aveline searched for anything she could use as a weapon. "Have you been out the entire time?"

Nodding, Therkla rubbed her head. "The last I remember, I was beating the shit out of you. I blame you for this, woman. I thought Aerik was reckless…"

"You can bitch at me all you want later. I'll even buy you an ale first." Aveline retrieved her trusty shackle and chain. "We need to find our gear."

Therkla counted on her fingers. "There can't be that many draks left. How many have you strangled to death with that so far?"

"Just two." *Three in the corpse room, plus the two outside.* "There's no telling how many there are, though, plus that nasty-looking wizard."

Therkla stretched, swinging her arms to get the blood flowing. "All right, let's find our stuff and bust some heads."

* * *

Tasha and the others led their horses across the hills. Since keeping everyone together seemed safest, she hoped to convince the three former prisoners to remain outside and guard their steeds. As they drew closer to the mine, the eastern sky brightened.

Her crows greeted them as they arrived at the makeshift camp just outside the mine entrance. Revan and Korbin, taking to the air, flew around the group before alighting on Tasha's shoulder. Feeling their mood within close proximity without effort, she determined the denizens of the mine posed no immediate danger to them.

"Vasco, how long will your spell hold the drak in that tent?"

The wizard counted on his fingers as he faced the eastern horizon. "I should reapply it if you intend on keeping him alive."

Jazeera and Raj inspected the two tents.

"This was Seventh." Jazeera waved her hand in front of her nose to ward off the odor of the dead drak.

"This is Fourth." Raj dragged the paralyzed drak out of the tent by his ankle, holding him for all to see.

"Seventh? Fourth?" Tasha furrowed her brow. "Are those their names?"

The faelixes took turns explaining how the draks called themselves the Hands of the Master, but, individually, they were numbered, like fingers. Raj tossed the drak to the ground so Vasco could reapply his binding charm.

"So, there are ten?" Tasha figured if they called themselves fingers, it would not make sense otherwise. "I don't suppose the master has feet too? Maybe another ten draks?"

Jazeera snorted. "No, just two hands, but he may have more draks down there. His hands are his closest, most trusted servants. Perhaps he doesn't count like we do."

"We slew three more before the master showed up." Vasco finished securing the drak, then shoved him into the tent.

Aerik spat on the earth. "Then you fled like a coward."

"I sought reinforcements." Sniffing, Vasco leaned on his staff. "What you call cowardice, I call discretion."

Tasha silenced them with an upheld hand. "So all we know for certain is there is a wizard down there who captured our friends who has at least three more draks serving him. Is that correct?"

Yun spoke to Raj. He swung a sword through the air, testing its balance. Tasha noticed familiar markings on the blade. It belonged to Aveline. The caprikin must have taken it from her saddle.

She took Raj aside. "What did he say?"

"Yun says he saw a few humans when he was helping carry bodies, and he said he would kill the drak if you didn't have the stomach for it."

Tasha glanced over her shoulder at the caprikin. He continued to move the blade around his body as he stretched muscles unused during his captivity. "That won't be necessary. Make sure he knows Aveline will probably want her sword back, though she doesn't really use it anymore. Let's check the area for supplies, rope, torches, anything that might help."

Raj nodded, then spoke to Yun while beckoning his sister. When they finished, Jazeera ducked into the tent with the dead drak, returning with two daggers and a length of rope.

She handed a dagger to her brother before flipping the other one into the air. "They're too light and small, Raj. We may need to use tooth and claw."

"Bah, I hate the taste of drak." Raj commented to Yun. The caprikin laughed.

Aerik drew a small blade from his boot. He handed it hilt first to Jazeera. "This might work better."

She accepted his dagger, then tossed hers to her brother. "Now we just need to find our possessions. They're in there."

She gestured toward the mine. "Somewhere."

Crossing her arms, Tasha shivered. She peered into the inky-black entrance. Revan and Korbin fluttered on her shoulder. The scar on her neck tingled. When she unconsciously scratched it, her fingers brushed against the amulet serving as her arcane focus before closing around it. Her thoughts returned to that day when Strom Lightbringer pushed her and Lorelei to assault a city of draks and minotaurs in the name of eradicating evil.

Strom, his squire Runt, and Yuri all died that day. She, too, nearly perished after a minotaur defending his home slashed her throat.

His home... we went there to destroy evil. I suppose we did, but we brought as much of it with us that day.

She commanded Revan and Korbin to watch over the horses. "If anyone wants to stay out here, now is the time."

No one accepted her offer.

Tasha removed her amulet, then held it before her. *"Fos."* Light from the gems in her talisman pushed away the shadows and darkness. She led the motley group into the mine, expecting the weight of the earth to press against her once the entrance disappeared from sight. Instead, to her surprise, Tasha felt comforted and safe. She placed her hand against the earthen wall.

The embrace of Gaia surrounded them, and Tasha understood. The Earth Mother called to her from this place. In an instant, she knew the layout of the mine and sensed all the life within—from the worms tunneling through the earth, to the spiders weaving webs in forgotten corners, to the Master Under the Mountain, his three remaining draks, and the slaves they kept. She felt the familiar presence from her visions as well as the disturbing force, and she felt the life-force of Therkla and Aveline.

It appeared to her as a scintillating burst of colors at first, then as cacophonous sounds, odors both sweet and sickly, and, finally, sensations of heat, cold, pain, and pleasure. Simultaneously, it revolted and fascinated her.

She recalled a history lesson from the Arcane University. "There's a chaos rift here."

Aerik's brow furrowed as his mouth fell agape. The faelix siblings tilted their heads, staring at her.

Vasco's wide-eyed stare told a different story. "You're certain? I feel something... but it is indistinct, distant."

"It is deep in the mine, but I'm certain of it." She gestured to the group. "Let's keep moving."

When they reached the first junction, Aerik pointed toward the right. "We went that way."

The left branch called to Tasha. "What's this way?"

Aerik grunted. "Therkla said a dead end, a shaft with a broken lift."

Tasha turned left. Just around the next bend, she saw the shaft, a black pit hewn from the earth and rock, plunging deep into the mountain. From the edge, she looked downward. Resisting the sudden and illogical urge to hurl herself into the abyss, she placed her hand on the wall to steady herself.

The familiar presence dwelt in that hole. She examined the pulley attached to the ceiling. It appeared strong enough to hold, but the attached rope, frayed and rotten, disintegrated at the touch.

"What are you thinking?" Vasco stood beside her. "This isn't the way we went. I'm not sure we were as far down as that shaft seems to go."

"I have to go down there."

Chapter 22

The farther Aveline and Therkla traveled beyond the rooms in which they'd been held prisoner, the more maze-like the mine became. Half-dug chambers connected to short, unlit passages, which led to dead ends or to twisting tunnels descending deeper into the earth. They remained in darkness as much as possible, dashing from shadow to shadow in tunnels where the draks left candles or lanterns burning.

At last, after what seemed like several arduous hours, the two women found a passageway that ascended. Therkla waited at the bottom of the tunnel, sniffing the air before nodding for Aveline to proceed. Not long after, she noted the odor, too, the familiar stench of decay and rotting flesh.

The brief reprieve from the fetor of the corpse room brought her no joy. However, its return heralded hope of escape. Areas of shadow to hide in became scarcer as they made their way upward through the twisting passages.

Approaching the all-too familiar room, Aveline held her hand out to stop Therkla. She heard voices ahead. Therkla indicated she heard them too. They crept forward together, drawing closer until the voices became distinct. Two people spoke in whispers, both men.

"Another one for the pile." The first one spoke with an accent that resembled Aerik's. "Can you believe that melted bastard's making us do this?"

"Eh, those two new ones killed a lot of his draks. The man's gotta make do." The second man's voice sounded more western to Aveline's ears, perhaps from Muncifer.

"Doesn't matter, I guess. We're still getting paid. He's letting us keep their effects too. Nice bonus, eh? Too bad we can't have some fun with them before he ruins them with his magic."

Therkla growled. Aveline put her hand on the oroq's arm to steady her.

The second laughed. "I'll admit, that oroq isn't half bad. Although the other is more to my taste, even if she is a northerner."

The first joined in the laughter. "I didn't know oroqs grew tits that big."

Flinging off Aveline's arm, Therkla charged ahead. For a moment, Aveline considered staying in the safety of the shadows. She sighed, tightening her grip on the chain, and joined the oroq woman in her rage-filled rush.

"You want a piece, do you?" Therkla burst into the room, a towering grey mountain of naked oroq fury. She howled. Calling out to Maris, goddess of war, she tackled the nearest of the two men. She rammed the top of her head into the man's jaw, following through with a punch to his midsection.

The other hulking, hairy brute wearing tattered leather breeches and a fur-lined vest, stood aside. Wide eyed, he witnessed Therkla slamming her opponent onto the floor with enough force to dent his breastplate. Catching his ear, Aveline swung her shackle across the side of the hairy man's face. Screaming, he clutched his bleeding ear with one hand while he fumbled to loose the mace hanging at his waist.

Therkla punched the first man. "Let me show you how we kiss." Closing her mouth around his nose and upper lip, she bit into him with an audible crunch. Shrieking, he thrashed, fighting to free his sword from a scabbard now pinned underneath him.

"How'd you… the draks…" The hairy hulk brandished his—no, Aveline's—mace backing away from her, ogling her naked body.

Aveline swung the shackle again. He raised the mace to block. The chain wrapped around the hilt. "That's mine."

She yanked on the chain, ripping the mace from his hand. Letting the chain fall free, she gripped the familiar weapon.

He regarded his now-silent companion while Therkla, straddling him, bashed his head repeatedly into the stony floor.

"Yield and you shall have mercy." Aveline raised her mace. "Therkla! He's done."

Responding to her name, the oroq rose from her fallen opponent, blood dripping from her face and hands. Upon rolling him over, she jerked her blade from the scabbard hung at his waist. Grinning, she regarded Aveline's opponent.

The blood drained from the big man's face. He glanced from warrior to warrior, as if assessing the odds of facing one or the other.

In no mood for games, Aveline set her jaw. "Surrender or die."

The man turned to flee. She swung her mace, catching the back of his head. Simultaneously, Therkla lunged forward. She pierced his side with her blade, shoving it through his ribs until it protruded from his back. He crumpled, blood pouring from his head and side. The oroq put her foot on him, shoving him away from her blade.

Therkla wiped her mouth with the back of her hand. "Two more for the pile."

Turning away from her in disgust, Aveline crouched at Therkla's opponent, careful not to look at his ruined face. The breastplate he wore, although dented, remained salvageable. To her dismay, she recognized it as hers.

"It doesn't even fit him." Aveline tugged at the straps, loosening the armor.

"We know the way out. We should go."

"Let's reclaim our gear. We might need it." She rolled the man out of her armor, then pulled the undershirt over his head, frowning when it collected blood from the myriad wounds covering his face. "The prisoners said nothing about these men. Who knows what else awaits us?"

"None of these clothes or armor is mine." Therkla kicked the hairy man's corpse. "I guess as long as I have my sword, I'm set."

"Take his breeches at least." Aveline pointed toward the hairy man's bottom half while she struggled to strip the man who wore her breastplate.

"Why? Does all this oroq flesh bother you?" Therkla licked a blood-crusted tusk, arching her back.

"Fine. Run around naked." Grunting, Aveline peeled off the man's breeches. "I don't care."

His clothes proved adequate, although tight, to wear under her armor. Turning, she noticed Therkla staring at her from beneath a lowered brow, smiling.

The oroq woman put her arms around Aveline, pulling her close, her breath laced with the metallic stink of blood. "When we get back to town, what say we get a nice, hot bath, together, and a bottle of wine. Make Aerik jealous?"

Aveline pushed her away, shaking her head. She felt blood rush to her face. Her mouth opened and closed several times as she struggled to respond in a way that didn't seem insulting. "One thing at a time. Let's just get out first."

The oroq smacked her lips, grinning as she passed Aveline. "All right, just think about it. There's no point in living if you can't feel alive."

* * *

Contemplating the abyss of the mine shaft before her, Tasha wiped her clammy palms on her tunic. The gaping hole reminded her of a great maw, waiting to devour her.

"Forgive me, but this seems an unnecessary diversion." Vasco held on to her arm, refusing to peer down the shaft.

Tasha withdrew from his grip. "Whatever is down there can help us."

"I think there are enough of us to deal with this wizard and however many minions remain." Vasco tugged at her sleeve. "Come, Aveline and the oroq woman need us."

"Aveline can take care of herself, Vasco." Tasha felt the energy of the presence at the bottom of the shaft calling to her. "What's down there can help with that chaos rift and whatever the wizard is doing with it."

"We could split up." Raj crouched at the edge of the mine shaft. "One could stay here with Tasha to help her down the shaft, and the rest could go search for your friends."

"I do not think that is wise." Using his staff, Vasco prodded the broken pulley protruding from the ceiling.

Tasha held her hand out behind her. "Pass me that rope we found." She hoped what they took from the camp was long enough to reach the bottom of the shaft.

Jazeera handed it to her. "Yes, it is terrible, this idea. We have a saying in Nakambe: don't follow two paths at once."

Tasha tossed one end of the rope down the hole, allowing it to unravel. "Someone needs to hold or secure this end. I'm climbing down there."

Aerik pulled Raj out of the way, then took the rope from Tasha. "I'll hold it."

Jazeera approached Tasha, bowing her head. "Perhaps you will allow me to go first. If there is danger there, you would appreciate the warning, yes? It's the least I can do to repay you for freeing us."

Tasha considered her offer. "Thank you. I would prefer not going down there alone." Nodding, she placed her hand on the faelix's shoulder.

"Hold fast." Jazeera gestured to Yun, who, nodding, grabbed the rope, helping Aerik hold it tight. The faelix twisted her arm around the line before shimmying over the edge.

Aerik and Yun grunted as Jazeera's descent tugged at the rope. Together, they kept it from slipping. Tasha observed it twitch with the faelix's movements as she disappeared from sight.

Raj watched from Tasha's side, peering over the edge. "She is making good progress. Do you know how far it goes?"

"You can see her?" No matter how much she strained, Tasha saw naught but pitch black beyond the boundary of their enchanted illumination.

"There is plenty of light for our eyes." Raj waved over the edge to his sister.

"The rope is not long enough." Jazeera's voice rose from the darkness. "It's a short jump to the bottom, though. There's a skeleton here. If you're coming, please hurry."

"My sister is nimble, but she doesn't take risks." Raj touched Tasha's arm. "It's not far from the end of the rope to the bottom."

Tasha gripped the rope to ease over the side. "I hate heights like this. It may as well be twenty leagues."

The glow from her amulet illuminated the wall of the mine shaft in front of her as she worked her way downward, bracing her feet against the earth as she descended. Within moments, her hands ached from her death grip on the rope.

Glancing upward, the magical glow from Vasco's staff eclipsed her view of the top of the shaft. Shutting her eyes against the glare, she lowered herself.

From below, Tasha heard Jazeera whisper words of encouragement. Risking vertigo, she glanced downward. The bottom, as well as Jazeera, remained out of sight. A wave of nausea overcame the sorceress. She squeezed her eyes shut, concentrating on calming the churning in her stomach.

Once the urge to vomit passed, Tasha resumed her descent. Proceeding hand over hand, she continued downward. The familiar presence pressed against her thoughts, urging her closer. In her mind, she felt the walls of the shaft, the ever-closer bottom, even Jazeera waiting for her and Raj and the others up top. She felt other life in the mine, the worms in the ground, even the people deeper in the mine.

So intent she was on searching for signs of Aveline, Tasha realized she reached the end of the rope moments before grabbing open air. Panic returned, and her hands slipped.

Time froze as Tasha fell. Crashing into the mound of detritus knocked the wind out of her. Gasping for breath, she lay motionless

Jazeera offered her a hand. "You should not let yourself get distracted when climbing."

With the faelix's help, Tasha rose to her feet. She shone her amulet around the bottom of the shaft. On the opposite side of the mound, near where she impacted, stark white bone reflected the light. The familiar presence she'd been feeling returned, stronger than before. Crouching by the bones, she noticed a shimmering black cloak beneath it.

"Is this why you needed to come down here?" Jazeera squatted beside her. "You knew this person?"

"I didn't know her, but she is why we're here." In her heart, Tasha recognized the body as that of the woman who fell down the shaft in her vision. She touched the cloak. *Feathers. Black feathers, like those of crows. Like the one I saw in my dream...*

With painstaking care, Tasha pulled the cloak from under the bones, careful not to disturb the woman's rest. She noticed the stitching holding the feathers to the backing seemed untouched by time. For that matter, even the fabric appeared to be in pristine condition.

"I am very confused why, in the middle of rescuing your friend, you needed to come down here for a piece of clothing." Jazeera crossed her arms. "What is so important about that?"

Tasha gathered the cloak in her arms. "I know it looks bad. It's... it's difficult to explain." She glanced upward at the tiny point of light pinpointing the location of their companions. "We should ascend first."

The faelix narrowed her eyes. "You go first. I will follow behind."

Tasha understood her behavior seemed strange to the faelix. She secured the cloak over her shoulder. Jazeera knelt beneath the line, preparing to boost Tasha. She let the faelix give her a leg up, grabbed onto the rope, and then ascended.

Her arms burned within minutes, even using her feet against the side of the mine shaft to aid her ascent. Her heart skipped a beat when the rope jerked in her hands as Jazeera caught hold. Tasha scrambled to gain a foothold, raining dirt and rocks on the faelix, as their companions pulled on the rope to aid their ascent.

By the time they reached the top, the sorceress's arms trembled, and her clothes, drenched in sweat, clung to her body. She sat on the ground panting.

Jazeera skipped past Tasha. "Let her catch her breath, but then we should ask why we just went through all that for clothes."

Chapter 23

Creeping through the shadows, retracing their steps from earlier in the day, distracted Aveline from focusing on Therkla's proposition. Despite the passages appearing familiar, the knight-captain remained vigilant.

The two made their way to the room where they first encountered the captives. After gaining their bearings, they identified the route leading upward toward the mine entrance.

Therkla held Aveline from starting up the passageway. "You hear that?"

Cupping her hand around her ear, she heard voices echoing in the higher passage. From the sound of it, Aveline judged the speakers to be near the mine entrance. They continued to follow the voices, weapons held at the ready.

As they drew closer, Aveline recognized one of the voices. Her heart skipped. Laughing, she broke into a run. She ignored Therkla's calls to slow down and come back. Light from outside grew brighter. Upon nearing the mine entrance, she realized the voices originated from the other passageway, the abandoned mine shaft with the broken lift.

Charging ahead, she rounded the bend, nearly colliding with Aerik. The three former prisoners surrounded Tasha, who sat on the floor. Vasco crouched near her. Spinning, Aerik raised his weapon in alarm before noticing Therkla who arrived behind Aveline.

"Ye gods, woman." Aerik lowered his sword, gawking. "This is no fit place to be running about naked."

"Aveline!" Tasha launched herself at the knight-captain, scrambling past her companions. The two embraced. Aveline felt tears welling in her eyes at the sight of her friend.

Therkla took Vasco aside.

"I feared I lost you." Tasha squeezed Aveline. The sorceress trembled, holding the knight-captain.

"It's going to take more than that. Thanks for coming after me."

Ra-Jareez crossed his arms. "It is fortunate you rescued yourselves. We were too busy looking for old clothes."

Spinning, Tasha glared at the faelix even as Aerik stepped forward with balled fists. "The Crow Queen does not answer to you. One life is nothing compared to all her responsibilities."

Aveline put her hand on Tasha's shoulder, shaking her head. The sorceress met her eyes.

Therkla, snarling, moved to strike Aerik. "One life? Perhaps you didn't notice I'd been taken too."

Raising his hands, Aerik backed away from the angry oroq. "I… I was worried for y… you, of course. I merely meant the Crow Queen was primarily concerned with the life of her lady friend there…"

"Yes, concerned enough to climb down an abandoned mine shaft in the wrong direction to retrieve a moldy old cloak from a pile of bones." Jazeera leaned against her brother as she, too, crossed her arms and stared at Tasha.

"Enough. Enough!" Aveline held up her hands. "None of that matters now; we're both safe." She pointed toward the entrance. "Vasco, you and Therkla come outside with me and drag that drak in here. We're going to get some answers." She pointed at the three former prisoners. "You three can help us or go wait outside with the horses, I don't care which. I'm going to get my spare breeches and shirt from Socks. When I return, we're going to go find that wizard, and we're going to finish this."

* * *

While Aveline stepped outside with Vasco and Therkla to retrieve their drak prisoner and re-equip themselves, Tasha examined the cloak she retrieved from the depths of the mine. Crouching near her, Aerik observed as she spread it out.

"The faelixes think retrieving that was a waste of time." He stroked the feathers. "What's so important about it?"

"I think"—Tasha smoothed the cloak as it lay over her lap—"this belonged to the Crow Queen. I think that is who is down there."

"Your predecessor? How did you know?" He stroked one of the feathers with a finger.

"When I commune with Gaia, I sometimes have visions. I see things, other places…"

"The future?" Aerik raised his eyebrows. "Visions of things yet to come?"

"Not yet." Tasha shook her head. "But I have seen the past. I don't know if the visions come from the Earth Mother or from a spirit."

"The Crow Queen serves more than just Gaia." Aerik placed his hand on the hilt of his sword. "Cybele, Artume, too, I think. Perhaps the visions come from one of them?"

Tasha ran her hand along the feathers of the cloak. "Perhaps."

She shrugged off her old cape, then pulled the feathered mantle around her shoulders. It wrapped itself around her as if alive, pulling itself snug and clasping around her neck. She felt the wooden toggle, carved in relief with leaves and vines. The cloak hung to just above her heels. It felt to Tasha like a mother's embrace.

"Let's check on Aveline and the others. Hopefully, Therkla hasn't throttled our prisoner."

Chuckling, Aerik led her out. Therkla held the snarling, pale, green-scaled drak at arms' length while Aveline pushed his head back with the head of her mace. Vasco kept watch for anyone approaching from the forest or the hills.

"The Master Under the Mountain will rend the flesh from your bones. He'll drink his soup from your skulls!"

Spitting, the drak thrashed, a futile effort against Therkla's iron grip.

"Yes, yes, and skewer our eyes and juice our livers." The oroq cast a sidelong glance at Aveline. "He has plenty of fight in him, but I don't think he knows much about the wizard or his plans."

Tasha approached her friend. "Perhaps I can help?"

"I don't think we're going to get much out of this one." Therkla shook the hissing drak. He flailed his legs in a vain attempt to kick her.

Taking Tasha's arm, Aveline led her away. "I'm reluctant to execute a prisoner…"

"I'm not." Therkla chuckled.

The knight-captain took several more steps with Tasha before resuming. "We can't just leave him tied up. You know draks better than I do. What would his kin do?"

Tasha glanced at Therkla tightening her grip on the prisoner, returning his snarls and snips with her own growls and gnashing teeth. "Draks in Curton follow the same laws we do. If his clan disapproves of his actions, they might banish him, but maybe all these draks belong to the same clan. If what he's saying is true, they serve a master of whom no draks I've dealt with would approve."

Aveline crossed her arms, glancing over her shoulder. "So, what do we do? I can't keep him in the jail forever, and I wouldn't inflict him on any of the draks in town to rehabilitate. What they've all been doing down there… you should see the bodies."

Regarding her feet, Tasha sighed. "Justice must be served. If you think the crime is worth the punishment, I doubt anyone here will be bothered if you carry it out."

Aveline lowered her head, meeting Tasha's eyes. "I don't care about the rest. Will you be bothered?"

Tasha faced the drak. He glared at Therkla with blood-shot eyes. Snarling, he snapped at his captor, spittle dripping from his jaws. She pulled her cloak around her, feeling a reassuring warmth from the feathers, then shook her head. "Do what you must. For the safety of Curton."

Nodding, Aveline returned to Therkla's side. "Take him away. Make it quick. We need to get this over with."

Therkla grinned. "About time you came to your senses." She carried away the thrashing drak, ducking behind some rocks as she drew a long, curved knife. "After I'm done with you, I'm going to gut a wizard."

"So, what's this?" Aveline ran her hand along Tasha's cloak. "Is this what was more important than finding your friend?"

"I—" Tasha, feeling her face grow hot, lowered her gaze. "It was calling…"

"Relax." Aveline pulled Tasha into a hug. "I know you'd divert your attention only if you thought it was important. You still came after me, and I'll never forget that."

Hearing her friend's affirmation, Tasha smiled. "Honestly, I'd hoped to never see the inside of a mine or cave again after Drak-Anor."

"I'm not fond of the dank underground myself." Aveline put her hand on Tasha's shoulder. "Are you going to be all right going in there? You can stay out here and watch over the horses."

Tasha shook her head. "No. I'm with you until the end." Therkla returned from behind the rock. Her blade dripped with drak blood. She wiped it clean on a tent flap.

Tasha felt a chill run down her spine at the sight. "I may not have lived in Curton as long as you, but they're my people too. They deserve justice, all of them."

* * *

After sharing a quick meal of jerky, bread, and cheese with the group, Aveline ensured everyone possessed functional weapons. Satisfied they were as prepared as possible, the knight-captain led the group into the mine. Despite complaints by both Ra-Jareez and Jazeera, Aveline insisted Vasco and Tasha provide them with light. If a renegade wizard indeed occupied the lower levels, then he surely knew they approached if, from nothing else, his quickly diminishing number of drak minions.

The group moved with cautious urgency through the familiar sections of the mine, descending through the chamber where they had first encountered the faelixes and caprikin before moving on to the corpse room. The winding tunnel leading deeper still from the corpse room narrowed, forcing them to travel single file. As they crept forward in silence, Aveline became painfully aware of the creaks and clanks of her ill-fitting, salvaged breastplate.

After a sharp descent that forced them to cling to one another to keep from falling, the passage opened into a glittering cavern. Crystals jutted from the walls, reflecting the light of Vasco's staff and Tasha's amulet like thousands of stars in a black velvet night. Pausing to stretch, they beheld the cavern's natural beauty.

"I never imagined such a place could be real." Aveline took Tasha's arm. They circled a gigantic crystal hanging from the ceiling like a faceted column. Glimpsing Tasha's reflection in the face of the crystal, Aveline witnessed its transformation.

Shimmering, the feathers of Tasha's cloak spread behind her like great wings. The sorceress's face became lined and worn with age, and her legs withered until they resembled that of a bird. Hearing a shriek echo across the cavern, they turned their attention away from the vision.

Ra-Jareez clutched his sister's hand as the stone floor enveloped her, drawing her into it. Wrapping his arms around Ra-Jareez's waist, Yun pulled. Vasco and Aerik rushed to their side to aid in the rescue.

Meanwhile, Therkla stood transfixed by a wavering image in a nearby crystal.

The floor around Jazeera's legs rippled like water as she sank deeper and deeper. Aveline and Tasha joined with the efforts of the four, pulling her loose. They tumbled backward on to the cool, wet cavern floor. Once freed, Jazeera scrambled away from the spot.

"Therkla? Hey." Aerik shoved his oroq companion who stared at her reflection.

The oroq licked one of her tusks. "I'm with child… yours?" Screaming, she fell clutching her belly.

Although the oroq writhed in horror at the image, Aveline caught her.

"It split me open! Tried to claw its way out." Therkla pushed Aveline away, glaring at anyone who moved to help her.

Shivering, Tasha examined the cavern. "We're close to the rift. It's affecting the environment and how we perceive it."

Vasco poked at the section of floor that entrapped Jazeera with the butt of his dragon-bone staff. Giving way under pressure, it coated the pole. It slid like thick soup when he lifted it. "Were our need not so urgent, I would love to study this rift. What it does is nothing short of wondrous."

Aveline glanced at Tasha. The sorceress seemed unaffected. She gestured toward a passageway leading deeper into the tunnels. "Wonder later. Let's get moving before these crystals drive us mad."

Chapter 24

The throbbing in her head, which Tasha first noticed in the crystal chamber, grew worse as they continued exploring. Buzzing reminiscent of a thousand angry hornets joined it as they approached the end of the tunnel.

Like a gaping maw, a dark hole opened into another cave emanating scintillating colors. It simultaneously reeked of carrion and wildflowers. In the distance, Tasha heard lilting bells underlaid with screaming.

"What smells like baked bread?" Vasco peered into the depths, holding his illuminated staff over the opening.

"Bread? Are you dense?" Therkla wrinkled her nose. "It smells like puke and that moldy cheese that farmer tried to give us in Brackeborg."

"It's the chaos rift." Tasha pulled Vasco away from the edge of the pit. "It affects everything around it. Try not to look at it while we're down there, and don't touch it."

"Yes, let's just concentrate on stopping the wizard, his cronies, and saving whomever he's holding prisoner." Aveline secured her mace at her waist and lowered herself to the edge, dangling her feet over the precipice. The faelix siblings tied a rope around a nearby protuberance of rock. Before they finished, Aveline slid off the edge, disappearing into the darkness.

"She's not keeping all the glory to herself!" Therkla, pushing past Tasha, jumped in after Aveline. Aerik followed suit with an eager whoop.

Tasha closed her eyes. "Foolish bravado."

Raj tossed the free end of the rope over the edge. "We'll take the slow way."

Once they reached the bottom, a short descent despite appearances, Tasha assessed the cavern. Crystal lined the walls, floor, and ceiling, creating a maze of reflective surfaces and bringing the coruscating light from the rift around a bend in the passageway. Therkla and Aveline advanced ahead, weapons drawn.

Tasha touched Raj's arm. "Once the battle is joined, maybe you, Yun, and your sister can free any prisoners you find. Getting between Vasco, me, and the wizard will be dangerous."

The faelix nodded. "Yes, I understand. We'll lend a claw when we can, but we'll make sure any captive townsfolk are safe first."

As they approached the chamber containing the rift, the passageway brightened. Beaming into the cave, Calliome's sun greeted them when they rounded the bend. They shut their eyes against the sudden glare. Between them and their quarry, the chaos rift, a miasma of kaleidoscopic colors, whirled in mesmerizing patterns. Attuned to arcane forces by her training, Tasha strained against the sudden onslaught of power from the massive, churning rip in reality. Easily the size of a small house, it dwarfed the cultists at the mouth of the cave.

"More interruptions?" The robed human kicked one of the draks. "You have failed me, my hands. Deal with these intruders, or I will feed you to the rift next."

The draks, raising their weapons, charged toward the group. Aveline, Therkla, and Aerik responded in kind, closing the distance before the draks reached the left side of the cavern. Raj, Jazeera, and Yun hugged the cavern wall to the right, keeping their distance from the melee while they searched for prisoners.

Vasco leapt forward, passing the faelixes and caprikin. Emerald tendrils of arcane power swirled around him, and the blade of his staff glowed red hot. Speeding to the other side, Tasha gripped her amulet. She dodged to the right as Aerik kicked the drak he fought into the rift.

"*K'teep'ma tis astrapis!*" Pointing at the wizard, Tasha directed a bolt of lightning toward him. He smiled as it splashed against an unseen shield, surrounding him in a bubble of dancing emerald electricity.

"That was powerful, girl. Maybe the lady knight isn't the one for whom I searched, after all." Raising his arms, glowing crystals burst from the earth, showering Tasha with shards of hot glass. Cries of pain from behind her indicated her friends caught as much, if not more, of the blast.

I'll bet they didn't teach you this at the Arcane University. Tasha reached out for Gaia, feeling the warmth of the earth beneath her feet. Digging her toes into the dirt, she chanted. "*Gwrāthiau a changhennau y goidwig, amthifyn eich was fythlon.*"

Penetrating the shield, vines and roots sprang from the dirt around the wizard. They wrapped themselves around his feet and legs. Failing to leap out of the way, he stumbled. Cursing as he struggled to free one of his legs, his skin sloughed off, leaving gore-covered vines. From the corner of her eye, Tasha observed Therkla throttling the drak she fought. She shook it like a rag doll until it hung limply in her hands.

"Foul abomination." Sliding to a stop, Vasco swung his staff in a wide arc before him. It slowed upon contacting the shield, but it stayed its course, slicing through the magical barrier. Allowing the momentum to carry him, he readied for a thrust, spinning in place.

"Look out!" Tasha shouted a moment too late. A thin spike of crystal shot from the ground in front of the wizard, piercing Vasco's abdomen.

Grimacing, he faltered before plunging his bladed staff into the wizard's chest. Together they screamed, locked in a bloody embrace, the wizard clawing at Vasco.

Tasha drew her knife, flinging it into the wizard's back. Her aim untrue, the hilt, bouncing off his neck, left a dent in the skin folds. He punched Vasco in the face, knocking the Maritropan to the ground. Spinning only his head, the Master glared at Tasha.

She recoiled from the sight of the wizard whose face resembled a melting candle. He lumbered toward her with his head on backward. Snarling, he opened his mouth, bile and blood pouring forth. Behind him, Vasco clutched one of the wizard's legs, but the flesh sloughed off in his grip.

Rough hands pulled Tasha backward. Therkla interposed herself between the sorceress and the wizard. A drak with his lower jaw hanging from his skull slid across the floor into the rift. Tasha assumed its crushed bones were courtesy of Aveline.

"Maris's bloody spear!" Roaring, Therkla punched the wizard in the mouth, snapping his head back. While he still reeled from the blow, the oroq lunged forward, then lifted him over her head.

The wizard clawed at her arms, leaving streaks of black oroq blood mixed with his own as his fingernails and flesh peeled away. She heaved, throwing him bodily into the glowing wound in reality.

A flash blinded Tasha, and she fell to the dirt. As she blinked away tears of pain, she felt the ground beneath her shake. Pebbles rained from the ceiling just before it collapsed.

* * *

The glare seared Aveline's eyes. She grunted, feeling Aerik pull her by the arm from the wailing groans of the rift and the terrible rain of falling rocks. Shaking herself free from his grip, she wiped the tears from her eyes until blurry sight returned and fresh mountain air filled her lungs.

The cave mouth scarred the side of the mountain, although dust and boulders now filled it. Therkla carried Tasha over her shoulder. The faelix siblings and Yun carried Vasco, limp in their arms. No one else exited the cave with them.

"Were there no prisoners? No one from town?" Aveline glanced around the hillside where they gathered themselves.

"We found... pieces of bodies"—Raj shook his head—"but he was the only one we could grab before the ceiling fell."

They laid Vasco on a flat boulder. Aveline's heart sank at the sight of his pale pallor and blood-soaked robes. She knelt at his side, then held her ear to his chest. A weak, ragged breath tickled the back of her head.

"Tasha?" Aveline searched for her friend. The sorceress held on as Therkla lowered her. She then made her way to Vasco's side.

"His wound is deep." Tasha winced as she peeled away tattered robes, revealing a bloody puncture through Vasco's stomach. Blood flowed freely from the wound. She tore strips of cloth from what dry material remained of his clothes, pressing them against the injury.

"We have a name for that kind of wound." Therkla coughed, spitting away from them.

"Not interested right now." Aveline put her hand on Vasco's cheek. His skin felt cool.

He took his final breath under the light of the afternoon sun.

"Damn it." Aveline sat back on her haunches, closing her eyes. *I didn't particularly like his lecherousness, but he proved his heart was true in battle. He didn't deserve this.* In that moment, she knew what her next task must be. Leaning forward, Aveline kissed his forehead.

"I suppose we should take him back to town." Tasha regarded the countryside toward the sun, shielding her eyes with her hand. "How far do you think our horses are? A league? Two?"

"Far enough that it'll be dark before we can get back here with them." Therkla wiped her blade on her breeches before sheathing it.

"We will stay with him." Jazeera crossed her arms over her chest. "Keep the carrion eaters away until you return."

"We should all go." Tasha gestured to the tree-covered hills. "We'll carry him. The rift is too close. I can still feel it."

"The Crow Queen is wise." Aerik tossed a pinecone toward Aveline. She gasped at its furry texture. Dropping it, she kicked it toward the collapsed entrance to the cave. After rolling to a stop, it sprouted six pairs of legs and scurried into a crevasse.

They wrapped Vasco in their cloaks and then lifted their fallen comrade. After putting some distance between themselves and the cave, they turned north and headed toward the mine entrance. Soon, they found a clearing adjacent to a small cliff overlooking hills leading toward the ocean. They stopped to rest and make camp.

Since their night vision proved superior to the others, Therkla volunteered to continue with the faelix siblings toward the mine and their horses. "I'll make sure nothing eats or steals them. Aerik and Yun should be enough to help you get Vasco the rest of the way in the morning."

Although Aveline's trust in the three remained shaky, she decided Therkla, at least, had done enough to deserve a chance. "Thank you. We'll continue at first light and meet up with you at the mine entrance."

Upon their departure, Aveline considered how best to communicate to Yun her needs without one of the faelixes to translate. After several minutes of pantomiming fire while holding up sticks, Yun grunted, nodding. He entered the forest to retrieve deadwood. Meanwhile, Aerik declared he would forage for nuts and berries to supplement what little dried meats they brought with them.

Soon after the sun set, the Great Whirlpool of Nethuns peeked above the eastern horizon, beginning its evening journey across the sky. Stars twinkled through the endless black of the sunless sky, becoming brighter as the night drew on. Tasha sat on the edge of the cliff, her hands resting in her lap. Aveline lowered herself to the ground alongside her friend, unsure of whether Tasha was meditating.

"I'm just checking on Korbin and Revan." Opening an eye, she peered at Aveline. "Everything is quiet there."

"Good. I was worried a bear or catamount would find Socks an easy dinner."

"The rift is probably keeping them at bay. We still have to deal with that, you know."

The thought of being in the proximity of the chaos rift again made Aveline's stomach lurch. "How, exactly, do we do that? How do you fight something like that? Is it even alive?"

"No, but chaos beasts can enter our world through it, and you saw what it did to the environment around it." Tasha rubbed the back of her neck. "I'll bet that wizard's condition was caused by working near the rift for so long."

"So, I guess I can seal the mine and station a command post here to deal with anything that might claw its way through the rocks." It pained Aveline that such a plan would require her to request a garrison expansion from Lord Mayor Koloman. He would, no doubt, make salacious demands in exchange for granting such a request.

"That won't solve anything for long." Tasha pursed her lips. "The rift must be closed."

"Do you know how to do that?" Aveline raised her eyebrow.

"I don't, but I'm sure there are those within the Arcane University who do. I'll send a message to the archmage and request assistance." Drawing her cloak closed around her, Tasha frowned.

"There's an unspoken 'but' there…"

"I have years of unpaid dues, and the nearest Arcane University is in Muncifer or maybe Maritropa. It will be several months before anyone could come out to investigate."

Turning, Aveline faced the collapsed cave. This late in the evening, darkness obscured any sign of the cavern. "Surely anything coming out of the rift would take that long to tunnel through the rocks, right?"

Tasha chuckled. "We can hope."

Aveline nudged her friend. "So, what's this Crow Queen thing you have going on, eh? Aerik's a true believer."

Groaning, Tasha put her head in her hands. "It's something I have to figure out. I don't know what's going on, why this cloak seemed to call to me, why these crows are following me, and why I know their names... I didn't even know crows could have names!"

"Pacha's having a laugh at our expense right now, I know it." Aveline didn't put much stock in the idea that the gods themselves had a hand in everyday misfortune, but strange events mounted too quickly for her to completely dismiss the notion.

"Pacha needs to mind his own business." Tasha patted Aveline's leg. "Let's go check on Aerik and Yun. I'm cold and hungry."

Chapter 25

Yun returned to camp with an armful of sticks and branches sufficient to start and keep a fire going through most of the night. Aerik's search for nuts and berries turned out less successfully. Among them, they shared only a handful of mealy walnuts and acorns. Fortunately, Aerik's propensity for carrying copious amounts of cured, dried meats provided enough to sate them.

Removing her feathered cloak, Tasha made herself comfortable sitting against a tree. She placed the mantle across her legs, watching Yun clean the weapons and armor procured from the draks and human guards at the mine. Although focused on his task, the caprikin noticed her attention and raised his head to view her.

"How did you get hired as a caravan guard without speaking the languages of the lands you're traveling to?" Tasha smiled, expecting little more than a grunt and nod in reply.

"Hire for sword. Not speak."

Aveline laughed. "You understood everything we've been saying this whole time?"

Yun shrugged. "Not all. Some." His mellifluous voice sounded deeper than Tasha expected. "No pay for listen or talk. Only pay for to keep Raj and Jaz safe."

"You should come to the Watches with Therkla and me." Aerik held up a strip of jerky, offering it to the caprikin. "Lots of trading goes on in Haefstaad."

The caprikin shook his head. "No meat. I go where Raj pays."

The three humans conversed with Yun late into the night. Tasha sensed Yun possessed greater intelligence than many might assume based on his limited vocabulary. As the conversation faded, they settled in. Tasha watched the evening stars wheel overhead until sleep overcame her.

When morning arrived, Yun roused them all. The sun peeking above the horizon greeted them. Tasha's body ached from the previous day's exertions. Forcing herself to get moving, she tried not to miss her own bed too terribly.

As they gathered their gear, Aerik distributed the last of his jerky to serve as their morning meal. While she ate, Tasha checked in with Korbin and Revan. One of the crows circled the mine entrance, as the other, perched on a tent, preened himself. Tasha identified Therkla and the faelix siblings, as well as their horses. Detecting no ill forces, she drew comfort from the quiet in their immediate area. Soon after eating, they were once again underway before the sun had fully risen.

Navigating the forested hills near the mine proved difficult, especially while carrying Vasco's body. Folk from Curton found the region east of the Iron Gate mountains too rugged to exploit, so there were no roads, only well-camouflaged game trails through the dense underbrush.

The sun continued its skyward climb, casting dappled light through the canopy of leaves above them, as they worked their way through the forest. A gentle breeze carried the scent of pine, as well as a familiar musk Tasha recognized as drak. She alerted the rest of the group, and they slowed their pace. As a precaution, Tasha summoned Revan and Korbin to her.

She reached out with her mind, feeling the teeming life of the forest around her, taking in the warmth of Gaia and letting it expand her senses. Within a few moments, she located the draks and understood why she could smell them. Just over the next ridge, a large group of the diminutive dragon kin congregated in a makeshift camp. Their life-force shone like a beacon against the background of the forest.

Further, Tasha sensed in an instant these were not the same draks as those calling themselves the Hands of the

Master. While she could not be sure why she felt confident in her evaluation of their motives, Tasha suspected her feathered cloak played a part in increasing her awareness.

Tasha glanced across a bush at Aveline, nodding, then gestured for the rest of the group to gather around. "I think we're safe. There's a large group of draks just up the ridge. They're not involved with the Master Under the Mountain."

Aveline adjusted her grip on her mace. "How can you be sure?"

"She is the Crow Queen." Aerik smiled. "She would know such things."

Tasha felt her cheeks grow hot. "I wouldn't be so sure about that. But, Aveline, I can sense them, and they don't feel... malevolent. Not like the ones at the mine."

"Fine." Aveline secured her mace to her belt. "We'll approach peacefully, see what they want. Maybe these are the draks the dwarves told me about."

As they lifted Vasco and prepared to climb the hill, Tasha paused. "Maybe I should approach alone. There's no need to carry Vasco up there if the draks are just passing through."

Aveline chewed on her lip. "Very well. Shout and we'll come running."

Tasha reassured her friend with a pat on the shoulder and a smile. She ducked beneath a branch, then made her way up the hill. Near the top of the ridge, a faint electric charge filled the air, lifting the ends of the feathers on her cloak ever so slightly and causing the hairs on her arms to stand on end.

Upon reaching the summit, Tasha turned in a circle, searching for evidence of the draks she detected. The air stood still, and she noticed the distinct lack of buzzing insects or singing birds. Closing her eyes, she focused her mind. While she stood not quite in the center of the area where she perceived the draks made camp, she continued to feel their presence. The longer she dwelled on the area, the more her sight cleared, and faint outlines of lean-tos and makeshift shelters appeared, along with ghostly, shimmering shapes resembling the diminutive dragon kin.

"I know you're here, draks. I'm not your enemy. I'm Tasha, an apothecary from Curton, to the west." Dropping to her knees, she bowed. She offered the traditional drak greeting. "May the strength of Rannos protect you. I'm… I'm sorry, I don't know the words in Drak."

A slight shimmer enveloped the area, and the electric tingling ceased. The shelters she perceived surrounded her as well as half-a-dozen, spear-brandishing draks. Scores more regarded her from behind neighboring trees.

One member of the group, a stout white-scaled drak limped toward her on a game leg. He held a glowing pinecone. "We want no trouble."

Tasha saw no sign of injury to the drak's leg. She assumed it was a malady of advanced age or lingering pain from an old wound that didn't heal properly. "Neither do we. We're returning home after… well, it's a long story. Dwarf traders told us about a substantial number of draks passing through the mountains. Maybe they were talking about you?"

Looking over his shoulder, he spoke in Drak to one of the warriors, who answered with a curt nod. The white-scaled drak returned his gaze to Tasha. "Our scouts saw a dwarf caravan in the mountain pass. We sought to avoid their notice."

"My friend is Captain of the City Watch"—licking her lips, Tasha rocked on her haunches—"so I must ask for her—why are you here? Are you just passing through?"

He gestured to the ever-growing crowd. "We fled our homes. Oroqs marched west along the mountains. We escaped before they slaughtered us."

Tasha furrowed her brow. "Did they give chase? Are they coming after you?"

"No." He shook his head. "They razed empty villages, too, for whatever they wanted and continued west. We seek a new life, away from oroqs and hairy men who drink too much."

Despite herself, Tasha laughed. "Dwarves or humans?"

The drak's expression remained stony. "Both."

"You're in human lands now. As far north as the great ocean. The elves of Raven's Forest are about the only bastion of fae, and they do not welcome outsiders." Spreading her arms, Tasha regarded the assembled draks. "But there is plenty of space in these lands. There are other drak villages. There are many of your kin in Curton and in some of the other cities. I'm sure you can build a home here."

Narrowing his eyes, the aged drak rubbed the bottom of his snout with the pinecone. "You can speak for the humans here?"

Tasha lowered her eyes. "In truth, no. But I have some influence with some of the leaders."

"Then we will stay here for now. Our scouts are getting the lay of the land. When we're ready, I may approach the town of which you speak and learn how hospitable you truly are."

The sorceress rose to leave. "Then I shall return to my friends and continue our journey. I will tell those in town who will listen that you are friendly, although I promise I shall keep your location secret.

Bowing his head, the old drak crossed his free arm over his chest. "Then, go in peace, Tasha the Apothecary. We will move, and you will not find us here again. Perhaps one day, you can explain how you penetrated my enchantment."

"Gladly." Tasha returned his bow. "May I know your name?"

"I am Klatt, High Elder of the Icescale clan."

"I look forward to our next meeting, Elder Klatt." Tasha bowed again before leaving. Feeling Klatt's enchantment as it camouflaged their makeshift village once more, she returned to Aveline and the others.

When she reached the bottom of the hill, Tasha found Yun watching over Vasco's body. Aveline and Aerik sat at the base of adjacent trees conversing. Aerik gestured toward Tasha.

Aveline rose to greet her friend. "Well? I assume they're friendly. Or, at least, indifferent."

"They're the same draks the dwarves saw." After Tasha took her place at Vasco's feet, they lifted their fallen companion. "They're fleeing an oroq march and just want some place to live in peace."

"An oroq march?" Aveline grunted when Vasco's weight shifted while Aerik sought a comfortable grip. "March to where?"

"They weren't certain. The oroqs marched west along the mountains. They took everything from the draks' villages, but they didn't pursue them."

"A war band." Aerik fell into rhythm with the rest as they resumed their journey to the mine entrance. "They march toward a foe beyond the drak villages, but they aren't above scavenging provisions along the way."

"What's west?" The lands south of the Iron Gate mountains remained unfamiliar to Tasha. As far as she knew, south of Curton lay a harsh land of boundless ice and snow. Anything beyond or adjacent was a mystery.

"I've never been there." Aerik shrugged. "Brackeborg is west, but it's weeks south of the mountains. Perhaps they mean to turn north where the Dragon Spines meet the Iron Gates and conquer the Western Wastes."

From the stories Tasha heard, the Western Wastes—a harsh, barren land filled with ash, lava, and demons—seemed the perfect place for a war band of oroqs to sate their bloodthirst without running afoul of militarized nations.

"Is there anything there even worth conquering? Fire?

Demons?" Aveline glanced at Tasha. The sorceress, having no answer for her friend, shrugged.

"Endless sand and rocks. Heat. Maybe they're going to hunt the great sand worms." Aerik chuckled. "I hear there are nomadic elves there with ships that glide on top of the sand."

"Are we talking about the same place?" Aveline glanced over her shoulder at Aerik.

"Well, I've never been there. Maybe your stories are more right than mine. Therkla might know what her kin are up to."

Ignoring continued speculation, Tasha concentrated on providing a somewhat smooth passage for Vasco as they carried him toward whatever would become his final resting place. By the time the sun reached its zenith, the entrance to the mine lay within their sight once more. Therkla and the faelixes led their mounts to them.

"Tasha, take Silvermane or Socks, whichever you're more comfortable riding." Aveline detached her saddlebags from the stallion. She slung them over her shoulder. "I know I can trust you to tell the pertinent people in town what they need to know."

"You can ride with me." Tasha mounted Silvermane, then held out a hand to Aveline. Shaking her head, the knight-captain stopped Aerik and Yun from slinging Vasco over Pepper's back.

"I'm not going back to Curton, Tasha. I'm staying here."

Chapter 26

Tasha searched Aveline's eyes for an answer to the unspoken question. *Why?*

"All those people in the mine, I failed them. It shouldn't matter who they are or how they earn a living. They're all under my protection. They all look to me for justice, and I failed." Aveline took Tasha's hand. "The dead deserve better than to be left in a pile in the belly of an abandoned mine."

"Don't be stupid." Therkla snorted. "You can't carry them all up here yourself. You don't even have a shovel, or an ax for wood."

"I don't intend to." Aveline kept her attention focused on Tasha. "Tell Lieutenant Valon to recruit volunteers. I'll need at least one grave digger. Any family of missing folk who want to try to identify their loved ones are welcome. I'll also need provisions, at least a week's worth. More if you can't arrange a regular supply run."

Tasha squeezed Aveline's hand. "I should stay behind too. To help."

"No." Aveline shook her head. "I need you in town to arrange all this. You know who to talk to and how. Leave Vasco here. He can rest with those he tried to save."

"Very well."

Aveline glanced toward the mine entrance. "Send several casks of ale and wine. I think we're all going to need it at the end of each day. When we've retrieved all the bodies, I'll post a guard to keep anyone from stumbling into the rift. At least until you've heard back from the Arcane University. If they won't help, we'll collapse the whole damned mountain."

"I'll take care of it." Tasha gestured for the rest of the group to prepare to move out. "What are you going to do in the meantime?"

Gesturing to the area behind her, Aveline sighed. "Clean up the camp, dispose of the wizard's minions, and gather as much equipment as I can. It'll keep me busy for the next couple of days, I expect. Certainly long enough for the first group of helpers to arrive."

"Be safe, Aveline. I'll have Korbin or Revan check on you regularly." Tasha pressed her heels into Silvermane's flanks. She led the group toward Curton.

Aveline watched them until they reached the top of the hill before turning her attention toward the camp. Already, the dead bloated and attracted vermin, so she gathered as many small branches and sticks as she could and built a small pyre behind the rocks to the left of the mine entrance. She started with the dead draks. The tent in which Therkla killed one of the sleeping draks when they first arrived swarmed with flies, so she broke the supports and added them to the pile.

When she finished building the pyre, Aveline set it alight. She then sought the camp's rain barrel, finding the water stagnant and fetid. Kicking it over, Aveline emptied it. Dark clouds moved on the horizon, and she hoped fresh rainwater would fill the barrel by morning. Lacking any for now, she resigned to hiking to the nearest stream to clean the blood off her hands and refill her waterskins. She recalled hearing a babbling brook between the drak camp and the mine. Retracing her steps, she found the stream without difficulty.

By the time she returned to the camp, the sun neared the western horizon. Her stomach grumbled, and she sorted through and inventoried what provisions she had left. While supping on a meal of stale bread and cheese, she cleaned out the remaining tent. Then she removed her breastplate, repairing the damage caused by the wizard's minions when they took it from her. When she could work no more, Aveline drifted off to sleep.

* * *

Leaving Aveline behind at the mine, Tasha pushed the group to journey as far as possible before stopping to rest. They traveled deep into the night, stopping when a rainstorm made it impossible to continue farther safely. The Queen, in her new phase, remained dark, and the light of only a single moon engulfed with cloud cover provided too little illumination during the downpour. While the others hunkered down to rest during the storm, Tasha prepared to send a magical messenger to the archmage and the council.

She lowered herself to the sodden leaves and cleared her mind, recalling the incantation, even as swirls of emerald ether surrounded her.

"*Ageliofedros.*" The wisps coalesced into a shimmering emerald bird. It cocked its head, awaiting her message. *A bird? That's not what happened last time. Could the cloak be affecting this magic?*

"Go to the Arcane University in Muncifer and find the archmage." Tasha introduced herself, explained the situation to the bird, and requested the archmage's assistance with the chaos rift. Then she sent the messenger on its way.

The next morning, as they rode, Tasha left the faelix siblings, Yun, Aerik, and Therkla to talk among themselves while she kept an eye on Aveline through Korbin and Revan. Although confident Aveline could take care of herself, Tasha worried undiscovered dangers lurking in or around the mine might pose a threat.

The walls of Old Town appeared as they broke through the forest and descended the hills. Tasha guided them south around the outskirts of the city expansion beyond the walls until they reached Miners' Gate. Although the guards gawked at her companions, they recognized Tasha and permitted the group to pass upon her explanation of the situation.

Tasha addressed her companions. "I have many people to contact here. I trust you will return our horses to the stable?"

Aerik cut off Therkla's retort with a bow of his head. "Of course, Crow Queen. Is there anything else we can do to help?"

"Not yet. I have a lot to do this afternoon." She glanced at the faelix siblings and Yun. "Maybe we could all meet up at the Bristled Boar tonight after I've taken care of it all?"

"Where is that?" Raj stared wide-eyed at the throngs of townsfolk moving between the gate and outlying buildings. In return, those close enough to notice the group stared at the cat-like faelixes and goat-like caprikin, pointing and murmuring to each other.

Tasha gestured down the street beyond the gate. "Not far. Aerik and Therkla can show you."

"I'm not going to play nursemaid to them." Therkla slid off her horse's back, eliciting a whinny of protest from Socks. "I fulfilled my obligation, and now I want to get paid."

Tasha frowned. "Well, I'm sure you know the way to Koloman's house. Your deal was with him, right?"

"No, we left that fool to clean up his own mess. Your lady knight offered to pay us for our help at the mine, remember?"

The conversation of several nights earlier, when the power of the Crow Queen first awakened in her, seemed fuzzy in Tasha's memory, although she did have a slight recollection of Therkla's deal with Aveline.

"I can't access the funds Aveline was going to use to pay you. I'm sorry." Tasha adjusted her seat. "You'll have to wait for Aveline to return or go back to the mine and help her deal with the dead if you're impatient."

Therkla seized Silvermane's reins to prevent Tasha from leaving. "Talk to her lieutenant then."

After fishing in her pouch and tossing a couple of crowns toward the oroq, Tasha dismounted. "I'm neither a member of the guard, nor do I have any influence over them. Stable the horses, then get a meal, a bath, and some drinks, and wait for me at the Bristled Boar."

Before the oroq woman could protest again, Tasha pushed her way into the crowd. After a short distance, she became aware she was being followed. Tasha glanced over her shoulder, seeing Ra-Jareez, Jazeera, and Yun jogging to keep up.

She moved away from the main flow of traffic to wait for the three to approach. "You don't need to follow me. Why don't you go with Therkla and Aerik?"

Raj gazed toward the city gate. "That large woman is not very good company right now. We would feel safer in this unfamiliar city with you."

A crowd gathered around Tasha and the travelers from the Far North. People pushed in around her, chattering and gawking at the faelix siblings and the caprikin. "Good people, please, let us through. I assure you, you have nothing to fear from my friends here. They have come far and need rest."

The crowd continued to build, eager for a closer look. Tasha searched the throng of curious townsfolk for familiar faces. None leapt out at her. As the crowd pressed in, her breath quickened.

A man wearing armor over furs moved to stand in front of her. "Give these folks space. Come on now, move away." Spreading his arms wide, he cleared the area around Tasha and her companions. She recognized him as the southerner who had come to her apothecary with a rash. His hair cascaded down his back, save for two narrow side braids.

Catching her breath, Tasha offered him a smile in gratitude. "How's your arm?"

He bowed his head toward Tasha. "Much better, thank you." He turned to address the crowd. "Go on now! Before you all hurt someone."

Spreading his arms again, he cleared a path for Tasha, gesturing down the street. Most of the crowd thinned before the bridge crossing the Copper Run toward the market. "Perhaps I'll have the good fortune to see you again soon."

"I'm indebted to you…" She smiled weakly as she failed to recall the man's name.

"Torben."

"Thank you, Torben.

Before the crowd decided to ignore the Watchman's instruction, Tasha guided her companions down the street, across the bridge, and through the market to Cybele's Church. She pointed toward the massive doors as they approached. "It should be quieter in there."

As expected, the church remained relatively deserted in the middle of the day. Mother Anya cleaned the altar at the far end of the sanctuary. Wisps of grey hair poked out from the unkempt bun in which she kept it. The matriarch, hearing the visitors enter her church, moved to greet them.

Tasha noted the slow pace the high priestess walked, as well as the pained expression on her face. "Please, don't let us disturb you, Mother Anya. We simply seek a respite from the crowds outside. As you might imagine, my companions"—Tasha gestured toward Yun, Jazeera, and Ra-Jareez—"are causing quite a stir."

The faelix siblings greeted Mother Anya. As if noticing them for the first time, the matriarch pressed a hand to her chest. "Oh my! It's been ages since I've seen folk from Nakambe and Hoseki." Bowing, she greeted Yun in his own language. She eyed Tasha's cloak. "You're dressing differently these days, Tasha."

Slack-jawed, Yun bowed to Mother Anya, returning her greeting.

"I must say, you surprise me, Mother Anya. I didn't know you spoke their language." Tasha did not expect the matron of Curton's only temple to be familiar with her companions. She hoped by diverting the old woman's attention to Yun, she could avoid conversation about her cloak or the Crow Queen.

"Only Xihani, dear. Remarkably similar to Nihansan." She nodded toward the faelix siblings. "I never had the chance to learn Haylan, or are you also from the Xihan region? You speak our language with an accent that sounds Haylish." She turned again toward Tasha. "I may be from Curton, child, but I haven't lived here my whole life." She sat in a nearby pew, a grimace on her face, and gestured for the others to join her. "You'll have to forgive me. This damp weather is making my joints ache something terrible."

Raj exchanged a glance with his sister. "We are from Shak-Hayla. Our family does much trading with the Xihani in the west. We met Yun at a market in Shan-tu, on the precipice of the Gods' Wound…"

Tasha held up her hand before sitting next to Mother Anya. "I used to have an herb for that pain, but I'm afraid my shop was destroyed in the flood." She glanced at Raj. "I would love to hear all about your travels later, Ra-Jareez, but we mustn't dawdle."

The three foreigners sat in the pew behind the matriarch, and Raj leaned toward Tasha. "Why exactly have you brought us here?"

"The crowd seemed unruly. I'm hoping they'll disperse in a bit so I can find Lieutenant Valon and get help for Aveline." Tasha took Mother Anya's hand. "Perhaps you'd be so kind as to help me find volunteers for a most unpleasant task?"

Tasha could not stop the tears from flowing as she apprised Mother Anya of the mound of bodies in the mine and of how they found no survivors from the town. She didn't see the need to tell the old woman of the chaos rift, at least, not until she'd heard back from the Arcane University.

"Of course, I'll help." Mother Anya squeezed Tasha's hand. "There are many in town who are lax in their duties to the church. I will see to it they volunteer, if not in body, then in supplies."

Raj threw up his hands. "Bah! You left out the most important part."

Glaring, she shook her head as Mother Anya's attention shifted to the faelixes.

"The hairy one, what is his name, Jaz?" Raj tapped a claw against the back of the pew, ignoring Tasha's silent protest. "The loud, angry woman's companion."

"Aerik." Staring at Tasha, Jazeera raised an eyebrow.

"Aerik thinks Tasha is a queen."

"A queen, indeed?" Mother Anya's eyes crinkled as she suppressed a laugh. "Is this Aerik a new suitor? I don't believe I've met him."

Tasha slouched in her seat. "He's a traveler from the Watches. He's not a suitor."

"Why does he think you're a queen?"

"He believes she commands the crows." Raj grinned.

Tasha narrowed her eyes, scowling. Mother Anya certainly knew the stories and lore surrounding the Crow Queen. Entering into a theological discussion with the high priestess of Cybele's Church was not part of her plan for the day.

"Crow Queen? Really?" Mother Anya recoiled from Raj. She examined Tasha's cape. "How did you come by this cloak?"

"She ignored—"

"Enough!" Tasha slammed her hand on the back of the pew. "You and your brother have helped enough today." Sighing, the sorceress related the tale of how she sought refuge in the abandoned, overgrown hut during the storm, how the crows began following her, and how she experienced visions that led her to the cloak in the mine.

Mother Anya listened, her brow furrowing first with suspicion then concern. Finally, she covered her mouth with her hands, gazing at Tasha. "You actually found Annika?"

"You knew her? The previous Crow Queen?"

"Of course. She disappeared many years ago. She left with her sister. But when Nika returned, she refused to speak of Annika." Mother Anya lowered her gaze. "From her injuries, we assumed they'd been beset by oroqs, but it seemed impossible Annika would die in such a case and Nika would live. At any rate, Nika fell ill, afflicted by horrible growths all over her body. Well, you know what happened with her son."

"Smith Piotr." Tasha heard the story from Aveline of how, during the past year, the knight-captain executed the smith for smothering his mother. Although she was sickly and many thought he showed mercy, the magistrate disagreed and condemned him for murder.

"I saw a vision of the two women in the mine. One was called Nika, and she killed an old woman. Said the old woman let a man called Dimas die after taking his child." Tasha tried to recall details. "I got the sense the two women were related, but one was ever so much older than the other. Maybe her grandmother?"

Mother Anya's eyes glistened with tears. "Dimas was my brother. He never could decide between the two sisters, Nika and Annika. He married Nika, sired Piotr, but also sired a child with Annika. Both he and his daughter from Annika fell ill when a plague ravaged Curton. Annika called upon her power as Crow Queen to save them and the town. It took a terrible toll on her. She aged a lifetime in a day. Still, she failed to save neither the man she loved nor her child."

Tasha lifted the edge of her cloak, running her fingers over the feathers. "People talk about the plague, but I had never heard the story. They speak of the Crow Queen like she's someone out of legends, not someone they might have actually known."

"The Crow Queen has always been known to us." Mother Anya put her hand on Tasha's shoulder. "If you came by this mantle truly, then we will be happy to know her once more."

Chapter 27

When morning came, Aveline awoke stiff and unrested. Dark images of decaying bodies filled her dreams. She crawled out of the tent in her smallclothes, then shuffled to the rain barrel. Last night's paltry precipitation did little to supplement the water she collected from the stream. A sodden, blackened pile of ash and bone stood as the last remnants of the previous night's pyre, a ritual Aveline knew she needed to repeat once she recovered the bodies from deeper in the mine. After breaking her fast, she donned her armor and strode through the entrance.

With no need for stealth, she reached the corpse room quickly. Assessing the pile, she decided moving even one victim alone would be foolish. She might be able to drag one person to the surface at a time, but the effort would exhaust her. She opted, instead, to mark the path to the room clearly, using the lanterns left behind by the wizard's minions. She then gathered as much equipment as she could carry, including the remaining pieces of her armor, before returning to the surface and preparing the camp for helpers Tasha would inevitably send.

Lacking an axe with which to chop wood or a bow with which to hunt, Aveline gathered deadfall for fuel and nuts and berries for sustenance. Using a helmet from the gear she recovered in the mine as a basket, she spent most of the morning foraging.

Aveline paused near the stream to wash the berries she had gathered. She squatted on a moss-covered rock, listening to birds sing in the distance, a lyrical accompaniment to the babbling of the brook. It was then she became aware of eyes watching her.

The snap of a branch betrayed the onlooker. Keeping her motions slow and deliberate, Aveline scanned the forest around her. Her eyes fell on a glint of stark-white scales contrasting against the deep green pines in which the drak concealed themself.

Aveline maintained her gaze on the diminutive dragon kin. "I'm not a threat to you. I'm just foraging for food and firewood. We're going to be working at the old mine, burying our dead."

The scout stood rock steady, having made no sign of hearing or even understanding her.

"Na par'ka Drak." *I don't speak Drak.* Aveline hoped her assurance, at least, would ease some of the drak's trepidations.

She watched as the visitor retreated beneath the pine branches, disappearing from sight. Sighing, Aveline returned to washing her berries, then gathered her supplies and returned to camp.

As the sun continued its journey across the sky, she passed time sorting through equipment, repairing that which could be repaired while discarding the rest. When she finished, she had scavenged three pickaxes and two shovels.

Utilizing one of the implements she recovered, she chose a spot within sight of the mine entrance and began digging.

* * *

At Mother Anya's behest, Tasha left the faelix siblings and Yun at the church so she could move about town unmolested. After checking with guards at both city gates, Tasha resorted to leaving a message at the citadel for Lieutenant Valon to find her in Drakton. There, she hoped to settle with Zadok of the Ashenscale clan. Whatever money the draks owed her represented the sum of her possessions following the flood, and she wanted to buy a few more sets of clothes before deciding how and where to rebuild.

It amazed her how resilient the draks were in the face of calamity. Already, mere days after the flood, most of the damage had been repaired, and one had to look closely to find any evidence of catastrophe. Despite their efforts, limited availability of materials meant Drakton still resembled a shantytown within the walls of Curton. *I wonder what they could do if they were given adequate resources to actually rebuild this part of town.*

She walked to the base of the tower where the Ashenscale clan had constructed their community house. She found Zadok there teaching draklings carpentry. She silently observed him explaining how to use a planer until he noticed her.

"I hope I'm not disturbing you, Zadok. Lady Aveline said she helped you get some supplies from my shop after the flood, and I wanted to settle up. I'm going to need to rebuild."

Zadok shooed away the draklings. "I understand. As you can see, we've had rebuilding to do ourselves."

"What you've accomplished in such a short time is impressive." Tasha observed a pair of draks constructing a door from a pile of scrap wood and attaching it to a building.

"We make do." Zadok clasped his hands. "Unfortunately, lack of support from the rest of the city means we've had to expend most of the money we set aside to pay you on building materials."

Tasha's heart sank, yet she maintained her expression. "I understand. To be honest, I don't think I'm going to rebuild my old shop anyway. Everything is rotting and moldy now. It needs to be razed."

"Where then will you go?"

The question burdened Tasha. As they proceeded, she drew her feathered cloak around her. Her mind drifted to the hut in the forest. *It's a ruin. I can't possibly right it.*

"For now, I guess I'll stay with Lady Aveline. Still…"

"Yes?"

Tasha realized she let her thoughts wander aloud. She felt a strong urge to return to the hut in the forest, despite knowing nature would surely reclaim it in a few years.

"My thoughts keep taking me to a hut I found in the woods. It was on its side and overgrown, but there was something about it." Tasha rubbed the cloak where its feathers covered her arm.

Zadok cocked his head. "There is something different about you. I admit, I don't know you well, and I don't believe I've ever seen you out of your shop…"

They passed a family of draks sorting a pile of debris. Tasha helped them move a couple of large timbers off the pile before resuming her walk with Zadok.

Unsure how much she should share with this drak, Tasha chose to keep her statement simple. "I discovered something important while I was helping Aveline search for the missing townsfolk. I may have to go away for a while."

"May I offer you some parting advice, for one who has been such a good friend to us all these years?" Zadok took Tasha's arm as they continued, reaching up to do so.

Tasha laughed. "I will always welcome your advice, though it isn't as though I'm going away to never return."

"I have a sense your life will change dramatically now. You'll be known far and wide. But you must be wary of fame. It's an empty purse. Count it? Go broke. Eat it? Go hungry. Seek it and go mad."

The sorceress patted the old drak's hand. "I've never sought undue attention. I don't see that happening now. Besides, Aveline, if no one else, will keep me grounded."

Parting ways with the drak, Tasha returned to the church to check on Raj, Jazeera, and Yun. When she arrived, she observed a crowd milling about in front of the church, no doubt hoping for a glimpse of the castaways from across the sea. Acolytes outside the doors of the church discouraged curious onlookers from coming too close.

Recognizing her, the disciples allowed Tasha to pass, despite cries of protest from the townsfolk. Ignoring them, she entered the church. Mother Anya had put the three visitors to work cleaning the main chapel with her. Over the years, pews moved out of place, and heavy decorations shifted. Too few of the townsfolk or farmers volunteered to help her on a regular basis.

"Is everything going well?" Tasha approached Ra-Jareez and Jazeera as they lifted a bust of Cybele for Mother Anya to clean under. Meanwhile, Yun worked at removing bent nails from a pew that showed signs of having been repaired too often.

"Oh yes." Smiling, Mother Anya nodded. "I decided to offer our visitors coin in exchange for some help around here. They're going to need clothes, food, and lodging."

"We know Cybele by another name in Nakambe"— Raj grunted as he and his sister struggled with the weight of the sculpture—"but her priests are generous every-where they serve."

"Hopefully, this inn we're meeting the others at tonight has a room and it's not too expensive." Jazeera took the weight of the bust from her brother, guiding it into place as Mother Anya stepped away from the pedestal. Once the sculpture stood firm, the faelix turned to Tasha.

"I owe you an apology. I was too harsh on you in the mine." Jazeera bowed her head to Tasha. "You had faith in your friend, and Mother Anya has explained the signifi-cance of your cloak."

Tasha put her hand on Jazeera's shoulder. "Really? Maybe she can explain it to me someday. This is all overwhelming."

Yun called Ra-Jareez over to help him with the pew.

"How much time do you have, child?" A smile overtook Mother Anya's face.

"Perhaps after I make sure Aveline receives the help she needs." Tasha did not doubt Mother Anya would proselytize all day, given the chance.

"Ah, yes." Mother Anya held up her hand. "I have sent several acolytes out to scour the city for volunteer grave diggers. I instructed them to assemble here as soon as possible. Were you able to find who you were looking for?"

"No." Tasha shook her head. "I left word for him to find me as soon as possible, though, either here, at the Bristled Boar, or at Aveline's home." She shrugged. "I guess I'm staying there since my own place was destroyed in the flood."

Raj glanced up from the pew he and Yun worked on. "We could help you rebuild."

Immediately, Tasha's thoughts strayed toward the abandoned hut in the forest. She shook her head to clear her mind. "Thanks, I… I think I'll stay with Aveline until we get everything sorted. There's a lot of work to be done at the mine."

An acolyte carrying a bundle of robes returned from the back rooms. "I found them, Mother Anya."

"Excellent. Here, friends." She distributed the robes to the faelix siblings and Yun. "They're going to be uncomfortably hot until the chill of winter is upon us, but they'll let you move about town without everyone gawking at you."

Once Yun and Raj finished repairing the pew, Mother Anya and Tasha helped the refugees into the garments. All three vanished within their voluminous depths.

Jazeera twisted this way and that. "They're hard to move in, and I cannot see that well with this cursed hood."

"Yes, you'll have to keep your heads down to watch your feet, and you won't be running in them." Mother Anya adjusted the sleeves of Yun's robe. "But everyone will dismiss you as acolytes running errands or perhaps pilgrims."

"I can't thank you enough for your kindness, Mother Anya." Tasha bowed to the old woman. "We should head to the Bristled Boar now."

"Think nothing of it. You'll be helping the people of Curton for years to come"—the matriarch smiled, returning Tasha's bow—"Crow Queen."

* * *

Wiping the sweat from her brow, Aveline leaned on the shovel as she gazed across Vasco's grave toward the setting sun. She hoped the rectangular pit she dug was deep enough to deter scavengers. She measured the depth using the handle of the shovel as a guide, figuring a hole as deep as the length of the shovel would be sufficient.

She hoisted Vasco onto her shoulder, then carried him over to the pit. She laid him on the grass before lowering herself into it. After pulling him over to her, she positioned his corpse at the bottom of the grave. Finally, she climbed out, catching her breath, before picking up her shovel and positioning herself at the head of the hole.

"I don't know what gods you prayed to, Vasco. Honestly, you never struck me as a pious man." Aveline studied the shrouded corpse below her. "Selene, perhaps? Maybe Pacha or Dolios? I know nothing about their funerary rites and precious little about those practiced here by the followers of Cybele and Adranus. Please don't think poorly of me for not having the tongue for this."

Sighing, Aveline bowed her head. "You fought beside us with bravery and sacrificed yourself for people you didn't even know. That makes you a hero by anyone's reckoning, and I'll make sure this place is marked with honor."

She plunged the shovel into the pile of dirt, then emptied it into the grave. "Wherever you dwell now, may you find that which eluded you in this life."

Night overtook her efforts to cover Vasco, and she finished by the dim light of the waxing moons. Once she had finished, Aveline plodded to the campsite, ate, and turned in for the night. The next day would bring fresh challenges—a day filled with cemetery design.

Chapter 28

By the time Tasha guided the faelix siblings and Yun to the Bristled Boar, she managed to shove her discomfort with Mother Anya calling her "Crow Queen" into a dark pit in her stomach.

Raucous laugher spilled into the street, evidence of a lively crowd within the inn and tavern. Sighing, she opened the door for her companions, urging them to seek out a corner table, if possible. To her disappointment, the only open table stood in the middle of the common area, near the bar. She scanned the crowd for Therkla and Aerik but did not see them, so she directed the siblings and Yun to the table.

At least my ale won't need to travel far.

As her three companions shrugged off their robes, a gasp circled the room. Tasha observed the assembled townsfolk whispering and staring.

Climbing upon a chair, she raised her arms. "Good people, these faelixes and this caprikin have traveled far and suffered much when they were stranded here. Please, do not be troubled by them. Let them enjoy a hot meal in peace."

"There'll be peace enough as long as you have coin to pay." The barkeep approached them, rubbing his hands with a grey, greasy cloth. The skinny, balding man glared at Tasha as he banged on the table. "Here now, get down off that chair. They're for sitting, not standing."

He scowled at the other patrons. "Go about your business. We'll have no trouble here, or you'll be out on your arses."

The barkeep circled the table as Tasha and the others took their seats. "We never had your kind here before. I don't know if our roast will be to your liking." He narrowed his eyes as he faced Yun. "It's mutton."

Raj rubbed his hands together. "Excellent. I have not had that in ages."

Grunting, Yun shook his head. "No meat."

"Mutton will be fine for the three of us, and ales all around." Tasha gestured at the caprikin. "I don't suppose you have any vegetables that weren't cooked with the meat for Yun there?"

The barkeep huffed. "We have some roots roasted with butter and some herbs, sweetened with maple. Potatoes, carrots, turnips, eh, others too, I reckon. I don't know what all the boy scrounged up today."

Tasha raised her eyebrows, glancing at Yun. "Will that be all right?"

The caprikin asked Raj a question. The faelix replied to him before nodding at Tasha. "Yes, that will be fine. Meat only for my sister and me."

"I'll have some of the roots, too, please." Tasha tapped the barkeep on the sleeve as he passed her. Grunting an acknowledgment, he returned to his place behind the bar, barking orders to two young girls. They rushed off toward the kitchen. The barkeep returned with four mugs of ale, setting them in the center of the table.

Tasha observed as Yun gazed around the room, taking stock of each person in turn. Noticing the sorceress watching him, the caprikin leaned forward. He nudged Raj, then spoke at Tasha in his native tongue.

"Oh, Yun says he's watching for robbers. Doing the job we hired him to do." Chuckling, the faelix whispered across the table at Tasha, "I don't know if he realizes we have no money to pay him now."

"We'll start earning coin soon enough, brother..." Jazeera regarded the armored man approaching their table.

Tasha recognized Lieutenant Valon standing at attention. "Good lady, Tasha." He bowed. "I sought you out as soon as I received your message."

"It took all day?" Jaz snorted into her ale.

The constable narrowed his eyes. "There's still much disorder from the flood."

"It's fine, Valon." Tasha pointed to the remaining chair at their table. "Please sit, there is much to explain."

After introducing him to the faelix siblings and Yun, she briefly explained how they came to be so far from home. Their meals arrived as she was taking Valon through the events of the last several days. By the time she finished, her supper was cold, and Valon sat with his head in his hands. The faelix siblings consumed the contents of each dish placed before them, beckoning for the barkeep to bring more. Yun seemed sated by his single plate of vegetables.

Tasha slid a mug of ale toward the constable. "Drink?"

Holding up his hand, Valon shook his head. "I'll pass, thanks." He pushed himself away from the table. "I'll round up strong backs from the citadel and gather equipment. We'll head out at first light."

"Aveline said to make sure everyone brings tools for digging. You'll need provisions too. And ale or wine." Tasha reached for his arm to gain his attention. "There are a lot of bodies, Valon. Some have been there a while."

"Understood." He forced a smile to his lips. "Do you have some way of letting her know we're on our way?"

"I'll let her know."

Valon left them to their dinner. Despite its tepid temperature, she nevertheless found it tasty and filling. Tasha appreciated eating in peace, even while she overheard snippets of conversation commenting on Raj, Jazeera, and Yun from time to time.

"So, what do you plan to do while your friend digs graves?" After Jazeera shoved away her empty plate, she leaned on the table, staring at Tasha.

Again, Tasha's thoughts drifted to the abandoned hut, and she pulled the feathered cloak tighter around her. "My shop flooded. All the inventory is spoiled. I don't even know if the house is salvageable."

If there was ever a time to start over…

"Our offer to help you clean and rebuild still stands." Raj picked at the remains of a mutton shank.

His sister slapped his shoulder. "We need to earn money for food, clothes. Think before you speak, Raj."

Tasha smiled. "I appreciate the offer. I need to evaluate what I actually have before I make plans. I—"

"There they are! I told you we weren't too late." Therkla shoved a passing patron aside to plop into the seat next to Tasha. Aerik gripped the back of her chair to steady himself.

"And I told you…" Aerik's words slurred together as he swayed. "We should have come here straightaway instead of going to Danica's Den."

"I needed to relax. No one told you to play drinking games while I was busy." Licking one of her tusks, Therkla glanced at Tasha. "We've come for our money."

The sorceress rubbed her brow. She neglected to mention Aveline's commitment to Valon before he left. "I told you already. I don't have access to Aveline's funds. You'll have to talk to Lieutenant Valon at the citadel. He should be there now."

Therkla snorted. "I figured you'd say that. We'll go in the morning."

"He and several others are leaving after dawn to go to the mine." Tasha reached for her ale, Finding the mug empty, she shoved it away.

"You should go with them." Raj picked at bits of meat stuck in his teeth. "Earn more money digging graves for all those poor, dead townsfolk."

"I'd rather spend the night in jail." Therkla slapped Aerik's chest, causing him to stumble backward. "Come, Aerik, let's pick a fight so we'll have a bed tonight."

Belching, Aerik shook his head. "I have enough money for that." Grinning, he patted his bulging pouch. "I won it… drinking."

"If you see that lieutenant, tell him we want to be paid before they leave." Therkla shoved the chair under the table, never taking her eyes off Tasha. "See you around, Crow Queen."

"Oh, I hope not." Tasha waited until they left before turning toward her three companions. "There's a hut in the woods. I need to go there and see what I can scrounge. It'll help me get the apothecary up and running." *I'm absolutely not going there to avoid Therkla and Aerik. Surely something in that hut will help me understand this Crow Queen thing.*

"Far from here?" Upon gaining the attention of a passing server, Jaz ordered more ale.

"Not really. Tomorrow, I can take you around to people I know, see if they have any odd jobs."

"That would be most appreciated." Raj bowed his head.

"Meanwhile"—Tasha pushed herself up from the table— "I'll get you rooms here for the night, then I'm going home. I'm tired. I'll be back in the morning, so don't go wandering."

* * *

Tossing and turning, Aveline found no comfortable position on her bedroll amidst the lingering stench of death. She found herself staring at the ceiling of her tent, trying not to envision the scores of dead in the mine below.

With a swear and a sigh, she crawled out of the temporary dwelling. Despite the light breeze, the night remained warm from the heat of the day. Yet, Aveline hoped whoever arrived to help brought extra clothing. She didn't fancy wearing only her shift at night while sharing the camp with townsfolk she may or may not know.

Stoking the smoldering embers of the fire, she coaxed a low flame to return. Aveline heard the flapping of wings behind her. Turning, she saw a crow alight on her tent, its eyes fixed on her.

"Tasha send you to check up on me?"

Cocking its head, the crow remained silent.

Spreading her arms, Aveline spun in a circle. "Well, here I am. Safe, nearly naked, and alone in front of a mine filled with corpses. Not quite how I like to spend summer evenings."

Crossing her arms, she regarded the preening bird. "When Dorian and I were first married, we'd go out to the fields north of town on nights like this."

Peering upward, she gazed at the whirlpool of Nethuns, its fine details obscured by moonlight from the King and Queen. "There was a grove of apple trees, and we'd lie there all night. Sleeping, talking, making love."

She laughed. "Tasha knows all this already. Can she even hear me through you, or are you just some random crow that stopped by to keep me company?"

The crow said nothing.

"I guess it's better than talking to myself, right?"

Evidently disagreeing, the crow took off into the night. Aveline lost sight of it in the darkness almost immediately. She had not thought of Dorian in ages. They weren't married that long, just a few months, when his horse, spooked by some raucous children playing in the marketplace, threw him onto the unforgiving cobblestones.

Shivering, she stopped her reminiscing and paced through camp. The fire sputtered and sparked, a dissonant accompaniment to the orchestra of crickets and distant wolf howls that filled the night.

As Aveline wandered, she saw points of light in the shadows around camp. Eyes, reflecting the dim firelight, watched her every move. She returned to the safety of the fire. The eyes seemed content to watch from a distance.

I hope those are just wolves, or maybe those draks are spying on me. Hurriedly, she ducked into the tent and pulled the flap closed. As she sat in the dark, she cradled her mace in her lap, holding her shield close. The sounds of night surrounded her. Through the music of insect and animal calls, she heard no footsteps approach the fire. After a time, she lay down.

Aveline shut her eyes, thinking of Dorian. Finally, sleep came for her as she let thoughts of her late husband transport her to comforting nights. After awakening with the dawn, she crawled out onto dew-covered grass. The remains of her fire still sent wisps of smoke from dying embers into the air. She considered coaxing it back to life, but she decided against it when she remembered she had nothing to eat but bread and cheese.

She found no evidence of her watchers from the previous night in the campsite. While dressing, Aveline concluded they must have been passing wolves, curious about the fire and her activity, but uninterested in confrontation.

Dew still clung to the grass as she returned to the future site of the graveyard. After verifying Vasco's grave survived the night undisturbed, she busied herself with planning burial plots for the unfortunate souls she arrived too late to save.

Chapter 29

A good night's sleep in Aveline's bed energized Tasha, but she still felt burdened by recent events. Though it lay out of the way, she broke her fast at the city market. As she bought her favorite treats from her favorite merchants, she inquired as to whether any needed help in their shops. Heartened by positive responses, she hurried to the Bristled Boar.

Raj and Jazeera awaited Tasha at the bar. Their heavy robes hung over the backs of their chairs. As she approached, they finished eating their morning meal of bacon and eggs. She did not see Yun anywhere in the common area.

"I see you've eaten."

Jazeera swallowed a hunk of bacon. "The rude man said this came with the room, but we would have to pay for other meals."

"I'll try to help you secure an income by the end of the day." Tasha gazed around the deserted room again. "Where's Yun?"

"A woman from Dadi"—Raj forced his lips around the unfamiliar name—"Dakida's Den hired him already. She said she needed someone strong to watch for unruly drunks."

"Danica's Den?" Tasha grimaced. While she had no issue with brothels or gambling establishments, Danica attracted the types of rough customers Tasha preferred to avoid in her day-to-day life.

"That's the place." Jazeera hopped off her barstool. "We could run games for her, but she said she doesn't need dealers, and I am not interested in selling my body."

"Things aren't that desperate, yet." Raj nudged his sister, then turned to Tasha. "Where are you going to take us?"

"I thought we might go to the market. Several of the vendors there indicated they might be interested in hiring some extra help. It might only be for the rest of the summer, or through the harvest, but it's better than nothing, yes?"

"Too bad our own wares were lost." Jazeera picked up their robes, then followed Tasha and Raj out of the inn.

"We'll be all right, sister. With steady work over the summer, I'll be able to get us set up doing something good by harvest."

Tasha hoped the faelix spoke true. She felt obligated to watch out for the castaways.

Although neither of the siblings wore the robes Mother Anya provided, the people of Curton seemed more at ease seeing the faelixes in town than they had the day prior. As they proceeded, Tasha pointed out shops and introduced the siblings to townsfolk she knew.

"You know, I suppose I should've asked if you have any skills." Tasha guided them over to Imrus the redsmith's stall.

"Just selling. Trading. Stealing." Raj shrugged. "We don't advertise that last one much."

"Imrus! These are the castaway siblings I told you about."

"By Adranus, I've never seen the like." Imrus wiped his hands on his already-dirty apron.

Jazeera leaned toward Tasha. "Which god is Adranus?"

"God of craftsfolk, smithing, fire, too, I think."

Imrus ran a hand through his sweat-matted, curly hair. Perspiration dripped down his face, showing dark streaks of skin through the coating of dust on him. "You've never heard of Adranus?"

"We know him by a different name—the Firelord." Raj examined Imrus's wares. "Nice pots. A little different than what I'm used to selling, but we can make this work."

Imrus turned toward Tasha. "I was actually hoping for someone to help with smelting and casting, Good Lady."

"Oh no, no, no." Shaking her head, Jazeera took Imrus's arm. "We have much too much fine fur to risk singeing it with the Firelord's tools."

"We will sell for you. You won't be able to keep up."

A portly man approached the stall, staring at the faelix siblings. He tore his gaze away from them long enough to settle on a small, footed cauldron. "That's an interesting design. Seems a bit small."

Imrus grunted. "Then get a bigger one. Or cook less."

Jazeera pinched the redsmith. "Listen and learn."

Raj grinned at his sister before taking the customer by the arm. "Excuse him, good sir, it is early, and he had a bad egg when breaking his fast. This cauldron is excellent for small stews and perhaps even potions. Notice the feet? You can set it over coals for quicker cooking or just set it on the side of the hearth. No need to hang it."

He guided the customer to a larger pot next to a copper skillet. "But this… this is for grand meals. You appreciate fine food, yes? There is no finer meal than what you'll cook in this pot. Stews and such. Of course, you'll need a skillet for a rasher of bacon, eggs, perhaps even a beefsteak, yes?"

Pulling the customer close, Raj glanced over his head. "There aren't any minotaurs about, are there? Don't want to be gored talking about cows." He lowered his voice. "They don't like when people eat beef, you know."

The customer stammered, turning his head to search the marketplace.

"Ah, no matter." Raj raised an eyebrow as he eyed Imrus. "How much did you say this set was, Boss?"

"Ten crowns for both."

"Oh my!" The customer stumbled backward. "I only need a pot."

"Oh, well, call it six for the pot. Six silver crowns…"

"Gold." Tasha giggled. "Crowns are gold. Talons are silver."

"That is what I said." Raj caressed the pot. "Six crowns. It is a crime to sell craftsmanship this fine so cheaply. The Firelord, er, Adranus should be insulted. But do we care?

No!" He clicked his claws in the customer's face. "We think you deserve to have the finest cookware when preparing opulent meals for you and your family."

Tasha watched Imrus. The redsmith's jaw hung agape.

"I live alone." The customer stared at the pot.

"Perhaps with cookware this beautiful, not for long, eh? Who could resist a man of such fine taste? I, myself, would be sorely tempted by a potential mate with finery such as this."

"I do enjoy cooking." The man patted his stomach before reaching into his money purse. "How much did you say again?"

"Seven crowns." Raj winked at his sister. "Seven crowns to honor Adranus's hand in this fine craftsmanship. Buying this is practically an act of worship."

The man counted out seven gold coins, dropping them into Raj's outstretched paw. Smiling, Raj handed the man his pot. "Cook well, and may your new mates give you many kittens!"

"Uh yes…" He stumbled away, struggling with the pot."

Turning to Imrus, Raj bowed. "That's how you sell."

* * *

By midday, Aveline finished plotting thirty graves. Digging that many intimidated her. She chose to wait for the helpers to arrive. Instead, she busied herself with further cleaning of the campsite. Without knowing how many volunteers Tasha recruited, her ignorance limited preparations.

Using what rope she had and canvas from the other tent, she constructed a makeshift litter. After donning her armor, she dragged the litter behind her into the forest. She tossed branches and sticks she came across on the forest floor into it as she proceeded.

She foraged until she reached the stream. After gathering all the nearby deadfall, Aveline sat on a rock and removed her boots. The frigid mountain water sent shivers up her legs as she dipped her feet into the rushing brook, but she grew accustomed to it after a couple of minutes. Examining her grimy hands, she decided to strip and bathe. While there was little she could do for her clothing, Aveline figured that which lay under it should at least be clean.

Gritting her teeth to gird against the shock of the chilly water, she squatted in the brook. One of the many streams feeding the Copper Run River, this tributary barely rose above her knees. She scrubbed her hands without the benefit of soap.

"Nethun's beard, this is cold. I miss my bed. I miss my hearth." She splashed water toward a bug-eyed frog on a nearby stump. "I miss a warm washtub, and I miss my mead." She decided to make building a roaring fire her first priority upon returning to camp.

Once the worst of the grime disappeared, Aveline stepped over to the bank, seizing a low-hanging branch to steady herself as she waded to dry land. She lowered herself onto a rock and rinsed her feet, then waited for the warm summer air to dry enough of her body so she could dress without her clothes clinging to her as if she'd been prancing through a spring shower.

After dressing, she dragged the litter back to camp. Approaching the mine entrance, she heard voices. Her heart skipped a beat, grateful for the arrival of help from Curton. She realized it was impossible, however, for whoever Tasha recruited to have traveled here so quickly. After dropping the litter, she drew her mace.

Creeping forward, she made her way toward the boulder at the edge of camp. The voices grew louder as she approached, and it became clear they conversed in Drak. She considered charging into camp. Instead, she decided to take a leap of faith, hoping they were the same draks with whom Tasha spoke and who were not actually hostile. Nevertheless, Aveline kept a tight grip on her mace as she entered the camp.

"Looking for something?"

The draks spun in unison, brandishing their spears. As she guessed, the draks' scales shone white in the midday sun. One barked orders at the other as he lowered his spear. His compatriots followed suit.

"I am Gral of the Icescale clan. We thought all your kind returned to your city."

These are definitely Tasha's draks. Aveline hooked her mace to her belt. "The others returned to Curton to get help. We have many dead to bury here. I informed one of your scouts yesterday, but I don't think he understood me."

The drak swept his gaze around the camp. One of the others chattered at him until he held up a clawed hand to silence him. "We see no dead here."

Aveline pointed toward the mine entrance. "They're in there. I haven't the strength to bring them all out on my own. That's why folk from town are coming to help me dig the graves."

The drak cocked his head. "Strange that your people leave one lone female to tend to the dead."

"My self-imposed penance. For failing them." Aveline hung her head, squeezing her eyes shut. "I'm Captain of the City Watch. I was supposed to protect them. Keep them safe. The least I can do now is ensure they're laid to rest with honor."

Gral turned toward the mine entrance. "Why are there so many dead in the mine?"

"A wizard was abducting people, using them for experiments. There's still"—she waved her hand in the direction of the mine—"evil there. My friend, Tasha, the one who spoke to your clan leader the other day, she has requested help from the Arcane University."

Aveline gestured toward the canvas structure. "I'd appreciate it if you'd move away from my tent. I'd like to stow my armor before getting back to work."

Bowing, the drak ordered the others to move to the other side of the camp. He leaned on his spear. "When you are finished, you'll begin digging here again? What is in this place?"

"It used to be a copper mine." Aveline tossed her shield and mace into the tent. "All the veins dried up years ago. The town abandoned it. That's probably why the wizard moved in."

"If we help you, perhaps my people could live there when it is safe?"

Aveline stared at the drak. She couldn't imagine the stench of death would ever leave the mine. Regardless, the decision did not belong to her. "Your help would be welcome. I can't make promises about the mine, but I will speak to the Lord Mayor of Curton about it on your behalf."

"Very well. I will speak to High Elder Klatt and return in the morning." The drak bowed, gesturing for his companions to follow him as he left the camp. A quick inspection showed they hadn't disturbed her things much, and Aveline set to work rebuilding her fire.

"Damn it. I should have asked them if they had any meat I could trade for."

Chapter 30

Tasha viewed the remains of her house. The smell of mold and rotting vegetation permeated the air. Taking shallow breaths to stave off the stench, she debated the value of entering it to salvage anything further. Her pack bulged, full of clothes that had remained dry. She hoped exposing them to the outdoor air would return them to wearable condition as they appeared to be unaffected by the devastation wrought upon her other possessions. Korbin and Revan observed from their perch on her roof.

"Lady Tasha! Lady Tasha!" A young boy rushed toward her. His sandy hair fell into his eyes when he stopped in front of her, panting.

"I'm not nobility." She placed her hand on the child's shoulder to steady him. "What do you need?"

"Lord Mayor Koloman sent me to find you." He gulped air in between words, like a fish flopping at the bottom of a fisherman's boat. "He wishes to see you at once."

Tasha sighed. "What does that fo—" She caught herself before insulting him in front of one who might relay her sentiments to the Lord Mayor. "At his home, I expect?"

"Yes, I am to bring you straightaway."

Of course. Never mind what I'm doing.

Lifting her pack, she gestured down the street. "Lead the way then."

As she followed the boy, her crows flitted from rooftop to rooftop, and her mind reeled with conjecture. Enduring Koloman's attempts at seduction sat pretty low on her list of desired activities for the day, preferable only to being stabbed. The child led her past the bakery where the aroma of freshly baked fruit pies wafted into the street. Feeling her stomach grumbling, she made a mental note to return there after her meeting with the Lord Mayor to purchase at least one pie for mood improvement purposes.

Soon after, they arrived at the gate of Koloman's estate. Rickon, who stood guard, opened the gate to let her pass. "Back to the stable, boy. There's stalls that need mucking out."

"I did that already."

"No lip." Planting a boot on the child's backside, the guard shoved him away. "Do it again."

Tasha glared at Rickon. "The next time you get an itch in your nethers, don't expect a salve from me."

"Heard your shop was destroyed in the flood, so I wasn't expecting it anyway. Unlike his lordship, who is expecting you." The guard pointed up the walk toward the house.

Shaking her head, Tasha entered the estate. The crows flew over the fence. Revan perched on the broken lamppost while Korbin alighted on her shoulder. Proceeding toward the entrance, she called toward Rickon, "You were nicer before you worked for him. He taints everyone around him, you know."

Alik pulled the door open before Tasha could knock. "Lord Koloman awaits you in his study."

"Thank you, Alik."

Nodding at Revan, he put an arm across the door before she entered. "Your... pet? I don't think Lord Koloman would..."

Tasha stroked Revan's neck. "Lord Koloman can deal with it. Things are different now."

How different, Tasha had yet to determine, but she would not allow her confidence to waver in front of the Lord Mayor or anyone associated with him.

"As I said, in the study."

"Thank you." Tasha turned down the hall. Koloman sat in the chair facing the cold hearth, a half-full glass of brandy in one hand and an open bottle in the other. His hair lay at all angles from his head, uncharacteristically unkempt.

"You wanted to see me, Lord Mayor?" Tasha struggled to conceal impatience and contempt from her tone.

He sat still in his chair. "I understand you and Lady Aveline went to the mine to rescue the abducted townsfolk?"

"Yes, a wizard performed foul experiments on them." Tasha circled his chair to face him. She recoiled from his rough appearance. Bags accented his bloodshot eyes, and several days of stubble covered his normally impeccably shaven face. "Unfortunately, none survived. Even now, Lady Aveline is organizing their burial. They deserve to be remembered with honor, at least. Perhaps they'll find peace in the next life."

"They were all whores, weren't they? Why bother?" He drained his glass, then filled it again from the bottle.

"How they earned a living is immaterial." Tasha clenched her jaw. Revan shifted on her shoulder. "How they died was terrible. They deserve better than to be left to rot at the bottom of an abandoned mine."

"I care not." He raised his head. "Dark have been my dreams of late. I have seen a man. A shadow in dark robes, like one of Aita's shepherds."

Tasha's brow furrowed. "Has this man a name?"

"He says nothing, but I sense he wants something from me." Koloman drank from his glass. "When I awake, I feel as though I have not slept. You will make a sleeping draught. One that will make me sleep with no dreams."

"I can't do that."

Koloman flung his glass, brandy and all, into the hearth where it shattered. "You will! I command it."

Tasha's amulet glowed with a dim green light, and she felt the cloak grow warm. "I cannot. My shop was ruined in the flood. I lost everything. And even if I hadn't, I am not an alchemist. You'll need to send away to Cliffport for it."

He drank from his bottle, then glanced at her, drawing a shaky breath. "Why is there a bird on your shoulder?"

"The Crow Queen has returned." As if in agreement, Revan cawed.

"She knows of dreams." He shrugged. "So the stories tell."

Uh-oh. Tasha bit her lip to keep from grimacing. "If I see her, I'll tell her you have questions about dreams."

"Fine. If you can't help, then leave. Tell Lady Aveline I wish to see her at once."

"Lady Aveline… yes, I will tell her when I see her." Spinning, Tasha left the study. Flapping his wings to maintain his balance, Revan settled when she slowed her pace in the hallway. She stroked Revan again, smiling as she passed Alik on the way out.

"Did you hear? The Crow Queen has returned." She straightened her feathered cloak as she stepped on to the porch. Tasha held out her hand toward Korbin, who left the lamppost to land in her palm. She turned toward Alik.

The old man stared, his mouth agape. "Annika died ages ago."

"I didn't say Annika was back. I told you, things are different now."

* * *

Invigorated with confidence following her visit to Lord Mayor Koloman's estate, Tasha returned to the bakery. She let Korbin and Revan fly free once Koloman's house was out of sight. Each time she told someone or hinted she was the Crow Queen, Tasha felt a surge of power from the feathered cloak. Approval, perhaps? It seemed obvious the cloak was no ordinary garment, that it exhibited a sort of awareness. If not true consciousness, then, at least, it possessed an empathic sense urging her toward certain actions.

It remained silent on the subject of pies, however, so Tasha chose a blueberry galette to take home and a couple of meat-filled buns so she'd have something savory to go with the sweet. She planned to keep a slice or two for herself, then share the rest with the neighborhood children. When she exited the bakery, she noticed several crows perched on nearby rooftops. They followed her as she navigated the winding streets, her own personal, feathered entourage. Approaching Aveline's home, Tasha noticed a group of young children darting here and there on the street as their parents tried to bring a semblance of normalcy into their post-flood lives.

Tasha enjoyed her slice of pie in the privacy of Aveline's home, setting aside an additional slice before cutting the rest of it into smaller slices than she served herself. She took the pie outside to sit on Aveline's stoop. Crows alighted on the roof and on those of the surrounding homes. Before calling the children over to share, Tasha sent Korbin and Revan to the mine so she could check on Aveline. Once satisfied the crows understood her instructions, she called to Aveline's neighbors and offered them slices of pie in exchange for stories about the Crow Queen.

A young girl with an unruly mop of dark hair framing her piercing blue eyes shoveled pie into her mouth with her hands as she spoke. "Me mother says the Crow Queen was a wrinkled hag what made the crops grow… but would eat your babies if you asked her for a favor."

"Nikki's wrong." An older girl with curly midnight hair, missing her two front teeth, offered an alternative. "She was a crone, all right, but she wouldn't eat babies for favors. She'd feed them to her wolves."

A third girl, shorter than the other two, with stringy blond hair, held out her hands for pie. "Who's the Crow Queen? Is she a giant bird?"

Laughing, Tasha ran a hand down the edge of her feathered cloak. "I don't think so."

"Here now, children. You shouldn't bother Lady Ave…" The man blinked, realizing his mistake. He carried the tools of a mason. "You're not Lady Aveline."

"I'm Tasha, the apothecary. Lady Aveline is kind enough to let me stay in her home since mine was ruined in the flood."

"Aw, bollocks. I was going to buy some wormroot from you this week."

Tasha offered him a piece of pie. "I'm sorry. All my stock was destroyed. I plan on heading out this afternoon to start restocking. I'll try to find some for you."

"I'd be much obliged." He accepted the pie with a nod of thanks. "The vermin's been awful since the storm."

"I hope to be able to help with that again soon." She peered into the man's eyes. He seemed familiar to her, but she could not recall his name. "You know, in exchange for the pie, each child had to tell me something about the Crow Queen. I don't suppose you have any stories you'd like to share?"

Exhaling, the man sat on the stoop next to Tasha as he ate. "Probably everyone in town of a certain age, or, at least, with parents of a certain age, has a story about the Crow Queen."

"I was born in Cedar Ridge." Tasha noticed by the man's blank expression he did not recognize the name of her childhood home. "It's near Almeria. I didn't grow up with stories about the Crow Queen."

"Oh, well, my father would have died as a babe without her. They were lucky she was around here when my grandmother gave birth."

"What did she do?" In all the years Tasha served Curton as an apothecary, she had never performed midwifery. She supposed she could learn from one of the midwives in town, if necessary.

The man scratched his head. "I'm not rightly sure. He was never clear on that. He came out wrong or something and was sick. She made sure he didn't die those first few nights. She left for about a year after, but she would check back now and then when she visited the area to see how he was doing. She was from Curton, you know."

"I've heard." Tasha regarded the children. "She doesn't sound like a crone or a nasty old hag."

He laughed. "She could be downright nasty if someone crossed her. The Crow Queen is motherly like Cybele, tied to the world like Gaia, and temperamental like Artume."

"You're quite knowledgeable."

He patted the tools on his belt. "I wasn't always a carpenter. It was a hobby. Kept my hands busy when I was one of Mother Anya's acolytes." Finishing his pie, he nodded toward a woman sweeping a porch down the street. She waved at him. "Then I met Daciana there during a moment of weakness at Danica's Den. We've been together ever since."

Tasha handed him the pie dish. "Take the rest of it to her and enjoy it with your family later, then."

"Thank you. She loves blueberries." He tousled the hair of the blue-eyed girl. "Like mother like daughter, eh, Sorie?"

"Can I take it to her, Papa?" The girl bounced on the balls of her feet while holding out her hands.

"Here. Don't drop it and don't eat any. We'll have the rest after supper."

Sorie bounded away, carrying the pie. Tasha smoothed her skirt before fluffing the bottom of her cloak. Glancing upward when the feathers caught his eye, the man noticed scores of crows perched on the rooftops. Twisting his head, he moved to get a closer look at the cloak.

"Cybele's tits… you're her… I mean, no disrespect…"

Smiling, Tasha clasped her hands in front of her. She felt her cloak pulse with warmth. "What is your name?"

"Vali, son of Razvan."

"You may be right, Vali, son of Razvan." Tasha bowed her head. "But I'm still finding my way, so don't expect too much too soon."

He stumbled to his feet. "Anything you need, anything at all, don't hesitate. I wouldn't be here if not for you saving my father as a baby."

Tasha put her hands on Vali's shoulders. "That was Annika, or her predecessor. I'm Tasha."

"The Crow Queen always has many names." Vali dropped to his knees. "It'll do this town good that you've come back."

She tugged at his shirt, pulling him to his feet. "That is not necessary, please." She turned him around before giving him a gentle push toward his wife. "I'll come see you when I've found some wormroot. Should be just a few days."

He staggered away, glancing over his shoulder at her after every few steps. After a moment, Tasha left the now-playing children behind and headed toward Miners' Gate. As she walked beneath the blazing midday sun, she realized the cloak did not make her feel too warm. *Maybe I can wear whatever I want under this if it's going to keep me perfectly comfortable all the time.*

As she entered the forest, Tasha considered the foolishness of leaving town in the middle of the day to find a derelict hut in the middle of the woods almost a day away from the town gates.

Pausing, she connected with her crows, learning they passed the workers from town who were traveling to help Aveline. The birds had found her well and alone in the camp. Tasha called them to her as she continued her journey.

"The sooner I can figure all this out, the sooner I can help everyone." She hoped the justification would prove true.

Chapter 31

After the draks left and Aveline finished piling all the foraged wood, she found herself with little to do. Venturing into the mines to search for additional supplies, equipment, and weapons proved fruitless. As she busied herself around camp, she spotted two dark birds circling overhead for a while, assuming Tasha sent the crows to check on her. *At least, I hope those are hers because roasted fowl sounds incredibly good right now.*

Her stomach grumbled at the thought of another meal of cheese, bread, and tepid water. Yet, being all she had, Aveline made do and forced herself to eat only enough to quiet her gastric rumblings.

This should serve as a lesson to be less impulsive, no matter how great an idea it seems at first. Aveline sat before the fire, polishing her armor, listening to the buzz of insects. *Maybe the draks will come by again. Even they would be better company than no one at this time. I should carry a bow when I leave town, in case I need to hunt.* The idea of chasing down an animal and beating it to death with her mace so she could eat seemed ridiculous to her.

Whatever animals spied on her the night before did not return, and she nodded off in front of the fire before retiring to her tent for the remainder of the evening. When morning came, she awakened to the sounds of horses and loud voices.

Pulling on her clothes, she then crawled out of the tent. Lieutenant Valon and at least two dozen townsfolk greeted her.

"Please tell me you have food. Mead?" Aveline returned the Lieutenant's salute with a half-hearted gesture.

"We brought wine and ale." He directed the people closest to him to unload he carts and set up a galley.

"Anything's better than water." She scratched her head. "I probably should have had them help me bury Vasco and then come back to town. To be honest, I think I was afraid someone would stop me from returning here."

She watched as a group of constables from the city watch unloaded picks and shovels, then carried them over to the graves she'd plotted.

"The Lord Mayor might have. He's been in a state the last few days. But we're here now, Lady Aveline. What would you have us do?"

"I've already marked thirty graves." She pointed toward the future site of the graveyard, then pointed at the mine. "I don't know how many people are down there. They're all in a pile. Bringing them out is going to be... challenging."

"A pile?" Lieutenant Valon removed his helmet. Scratching his head, he glanced toward the mine entrance. "How many are there? There were only a handful noticed missing from town."

"The prisoners we freed, the faelixes and the caprikin, indicated the wizard was taking travelers too. There's no telling how long he was down there, and I fear we may not be able to identify any of the bodies."

Valon nodded at the mention of the castaways. "I saw the three when Tasha came back to town. She looked different."

"Different?" Aveline accepted a tankard of ale from a woman who carried several toward a table someone from one of the taverns set up.

"Not bad, mind you. But different. Like she wasn't her anymore, but someone else, but still Tasha." Valon shook his head. "I'm not making any sense."

"Tasha thinks she has some connection to the Crow Queen. She found a body at the bottom of a shaft and a feathered cloak that looked almost new. It must've been down there for ages."

"The Crow Queen had a cloak like that. Birds would follow her around, and she'd come to town in a hut that walked on legs. She'd set it down outside Mudders' Gate and help people that came to her, favors and such." Staring at his feet, Valon kicked a pebble away. "At least, that's what my mother used to tell me."

Aveline sighed. "Well, that's nothing we need to be concerned with right now. Tasha wants us to retrieve the bones, though, give them a proper burial."

"Right. I'll start sending lads down into the mine to haul bodies up. How do we find them?"

Aveline drained her ale. "I'll lead them down there." She held up her mug. "We're going to need a lot of this by the time we're finished."

* * *

Despite the forest canopy obscuring the dim light of Calliome's waxing moons, Tasha navigated the trails without difficulty. Not only did she feel an instinctive sense of where to go, but she also noticed a sort of faint light infused everything around her. She heard deer bedding down for the night, even though she could not see them. She heard and smelled a wolf pack hunting. The dirt beneath her feet pulsed with the life of the Earth Mother.

A quick experiment of removing the cloak, plunged her into the pitch black of night, confirming her suspicion the feathered mantle itself facilitated her passage in the dark. Her connection with Gaia remained strong without the cloak, and she basked for a moment in that connection for reassurance. When she pulled the cloak around her shoulders once again, she immediately felt oriented and confident in the direction she needed to travel. She continued her trek.

Knowing where to go shortened her search, although she sensed dawn was still several hours away by the time she approached the clearing where she first found the hut. This time, however, no bones jutted from the ground. Instead, a pair of legs, giant avian legs, stood in the clearing. On top, she found the hut she last saw lying on its side. Smoke rose from its lone chimney, and a dim amber light shone through its windows.

Tasha stared at the hut for what seemed like minutes before stairs rose from the earth, creaking and cracking with the sound of churning rocks, soil, and wood. After they met the entrance, the door opened.

Accepting the invitation, Tasha climbed the stairs. With each step closer to the top, she felt the world's life-force flow through the stairs and into the hut through her connection with Gaia.

Once inside, Tasha dropped her pack near the door and examined the furniture arranged along the walls. A carved stump in the center of the floor served as the focal point in the room. The sides of the stump featured relief carvings of birds surrounding the Tree of Gaia, the Sacred Cow of Cybele, and a depiction of the Huntress Artume; the same iconography on the altar she saw before, although she didn't see it anywhere. The top sloped inward, creating a natural, carved bowl in which Tasha saw clear water. A low fire burned in the hearth, and she smelled smoldering sage and rosemary coming from bundles tied above the flames. A ladder positioned between the hearth and the bed led to a hatch in the roof. Next to the bed, there was another door, which Tasha assumed led outside.

She circled the central stump, stopping at a cabinet opposite the bed. Upon opening it, drawers upon drawers of reagents, shelves of papers and books, and drawers containing dozens of vials revealed themselves. A red, leather-bound diary, protruding from the rest, beckoned to her.

Tasha opened the book. Strokes made with a bold hand indicated the diary belonged to Annika. Carrying it over to a chair, she settled in to read. A mundane journal at first, it chronicled day-to-day oddities of a woman who relished using the power of the Crow Queen to heal sick livestock, help with difficult births, bless new crops, and encourage favorable weather when droughts or precipitation tarried.

As she flipped through the pages, a single line drawn with a shaky hand caught her eye: *My daughter is dead.*

Stains marred the next few blank pages. Once the writing resumed, the bold hand included a noticeable tremble. Tasha read on.

The plague took half the city before I could stop it. Nika blames me for the death of Dimos. She doesn't know. No one knows, though Anya suspects. I used my own life to stop the plague.

It was worth it.

If you're reading this, you've found my hut and my mantle. I don't know where you found it, and it doesn't matter. It has accepted you, although it was meant for my daughter.

You're Crow Queen now.

Tasha dropped the book. It remained open to the last page she'd read. The words, written decades ago for her eyes, burned into her mind. Drawing a shaky breath, Tasha leaned forward and picked up the journal.

I don't know what challenges you'll face. I don't know what kind of person you are. But you'll read no more of my life in these pages. Instead, I will tell you everything I've discovered about the mantle, the hut, and what it means to be Crow Queen.

This is what I meant to teach my daughter. Stories you hear from others will be full of half-truths and embellishments. You're not a queen (unless you actually were born into nobility and have a title, of course), you're not a goddess. People will say you're a witch. Maybe you are. I was; it's not a bad thing necessarily. People will say you're supposed to be a vile old hag. You can be if you so desire. Depending on how long I've been dead before you read this, you may have an entirely blank slate to work with. If I have faded into legend or obscurity by the time the mantle finds a new bearer, then you have an opportunity to create a new myth.

One last personal note, and then every page henceforth will be instructional: I encourage you to be good. Help others. The feathers on the mantle were gathered by Artume, woven into flax grown by Cybele in the soil of Gaia herself. You could be as tempestuous and uncaring as the natural world. But, you will have a happier life if you choose to be more selfless than that. Perhaps you will have a family, as I tried to have. You will find the hut will accommodate you. It can change, grow, and it can take you places you never imagined existed.

Your journey begins on the next page, Crow Queen.

Tasha closed the journal, rocking back in the chair. She stared, wide-eyed, at the flames in the hearth as a swirling torrent of thoughts raged in her mind. *What have I gotten myself into?*

"Caw!" Revan flew through the open door. He perched on the edge of the stump, followed by Korbin. After a moment of preening, they huddled together.

"I guess we're on this journey together." Tasha tossed the diary on the bed. She approached the door through which she'd entered. At the bottom of the stairs, the forest floor appeared dangerously distant. She shut the door, taking a moment to appreciate the intricacy of the carved wooden handle, before moving to the window. The stairs collapsed, disappearing into the earth as though they'd never existed.

"Well, that's handy for keeping unwanted visitors away." Tasha circled the stump, making her way to the other door. Between the window and the cabinet was a fully stocked larder. Wondering where the provisions had come from, she continued to the other door. Unlike the entry door, this one featured no knob or handle. Her eyes scanned the frame and the door itself.

"How odd." She moved to stroke the moss-covered wood. "How does a door with no handle…"

The door vanished, and a shimmering cascade of rainbow light took its place. Recoiling, Tasha shielded her eyes with her hands. "It's a portal, not a door."

After taking a few steps backward, the light vanished, and the door reappeared. Tasha returned to the bed and sat. Korbin and Revan remained perched on the stump, appearing to be asleep. Tasha stifled a yawn.

"I guess with no stairs and the doors all the way up here, no one is going to break in if I rest a bit." She made herself comfortable on the bed, staring at the ceiling. Thick wooden beams separated panels of thatch, much as the roof appeared from the outside. Her eyelids grew heavy, and she allowed sleep to overcome her.

Chapter 32

Two days of digging graves and hauling putrid bodies followed by nights sleeping on the ground spared no part of Aveline's anatomy from aches and fatigue. Plastering her tight curls to her scalp, sweat poured down her face as the relentless heat of the sun baked the foothills. Aveline passed her shovel to a fresh worker before making her way toward the encampment.

Since Valon arrived with help from the town, the site took on an entirely different appearance. Tents for sleeping were pitched to one side of the mine entrance, around the area near Aveline's. A straight path, or as straight as it could be considering the terrain, led from the mine entrance to the grave plots she'd mapped over the last several days. Behind the tents for sleeping, other workers from town had built tables from scrap wood, as well as from trees they felled for that purpose. They built two cooking fires there, then kept them running day and night. Finally, behind a small field of boulders, they'd dug the latrines.

She approached the cooking fires where two women, Magda and Silvie, eyed the bubbling cauldron suspended over the flames. Joining them, she peered into the pot. A mass of sand-colored goop roiled within.

"Dare I ask what that is?"

Magda snorted. "You can ask."

Silvie poked at the flames with a fire iron. "I think it's supposed to be porridge. Eventually."

"Hm." Aveline did not oppose porridge in principle, although presentation counted for a lot. "Oats and water. Can't argue with efficiency."

"I reckon it'll be all right if we can find some fruit." Magda stirred the sludge with the protruding spoon. "Hopefully, what we brought isn't all gone yet."

Silvie thrust the fire iron into the dirt. "Too bad there's no cream. I heard there's draks in the forest nearby. Do you think they have any goats?"

"They seemed more the hunter type." Clasping her hands behind her back, Aveline stretched. "I'm surprised we haven't seen them yet. They told me they were going to help us."

"Help us? With what?" Magda furrowed her brow. "Digging holes or carrying bodies?"

Glancing at the mine, Aveline observed two men, retching as they hauled a dripping, blackened body from the darkness. A light breeze caught the stench of putrescence, wafting it over the cauldron. Closing her eyes, she concentrated on ignoring the intermingling scents of rot and gruel.

"Um"—Aveline swallowed rising bile—"draks can be industrious diggers, but maybe they can hunt a deer for us."

"Mm, or a ram." Silvie tapped Aveline on the arm. "There's big mountain sheep around here. Remember when my brother brought one home last harvest and it fed us all through the winter?"

"Either would be good." Aveline forced a smile through her nausea. "But I do appreciate everything you folk managed to cobble together to bring on such short notice."

"Honestly, m'lady"—Silvie lowered her head—"we can't tell you how much it means you stayed after we arrived. You've been working twice as hard as anyone else here."

Magda nodded. "You shouldn't push yourself so hard."

Shaking her head, Aveline held up her hand. "No, I must. I failed the town. I failed you. I tarried too long in taking the abductions seriously. I let myself put a lesser worth on the missing people because they were ladies of the night, vagabonds, and passing travelers." The knight-captain wiped away a tear. "How many died needlessly because I thought less of them due to their circumstances?"

"It's done." Magda put her hand on Aveline's shoulder. "You can't change it."

"But I can atone."

"We're lucky to have you watching over us, Lady Aveline. You think Lord Koloman cares? He wouldn't give us a pot to piss in." Silvie spat when she mentioned his name.

"Pompous bastard." It was Magda's turn to spit. "Do you know he kept trying to hire me even years after I told him I stopped whoring? After I was married, even. The bastard."

Silvie put her arm around Magda's waist. "Then when she found out who you was married to, he propositioned both of us."

Aveline pinched the bridge of her nose. "Well, you should pray for the poor soul who has to explain all of this to him. It'll probably be me."

Silvie giggled "Want to pray to Dolios for luck or Maris for—"

A commotion arose on the other side of the camp. Aveline noticed people moving away from the graves, pointing and talking among themselves. She jogged toward Lieutenant Valon, grateful to put distance between herself and the stench wafting from the mine.

Aveline observed with a mixture of confusion and awe. A thatched roof hut crested the hill, strutting forward on a pair of black crow's feet. Soon, everyone stopped working to gape.

"Have you ever seen the like?" Valon, standing alongside Aveline, wiped sweat from his brow. She could only shake her head in response. The hut stopped in front of the crowd and seemed to settle, in the same way a dog settles on its haunches.

The door opened, and a familiar figure waved from above.

"It's Tasha!" Aveline grinned, waving both arms over her head. "Tasha!"

Earth and vines erupted from the earth, growing skyward. Approaching the door, the mass formed into a staircase. When they reached Tasha, she fluffed her cloak, striding forward. She descended the steps, like a queen approaching her subjects from on high.

Then she fell.

Catching her left foot on the hem of her cloak, Tasha tumbled down the bottom half of the stairs. Aveline rushed forward, skidding to a stop on her knees in the mud as she reached her friend.

"Everyone, keep back. Tasha?" Holding out her hands to keep others away, Aveline regarded the sorceress.

"Ouch."

"Are you all right?" Supporting Tasha's back, Aveline helped her into a sitting position.

"I think I'll be sore for a few days." Tasha arched her spine, rolling her neck. "I'm not hurt, just humbled. I'm pretty sure someone sent me a message just then."

Aveline pulled Tasha to her feet. The knight-captain then wrapped her friend in a hug. When they parted, she held her friend at arm's length, gesturing toward the hut with her head. "What is going on?"

Smiling, Tasha glanced at the crowd. "I'm sure most of them could tell you. They've heard stories. Haven't you?"

Murmurs of affirmation circulated through the crowd. Valon approached, raising his hand in greeting to Tasha. "Surely you recognize it, Captain? That's the hut of the Crow Queen."

* * *

"It is, indeed, Lieutenant." Spreading her arms, Tasha raised her voice. "The Crow Queen has returned."

Korbin and Revan swooped in, passing Tasha's head and circling over the crowd before landing on her outstretched arms. After dismissing her birds, she clasped her hands in front of her.

Clearing her throat, she glanced at Aveline. "Just go easy on me right now. I'm still learning what all this means."

"By the gods"—Lieutenant Valon stared first at Tasha, then the hut, before returning his gaze to Tasha—"you're the Crow Queen? She... we... I... this..." Moving his mouth in silent confusion, words failed him. Several people in the crowd fell to their knees.

Tasha rushed forward. "Oh, no, no, no. We don't do that. No. I'm still just Tasha. You used to come to me for herbs and poultices." She gestured behind her toward the hut. "I just have a new home now. A new shop."

She glanced over her shoulder at the hut before returning her attention to the crowd. "With legs. That walks around. And is... full of... I don't know... I didn't think this through..."

Suddenly, Tasha felt the weight of the cloak. Gasping for breath, she turned on her heels and ascended to the hut. She heard Aveline call after her, and she sensed her following. By reflex, she grasped the door handle to shut it, but she saw her friend climbing the stairs and didn't want to find out how quickly they would vanish if she closed the door before Aveline reached the top.

"Fine, come in." Once Aveline crossed the threshold, Tasha shut the door, then she collapsed on the bed.

"Well, this is impressive."

"I remembered where it was, and I needed to start rebuilding my shop. I figured maybe there'd be something here I could use, but when I got here, it was upright again, standing on crows' legs." Tasha's mind racing, she babbled about the diary and the door of light, repeating herself and talking in circles until Aveline, taking her hand, sat alongside her.

"So, what do you do?"

Rising, Tasha swung her legs over the edge of the bed to sit next to her friend. "I don't know, Aveline. The diary

I found tells me everything I can do with the mantle, the hut, all that. But she was dying when she wrote it, and she intended to teach all of this to her daughter. It's like learning how to be a smith from reading stories about how Adranus forged the world.

"Annika's instructions in the diary read more like anecdotes than lessons. It's clear from the way she wrote that she knew she didn't have much time. The diary skips from topic to topic, sometimes spending pages talking about how Annika helped someone with what she had started to describe, but she failed to finish describing how to accomplish it."

Aveline nodded. "You know what you can do, just not how. Or why. Or when."

"Pretty much."

Rising, she patted Tasha on the leg, then started pacing between the bed and the window. "Well, why not just help people the way you always do? Just be yourself? And when you feel like you can do more, then do so. No one is expecting you to perform miracles."

Tasha snorted. "They might. The last Crow Queen cured the plague that ravaged Curton. And not just in one or two people—I mean the whole town. At once."

Crossing her arms, Aveline leaned against the larder. "That sounds pretty hard to top. The plague was so long ago. There can't be more than a handful of people alive who even remember it."

"Mother Anya. People remember their parents talking about it."

"Just stories to most folk now." Aveline cocked her head, examining the basin in the central stump. "So, Tasha, how does this even work? The hut was walking."

Tasha slid out of bed, moving to retrieve the diary from the bedside table. Holding it up, she grinned. "That was the first thing I tried."

She pointed at the stump. "The whole hut is grown around that. Grown, built. However you want to describe it. I can use the basin to scry, though I haven't quite figured that out yet. It replenishes itself, too, so I always have a source of clean water. So, I just need to climb up here"—she patted the flat edge of the stump—"and sit. I levitate above the pool, and I sort of… feel the hut as if it were me. Then, I just… walk wherever I want."

Aveline pushed out her bottom lip, nodding in appreciation. "Silvermane will be crushed."

"I know it can do more." Tasha tossed the diary onto the bed. "Aveline, I can take the hut to the other side of the world"—she clicked her fingers—"just like that. I don't know how—yet—but whenever the stories talk about the Crow Queen just disappearing for weeks or months at a time, she was just somewhere else. Hoseki. Nakambe. The Four Watches. I could go to the far side of the Western Wastes, see if there really is anything over there."

"You could give that caprikin and the faelix brother and sister a ride home."

Tasha rocked back on her heels. "I could. I didn't even think of that."

"Where are they, by the way?"

Tasha chuckled. "I got Raj and Jazeera a job helping Imrus sell his wares in the market. Yun's working at Danica's Den. Probably throwing out rowdy gamblers."

Aveline raised her eyebrows. "Really? Huh… I didn't expect that."

"Therkla and Aerik will no doubt be very angry by the time you get back to town. She wanted her payment. I couldn't access the funds, and neither she nor I could find Lieutenant Valon at the time, so I guess she never got paid." Tasha shrugged. "Oh, and I spoke to Koloman." Tasha chewed her lip as she decided how much to tell Aveline. "He wants to see you as soon as possible."

"That oroq woman…" Aveline pinched the bridge of her nose. "About what? What does Koloman want now?"

Tasha gestured toward the door. "About what happened at the mine. He was haggard, Aveline. Wanted me to fix his recent nightmares, give him a sleeping draught that would keep him from dreaming. There wasn't anything I could do, of course. I'm not an alchemist."

"Can the Crow Queen fix bad dreams?"

Tasha shrugged. "I haven't read anything about that yet. He has no idea that I've taken the mantle. Well, he might now. I told Alik as I was leaving. I don't know if the old man believed me or not."

Rubbing her chin, Aveline moved across the room to look out the window. "Normally I would say I don't care about Koloman's bad dreams. But the last time I didn't care about someone, a lot of people died in the mine. If he had regaled you with stories of his dreams of debauchery it would be different, but you said he was haggard looking?"

Tasha nodded. "Despite his vanity, he appeared as though he hadn't had a good night's sleep in at least a week."

"We have things under control here." Aveline approached the bookcase. "Maybe see if there's anything in any of these books or scrolls that can help him. He's a right bastard, but if he's not sleeping, he might make worse decisions than he normally does, and I don't want him doing anything to hurt the town."

"First thing tomorrow, I'll approach the town discreetly and see what I can do for him." Tasha sighed. "I guess I have a lot of reading to do tonight."

Chapter 33

Aveline left Tasha to her research and returned to work. While half the workers proceeded with their tasks, the other half still clustered near the Crow Queen's hut, gawking at it while whispering to each other. She dispersed them, bidding them to resume work, then went to speak to one of Cybele's acolytes ministering to the dead.

The sheet covering the body clung where fluids soaked through the fabric. No number of wildflowers, of which copious amounts had been scattered in the area, could mask the odor. Wispy clouds sliding across the sky provided no protection from the merciless sun beating upon the already-tortured corpses in the field.

Acolyte Dumitra bowed as Aveline approached. "Something you need, m'lady?"

"How many are we up to now?" Aveline shielded her eyes with her hand, scanning she scanned the graves. Too many workers occupied the area, making counting difficult.

"This one makes twenty-five." Her sandy-blond hair clung to her head, matted with perspiration. "There's at least ten more in the mine from what I hear. Lieutenant Valon has ordered more graves to be dug."

Thirty-five. Aveline knelt by the body, closing her eyes. "Have we been able to identify any of them?"

"Not yet. Brother Dorin has been keeping a ledger with detailed descriptions, so we can continue the work after they're in the ground."

"Good." Aveline covered her nose with her hand in an attempt to block some of the stench. She bowed her head. *I'm sorry I failed you. I'm sorry you're going to be anonymous as we lay you to rest.*

Dumitra put her hand on Aveline's shoulder. "It's not your fault. No one blames you."

"I would. I was responsible for keeping these people safe. I failed."

"By that logic, you should be blamed every time a child falls and scrapes their knee." Dumitra knelt next to Aveline, lowering her head and pressing her hands into the earth. "Blessed Cybele, Mother of Mothers, she who brings bounty to this land, we offer you this shell to feed the land and make it fertile. While we do not know the soul to whom this shell belonged, we know Aita's shepherds will welcome them into her bosom and guide them where they belong. Glorious Anetha, give comfort to our honored Lady Aveline. She punishes herself so for events she cannot control. She watches over us as best she can, and we are grateful for her."

Biting her lip, Aveline took Acolyte Dumitra's hand. "Thank you."

Dumitra smiled, nodding, but then her expression fell. "I think someone is here to see you."

Aveline glanced up. Half-a-dozen white-scaled draks approached from the forest. From the group, two, Gral and High Elder Klatt, strode ahead of the rest. Aveline headed to meet them.

"I was beginning to think you'd changed your mind."

Gral bowed his head. "Apologies. The High Elder was not certain of your intentions."

The wizened drak clicked his teeth together. "With good reason. The humans of the Four Watches are not charitable toward us. I have no reason to believe you shall behave any differently."

"We are not Watchfolk. But I know my words won't convince you that we desire peace. All I can ask for is patience while we prove ourselves through our actions." *Tasha's better at this than I am.*

"That is what Gral said." Nudging the younger drak, Klatt examined the freshly dug graves. "He says you told him we could live in the mine. But all of these people came out of the mine. It does not seem safe to me. Perhaps that's why we're welcome to it?"

Clearing her throat, Aveline beckoned to Acolyte Dumitra. "Perhaps you could fetch Tasha for me?"

The color drained from Dumitra's face. "You want me to summon the Crow Queen?"

Clenching her jaw, the knight-captain faced the acolyte. "Just think of her as Tasha the apothecary, and it'll be easier. I need her. Please."

Dumitra bowed. "Yes, m'lady."

As the acolyte hurried away, Aveline returned her attention to the draks. "A wizard was abducting townsfolk and travelers. We dealt with him. The mine ran dry, but it's stable. As far as I know, the main chambers are in no danger of collapse. My friend can explain what happened in more detail."

"We have heard of this Crow Queen, though it has been a generation or more since she last visited our people." Klatt lifted the cloth covering the nearby corpse with the butt of his staff, recoiling when he observed the state of decay.

"It's an unpleasant task, but necessary. We should have retrieved all the bodies by tomorrow." Aveline made a mental note to instruct Valon to have his men scour as much of the mine as possible for equipment used by the wizard and remove it.

Gral turned his gaze on the High Elder. "Then it seems we are too late to help."

If they intended to help with the bodies, Aveline agreed. She considered another alternative. "Not necessarily. Do you have hunters?"

Klatt sucked in breath through clenched teeth. "We do. Why?"

"We could use some fresh meat. We've had naught to eat for days but oats, cheese, and jerky. My people left town with little time to prepare, and they brought only necessities with them. I don't suppose you have any goats or cows?"

"No." Klatt tapped a claw against the shaft of his staff. "And in exchange for this meat, you will let us stay in the mine?"

Aveline raised her hand. "I can't speak for the Lord Mayor, but I will speak to him on your behalf and strongly encourage he allow it. The town has abandoned the mine. I can't imagine why he'd refuse." *And if he does, I'm sure Tasha and I can figure out some way to convince him otherwise.*

"This Crow Queen is a servant of Gaia, as I understand. As she was the mate of Rannos Dragonsire, I would like to speak to her before I make a decision." Klatt turned to Gral. "Take the others back to our camp. I will follow shortly."

"Yes, High Elder." Gral bowed his head, then sprinted toward his kin. Gesturing for them to follow him, he headed into the forest.

"I'll go see what's keeping her." Aveline glanced over her shoulder toward the hut, most of which lay obscured by a hill.

"I will walk with you."

Together, they left the graveyard. She heard him suck in his breath as they crested the hill. The hut came into full view, legs and all. He continued forward, however, and Aveline decided not to volunteer further information.

Acolyte Dumitra, a short distance away from the hut, jumped up and down, waving her arms.

"Have you tried shouting?" Aveline called across the field to her. Gathering her robes, Dumitra jogged to join her and the drak.

"I didn't want to cause a scene. Her door is closed." Several workers on break joined Aveline, watching Dumitra do just that.

Aveline cupped her hands around her mouth. "Tasha! I need you."

After a moment, the door opened. The earth roiled and churned, forming stairs. The gathered workers shuffled backward, but they kept their eyes on the hut with legs. Aveline gestured for them to disperse. They ignored her.

Tasha descended. "It's going to take me a long time to find information about dreams with people shouting at me."

Noticing the elder drak, she bowed her head. "Good to see you again, High Elder. I'm happy you've come."

"You are the Crow Queen." Klatt rubbed his chin with his claw. "Strange that you came to us so humbly the other day, Tasha the Apothecary."

"Not so strange. Tasha has a soft spot for your people." Aveline chuckled and tapped Acolyte Dumitra on the shoulder. "You can return to your duties if you wish."

Dumitra curtsied. "Thank you, m'lady. Crow Queen."

Tasha's cheeks grew rosy at the deference shown by Dumitra. "What can I do for you?"

"High Elder Klatt wanted to speak to the Crow Queen before he decided if the clan was going to help us in exchange for living space in the mine." Aveline spread her arms. "So here we are."

Eyeing the hut, the old drak craned his neck to examine it.

"I'll leave you two alone, then." Aveline winked at Tasha. "I'm sure Lieutenant Valon needs me." Tasha raised her eyebrows.

* * *

"Thanks, Aveline." Tasha pursed her lips as her friend abandoned her to the elderly drak. He continued to alternate his gaze between her hut and her. He reached for her cloak, but he paused. Tasha noticed his clawed hand trembling.

"May I?"

Shrugging, Tasha held out the hem of her cloak. He rubbed it between his fingers and ran his hand down the hem, smoothing the feathers.

"Your connection is strong. The Earth Mother, mate of Rannos Dragonsire, indeed speaks through you." Klatt withdrew his hand, bowing his head "Strange that I did not feel it at our first encounter."

Tasha chewed her lip before responding. "I think perhaps that is because I had not fully accepted the mantle at that point. I felt a calling. To this mine." She gestured toward the entrance. "I found the… my predecessor in there, and I claimed the mantle at that time. It was not long after that we met."

Klatt clicked his teeth together. "You claimed the mantle, or the mantle claimed you?"

Ever since Tasha first felt drawn to find the cloak, she wondered how much choice she had truly had in the matter. She chuckled. "Maybe a little of both."

"The Earth Mother's power is not taken, but it is given." Klatt drew himself up. "We will help your people. Then, we will wait to see if your leader will let us make this old mine into a home."

Tasha knelt to put her hand on the old drak's shoulder. "He will agree. Or I will convince him. I can promise you that."

Klatt shook his head. "We do not wish to live where we are not welcome."

She offered him a smile she hoped appeared reassuring. "He is one man. The people of Curton will welcome you."

"Hm. We shall see." Klatt brushed her hand off his shoulder. "I will tell our hunters to bring you some game. The rest of us will wait in the forest until you are finished honoring your dead."

Without waiting for Tasha to respond, he left her and returned to the forest. She started after him, but she paused, facing the hut. As if reading her mind, the door shut of its own accord. The stairs collapsed, melting into the earth. *Does it know, or am I actually controlling it?* Despite her growing familiarity, many questions remained.

After a quick glance around the camp in search of Aveline, Tasha informed Lieutenant Valon the draks would bring fresh game soon. She returned to the hut and continued scouring Annika's library, searching for any reference to dreams.

While the history and geography texts provided no help, Tasha found a reference in one of the scrolls. By now, the sun sat near the horizon, dimming her available light. After she lit a triple-candle sconce, she continued reading. The scroll offered a brief overview of oneiromancy, a discipline closely related to divination and enchantment. It did not, however, provide Tasha with any instructions.

She glanced at the basin of water. *If I can use that to scry, then maybe I can use it to scry into dreams. I suppose it's worth a shot. Of course, I'd have to know Koloman was sleeping first. Otherwise, I'd just be spying on him, and Selene knows there are some mysteries I don't want the answers to.*

The thought brought other questions to Tasha's mind. That the hut possessed powerful magic was obvious even to the layperson, and it was more than just the mystical power of Gaia. Selene, goddess of magic and secrets must have had a hand in its creation. Tasha scrunched her face, disappointed she didn't pay closer attention during classes on the history of magic at the Arcane University. *It would have helped if some of those instructors were interesting.*

Putting aside her reminiscences, she skimmed through the diary, searching for the pages on which Annika wrote about using the basin for scrying. The instructions seemed frustratingly vague—*Look into the still waters while calling upon your power, then concentrate on the subject.*

In Tasha's experience, divinations were never as easy as that, nor were they particularly accurate. She had no experience with direct scrying, however. While other types of divination focused on predicting future events or uncovering forgotten lore, scrying simply involved viewing current events as a bystander.

She decided to start small, locally. Placing her hands on the stump, Tasha leaned forward, peering at the pool. Clearing her mind, she focused her energies on the water. Verdant wisps of aether flowed into the basin swirling the liquid within. She redoubled her efforts, allowing the wisps of arcane energy to calm the whirlpool and flow into it with as gentle a motion as possible.

When the water stilled, Tasha dared to allow her attention to lapse enough to think of Aveline. She called her friend's face to mind. Shimmering, the water in the basin formed a misty scene beneath the surface. At the head of a grave, the knight-captain helped workers inter a body into the hole. An acolyte spoke an incantation—silent to Tasha's ears—then stepped aside, allowing the others to cover the grave with dirt.

Continuing to observe until they filled the hole, Tasha kept her focus on Aveline until the mist cleared and the scene came into sharp focus. Via the basin, she heard the metallic clang of shovels piercing mounds of soil, the twang of earth sliding off steel, and the wet thud of mud falling into the grave. The workers made small talk and macabre jokes—days of digging and scores of bodies required some measure of levity.

She watched until they finished. Aveline hammered a marker into the ground at the head of the grave, then clapped one of the workers on the back. "I think that's all for tonight. The draks brought some deer. Time for venison and ale!"

Venison, nice. Tasha's stomach grumbled. The distraction caused the scene to vanish into the basin with a splash. She jerked backward, her heart racing.

She flung open the door. After stepping through the threshold, she pulled the door shut behind her, waited for the rising staircase to meet her, and descended the steps. It collapsed after she reached the bottom. Tasha jogged over to her friend. While holding a mug of ale, Aveline ushered dirty, sweaty workers through the line. Two larger fires crackled behind the regular cooking fires, and men Tasha recognized from the city watch alternated turning deer on spits.

"Tasha, the draks came through. It's a veritable feast tonight." Aveline clicked her fingers at Silvie. "Ale for the Crow Queen."

The dark-haired woman bowed her head as she presented Tasha with a foaming mug. Tasting it, she grimaced. She took pains to replace the grimace with a smile before anyone noticed.

"I know, this batch is a bit muddy." Aveline chuckled.

I guess I wasn't fast enough.

"It was too much to expect that someone would donate a few barrels of the good ale." Aveline took Tasha aside. "With all we've seen and smelled the last few days, no one cares if the ale is a bit muddy, to be honest. How goes the research?"

Tasha drank from her mug. Small sips seemed less offensive. "I figured out how to scry through the basin. I think I can use that to access dreams."

Aveline furrowed her brow. "So, scrying lets you basically spy on people, right? You can see and hear them from afar?"

"Right."

"Dare I ask who you practiced on?"

Tasha felt her cheeks grow hot, and she lowered her eyes. "You. I watched you and the others bury that last body."

"Funny." Aveline rubbed the back of her neck. "As we were finishing up, I had the distinct feeling someone was watching us. Obviously, people could see us, we were standing right there in the open, but this was different, you know?"

Tasha had heard that sometimes especially perceptive subjects sensed someone scrying upon them. The revelation from Aveline, one of the least magically adept people Tasha had ever met, surprised her.

"It's not impossible that you felt me. I'm not very good at it yet." Tasha shrugged. "Anyway, oneiromancy, that is, magic dealing with dreams, is supposedly related to divination. They don't teach it in the Arcane University."

"Why's that?" Aveline glanced at the food line, gesturing they should make their way toward it.

"I don't know. At least, they didn't teach it in Muncifer. It's supposed to be big up north, especially in Nakambe. In Muncifer, the only person we knew of who practiced it was this creepy old man. Everyone said he used it to watch young lovers dream… and, sometimes, watch them when they weren't dreaming."

Aveline scowled. "Ugh. I don't suppose there's any way to prevent wizards from doing that to us?"

They shuffled to the end of the line. Magda slopped spoonfuls of porridge into bowls, thrusting them toward people passing by. Another man Tasha recognized as an infrequent customer, Radu, offered workers plates with piles of sliced venison. Tasha took one of each.

"There are fetishes and charms one can hang in their homes that can prevent such casual scrying." Tasha carried her plate to one of the tables. People scooted over to make room for her and Aveline. "I could make you one if you like. It takes a lot of effort, the scrying, I mean. I've never known a wizard who performed it casually. It requires total concentration, so you're really vulnerable. You can lose yourself in what you're watching."

"Well, I trust you not to do that." Aveline raised her mug. "Not sure I'd say the same for Vasco, Aita take him. Hopefully, he's resting peacefully."

Nodding, Tasha raised her mug, tapping it against Aveline's. "He's with Selene now, or maybe Dolios. Of course, he seemed like the type to revere Pacha, as well." She laughed. "Wherever he is, I'm sure there are women and wine."

Aveline smiled. "Wine, women, and song. That's a Pacha party." She climbed on the table. The dining workers hushed, fixing their attention on her. "To Vasco Dragonblade! He gave his life trying to give these people some measure of justice. May his afterlife be a never-ending party with Pacha!"

Chapter 34

Once they finished eating, Aveline and Tasha returned to the hut. Aveline stared at the closed door. Dim orange light flickered in the windows. "So, how do you get in when it's like this?"

Tasha caught up to her. "Oh, it just opens when I want to go up."

Stairs erupted from the earth, showering pebbles, sticks, and grass into the air as they rose to meet the door.

"See?"

"That's never going to get old." Aveline followed her friend up the stairs, closing the door behind them once they entered the hut.

"You could stay here until I leave, you know." Tasha patted the footboard of the bed as she passed it. "It's big enough and a damn sight more comfortable than sleeping on the ground."

Aveline rubbed her lower back. "I'm not going to argue with that, but the way I see it, the discomfort is part of my penance for failing all those folks we're putting in the ground."

Selecting an iron kettle from the hearth, Tasha then filled it with water from the basin and hung it above the crackling fire. "Isn't there a sect of Anetha that believes suffering, particularly self-inflicted, is the only way to cleanse the soul of sin?"

"Probably." Aside from having memorized the pantheon, Aveline lacked extensive knowledge of theological practices. "I don't know anyone who follows that. Of course, we don't have many worshipers of Anetha in Curton anyway."

"Isn't there a shrine to her in the citadel?" Tasha stepped over to the apothecary cabinet to rummage through the drawers.

"It wouldn't be a hall of justice without it. We keep it clean and sanctified. Even the full-time guards have families with farms, though. You're going to be a big hit when you get to town." Aveline hoped the town wouldn't expect Tasha to deliver a miraculous reversal of fortune.

"Tea?" Tasha held up a pouch containing blackened leaves.

Aveline shook her head. "No thanks. I don't want to drink too much before turning in for the night. It's dark out here without at least one full moon, and I don't want to stumble around outside this late." She laughed. "I hope you don't have to wait on those steps if you ever have an emergency."

Tasha paused, mid-measure. "I never considered that. I wonder if the former Crow Queen kept a chamber pot around here somewhere."

"You can buy one in town."

The Crow Queen finished measuring her tea into a sachet, then dropped it into the now-steaming kettle. "I'm sure Raj knows just the pot I could buy from Imrus for that purpose."

Envisioning the redsmith's indignation upon learning of the defilement of one of his prized copper pots, Aveline stifled a snort. "Aren't you fancy now? Buying a solid copper pot to piss in."

"Nothing but the finest for the Crow Queen." Laughing, Tasha flipped the bottom of her cloak outward. Aveline traced her hand around the doorframe opposite the entrance. She noticed it possessed neither a handle nor knob.

"Where does this door go?" She glanced at the nearby ladder. "I'm guessing that goes to the roof, but this is a door, right? This hut doesn't look big enough for another room."

Tasha rummaged through the cabinet for a cup. "I don't know where that goes. I opened it when I first found the hut. It was a doorway of light. Rainbow light. I decided I could investigate that some other time. For all I know, it'll suck me into the Fae Realm and leave me there."

Aveline had heard stories of the ancestral home of Calliome's faeries. She thought all the talk of purple skies and talking animals sounded a bit daft. Elves rarely passed through Curton, so, with no one who might have firsthand knowledge to ask, it remained a subject of mystery to her.

She regarded the basin. "But that water there, it worked for scrying?"

"Quite well, once I got the hang of it. I'm going to try again tonight. Maybe see if I can scry out farther than the camp. I thought I'd see if I could look in on Curton." Tasha poured her tea. "I don't suppose you'd let me try to view your dreams tonight? I don't want to try Koloman unless I'm sure he's sleeping, lest I see something I'd rather not."

Aveline laughed, despite her discomfort at the request. "I can understand that. You know, if anyone other than you were asking, I'd tell them to sit on Maris's spear."

Sitting at the table, Tasha cupped her tea in her hands. "I don't think I'll be able to manipulate your dreams, or even communicate with you in them. I certainly have no intention of trying."

The knight-captain joined her friend at the table. "I'll help any way I can, Tasha. Maybe give me an hour or so after I leave here? I plan on turning in straightaway, but it's been hard to get to sleep."

Tasha nodded at her bed. "The offer still stands. You'll be more comfortable here."

"Don't tempt me." Aveline gazed at the bed with a longing she previously reserved for her late husband. "I'm trying to be properly penitent."

The Crow Queen smiled. "All right, it's your choice. I'm not going to stand in the way of your self-flagellation."

"Ugh, it's not as bad as all that." Aveline stifled a belch, the legacy of several mugs of ale. "Maybe having that venison in my belly will help. It's been nothing but porridge for days, and bread, cheese, and jerky before that."

"I can give you something to help you sleep. The drawers are constantly stocked with everything I need. It's amazing.

Whatever magic imbues this building, it's beyond anything I've ever encountered."

The admission caused Aveline's skin to crawl. "I don't want anything to help me sleep. All this digging is doing fine with that. Just be careful with this place, all right? I'm not sure you should trust strange magical homes."

After extracting a promise she'd be careful, Aveline left Tasha to her tea. As she turned in for the evening, she hoped Tasha proved correct about not being able to manipulate dreams. She loved her friend dearly, but she preferred her dreams to remain her own.

* * *

After Aveline headed to her tent, Tasha returned to poring over the books and scrolls left by Annika for more information about oneiromancy and using the basin in the hut for scrying. While she managed to figure out basic scrying on her own, she hoped to find a nugget of wisdom that could reveal more insight.

To her dismay, she found nothing before she finished the tea. Finally, the time to attempt scrying into Aveline's dreams arrived. She put away the books and scrolls before pulling up a chair by the stump. Tasha leaned over the basin, focusing to keep the water still even as she conjured arcane energy to power the divination.

Tasha found success more quickly than during her first attempt earlier in the day. Within a few moments, she viewed her friend's sleeping form. Unsure of how to proceed, the Crow Queen fixed her attention on Aveline's head, thinking the knight-captain's mind might open to her if she exerted sufficient mental effort. Her head filled Tasha's view, growing larger and larger until it filled her sight.

Yet, Aveline's mind remained closed. Tasha continued to concentrate on breaking through, seeing Aveline's thoughts, her dreams, but she accomplished only staring at her friend's forehead until her back ached from hunching over the bowl. Slumping her shoulders, she winced, breaking the connection.

"It figures it wouldn't be that easy." Tasha leaned back in her chair, catching a flutter of movement out of the corner of her eye. Korbin and Revan perched on the open windowsill. As yet, Tasha found no way to close the windows. There never seemed to be a breeze coming through the opening. Despite having a roaring fire, the interior of the hut maintained a comfortable temperature.

"I suppose there's no shame in asking for help, eh, guys? Girls?" Tasha smirked as she regarded the birds in her windows. "I suppose I should figure that out sooner rather than later."

She grasped her necklace, pulling wisps of aether toward her. "*Ageliofedros.*" An emerald crow formed from the aetherial threads hopping onto the stump as it awaited her message.

"Seek out the archmage of the Arcane University in Muncifer. Try to catch up to my previous messenger. I need a book, a scroll, even an instructor in oneiromancy. I... I realize you've no obligation to assist me, but if you've heard of the Crow Queen, well, her mantle has been reclaimed and she's back, helping the people of Curton. I'm assisting her with this."

Tasha figured the lie would play better than just saying outright that she, herself, took possession of the mantle and was the Crow Queen. "At least tell me if I'm on the right track in using a scrying apparatus to access dreams. I'm not seeking to manipulate, or enter them, I've just been asked to help someone, the Lord Mayor of Curton, deal with some disturbing dreams, and he's very vague on what they entail. I thought if I could see them for myself, I'd maybe have a place to start. When our current... crisis... is over, I'll be happy to compensate the Arcane University in whatever way you think is appropriate. Thank you."

She sent the messenger on its way. After she did so, a thought occurred to her. Headmasters of the various Arcane Universities possessed Herald Stones, magical devices that allowed them to communicate with their peers across vast distances. They allowed the Council of Wizardry to meet, even if their members lived in remote cities.

Tasha activated the scrying basin again, this time, focusing on moving across the countryside toward the Arcane University in Muncifer. She kept one thought in her mind as she did so. *Herald stone, herald stone, herald stone.*

After a few moments of flying over fields and foothills, the craggy mountain city of Muncifer came into view. Towers flanked massive granite gates, beyond which lay rows of block-like buildings. A crescent canyon split the city. Lights from homes and shops dotted the rim and down into the canyon in some places. A citadel, which appeared to have been sculpted from the very mountains themselves, overlooked a city.

Tasha focused on the inner city, toward an area with spires and tall buildings. She approached a walled compound containing several of the spires. A force slammed into her, throwing her backward and breaking the connection.

She crashed into the floor, flipping her chair, before she landed on her legs. Squawking from the window revealed the event had not gone unnoticed by Korbin and Revan, but by the time she picked herself off the floor, they had flown away.

The room spun. Tasha grasped for a handhold within reach to keep her feet, collapsing onto the bed as darkness took her.

Chapter 35

Aveline awoke to the crash of thunder. Rain pelted her tent. The downpour seeped under the staked edges, wicking into her bedroll. Swearing, she pulled on damp clothes before crawling out of the tent into the muck. Observing most of the workers huddled in the kitchen and dining area of the camp under the pavilion tent, Aveline entered the crowd to search for Valon.

She found the lieutenant near the fire, hugging another man from town. The sky flashed with light, and another roll of thunder soon followed.

The knight-captain rubbed her hands before the fire to dry them as she greeted Valon and his friend. "I was hoping to finish up today."

"Bloody weather. Couldn't hold out for one more day." Valon's friend scowled, leaning toward the lieutenant.

"I don't believe we've met." Aveline regarded the man standing alongside Valon. Possessing arms like tree trunks and a head of short, wiry black hair, he stood slightly shorter than the lieutenant. "Care to introduce us, Valon?"

The lieutenant glanced at his companion. "Sorry, Captain. This is my betrothed, Skender."

"Oh, first I've heard." Aveline offered her hand to the man. "Congratulations to you both, nice to meet you, and I couldn't agree more about the weather."

Skender clasped her hand. "Thanks. Valon doesn't talk about work much at home, and vice versa."

Staring into the fire, Valon lowered his head. "Oh, uh, the stone masons should arrive later today. They'll be able to start work on the monument and more permanent grave markers."

"Good. Their first priority should be the grave markers." Aveline remained unsure what form the monument should take, if any. "I don't suppose we've identified anyone at all yet?"

Valon's expression brightened. "Two yesterday, just before dusk. They found the young girl, Innya, and one of the working ladies from Danica's Den who'd gone missing."

"Yana." Skender lowered his gaze, shaking his head.

"You knew her?" Biting her lip, Aveline maintained a neutral expression upon hearing the name of the butcher's daughter. "Yana, I mean?"

"I ran into her a few times at the Den." Skender shrugged. "She was an unpleasant woman. Everyone assumed she just ran off with some trader passing through, chasing the promise of gold or a better life. Most people assumed it was gold."

"That may be how they lured her out here." Aveline chewed her lip. "At least they won't all be anonymous. I suppose we should make sure Butcher Myasnik knows we've found his daughter, at last."

Valon exhaled. "Make sure he doesn't have any knives within reach. Do you think they'll want her back in town? Bury her there?"

Nearly on top of the blinding flash of lightning, a peal of thunder shook the earth. The downpour showed little sign of abating. Aveline rubbed her eyes. "I don't want to deal with hauling a body that's been dead for weeks to town. It'll attract animals from all over these hills. We'll be fighting off wolves the entire trip, maybe worse."

Skender raised his eyebrow. "You don't think wolves got better things to eat than dead girls?"

Valon shrugged. "She's really ripe. Sorry, but she'd been dead long enough that there's no other way to say it."

Aveline glanced at the sky. "Maybe it'll let up enough we can finish digging. The rain will help keep the stench at bay. It'll be better than when the sun's beating down on us."

"Thank Tinian for that." Skender raised a finger to the sky. "Though we could do without the lightning."

Aveline ran her fingers through her hair, squeezing some water out of the tight curls. "Maybe it'll blow over soon. It seems to be moving through pretty fast."

"Maybe your friend can help with that." Nudging Aveline, Valon gestured toward the hut in the distance.

I don't think Tasha's up for that. However, she didn't want to diminish anyone's confidence in the newly returned Crow Queen. "Don't the stories tell of the Crow Queen only stepping in during catastrophic storms, not just everyday squalls?"

"Yeah." Skender grinned. "But she weren't around yet when Curton flooded, so maybe she owes us one."

Aveline looked daggers at Skender. "I'll remind you Tasha lost her home, shop, and nearly her life in that flood. She wasn't Crow Queen yet, besides."

"Can't hurt to ask. She's not going to turn you into anything unnatural. You're her friend."

Valon nudged his betrothed. "Stop it. Lady Aveline will do what she thinks is best."

"Yes." Aveline nodded at Valon. "I will." She glanced over her shoulder at the hut. "I think I'll go see if Tasha can do anything about this rain."

Having borrowed a cloak from a nearby worker, Aveline pulled the hood over her head and strode into the soggy grass. While others praised Tinian for rain suppressing the ever-present stench of rot, Aveline cursed him in silence for not waiting until they had finished interring bodies for the day.

The hut squatted above the sodden turf. Despite it sitting lower than it had the night before, the door still stood out of reach. No earthen steps led up to it.

Aveline cupped her hands around her mouth. "Tasha! Tasha Crow Queen!" Upon hearing no response, she continued shouting until the rain penetrated her cloak. Finally conceding defeat, Aveline returned to the crowded food pavilion, returned the now-soaked cloak, and joined Valon and Skender by the fire.

"I couldn't get her attention." Aveline rubbed her hands over the fire to dry them. "For all I know, she can't hear people outside, even if the windows look open. That hut is… very strange."

Aveline's stomach grumbled, and she let others take her place by the fire while she sought out sustenance. Porridge was the meal of the morning, as usual, although someone had possessed sense enough to add berries to it. As Silvie slopped a ladleful into a bowl for Aveline, the knight-captain assessed the array of cups, mugs, and bowls on the table.

"Still no cream?"

"I guess the draks only brought us two deer last night." She thrust a steaming bowl at Aveline. "You could pour mead over it."

"I don't think I'm ready for that, thanks." Aveline took the bowl, then sat at the first table that made room for her. As she broke her fast, she did the only thing she could do— wait for the rain to stop.

* * *

With a groan, Tasha rolled over. Thud. She lay motionless, wondering why the floor chose to attack her before realizing she had fallen out of bed. Sitting up, she felt a sharp, stabbing pain in her skull. Dim grey light filtered in through the window, and she heard thunder in the distance.

Risking a peek at the window through a cracked-open eye, Tasha observed her crows huddled together, still perched where she last saw them when she attempted to contact the Arcane University in Muncifer via the basin.

Closing her eyes again, she sat on the hard wooden floor for a moment. Her headache grew less intense. When it subsided to a pounding sensation, she gripped the bedframe and pulled herself to her feet.

Upon standing, the pain returned. She climbed into bed, pulled the covers over her head, and basked in the darkness. Burying her head under fur blankets despite the heat of summer, Tasha drifted in and out of consciousness.

She became aware of a rhythmic pain on the back of her hand. A sort of pecking sensation. Tasha removed the covers from her head, cracking an eye to view the offending appendage.

"Caw!" Korbin hopped away from her hand and into the air, flying out the window.

Rubbing the back of her hand, Tasha rolled over, then sat on the edge of the bed. Feeling no pain in her head when she stood, she shuffled to the window. Outside, she noted evidence of an earlier storm, and she judged it to be midafternoon based on the location of the brightest area of the overcast sky.

Stifling a yawn, she retrieved the kettle from the hearth. Tasha filled it with water, then rummaged through the apothecary drawers. She made a small sachet containing willow bark, turmeric, and cloves before dropping it into the kettle.

While waiting for the tea to brew, she stretched. "I could use a bath."

Shimmering, the mysterious doorframe displayed an image of a sylvan glade. Tasha craned her neck, peering through it. Trees with brilliant purple and cerulean leaves swayed in the breeze against a pastel sky streaked with rosy clouds. Water cascaded down a cliff into a crystalline pool, and the scent of lilacs and lavender wafted into the hut.

When she reached the door, Tasha extended her hand. It passed through with only a hint of resistance. The air on the other side felt comfortable and warm. For a moment, Tasha considered exploring the glade.

"No… I don't know enough yet. What if I can't get back?"

She returned to the hearth to pour her tea. The bitter brew would chase away any lingering traces of her headache. While she sipped the hot liquid, she searched through the larder. She settled on a block of hard, yellow cheese, finger-sized dried sausages, and an apple. Without bothering to find a plate, Tasha set them all on the table. She noted the doorway to the wooded clearing reverted to its plain appearance sometime during her search for nourishment.

After she ate, Tasha splashed water from the basin onto her face, made her hair appear as though she hadn't just rolled out of bed with a hangover, and left the hut to search among the workers for Aveline.

Tasha contemplated her discarded boots as she traveled through the camp, acknowledging her connection with Gaia was stronger without foot coverings. Forcing herself to ignore the discomfort, she hoped, in time, she'd become accustomed to the sensation of wet grass and mud squishing between her toes.

Tasha found Aveline talking with Lieutenant Valon near the mine entrance. She waited for them to finish their conversation before approaching and greeting each in turn. Valon bowed and went about his business.

"Where have you been? I tried shouting up at you during the storm this morning." Aveline's clothes still remained damp from working in the rain earlier. A streak of dried mud stained her cheek.

"I'm sorry. I was… out."

"Out where?"

Tasha pursed her lips. "Out. Unconscious. I had a brilliant thought last night."

"Oh, what was that?" Aveline's face remained expressionless despite Tasha's revelation.

"Well, I sent a message to the Arcane University asking for help with dream magic. Then I remembered all the headmasters have Herald Stones." Tasha clenched her hand.

"They're magical crystals about the size of my fist that let them communicate across great distances. I thought maybe I could use the basin, find one by scrying, and communicate to the Arcane University directly."

Aveline shook her head. "I have no idea if that makes sense or not." Crossing her arms, she leaned against a boulder.

"The principle is logically sound." Tasha nodded in assurance of her conviction. "I successfully scried on Muncifer, but I think the Arcane University has a scrying shield or something. When I got close to it, it was like I suddenly slammed into a wall."

Tasha punched her palm. "It broke the connection, and I was thrown backward. It was all I could do to make it into bed before I passed out. When I awoke, it was raining, but I had the worst headache of my life. I pulled the covers over my head and fell back to sleep until just a little while ago."

Aveline patted her friend's arm. "But you're all right? You're not hurt?"

Holding up her hand, Tasha shook her head. "I'm fine. The headache is gone. But I discovered something new about the hut."

"Dare I ask?" Aveline raised an eyebrow. "I'm wary of that thing, you know."

"I haven't sensed any malevolence from it. It just... is. Anyway, I thought about how much I'd like to have a bath, and that back door that isn't a door disappeared. I saw a glade through it."

"Like a forest or something?"

Tasha ran her fingers through her tangled hair. "The colors were bright and otherworldly. There was a waterfall and a pool. It looked so inviting and warm. Like a secret pool just for me. That doorway is a portal of some sort. It might be one way the Crow Queen always seemed to travel to so many places so quickly in the old stories."

Aveline exhaled. "Well, I don't know anything about that. You didn't go through it, did you?"

"No." Tasha shook her head. "I was afraid I wouldn't know how to get back."

"Good thinking." Aveline pointed at the cemetery. "We're almost finished here. We're going to start packing up tonight, break camp tomorrow, and head back to town. Then, I guess after we leave, the draks are going to move into the mine. I've got some folk down there now making sure the passages to the crystal cave and such are all blocked off."

Tasha worked a knot out of her hair. "I suppose someone should tell the draks about the chaos rift."

"You got here pretty quick. You found the hut about a day out of town, right, in the other direction?"

Tasha nodded. "Yes."

"Stick around, explain the situation to the draks, then meet up with me in Curton. I bet you'll pass us." Aveline snorted. "I'd kind of like to see how that hut actually moves."

"I could do that. It'll give me some time to practice scrying before Koloman catches up with us again."

"Good." Aveline pulled Tasha into a hug. "I'm heading down into the mine. Do your thing, and if I don't see you again today, we'll catch up in town."

"All right." Tasha watched her friend leave.

Aveline called to her before disappearing into the darkness, "And don't go through any strange portals!"

Chapter 36

The sun blazed high in Calliome's sky by the time Aveline and the workers finally broke camp and started their trek back to Curton. The stonemasons had everything they needed for the short term, since they were staying behind to construct the monument and permanent grave markers. Aveline trusted they could work around the draks, should they arrive before the masons finished. She promised them she would arrange a regular flow of supplies once she returned to town.

Aveline rode with Valon in a cart near the front of the procession, but as the wagon bounced over every rock and divot, she soon regretted not choosing to walk. When they finally stopped for the night, she ached. Even an extra mug of muddy ale did little to dull the pain. Despite her discomfort, she slept soundly. The next day, the workers made an early start. Fair weather held all morning, and by midday, the entrance to Curton once again came into view.

Aveline split from the group as soon as they passed through the gate and rushed to her home. She didn't bother closing her door behind her before rummaging through her wardrobe for a change of clothes. Gathering them into a bundle, she then went into Old Town, making her way to the riverside bathhouse.

By the time she finished bathing, her clothes were returned to her freshly laundered, although still damp. She took them home, donned her armor and city watch tabard, and returned to the streets of her town to head to the citadel.

Even though she'd been gone barely ten days, the hard work folks put toward cleaning up from the flood made Curton appear, if not new, at least, not like it had just suffered a catastrophe. Gone were the groups of people cleaning debris and repairing structures. In their place, folk bustled, going about their regular business.

As she passed through the market, she heard a familiar voice hawking Imrus's fine Curtonian copper pots. Ra-Jareez's embellishments of Imrus's skilled work gave one the impression he sold the handiwork of Adranus himself. She took a circuitous route down a different row as to not become distracted by the faelix's salesmanship.

"Hey, Lady Captain!" The gruff, bellowing oroq voice felled Aveline's good mood.

Gritting her teeth, Aveline turned. Therkla jogged toward her, a hand on the hilt of her sword. Aveline waited until the oroq woman reached her, then extended her hand.

"Good to see you again."

Narrowing her eyes, the oroq stared at the outstretched hand as if it were a viper poised to strike. "You owe me money."

"So I do. Your friend, Aerik, too. Is he around?"

"He's at Danica's Den."

Aveline gestured for Therkla to accompany her before resuming her route. "I trust I can give you his payment as well and you'll see that he gets it?"

"Of course."

"I'm headed to the citadel now. Come with me, and I'll get your money." Aveline was not averse to paying Therkla her promised reward. However, part of her had hoped the oroq woman would consider her labor a gift to the townsfolk of Curton, chiefly because they didn't actually save anyone.

"I was beginning to think you weren't ever coming back. Aerik and I would have left town by now were we not waiting on our money."

Aveline stifled her initial reply. "Your dedication is admirable."

"Think what you will. Mercenaries get paid." Therkla hawked a gob of spittle into a nearby puddle. "Besides, we heard of an expedition down south we want to join. This money will help us get there."

"What expedition would that be?" The more Therkla spoke, the more resentful Aveline grew that the woman remained so adamant about being paid. "A quest for snow?"

If Therkla detected Aveline's contempt, she made no sign of it. "I've been hearing of my folk heading west, looking for Ankor. Whole strongholds are emptying out. I want to try to catch one of them before summer ends."

Aveline had heard stories about the riches of Ankor—the ancestral home of the oroqs, lost since The Sundering—reward to whoever proved brave enough to travel across the Northern Watch through to the southern tip of the Western Wastes. Every story told of different horrors—feral dragons, demons, hordes of boggins descending upon unwary travelers.

The citadel loomed before them. Seizing Aveline's arm, Therkla stopped the knight-captain from opening the door. "You'll understand if I don't want to see the inside of your jail again. I'll just wait here for you, if it's all the same."

"I don't keep the money inside a jail cell, but whatever suits your fancy. I'll be right back." Aveline trudged up the steps, then entered the building. A strongbox in a vault past the armory contained the city watch's funds. She and Lieutenant Valon carried the only keys. She greeted the constables as she passed, retrieved the promised payment, and met Therkla at the bottom of the steps by the front door.

She counted out the coins into Therkla's hand. "No one who goes looking for Ankor has ever returned, you know."

"So I hear." Gazing at Aveline, Therkla licked one of her tusks. "This might be the last time you see me. Want to have a wild night? You'll never forget it."

"I don't doubt it, but I'll pass."

"Your loss." Grinning, Therkla shoved the money into her belt pouch. "The stories are all boggin spit anyway. If no one ever comes back, where do the stories come from?"

"You make a good point."

"Besides, the wastes aren't the end of civilization. There's good farmland between the western mountains and the ocean, I hear. Skogn is even further west than Ankor is supposed to be, and the Watchfolk there do fine." Therkla offered her hand to Aveline.

The knight-captain clasped the oroq's hand. "Safe journeys. I hope you find what you're looking for out there."

"Fortune and glory, Lady Knight. Fortune and glory."

* * *

By the time Tasha met the draks and explained the situation with the chaos rift, the caravan of gravediggers had already begun its journey back to Curton. Once underway, Tasha found not overtaking them a difficult challenge. To keep from passing them and arriving in town a full day ahead of Aveline, she veered south into the more difficult terrain of the higher foothills.

Despite the dense foliage, the hut seemed to bob and weave of its own accord, fitting through spaces Tasha judged too narrow. She needed only to focus on where she wanted to go, and the hut selected its own path. Yet, despite the bumpy topography, the interior of the hut remained still.

By dusk, Tasha found a clearing between Miners' Gate and the river. Although Aveline's caravan would not arrive until sometime the next day, she settled in for the night despite wanting desperately a bath. She considered entering the sylvan glade, but Aveline's warning echoed in her thoughts. Tasha's own trepidation about being able to return reinforced her decision to patronize the public baths in Old Town in the morning.

When dawn came, she checked on Aveline's progress with Revan, then sent Korbin to check on Lord Mayor Koloman. She caught the caravan as they were breaking their fast, but all else seemed in order. Koloman's estate seemed quiet, as well.

After leaving the hut, she headed toward town, joining the road just out of sight of Miners' Gate. Even early in the morning, the town seemed abuzz with gossip, much of it centering around a woman claiming to be the Crow Queen. Tasha, attempting to appear uninterested, focused on her destination.

After a refreshing visit to the baths, she stopped at the bakery for a sweet roll, then headed for the market. She crossed the river only to find all the stalls closed. Tasha frowned in dismay, cursing herself for losing track of which days were market days. She'd hoped to visit Imrus's stall to check on Raj and his sister. Not knowing the location of Imrus's workshop, Tasha headed to Danica's Den to check on Yun.

Proceeding along River Road, she saw her old home and apothecary across the river. Living there had been lonely when she first arrived in Curton over a decade ago, but she'd made do. Within a year, it truly felt like home. She met Aveline about the same time. From the side of the road, Tasha stared at her house, brushing away hair the light breeze blew across her face.

So much has changed in such a short time. I know more now than I did then. Yet, I feel like I have no idea what I'm doing. She became aware of someone speaking to her.

"I say, you're the apothecary, Tasha, yes?"

"Yes, yes, I am." Tasha turned to regard the person who had spoken. An older, taller man, with thinning grey hair, gazed upon her. She recognized him as a member of the town council, but she did not recall his name.

"I thought your shop was on the other side of the river."

"It is." Tasha pointed. "Just there. Everything was ruined in the flood."

"Yes, I noticed you've been closed. I've been trying to find you." Holding up a gnarled hand, he flexed it. "My joints have been aching something awful, and I was hoping you had a remedy."

He glanced across the river, then at her. "I suppose if it's all ruined, though, I'm out of luck."

Tasha cupped his hand in hers, noticing his extremity felt unusually warm. "Not necessarily, Councilor. I found a new place, and I've restocked. It's just outside Miners' Gate, in a clearing between the gate and the Copper Run."

Furrowing his brow, he blinked. "In the forest?"

"Yes, but it's not far, just a few minutes from the gate." She patted his hand. "Come see me this afternoon. I have a few errands here in town to take care of."

"I will, thank you."

A raucous roar arose from Danica's Den, just up the street. The councilor frowned. "Though, I don't know what business you'd have in this part of town. All sorts of unsavory types are around these parts."

I might wonder the same about you. Tasha offered him a smile instead of a retort. "A friend of mine was down on his luck. He got a job at Danica's Den. I thought I would see how he's coping."

"Of course. I didn't mean to imply you'd be involved in anything untoward." He touched her arm, recoiling slightly when he felt the feathers of her cloak. "Would you mind if I told some others where to find you? We've been sorely missing you. The other herbalists in town just don't measure up."

"I don't mind." She bowed to him. "That's why I'm here."

After the councilor departed, Tasha crossed the street in front of Danica's Den. It had been years since she stepped foot in the place. The commotion coming from the building surprised her. Tasha expected the establishment received most of its business later in the evening. The structure resembled a nondescript warehouse someone stuck a windmill on top of. She suspected it was once a utilitarian building that Danica had added onto over the years.

A young dwarf held the door open for her. A recent arrival, Tasha had seen him around town and believed he worked to repay a debt of some sort. Thanking him, she entered the dark, smoke-filled tavern. Four townsfolk clustered around one of the gambling tables. The rest of the bar area was empty. A cheer arose overhead.

She nodded at the bartender as she approached. "I'm looking for Yun, the caprikin?"

The barkeep, wiping sweat off his brow with a dirty rag, pointed toward the ceiling. "Upstairs. All betting is off, though."

"Thank you." Tasha hurried away, having no intention of drinking or betting. Several wrought-iron spiral staircases led to the upper levels of Danica's Den. She chose the nearest and ascended. Pipe smoke mingled with the musty scent of burning herbs. Although the stairs continued to a third floor, a crowd of howling townsfolk clustered around a fenced-in arena comprising most of the second floor. Danica herself, a matronly woman with a mane of greying black hair, stood on a box overlooking the arena. Wearing a red-leather-trimmed black dress, she resembled a seductive sorceress one heard about in stories.

Her fashion choices deliberately led one to such impressions; of that, Tasha harbored no doubt. She wound her way through the crowd toward the arena. Two men challenged Yun, who, bare-fisted and bare-chested, wore only a loin cloth.

Feeling rage rise from the pit of her stomach, Tasha shoved her way through the crowd toward Danica. Out of the corner of her eye, she saw Yun clobber one man with a right hook. Spinning, he shoved the other man with a cloven hoof on his riposte. The first man roared, charging. Lowering his head, Yun, braced himself.

The man, upon colliding with Yun's horns, collapsed to the floor, where he lay motionlessly. Upon Yun raising both arms, the crowd roared in delight.

Tasha seized Danica's arm, spinning her. "What is the meaning of this?"

Her voice reverberated through the arena, louder than she expected. The crowd fell silent, backing away. Tasha's cloak billowed behind her, appearing for a moment as a massive pair of crow's wings.

Danica glared at her, a mixture of fear and defiance in her steel eyes. "How dare you come into my establishment…"

"Crow Queen." Yun approached the women, bowing.

"I was told Yun worked here." Tasha felt bile rise in the back of her throat. "I come to visit, and I see you forcing him to fight for the amusement of the townsfolk?"

Danica threw off Tasha's grip. "Force? What sort of establishment do you think I'm running?" She gestured at the caprikin. "This was his idea."

"Yun fight. Make good money. People here"—Yun bared his teeth at the nearest spectator—"soft as mud."

The man laughed. "Ha! I won five crowns on you!"

Tasha's cheeks grew hot. "This was your idea, Yun?"

Bouncing his head up and down, the caprikin accepted a mug of ale thrust at him from behind Danica. "Warrior. Need practice. Throwing out drunks not practice."

"Here, move out of the way. It's my turn." Aerik shoved spectators aside, stopping short when he saw Tasha.

He bowed, pulling the nearest man down with him. "Crow Queen. Come to see us fight? I am honored." Rising, he belched. "Just passing the time until Therkla gets back with our money so we can leave town. Yun thinks he can take me. Well, I'm about to show him what Watchfolk are made of!"

"Ice and stone," a man in the crowd shouted.

"Ice and stone, fire and steel!" Aerik raised a fist above his head.

"Yellow snow!"

Aerik spun on the man behind him, then pushed him backward. "Maris take you repeatedly with her bloody spear. Come to the Watches and see how you fare, mudder."

"Silence!" Raising her arms, Danica shouted. She then sneered at Tasha, "Well, 'Crow Queen'? Will you permit me to continue to run my business as I see fit?"

Tasha lowered her eyes. "My apologies. I misunderstood what was going on here."

"Stay and watch." Aerik took her arm. "I'll win for you, Crow Queen. Maybe you'll favor me, eh? Therkla and I have a long journey ahead of us."

"I have no desire to watch blood sport." Tasha extracted herself from Aerik's grip. "I wish you well on your journey. I have a place in a clearing between Miners' Gate and the river. Perhaps you and Therkla will stop by on your way out of the city."

"Yun?" She turned to the caprikin. He wiped foam from ale off his lips. "Come see me if you need something for bruising or aches. There's a glade outside of Miners' Gate, toward the river. Understand?"

Yun thumped his chest. "Put money on Yun. You win."

Tasha left the men to their fighting, descending the stairs two at a time, stopping for no one until she reached the safety of the street.

Chapter 37

Aveline returned to the citadel after paying Therkla. She propped her feet on her desk, reveling in the first moment of relative peace since she left for the mine. *Home would be better, but duty calls.*

Lieutenant Valon entered carrying two stoneware jugs. He placed one on Aveline's desk. "Fresh cider from Rockbreak Orchard, m'lady."

Midsummer rock apples from the orchard provided the only source for cider this time of year. Aveline often wondered how they managed to ripen such delicious fruit so early in the season. Every time she asked, the dwarf Ogden Rockbreaker only smiled his gap-toothed grin and said, "Magic."

"Magic cider from magic dwarves." Aveline popped the cork. Bringing the bottle to her nose, she inhaled spicy-sweet and floral aromas. "Has anyone seen Tasha? She should have been back by now."

"There have been sightings here and there. The bakery, the baths, the market."

Aveline corked the cider jug. "The market's closed today, isn't it?"

"Yes, maybe she forgot."

Sighing, Aveline leaned back in her chair. "I could sleep for a week."

"Go home, then." Valon opened the door to the larder. "It's quiet here. I can send someone to fetch you if something happens."

"It's all the way across town. Maybe I'll bunk here."

The door slammed open. A moustached, short-haired man, entered. The tabard he wore bore the markings of the same knightly order to which Aveline belonged. She noticed a short, triangular-shaped blade where his left hand .

She remained in her seat with her feet propped on the desk. "Shut the door."

Ignoring her, he strode forward. "I am Sir Maxim Arshavin, Knight of the Order of the Shield, duly appointed by Her Highness Princess Valene of Almeria. I have been to Dawnwatch, and I found it to be in shameful disrepair. I demand to see the knight-commander of the garrison."

Aveline pushed herself away from the desk. "I am Lady Aveline, Knight-Captain of the Order of the Shield, Watch Captain of Curton, and Dawnwatch has no garrison, you pompous git. It was abandoned by Prince Gavril over twenty years ago."

"Gavril is dead, a traitor to the land. Valene rules Etrunia—"

"I'm not stupid." Glaring at the man, Aveline returned to her seat. "We do hear news out this far. Now, what do you want, Sir Maxim?"

"Princess Valene is taking stock of her lands. I've been charged with inspecting the garrison, woman."

Slamming her fist on the desk, Aveline snapped to her feet. "I will have my rank from you. You may address me as 'Lady Aveline' or 'Knight-Captain Aveline.' Do you understand?" Normally, she did not stand on protocol, but pompous outsiders condescending to her caused a rare fury to rise in her belly.

"Of course." Maxim crossed his fist over his chest, standing at attention. "My apologies, Lady Aveline. I was not informed a member of the peerage was stationed in this mudhole, though I must wonder why you have not taken charge of Dawnwatch as would be your duty according to the charter—"

"Look around you. How many knights do you see?" She gestured to the room. Valon moved behind the desk to stand at her side. "The citadel belongs to the city watch. I am the only knight of Etrunia remaining in Curton. Sir Agnar died many years ago after watching Etrunia neglect Dawnwatch's garrison for decades. They never sent reinforcements, never responded to his requests for aid. One old man and his ward could not garrison Dawnwatch by themselves."

Not that I have to explain myself to you. Aveline gritted her teeth, too tired to deal with people like Maxim.

The knight reached into his satchel, produced a document secured with wax bearing the royal seal, and thrust it at Aveline. "Our orders. Times have changed."

Taking the document, Aveline sat. After breaking the seal, she skimmed its contents. "This doesn't apply here. Dawnwatch fell into disrepair over twenty years ago. There hasn't been a garrison in that long."

"One could argue Sir Agnar abandoned his post." Maxim maintained his stone-steady stance of attention.

"A fool could argue that." Aveline rolled the document, then tossed it on her desk. "One should, instead, argue that Sir Agnar and his ward were abandoned by the crown to fend for themselves, and they did so by taking charge of the Curton constabulary. I have protected these people, and I've dispensed justice here most of my life."

"Nevertheless, our mission is to rebuild the garrison."

"That may be *your* mission. I will not abandon my charges here."

"Indeed." Valon put his hand on the back of Aveline's chair. "Lady Aveline is our primary defense against the odious troll who calls himself Lord Mayor of Curton. He'd have us all toiling for his own enrichment were it not for her and the Crow Queen, Lady Tasha."

"Lady Tasha? Crow Queen?" Maxim raised his eyebrows. "Another member of the peerage this far from Almeria? To which family does she belong?"

"'Lady' is a moniker of respect. Tasha is just an apothecary who is well-regarded by the townsfolk."

"And she is the Crow Queen reborn." Valon's voice carried a hint of protest.

Aveline held up her hand. "Which probably means nothing to one such as Maxim who grew up pampered, raised in privilege at court."

"I protest, m'lady." Maxim glared at Valon. "I was not raised at court. I earned my knighthood."

"As did I." Aveline rose from her desk. "Valon, set up Sir Maxim with quarters here in the citadel. I'm going on my rounds"—she glared at Maxim—"as duty demands."

* * *

Embarrassed by her misinterpretation of events at Danica's Den, Tasha hightailed it to the hut and awaited the few people she expected the councilor to bring with him. She instructed Korbin and Revan to keep watch for anyone approaching while she acquainted herself with all the reagents in the apothecary cabinet.

In addition to the herbs and compounds she was already familiar with, the cabinet contained numerous powders she had not previously encountered. While she waited, she found a quill, ink, and parchment, then made a note of which drawers contained unknown substances. Tasha hoped she wouldn't need to conduct alchemical experiments to determine what they were. When she finished, she reread as much of the diary's instructions as she could.

"Caw, caw, caw!"

Tasha closed the diary, glancing toward the window. Korbin hopped back and forth on the sill, seemingly agitated.

"What's out there..." Tasha's jaw dropped as she watched a procession of townsfolk approach the hut. Each carried with them an offering. Some brought food, others small casks of what Tasha assumed were ale or mead, while others brought livestock. Revan hopped out of the window and flew away. Taken aback at the sight of the multitude below, Tasha realized she could not recall even one of the diary's instructions on how to serve petitioners.

That sylvan glade looks really good right now, one-way trip or no. From the corner of her eye, she saw the back door transform into a portal.

"Oh, for the love of Selene, I didn't mean I was actually going to run away." Tasha waved at the door, hoping it would revert to its normal appearance. After a moment, it did. She circled the central stump, wracking her brain on how best to handle the crowd forming below.

"I wish I'd paid more attention when people talked about the old days and the Crow Queen in the tavern." Taking in a deep breath, she pulled open the door. Once the stairs formed, she descended, carefully taking one step at a time while scanning for familiar faces. A few townsfolk stood out in the crowd that comprised mostly people she had not met.

The councilor to whom she'd spoken earlier in the day stood near the front of the crowd. A few steps from the bottom, she clapped her hands to gain everyone's attention. "I wasn't expecting so many. Those of you who were customers of mine at the apothecary in town and need more teas or balms, form a line to my right."

She pointed to avoid confusion. "Those of you who came for the Crow Queen's help with something you think I should be able to help with because of stories you've heard, form a line to my left."

"Finally, those of you who just want to see the Crow Queen for yourself, stay where you are." She spread her arms. "Now you've seen me. I am not Annika, but the Mantle of the Crow Queen has chosen me. I will tell you now that I am still learning what all this means."

She whispered, "So, go easy on me."

Tasha gestured toward the councilor. "If you will, sir. I believe we had an appointment. Step forward."

"Ah, yes." He approached her, rubbing his hands together. "You mentioned you had something to help with my joint pain."

"I do." She raised her voice to project over the crowd. "Is anyone else here for relief from joint pain or other aches?"

Several voices murmured their assent. Tasha bade them to come forward and join the councilor at the bottom of the steps. She took a head count, eyeing the piglet one of her customers held. "I'll be back momentarily. I don't have anywhere to keep livestock at the moment, so if you could just pay me a talon each, that will be sufficient."

She returned to the hut. "Korbin, let me know if anyone tries to come up."

"Caw!"

She prepared several small bundles of turmeric, white willow bark, cloves, cat's claw vine, and rosemary, then carried them down and handed them to each person waiting. "Brew a tea with these sachets and drink it once a day. It should help. There's enough for three or four brews, depending on how strong you make it. I should have more by the time you need it."

Thanking her, they each departed. She worked through more than half the crowd in a similar fashion, taking care of everyone with a commonplace ailment such as she would have seen in her apothecary.

Tasha called over the first of the people specifically in need of the Crow Queen's aid. A blonde woman with rosy cheeks waddled forward, holding her swollen belly.

I hope she's not expecting me to midwife. "What can I do for you?"

"Me ma told me you could help me with me baby." The woman beckoned for Tasha to lean closer, lowering her voice. "I want to know if it's a boy or girl… and who the father is."

"Who the fa… you don't know?"

The woman bit the tip of her finger. "Well, it could be Bela. But there was that dwarf about the same time. He looked so handsome, and I'd had a bit too much to drink, so he looked even more handsome. And he had a big nose—you know what they say. Nice fella, but he up and went home the next morning. Said he was just passing through."

Tasha remembered reading something about using the basin to sex babies. She took the woman's hand. "Come with me, and I'll see what I can tell you. What's your name?"

"Ioana."

Once they were inside, Tasha shut the door. The woman gazed around the hut, whistling in appreciation. "This is nice."

"The good news is the father is Bela, unless there are other men you've been with you haven't mentioned."

The woman's eyes widened. "You know just from holding me hand?"

Tasha took her hands, shaking her head. "Dwarves and humans can't have babies together."

Ioana breathed an audible sigh of relief, and her shoulders sagged. "Oh, thank Cybele! I'd been envisioning this little runty thing coming out looking like a toothless boggin."

Shaking her head and suppressing an exasperated sigh, Tasha pulled over a chair for Ioana and directed her to sit. She stepped to the opposite side of the basin. "I've never done this before, so I don't know if it's going to work."

"Will it hurt?"

Tasha shook her head. "You won't feel a thing." *Probably.*

According to the diary, sexing an unborn child essentially involved divination, but Tasha wouldn't actually need to utilize the basin or invoke any spells during the process as long as she remained in the hut. She lowered her head and closed her eyes, concentrating on the water much as she had the last time she'd attempted to scry.

She focused on the woman, then on the unborn child in her belly. In a flash, she saw the boy. His club foot drew her attention. She gasped, in spite of herself. The vision vanished.

"What? What did you see? Am I going to die in childbirth?"

"I did not see that." Tasha avoided Ioana's gaze. "I saw a boy. He will be born with a deformity. A club foot."

"Oh, well, that's all right. Me brother was born with two of 'em. Me ma knows how to fix them well enough." Ioana rapped her knuckles on the flat part of the stump. "'Ere, me ma says you want a price for such information. She said you'd want me baby, but I thought that sounded steep. I knowed I should have asked before you did your magic, but I wanted to know."

Tasha smiled. "I don't want your baby. I'm not going to exact a blood price for anything. I can't imagine ever doing that."

"I can bring you a leg of mutton. Me da's slaughtering one of our sheep in a few days."

"That would be fine." Tasha led Ioana to the door, then opened it, detaining her until the stairs fully formed. "I enjoy roast mutton."

She glanced at her hearth to make sure she could indeed cook a roast over it, noting hardware for affixing a spit above the fire. *Did I not notice that before?* "Send the next one up, if you would, please, Ioana."

"Thank you, Crow Queen. I told me ma you weren't a bad sort. She only listens to the bad stories. I like the good ones instead."

Chapter 40

Aveline's started her rounds by heading straight for Tasha's favorite bakery so she could inquire as to the whereabouts of her friend. While the staff confirmed Tasha stopped by for pastries, they couldn't tell the knight-captain where she went afterward. A customer spoke up as he handed over several talons for his bread.

"I heard people saying she's calling herself the Crow Queen now. She's holding court in the clearing just outside Miners' Gate." He collected his loaves. "You know the one, close to the river? Bunch of bollocks if you ask me."

"I know the clearing." Aveline contemplated the egg-washed buns sitting on the counter. The bakers often filled them with a hash of eggs, sausage, and potatoes. She pointed, holding up two fingers.

"She *is* the Crow Queen, by the way." Aveline chuckled. "I can hardly believe it myself. But I've seen… I never thought I'd see a walking hut."

The customers in the bakery chattered, rehashing most of the rumors Aveline grew up hearing. She tossed a talon on the counter after selecting the buns. "Times are changing, I guess."

Aveline carried the pastry with her through Miners' Gate. Finding the clearing proved easy, as steady streams of people traveled toward and away from the site. Gathered nearby, the crowd seemed content to observe as each person, in turn, ascended the steps. Some folk brought livestock, baubles, or baked goods. She regarded the buns she held. *She probably has her fill.*

Making her way to the crowd, she spotted a crow overlooking the clearing on a nearby branch. "Hey, are you Revan or Korbin?"

"Caw!"

"Go tell Tasha I'm here." Aveline did not expect the crow to follow her command, but the bird hopped into the air, then flew through the open window.

As she waited, Aveline became aware of people glaring at her. She displayed the pastries. "I'm not jumping the line. I'm just making a delivery."

In truth, Aveline had intended to spend some time with Tasha. Having buried thirty of Curton's townsfolk, she needed time with a friend, and the Crow Queen remained the closest one she had.

Tasha appeared with an old man at the top of the stairs. She smoothed his wispy white hair, then helped him descend to the forest floor. As he left, she eyed the contents of Aveline's hands. "Are those what I think they are?"

"Fresh from the bakery." Aveline brought one to her nose, inhaling the delicious aroma. "Sausage, egg, some herbs. I was hungry, and I thought you could use something to eat."

"Come on up for a minute. I don't have a lot of time." She turned to the people in line. "I'll be just a moment. Lady Aveline is a dear friend, and I need to speak with her about something very important."

The knight-captain preceded Tasha up the steps. "Here." Aveline placed the buns on the table. "I see plenty of people have brought offerings." She pointed at the gifts scattered about—several pies, small casks of ale, and two bottles of wine.

Tasha laughed. "One woman was told I was going to take her unborn child."

"So is this how this works?" Aveline examined the pies. "People bring you treats, and you cure all their ills?"

"I don't know how it's supposed to work. So far, I've been doing minor prognostications along with the type of herbalism work I used to do in town." Using a knife she retrieved from the larder, Tasha cut into one of the buns. She handed half to Aveline.

The yeasty dough provided the vessel for the savory fillings within. It took much of Aveline's self-control to keep from shoveling it in.

"I'm going to move."

Aveline stopped mid-bite, peering at Tasha. "Hmm?"

"I can't have crowds like this. I can't learn what I'm supposed to be if I'm constantly guessing the sex of people's babies or telling them if their son is ever going to marry. There are fortune-tellers at the market for that."

Swallowing, Aveline reached for one of the bottles of wine and uncorked it. She poured a goblet for Tasha and one for herself. "What if you're only supposed to be what you're comfortable being?"

"Thinking about that makes my head hurt." Tasha guzzled the wine. "I'll stay close, but I'm not going to advertise my whereabouts. People will need to seek me out. I'll send Revan or Korbin to you with a note or conjure one of my magical messengers, though, so you'll always know where to find me."

"I appreciate that." Aveline refilled Tasha's glass. "I'm going to miss stopping by on my rounds."

"You're always welcome. I wanted to ask you something."

"What?"

"The diary hints at a lot of things, but it doesn't outright say much." Tasha sipped her wine. "Annika didn't finish it before her sister killed her, but she indicated she used the portal in the hut to travel."

Aveline narrowed her eyes. "You aren't considering…"

"I'm going to start small at first." Tasha put her hand on Aveline's. "From here to your house, with your permission. If it's a one-way trip, at least I won't have far to walk. I promise you I won't try anywhere farther until I'm absolutely certain I can get back."

Aveline waved her hand toward the door. "Where would you go? That sylvan glade for a bath? You can do that in town."

"There, yes." Tasha chuckled. "But, more importantly, I could go to the libraries of the Arcane University and try to learn as much as I can about the history of the Crow Queen. What this all means... there has to be some information somewhere."

"The Crow Queen is supposed to be a servant of Cybele, right?" The solution seemed obvious to Aveline. "Ask Mother Anya."

"Yes, I will speak to her. The Crow Queen, er, I am supposedly also a servant of Artume and Gaia. Selene must be involved somehow too. The number of enchantments in this hut alone indicates that. There's a temple to Selene in Muncifer, the biggest I know of. They must know something or know someone who does."

Aveline sighed. "That's so far away."

"But if the portal allows instantaneous travel, it won't take any time at all." Tasha squeezed the knight-captain's hand. "Aveline, I have to figure this out. I need to know why... why me?"

"I've been wondering that myself." Aveline loved her friend dearly, but the sorceress didn't seem particularly special to her. Even with the feathered cloak, she was just Tasha. Besides which, Aveline did not believe people possessed special destinies.

"Honestly, I don't think you can help me find the answers. Mother Anya might be able to give me some clues, but I think she's just as puzzled as I am. Or she accepts it as being Cybele's will."

Aveline agreed Tasha made a good point, and she took no offense at the suggestion she could not help find the answers the Crow Queen sought. "All right, well, look. Just... come by my place tonight. I'm planning on going home around dusk. We'll discuss it more then."

"I'll bring a pie." Smiling, Tasha glanced at the table. "Or two."

Aveline laughed. "We can eat ourselves to sleep." She moved to leave.

"Send the next one up, would you, please?" Tasha pressed her hands together. "Maybe do another favor for me, and tell everyone I'm tired and need rest after that one?"

"It'd be my pleasure." Aveline trotted down the steps, her armor clanking as she bounced to a stop. She pointed at the nearest petitioner. "You there, the Crow Queen will see you now. The rest of you, go home."

The command caused a round of protest to arise from the crowd. "She needs rest and time to eat and bathe. None of you are entitled to demand more of her time than she's willing to give." Aveline clapped her hands together. "Now, disperse. Don't make me bring the city watch out here."

Despite their grumbling, the crowd complied. A few people lingered, hoping to catch the Crow Queen's attention, but Aveline offered them a withering stare. Approaching each one in turn and physically turning them around, she pointed them toward town with a final command to return home.

Aveline followed the stragglers, ensuring, under her watchful eye, they all reached the city gate. Observing the sun still fairly high in the sky, she resigned herself to continuing her rounds.

* * *

After the last petitioner reached the bottom of the staircase, Tasha shut the door. She organized all the gifts people brought her, storing the wine and ale in the larder, and arranging the pies on the table, a half-dozen in all. Fortunately, no one brought her any uncooked meats as of yet.

Contemplating the back door, she pulled the cloak tight around her. She never felt too warm, even when wearing it inside the hut on a hot day.

"So, do I just think or speak a destination?" Tasha decided to test her idea. "I want to go to Muncifer."

The door shimmered before it shifted to a street scene. Stonework buildings lined a cobblestone road. Humans, draks, and minotaurs shuffled past, unaware anyone watched from afar. A striped drak with wings wrestled with an infant, and he glanced at a passing minotaur pushing a cart of potatoes. She couldn't hear their conversation, but she observed the drak laugh at something the minotaur said.

No, maybe I'd rather go to the Cybele's Church, in Curton instead. Merely thinking her desire resulted in a similar effect. Instead of a city street, Tasha viewed the interior of the church. Standing near the altar, Mother Anya lectured to several acolytes listening intently.

Revan flapped in from outside to perch on the edge of the basin. Cocking his head at her, he preened himself.

"Well, that's convenient. But if I go through, how do I get back?" She glanced at Revan. "I don't suppose you could tell me?"

"Caw!"

"That's what I thought."

Tasha collected four pies, cradling two in each arm, and strode toward the doorway. Noting the portal offered no resistance, she stepped into Cybele's Church. She found it as easy as passing through an open door. Mother Anya shrieked upon Tasha's sudden appearance.

"Cybele's ti… by the Grace of our Mother, the Crow Queen!" Mother Anya put a hand on her cheek, blushing crimson at her near blaspheme. The acolytes, gasping at her outburst, spun to face Tasha before falling to their knees.

"Get up, all of you." Tasha regretted the forceful command as soon as she said it. "Don't kneel to me. I brought pie."

The acolytes' eyes widened. Mother Anya stood motionless. "Pies?"

Tasha offered them a smile. "People needing my help and advice brought them. Payment, I guess. I can't eat all of these myself, and I wanted to ask you some questions, Mother Anya. I thought, perhaps, you and your brethren would like to have these."

Mother Anya directed the acolytes to take Tasha's offerings. "That is most generous of you, Crow Queen."

Reserving the wild berry pie for herself and Aveline, Tasha handed the other three to the acolytes. "Is there somewhere we can speak privately, Mother Anya?"

"Of course, child." The matron gestured toward a door behind tapestries near the altar. "Let us retire to my chambers."

Tasha followed Mother Anya. The room, not much larger than her own hut, featured a small desk, two simple armchairs set before a wood-burning stove, and a bed. A hand-carved bull's head, symbol of Cybele, hung above the bed. Mother Anya pulled the chairs together and sat, patting the seat of the empty chair.

"I need you to tell me everything you know about the Crow Queen."

The corners of Mother Anya's mouth upturned. "In truth, I don't know you very well. You're not one of our regular parishioners."

Tasha shook her head. "Not me, Mother Anya. The Crow Queen... as a figure, a servant of Gaia, Cybele, and Artume. I'm, well, to be honest, I am at a loss. I don't even know if I can return to the hut using the means that got me here. I didn't grow up hearing the stories, how she came about, what her history is. Yet... here I am. How did Annika become Crow Queen?"

"Annika received the mantle when her mother died." Anya pursed her lips. "As far as I know, it has been passed from mother to daughter for generations."

"Never mother to son? Father to daughter? Father to son?" Tasha understood Gaia, Cybele, and Artume predominantly encouraged feminine priesthoods owing to their own gender identities; yet, neither Gaia nor Cybele outright prohibited men from the priesthood.

"Unless Artume forbids it, it's not impossible, though any men who took up the mantle were not identified as such in the old stories." Mother Anya slumped in her chair. "I'm sorry I'm not much help, dear. The Crow Queen is enigmatic. She helps, or she doesn't. I knew Annika, yes, but not well. She always seemed distant to me. I didn't know her mother was Crow Queen until after she died when Annika showed up one day when she was expected at High Harvest."

Tasha considered her words. "Do you know any priestesses of Artume?"

"There is a young huntress, Vasilisa. She spends most of her time in the wilds east of town, though she does come in for the Dusk of Autumn festival."

"At the equinox. That's"—Tasha counted to herself—"fifty days away."

"And with Abarron gone"—Mother Anya gestured toward Tasha—"you're our foremost authority on Gaia."

The words sat in Tasha's breast like a lump of wet clay. "Great. Well, did you ever see Annika come and go, like I just did?"

"I never witnessed it myself." Mother Anya leaned forward to take Tasha's hands. "You'll learn. You'll make mistakes. Don't hide from them. Think of yourself as a village witch. Only, you're young. You have plenty of time."

Her reassurances did little to assuage Tasha's anxiety.

Chapter 41

When the afternoon gave way to evening, Aveline returned to the citadel to ensure no tasks needed her immediate attention, then she went home by way of the butcher and bakery. While she waited for Tasha, she started a fire. She placed a chicken in a pot, then added a bottle of wine, fresh herbs, and cut vegetables before she covered it and set it in the hearth.

While the stew cooked, she removed and polished her armor. Sleeping outdoors for several days immediately following the abuse it suffered in the mines did it no favors. Appearing dull and spotted with rust, it no longer possessed a silvery sheen.

She finished scrubbing and oiling her mail, then worked at hammering out the dents in her breastplate. About halfway through, a knock at Aveline's door interrupted her. Putting her work aside, she opened it. To her surprise Tasha, holding a pie, greeted her from the bottom step.

"I expected you to just appear inside, out of thin air." Aveline took the pie, moving aside so Tasha could enter.

"I visited Mother Anya first. Couldn't figure out how to teleport back to the hut, so I walked here."

Aveline smelled the pie. Berries. "Just one?"

Tasha laughed. "Can we even eat more than just part of this one? I took three to the church."

"That was nice of you." Aveline set the pie on the table before checking the pot in the hearth. The dish still required more time in the fire. "In lieu of tithing?"

"I was hoping Mother Anya could tell me more about previous Crow Queens or share stories that were more than just bedtime tales about hags and crones." Tasha plopped into a chair. "No such luck. She said I should think of myself as a village witch."

As far as Aveline knew, village witches did not have to concern themselves with as many people as lived in Curton. The stories she heard about the Crow Queen indicated she hadn't confined herself to just the city, in any case.

"So, act crotchety, yell at children, and only help the handful of people you know?"

Tasha giggled. "That must be what she meant." She brushed a stray lock of hair away from her eyes. "You know, growing up, our village witch wasn't that old. No older than you or I am now, if I had to guess. She mostly made fetishes for folk looking to ward off evil, and she made the occasional unguent."

"How long until you hear back from the Arcane University?" Aveline appreciated Tasha's magical messengers traveled faster than a rider on horseback could, but she did not understand how that related to the time it would take to travel to Muncifer and back to Curton.

"Could be weeks, assuming they answer right away. If they don't…"

Aveline popped the cork on a bottle of mead, then poured a goblet for each of them. "So you're stuck waiting."

"Unless I go there myself." Tasha took the goblet, then sipped her mead.

"Using that door? You'd be mad to do that without knowing how, or if you could even get back." Aveline expected if Tasha became desperate, even that uncertainty wouldn't stop her.

"I was hoping Mother Anya would have some insight. If she could describe what effect she noticed when Annika used the door, I thought I might be able to figure it out, but she never saw her travel that way."

"Have you tried clicking your heels together and commanding the cosmos to take you home?"

"Somehow, I don't think it works that way."

Aveline snorted. "Well, make a flourish with that fancy cloak when you do it, so you look like a proper, mysterious Crow Queen."

"Ha! Things are never that simple. But once I figure it out, I'm going straight to Muncifer."

"You could always walk the hut to Muncifer." Aveline glanced at the pot in the hearth. Steam sputtered out from under the lid. "I'm not keen on you being away that long, though. Not with Koloman having these problems and this new knight in town."

"New knight?"

"You want any of this chicken?" Aveline went to the hearth to lift the lid of the cauldron. Steam rose from the pot, caressing Aveline's face with savory aromas. "It's not fancy, but it's cooked in wine and herbs. It's better than nothing."

"Are you suggesting I should eat more than just pie tonight?" Tasha laughed.

"Eat what you want. I'm not your mother." Aveline stabbed at a chicken thigh with a fork, extracted it from the pot, then shook it off onto a plate. She scooped some vegetables alongside it, set the dish on the table, then repeated the procedure with a second plate.

"I'll have some chicken, thanks."

As they ate, Aveline told Tasha about Maxim's arrival and his orders. "He's a pompous arse, but I can't just ignore him."

"I suppose asking you to come with me is out of the question, then." Tasha poked at a carrot with her fork.

"I would love to, but I can't." Aveline's lip curled at the thought of having to deal with Maxim on a regular basis. "I can't risk Maxim conscripting half the city watch to rebuild Dawnwatch. I'm not really keen on you going alone, though."

"I can handle myself, Aveline."

"Yes, you can." Aveline sipped her mead. "But it would make me feel better."

Tasha waved her hand. "I'll be all right. I promise I'll wait until I figure out how to use the portal both ways, then I can return to Curton each night. How's that?"

Resting her hand on her chin, Aveline regarded her friend across the table. Dark circles smudged beneath Tasha's honey eyes. "I don't know anything about this arcane lore or mysticism. I wish I could be of more help."

"You help plenty."

"Right now, I want to help eat that pie." Aveline pulled the berry-filled pastry toward her.

"A fine idea, m'lady!"

* * *

Their appetites sated and the moons rising high into the sky, Tasha decided to depart for the evening. Yawning, Aveline stretched before hugging her friend.

"You know, I think I'll try it." Tasha stepped away from Aveline, flipping her cloak around her body as she clicked her heels together. "Send me home!"

Aveline burst into laughter. "It was worth a try."

Warmth faded from the mantle. Tasha ran her hand along the hem. "You know, I think you were on the right track."

"You're joking." Aveline leaned on the back of a chair.

"No. Everything so far has responded to my thoughts, my desires." Tasha spread the cloak. "Why should this be any different?"

"So… what are you going to try? Do I need to move anything?"

"No, just stand still. If it works, well, you'll know instantly." Tasha glanced around her to make sure she wouldn't hit any furniture or catch her cloak. Closing her eyes, she visualized the interior of the hut and then snapped the cloak closed around her.

Hearing the calls of a hundred crows, Tasha felt herself moving along at an incredible rate. She dared to open her eyes, viewing Curton passing beneath her in a blur.

And then, she stood inside her hut. Laughing, she spun in a circle. "It worked! I can't believe that worked. Aveline, did you see…" She realized her friend was still in Curton.

"I want to go to Aveline's home."

Shimmering, the back door showed Aveline sitting dazed on the floor near her hearth. Tasha rushed forward, stepping through the doorway to offer a helping hand.

"You're back?" Aveline sputtered several half-expletives, unable to complete a thought.

"I was in the hut in an instant. I wanted to come back to hear what you saw and to let you know." She grasped Aveline's arm, steadying her friend as she collected herself. "Did you fall?"

"You flipped that cloak around, and it exploded into scores of little crows. They flew all over. I stumbled backward, then, suddenly, they were gone. By the time I noticed, you were stepping into the room out of thin air." Aveline fumbled for her goblet of mead, draining it in one gulp.

Tasha pulled her friend into a hug. "Looks like I'm going to Muncifer after all, thanks to you."

Aveline pressed her hand to her forehead. "I'm glad I could help."

"I hear there are some good meaderies around Muncifer. I'll bring you a bottle or two tomorrow." Tasha clutched the edges of her cloak. She didn't know if the flourish helped, or if it was merely a pointless affectation, but she enjoyed it.

"You're leaving now?"

Tasha stopped. "No, in the morning. I doubt they'd let me in the Arcane University library this late. No one there even knows who I am."

Aveline spread her arms. "No one will know who you are in the morning, either."

"True, but I can present myself properly. I did attend the Arcane University in Maritropa. I know the protocols."

"Let me know when you get back."

Tasha hugged her friend again. "I will. Sleep well, and don't let people like Maxim and Koloman aggravate you too much. They're not worth it."

"Don't worry about me." Aveline nodded. "Worry about *them*."

Grinning, Tasha took hold of the edges of her cloak. "I have to admit, I kind of love this." She thought about her hut, whipping her cloak closed. In an instant, she arrived home. Korbin and Revan huddled together on the windowsill, their sleep disturbed at her arrival, shuffling and tittering before settling themselves.

Stifling a yawn, she approached the bed, but she paused. *I wonder… can I just use the cloak to travel?* She pulled the cloak closed around her and concentrated her thoughts on the city market. A feeling of warmth enveloped her. When she opened her eyes, she remained within her hut, although the back door now showed an image of Curton's deserted market, pale light from the King and Queen illuminating the empty and shuttered stalls.

"Oh well, it was worth trying."

She changed out of her clothes, doused the lights, and crawled into bed. Despite her mind racing with the infinite possibilities instant travel provided, Tasha succumbed to sleep within minutes of her head hitting the pillow.

Upon awakening the next morning, Tasha heard the chatter of people down below. Scattered sunlight streamed in through her windows, beams of light broken by the branches and leaves in their path. Neither Revan nor Korbin remained in their windowsill perch. Cramps in her lower abdomen reminded her that her time to pay Cybele's price drew near. *Damn. I should have moved the hut last night.*

Rather than face the horde of townsfolk seeking quick prognostications, Tasha instead thought of a warm, relaxing bath. The back door shimmered, revealing the sylvan glade she first saw several days earlier. She rolled out of bed, pulled on her skirt, a tunic, and her cloak, then stepped through the portal.

Upon striding through the doorway, she smelled floral scents on the warm breeze. Although no sun shone in the sky, diffuse light spread across the heavens, illuminating the clouds and treetops with a pastel rosy color. It was at once dawn and dusk, a perfect time for birdsong and the chittering of forest animals. Ahead, Tasha saw the waterfall-fed pond she remembered from her first glimpse through the portal.

Apart from the clearing around the pool and the cliff over which water cascaded, trees surrounded the area. All around her, Tasha observed pines with needles of rich burgundy, oaks bearing silver leaves, and myriad other flora she'd never before encountered.

"Crow Queen, you've returned!" A high-pitched voice cheered from a nearby shrub. The leaves rustled, and a crimson vixen emerged.

"Returned?" Tasha pointed at the fox. "Did you just speak to me?"

"Of course I did. There's no one else here." The vixen bounded toward her, then sniffed her foot. It regarded Tasha, blinking its green eyes slowly. "You smell different."

"I don't think I'm who you think I am." Despite remaining unsure of the wisdom in admitting ignorance to strange talking animals, Tasha felt honesty might serve her well in this case. "What is this place?"

"I know it's been a while since you've visited, but surely you haven't forgotten. Terath Balénor." The vixen huffed. "The Fey Realm?"

Tasha gasped, placing her hand over her mouth. "The Fey Realm?" She gazed at the strange trees all around and at the alien sky.

She knelt before the fox, who sat on her haunches peering at her. "I am a new Crow Queen. I'm still learning what all this means. This is my first time here. My name is Tasha." She held out her hand.

The fox sniffed it. "I knew you smelled different. My name is Tika. You… the other you, used to come here to bathe in our pond. It's been a long time since she visited, though. What happened to her?"

Tasha withdrew her hand. "She was killed. The mantle was lost for a very long time."

"That's too bad. She used to bring me fish from the mortal world." Tika snapped her jaws, licking her lips. "They were juicy sweet." Leaping in circles around Tasha, she yipped. "Welcome, welcome, welcome, new Crow Queen!"

Tika bounded into the underbrush. Tasha waited for a few moments. When the vixen's return seemed unlikely, she approached the pond. The earth beneath her feet felt soft and loamy. Crouching at the edge of the pond, Tasha dipped her fingers into it. The water felt warm against her skin, a perfect bath beneath magical skies. She shrugged off her clothes before slipping into the pool.

The warmth she learned long ago to associate with Gaia; however, here in the Fey Realm, it required little effort for her to experience the goddess's presence. Closing her eyes, she floated, allowing the current to carry her. The warm waters of the pond eased the cramping in her abdomen. When she opened her eyes, she found herself near the center of the pond, gently turning in a circle. The dull roar of the waterfall provided a droning background chorus against which unseen birds sang lyrical tunes.

She dove underwater, kicking to propel herself toward the shore. When she surfaced, she faced pale, sky-blue legs. Yelping, Tasha submerged to her neck as she swam away from the intruder. Following the pair of legs up the ragged edge of a diaphanous gown to a face framed by a cascade of ginger locks, her gaze met smiling, cerulean eyes. The Crow Queen knew the face, although she had not seen it in over a decade.

"It's good to see you again, Tasha."

Chapter 42

The next morning, Aveline awoke to the realization she had overslept. Cursing, she rolled out of bed and set to work. She stole bites of bread and cheese while she wrangled hair made unruly by pillows and blankets. When she finished, she pulled on clean clothes and donned her armor. She set out into the streets of Curton to do her duty keeping people safe and dispensing justice.

At her first stop, Miners' Gate, she viewed a steady flow of people exiting the city. Chattering as they waited their turn to consult with a Crow Queen apparently holding court, their excitement was palpable. Aveline followed them all the way to the hut, to ensure they did not become unruly.

People crowded in the clearing in which the hut sat. Dim orange light shone in the window, and a thin stream of smoke wafted from the chimney. People called for the Crow Queen to show herself.

"What's going on here?" Aveline pushed her way through the crowd.

"She won't come out!"

"We've been waiting all morning!"

Aveline banged a mailed fist against her shield until the crowd fell silent. "The Crow Queen isn't at your beck and call. Maybe she went to the market, maybe she went to visit a friend in town, maybe someone in town needed her help, you don't know. Instead of waiting around, stomping all over the forest, I suggest you go back to your lives."

A man pointed at his foot. "But I have a painful bunion."

Another man pointed at his head. "I'm affected by a bald patch."

A woman patted her pregnant belly. "I need her to bless my child so he doesn't look like his father who isn't my husband."

"Go." Aveline shooed the people away. "Go to a fortune-teller or soothsayer in the market. You'll get the same results, and you won't disturb a woman who's trying to do important things, like... keep another plague from killing half the town."

Of course, Aveline knew full well Tasha's labor involved nothing of the sort. The townsfolk were none the wiser, though. She repeated her commands for the people to disperse.

"Here, you just want her to yourself!"

"Everyone knows you two are lovers!"

Aveline spun on the woman. "So what? If we are, don't we deserve some time alone? I don't come around banging on your door when you're with your husband. Now get out of here!"

Glaring until the woman left in a huff, she turned her gaze on the remaining townsfolk. Aveline waited until they disbursed before she shifted her focus to the door of the hut, high above the forest floor.

"Tasha?" Aveline called to her friend, but she received no response. The knight-captain shrugged. "I guess she went off to Muncifer already."

She hummed a bawdy drinking song as she returned to town. Stopping at the gate, she beckoned the sergeant over to her. "Discourage people from going to see the Crow Queen, please. She's not receiving visitors right now, and we wouldn't want anyone turned into frogs." Aveline stopped short of telling the guard Tasha wasn't home; she didn't want people holding days-long vigils awaiting her return.

The sergeant saluted. "Yes, m'lady."

On her way to the citadel, Aveline passed through the market, purchasing a freshly cooked sausage to slake her hunger. She had the merchant thread a skewer through it so she could eat it while walking.

"Ah, our lovely lady knight." Ra-Jareez's voice cut across the crowd. "Perhaps you would not have to eat such messy foods if you had one of these wonderful cooking vessels in your home."

Wiping grease off her chin, Aveline approached the faelix. He stood alone in Imrus's booth. "Where's Imrus? And your sister?"

"Master Imrus is in his workshop, making more excellent wares." Raj tapped his claw against the side of a gleaming copper pot. "Jazeera is taking a cart of seconds through Drakton."

Chewing her way through a piece of gristle that hadn't been ground finely enough in the sausage-making process, Aveline nodded. "You seem to be settling in well."

"We are nothing if not adaptable." Raj bowed to a passing customer. The man moved on without stopping.

"Good. Stay out of trouble."

"Wait, Lady Aveline." Raj reached toward her but withdrew his hand when she stopped to face him. "Perhaps you could tell me… Tasha, this bird princess woman…"

"Crow Queen."

"Yes, I understand she had a home here in town, yes? Ruined in the flood?" Raj pressed his hands together as his ears twitched. "What are her plans for it now that she has this marvelous hut that is the talk of town?"

News travels fast. "You'll have to ask her about that. It needs to be gutted and have all the mold scraped from the interior. Why?"

"Jazeera and I, perhaps Yun, too, cannot stay in inns our whole lives." He rubbed his ear. "We are no strangers to hard work. Perhaps we could make the necessary cleanings."

"That's between you and her. She might have a way to send you home, though." Aveline assumed people other than Tasha could use the portal in the hut.

"Home? To Nakambe?" Chuckling, Raj scratched under his chin. "We… we left to trade, and I've only just begun… I was hoping we would be welcome to stay here a bit."

Aveline patted the faelix's shoulder. "Stay as long as you like. I'll let Tasha know you want to talk to her."

"You are most kind." Raj bowed, then smiled at a young woman who picked up a nearby kettle. "Ah, fine lady, that is a most excellent choice…"

She left Raj to his business as she continued to the citadel. Finishing her sausage, she tossed the skewer into the gutter before entering the building. To her dismay, Maxim sat behind her desk, poring over maps covering the surface. She slammed the door, startling him.

"My seat. Move." Aveline loomed over him until he gathered the papers and slid out of her chair. After stowing her shield and mace in the weapon rack, she sat behind her desk and put her feet up. "Aren't you supposed to be going to Dawnwatch?"

"I've already been there." He struggled with the maps as he backed away from her. "I was looking over the original construction documents. Your Lieutenant Valon was kind enough to help me retrieve them."

"That was nice of him. Make a list of what you need, and I'll see what we can spare." Aveline crossed her arms over her chest.

"I need about twenty strong men to get started on the cleanup."

Aveline pointed at the door. "I can't spare any of the city watch. Recruit townsfolk. I assume Princess Valene is sending funds, because you are not to conscript anyone."

"Certainly not." Maxim thrust his chin upward, sniffing. "The garrison funds…"

"Were depleted twenty years ago. I will not steal money from the town for a rundown old keep. If it's so damned important, the princess can answer our requests for supplies and funds for workers."

Maxim threw the maps on her desk, snatching one that threatened to roll off. "You are not being reasonable."

Aveline poked him in the chest. "Reasonable stopped when you barged in here yesterday making demands. Check your attitude, put together a list, and maybe I'll see if I can get some volunteers to go with you. It's unlikely many will be available for free, however. Their families are going to need them on their farms."

Leaving him, she headed to the larder to retrieve a bottle of stout. Fortunately, this bottle avoided the muddy aftertaste she'd encountered while at the mine. When she returned, Maxim had nearly finished straightening the documents.

A guard opened the door, pushing a bloody-faced mudder in front of him. The man weaved and staggered. "He looks worse than he is. Lost a fight in the Den and tried to drink away his shame, but then started breaking the furniture."

Aveline gestured toward the cellblock. "Have him sleep it off. I assume you have a list of damages?"

"Danica said she'd bring it by."

Maxim finished rolling the final map before setting it on her desk. "Lady Aveline, perhaps you could lend me a woodworker and a stonemason. Surely folk with such skills serve on the watch?"

"Lend?"

"The keep needs much work, but I am not knowledgeable enough to give a full accounting. I will take them there, spend a few days making your list, then return." Maxim clasped his hands in front of him as he spoke.

"We may have some craftsfolk serving on the watch." Aveline knew full well they did, although she couldn't recall names offhand. "I'll speak to Lieutenant Valon about it."

"Thank you."

"In the meantime, I suggest you write to the princess and explain the situation here. I'm sure I can find a courier to hasten the letter. Perhaps we'll receive funds to rebuild the garrison before winter."

"Winter?" He shook his head. "It cannot remain unstaffed that long."

"What's the rush?" Aveline pulled her chair over to her desk and sat. "It's been unstaffed for decades. There's nothing between here and Cliffport but farms."

"Oroqs and draks from the hills—"

"Have never been a problem. Oroqs from the mountains haven't been a problem in decades, and I hear they're moving west now on some crusade in the Western Wastes. Dawnwatch is out of the way and pointless. It was out of the way and pointless even when a garrison occupied it." She recalled from her time living there that mostly trade caravans heading inland from Cliffport used Dawnwatch as an overnight shelter, and she didn't see much other use for it. "Put that in your letter."

"The princess feels we should inspect trade goods coming in from Cliffport, particularly those from Hoseki and Nakambe. Perhaps even levy taxes on such goods."

To keep from rolling her eyes, Aveline gritted her teeth. She pulled open a drawer, removed a sheaf of parchment, an inkwell, and a quill, and thrust them at him. "You can use a table in the dining room or your quarters."

Maxim took the writing implements, then stalked away to write his letter. Aveline leaned back, propping her feet on her desk. "Save me from greedy nobles."

* * *

Gaining a foothold in the pond, Tasha wiped the water off her face. "It can't be... Lorelei, you died... I saw you..." She felt her legs give way. Lorelei darted into the pond, catching Tasha under the arms and holding her head above the water.

Wrapping her arms around the elf, Tasha buried her head in her ginger hair. The perfume... her scent smelled just as she remembered it. Choking back a sob, she squeezed her lover tight.

Lorelei unwrapped Tasha's arms and stepped backward, keeping hold of her until she was certain Tasha would not collapse into the water. "It's been a long time."

"How is this possible?"

The elf released Tasha. Moving through the water with the fluid comfort of one who spent years near the sea, Lorelei rested against a rock. "When I died, my mortal body on Calliome died. My spirit came to rest at the side of Gaia. When you came here, she released me into Terath Balénor."

"Resurrected?" Hinted at in legends, resurrection magic was largely regarded as impossible. Tasha swam toward Lorelei.

"No. Fey are immortal here, in the Fey Realm. Only my mortal body died."

"There's still a Fey Nexus in Raven's Forest. You could go there." Surely the elves there would not deny the hut of the Crow Queen, a servant of Gaia. "I can meet you—"

"Tasha…" Lorelei held a finger to the Crow Queen's lips. "My mortal body died. I cannot return to Calliome. I remember you. I remember how I felt about you. But that part of me is dead."

Tears welled in Tasha's eyes. "What are you saying? It's been so long, Lori…"

"I know. I'd hoped that, by now, you'd have moved on."

Tasha wiped her face. "I thought I had. But seeing you again…"

Over Lorelei's shoulder, Tasha saw a family of foxes chasing shimmering butterflies. Lowering her eyes, the elf shook her head. "I had concerns about appearing before you like this, but when the Earth Mother asks of one a favor, one obeys."

"What favor?"

"The Mantle of the Crow Queen is passed down, usually from mother to child. A childless Crow Queen finds a suitable surrogate. When they take the mantle, they already know that which they need. The Earth Mother is incredibly pleased you found your way here by yourself, and so quickly. But she wants me to pass on to you the knowledge you need to carry out her will on Calliome."

So, she's not here because she wanted to see me again but to teach me. "Why me? I'm no one special. I'm just an herbalist now."

"We could spend years talking about the history of the Crow Queen. You are a trained sorceress. You have learned the mysticism of Gaia—Abarron sends his regards, by the way—The Crow Queen is the embodiment of more than just Gaia. But also, of Cybele, Artume, and, to a lesser extent, even Selene, Aita, Nethuns, and Tinian. The way the Bonelords represent Aita and death as the natural end to life, the Crow Queen represents the natural world and how the people live within her."

Lorelei spread her arms. "Calliome is Gaia. But so is the Fey Realm. The Fey Realm is within Gaia but lies apart from Calliome, although they are connected in ways."

Tasha's mind reeled. "I don't understand."

"You will, when you move on to the next life." Lorelei took Tasha's hands. "It's difficult to explain all this in a way you'll understand and won't take all of the time we have."

"Well, just start with what it means to be Crow Queen." Tasha would have been more than happy to spend the rest of her life with Lorelei if that's how long it took for her to understand.

"The gods cannot interact with the world directly. They act through agents." Lorelei counted them on her fingers. "The Bonelords. The Crow Queen. The Athantoi…"

"Who? I've never heard of the Athantoi."

"Immortals. Physical manifestations of the divine." Lorelei rubbed her chin. "I don't know them all. The Keeper of Mysteries, The Grim Shepherd, Nightblade, Forgemaster... it doesn't matter. They wander, keep to themselves. You're unlikely to ever meet one, although perhaps Harvestwife will seek you out. She—it's usually a she—is Gaia's avatar. The Athantoi are the eyes and ears of the gods; the gods hear prayers, of course, but contrary to popular belief, they can't focus on the entire world at once."

"What do they have to do with me?" Tasha brushed her wet hair away from her face.

"Like them, you are an agent of Gaia now. And Cybele, Artume, and the others I mentioned to a lesser extent. You bring their bounty to the people you serve. You help, in their names. It's that simple."

"I've already been doing that." Tasha questioned whether her responsibilities were as straightforward as Lorelei stated.

"Calliome is still healing from The Sundering. You have the power to help that healing along. But you are free to be the kind of Crow Queen you want to be." Lorelei gazed at her, drawing Tasha into her cerulean eyes. "When the mantle is lost or abandoned, it's often found by someone who desires power to rule over others. That's where the stories about evil hags and crones come from. The power corrupts them. You will not be like that."

"I want to help people." Tasha nodded. "Tell me what I must do."

Lorelei shook her head. "No. I'm going to teach you what you *can* do."

Chapter 43

At the end of the day, Aveline returned to Miners' Gate to find out how many townsfolk had ventured to see the Crow Queen over the course of the afternoon. The guards indicated most people got the message, but they stated a few insisted on hiking out there to hear it for themselves from the source.

Aveline muttered obscenities under her breath as she traveled the forest trail, sending stragglers home. When she reached the hut, it appeared much as it had that morning, except Raj, Jazeera, and Yun stood in front of it, talking among themselves.

"Ah, Lady Aveline." Jazeera bowed, tugging the shirts of Raj and Yun to pull them downward into a semblance of a bow. "We have been trying to get the Crow Queen's attention, but she does not answer."

"This hut is most impressive." Raj spread his arms. "How does it stand on such skinny chicken feet?"

Yun said something in Xihani. Raj and Jazeera laughed. "What?"

"Yun wonders if the legs can be removed and cooked"— Jazeera put her hand on Yun's shoulder—"in case she's hungry."

Aveline pinched the bridge of her nose. "Has it occurred to you that Tasha isn't home?"

"You see?" Jazeera slapped her brother's shoulder. "I said that. We've wasted precious eating time for nothing."

Yun grunted what Aveline surmised was an expletive from the way he glared at Raj before stomping past the faelix siblings and heading down the path toward Curton.

"When will she be back?" Raj rubbed his shoulder, stepping toward Aveline. "We wish to speak to her about the house in town."

"I assumed sometime tonight, but I'm not her keeper." Aveline gestured for the faelixes to follow Yun. "I told you

I would pass your request on to her. I'll ask her to come see you when she gets back or at least send one of her birds to come fetch you." She glanced around the clearing, but she saw no sign of the two crows. "By the by, have you seen either of them?"

"I have not." Jazeera rubbed her stomach. "Just as well, I might have eaten one."

"Head back to town. I'm going to check a few things here and then go back myself. Don't linger; they like to lock the gates at dusk."

Nightfall arrived earlier each day, and Aveline yearned for autumn when the winter squashes ripened and every orchard around town sold their cider. As autumn matured, nights lent themselves to mulled cider by the fireside, and farmers distilled sweet cider into apple brandy

Maxim left for Dawnwatch the next morning, and Aveline gave him no thought for the next several days. Each morning and afternoon, she visited the Crow Queen's hut, shooing away the ever-diminishing crowd of hopefuls and growing more concerned each day her attempts to gain Tasha's attention went unacknowledged.

Despite Tasha's seeming absence, the townsfolk's faith in their Crow Queen only grew stronger with each passing day. They grew up hearing tales about the Crow Queen's comings and goings; sometimes, she'd vanish for an entire season. Aveline grew up with no such stories, however, and the mysterious disappearance of her friend provided a genuine source for concern.

Aveline kept herself busy in an attempt to keep her mind off the most serious possibilities. She kept telling herself, at worst, the cloak couldn't transport Tasha back from Muncifer; the distance was too far. Certainly, she had no reason to believe the Crow Queen faced mortal danger. While Aveline's familiarity with Muncifer remained limited to what she'd heard from passing traders, their stories did not indicate the mountain city to be a hotbed of murder and robbery.

However, logic rarely ruled hearts. Sleep came to Aveline with increasing difficulty as the days passed without evidence of Tasha's arrival. Maxim's inevitable return provided her with a welcome distraction. The list he provided her seemed reasonable at first glance.

"We have craftsfolk in town who can provide all of these materials and services." After rolling the parchment, Aveline returned it to Maxim. "You'll have to pay them out of the garrison fund, though."

Maxim huffed. "There is no garrison fund. I was dispatched under the assumption I'd be joining an existing garrison."

"Yes, instead, you're going to get to build a new garrison from scratch." Aveline laced her fingers behind her head, leaning back in her chair. "Isn't it exciting?"

"I hardly think this is what the princess had in mind."

Aveline cared little for what Valene expected. "No one in Almeria cares about Curton until they do. Koloman is supposed to send a portion of the taxes he collects to the royal treasury. As far as I know, he hasn't sent a caravan that way in years. Perhaps you could ask him to divert some of those funds to the garrison?"

"The Lord Mayor?" Maxim considered Aveline's suggestion. "That is a sound idea. His estate is in Old Town, yes?"

"Just outside the city walls." Aveline did not believe for a moment Koloman would honor his duty to the crown. She suspected he'd been keeping that money for himself for years, although she'd be pleased to be proven wrong. When she questioned Koloman about it once, he reminded her that serving the town was her mandate, and he stated the question of taxes going to Almeria was an issue between him and the crown. As the crown had never given her a mandate to investigate tax collection, Aveline accepted there was little she could do about his embezzlement.

Deciding not to wait to learn of Koloman's answer, she penned a petition on Maxim's behalf to Almeria for funding. Writing the letter took her mind off Tasha.

* * *

"It's a lot to take in." Now clean and dry, Tasha reclined in the meadow. Multicolored birds soared across the pastel sky. Even though she felt as if she'd been there for hours, the illumination of the sky never changed.

"You'll remember when you need to." Lorelei sat cross-legged, her gown splaying around her on the earth next to Tasha like a pool of gossamer lace. "Let the mantle guide your decisions. It will never lead you away from the path."

"I've noticed it feels warmer when I do something that seems like a thing the Crow Queen should do."

Lorelei ran her pale-blue hand along the sleek black feathers. "It speaks to you, if you know how to listen."

"Lori"—Tasha gazed at her former lover—"did you know all of this before? When we were together?"

"No. Yes. Some of it I knew, but I would never have thought to volunteer unless it became relevant. Most of what I taught you today, however, was given to me by the Earth Mother and your predecessors when it became clear someone was going to have to pass the knowledge on to you."

"Did they think I wouldn't learn it on my own?"

"You may have, eventually." Lorelei brushed a lock of hair off Tasha's face. "It is safer this way."

Tasha closed her eyes at Lorelei's touch. She moved to take the elf's hand, but Lorelei pulled it away.

"It can never be the way it was." Lorelei gazed at her. "When you leave here, Tasha, I will return to the bosom of the Earth Mother. We will not see each other again."

Tasha forced herself to meet Lorelei's passionless gaze. "I suppose it would be distracting if you were here every time I wanted to bathe in the pool."

"Indeed." Lorelei glanced over her shoulder. "I cannot say the same for Tika. I suspect she and her family will always be here."

"I think I can handle that." Tasha watched the foxes frolic in the pasture on the opposite side of the pond. "What's beyond the trees? Can I return and explore this realm more someday?"

Lorelei offered a hand, helping Tasha to her feet. "Beyond the trees are endless forests, meadows, and rolling hills. As a mortal, your life-force is tied to Calliome, and you would not survive long enough to reach Daermoch Chanel."

"That's a shame." Tasha smoothed her skirt. "I assume I return home using the cloak, like I did when I used the doorway to visit Aveline?"

Nodding, Lorelei raised her hand in farewell. "You know the way."

Tasha closed her eyes, thought of the hut, and snapped the cloak closed around her. After a brief period of the now-familiar rushing sensation, she opened her eyes to find herself inside her hut. The fire burned low in the hearth, barely more than embers, flaring as she approached it. Candles around the hut provided dim orange illumination, the only source of light. Outside, crickets played their evening songs. In the distance, a wolf howled at the twin moons.

"Night? I wasn't gone that long…" Tasha leaned out the window, barely able to see the forest floor below, in spite of the light provided by the King and Queen. Her stomach knotted, clenching like a fist in outrage. *I guess I was gone all day.*

Tasha fed her complaining belly and found she did not feel the need to sleep, despite the late hour. Taking a moment to locate Revan and Korbin, she found the birds sleeping together in a tree nearby. Choosing to not disturb them she entered the forest.

Using techniques Lorelei described, she used the mantle to aid her focus on the forest around her. She sensed a deer slumbering in the distance, bedded down in shrubs. Likewise, dozens of birds nested in the canopy all around her, and an owl glided with silence through the trees, diving to catch a hapless mouse exposed in the open.

Tasha made her way through the forest until she arrived at the edge of the Copper Run. Little evidence of flooding remained; this part of the waterway ran within deep banks. From a protruding rock overlooking the river cascading around a fallen beech, she enjoyed the yellow-white moonlight from the waxing Queen dancing upon the water.

Across the bank, a pack of wolves trotted by, climbing down an embankment to drink from the river. One of the wolves stared at her, its eyes glowing with reflected light. When the pack had drunk their fill, they loped away. She lowered herself to a sitting position, letting her legs dangle off the edge of the rock. Mist from the rushing water sprinkled her feet now and then, reminding her a dunk was only a short drop away.

Tasha pulled up her feet, crossing them beneath her. Closing her eyes, she focused on the Earth Mother, the life all around her, the world. Her mind opened to the forest on both banks of the river, then the town, the farmland beyond, and the nearby mountains.

In the mine, she felt the chaos rift, like an open wound cutting deep into the world. For now, it remained contained, surrounded by tons of rock. She sensed the draks working late into the night transforming the mine, once a pit of death, into a haven for life. Humans slept nearby, the remaining stone masons who worked on the graveyard's monument.

Her eyes snapped open as the hair on the back of her neck rose. She felt eyes upon her, not malevolent, but they belonged to a predator nonetheless. Glancing over each shoulder, she spotted nothing. Tasha stood, using slow, deliberate motion. Turning her back to the river, she saw a pair of honey-colored eyes staring at her from the gloom. The creature padded forward.

The wolf-like creature emerged from the darkness. Shaggy, it stood half again as tall as the largest wolf Tasha had ever seen. Snarling, it retracted its lips to reveal gleaming teeth, bits of its last meal still caught between them. It reared on its hind legs, howling. Spreading its front paws in a mockery of human arms, it bowed.

A werewolf.

Tasha's blood ran cold. She thought of home, snapping her cloak shut around her.

Nothing.

She smelled the metallic reek of blood. Its curved claws, as long as her own fingers, appeared capable of disemboweling a person with one blow. Widening her stance, she spread her cloak.

"Begone, Cursed One. I am the Crow Queen." Feeling the cloak grow warmer, Tasha noticed the lycanthrope seemed to shrink before her. "The people who dwell here live under my protection."

It growled, snapping its teeth at her before bolting on all fours into the forest. Tasha, likewise, ran, stopping only when she returned to the clearing where her hut stood. Once inside, she leaned against the door until she caught her breath and her heart stopped pounding.

When she felt calmer, she took her place at the basin. An image of the forest around the hut formed almost immediately, and she focused on the werewolf. As soon as it came into focus, the beast turned around, as if detecting Tasha watching it. She recoiled by reflex when it swiped a paw in her direction. The connection severed.

"Damn it."

Chapter 44

As she had so many previous mornings, Aveline trekked to the Crow Queen's hut. Outside it, a figure clad in a dark cloak chatted with a green-scaled drak.

"Tasha?" Aveline increased her pace. The Crow Queen waved at her, and the drak took his leave.

"Good morning." Tasha held open her arms.

Aveline gathered her friend in a hug. "I've been worried sick. Where have you been?"

"I went to that glade for a bath. I admit, I was gone a little longer than I intended, I met—"

"A bath? For a week?" Aveline held her friend at arm's length. Something seemed different about her, although Aveline could not tell what.

"I was back last night." Tasha looked down the road past Aveline. "I have to admit, I expected more people here by now."

"You were gone seven days, Tasha."

The Crow Queen's expression fell. "Seven…" Shaking her head, she clutched at Aveline's sleeve to keep her balance. "Seven days?"

"You'd better sit down." The knight-captain slipped her arm around Tasha, helping her friend up the stairs.

"I was in the Fae Realm." Tasha settled into a chair. Aveline pulled over the second one and sat with her. "I saw Lorelei… or at least someone who looked like her. The way she acted, you'd think we were simply good friends, not lovers planning a future together."

"Wait… you saw your dead lover there?" Aveline tried to wrap her head around the idea of encountering dead people in a different realm. After removing her gloves, she rubbed her temples.

"It's hard to explain."

Aveline didn't believe Tasha evaded her question, but neither would she let her friend off the hook that easily. "Try."

Tasha's tale of the Fae Realm, being reunited with an emotionally distant fae former lover, and the ensuing instruction on how to best use her power as Crow Queen made Aveline's head swim. When Tasha finished, Aveline still didn't understand what occurred to cause her friend to vanish for so long, but she accepted Tasha didn't quite understand it either.

"You feel like you only chatted for an hour or two?" Aveline furrowed her brow, considering how several hours could translate into a week.

"I was with her for only a few hours. I left in the morning, bathed, talked to her, and, when I came back, it was the middle of the night." Tasha shook her head. "I've heard time passes differently in the Fae Realm, but seven days for a few hours?"

Leaning back, Aveline sighed. "Well, it explains all those stories where the Crow Queen just vanished for an extended period of time."

"I don't think it explains all, but I'm sure it contributes to some." Tasha stretched. "Well, this is as good a time as any to move the hut. Want to stick around?"

Aveline shook her head. "I don't want to hike all the way back to town from wherever you end up."

Tasha pointed to the inactive portal. "Use the back door. You'll be home in an instant." Smiling, she climbed into position, levitating above the water in the basin. Aveline's eyes widened. Circling the stump, she turned her head, checking under Tasha and seeing for herself that her friend was, indeed, unsupported by any visible means.

"That is amazing." Aveline glanced at the back door. "All right, my curiosity has the better of me. I'll risk that damned back door thing to watch this."

Tasha closed her eyes. Aveline felt the floor beneath her shift slightly before it settled into an almost-imperceptible rhythm. The knight-captain moved to the window and watched the trees speed past at a shocking rate. From her vantage point inside the hut, the structure seemed to sprint through the forest, bobbing and weaving to avoid trees and leaping over fallen logs and boulders.

Aveline stepped away from the window as her head swam and her stomach roiled in protest. Stumbling into the nearest chair willing herself not to vomit, she held her abdomen. After a few minutes, the sensation passed. Nevertheless, she remained seated until Tasha, opening her eyes, hopped to the floor.

"You look a little peaked."

Aveline lifted her head just enough to regard Tasha. "Going to the window to watch was a bad idea. Where are we?"

"In the hills southwest of town. You should be able to see Curton." Tasha brought her friend over to the window. "There, see it?"

Tasha pointed to the city in the distance. Facing northeast from their current position, the skyline of Curton resembled a cluster of wooden blocks straddling the river surrounded by trees on the near side and fields on the far side.

"A little far, isn't it?" Aveline shielded her eyes from the sun. "It'll take people days to hike out here."

"That'll weed out the ones looking for me to tell them who the father of their baby is, won't it?"

Aveline laughed. "It will at that, but it'll make it difficult for the ones who want you to cure their bunions."

Tasha filled her kettle, then set it over the hearth to brew tea. "Yes, well, that's not so life threatening they can't wait until I'm closer to town. I learned so much while I was gone, Aveline. Curton will need another apothecary."

She spread her cloak, the feathers shimmering as they caught the firelight. "I need to be so much more than the village witch or town herbalist." Sighing, she lowered her head. "I have to take care of more than just Curton now."

Aveline approached Tasha, then put her hand on her friend's shoulder. The feathers felt warm, as though they'd been sitting in the sunlight for hours. "I don't know what to make of all this, but I believe in you. Somehow, my friend is the Crow Queen. You do what you need to do, for the good of everyone you're supposed to serve. Be they gods or us puny mortals."

Tasha put her hand on Aveline's and squeezed. "I'll always be here for you. Even if I'm away, if you need me, I'll come. We'll figure out a way."

"I don't suppose you learned anything about dreams while you were frolicking with the faeries?"

Tasha snorted. "They didn't teach oneiromancy in Introductory Crow Queen. After I've had my tea, I'll go to Muncifer."

"All right." Aveline nodded toward the back door. "How does this thing work?"

"I can just think of a destination." Tasha glanced at the door. It shimmered before displaying the interior of Aveline's home. "How's that? Or would you rather go to the citadel?"

Aveline peered at the glimmering image in the door-frame. The view of her living area appeared as though she stood just inside her own front door. "Home is fine. I came straight here, so I need to walk Old Town this morning."

"Oh, Aveline. I… saw a werewolf in the forest near town last night."

"A what?" Spinning to face Tasha, Aveline's hand dropped to her mace by reflex. "Where?"

"Down by the river. I think I scared it off, but you might want to warn people."

Crossing her arms, Aveline chewed her lip. "Neither moon was full last night."

"That just means they can control their transformations. They have accepted their curse." Tasha poured her tea, then cupped the mug in her hands. "That might mean they're a perfectly reasonable person and hunt only animals in the forest."

"It could also mean they like killing." Particularly from Watchfolk, Aveline had heard stories of werewolves living perfectly normal lives as the main hunters for their villages.

"It might even be someone from town. They know they're afflicted, and they go into the forest, so they don't risk others when they hunt. They might be trying to do the right thing."

"All right." Aveline paced before the portal. "I'll let the guards know to warn people leaving town to be wary of the forest at night. They only come out at night, right?"

Tasha pursed her lips. "Well, if they can control their transformations, they could be hunting during the day too."

"That's fantastic." Aveline pondered what sort of trouble she'd have if she closed the town entirely.

"Look, just start gathering wolf's bane, and don't let anyone go into the forest without it." Tasha shuffled over to her apothecary cabinet, then searched through the drawers until she found a bundle of dried leaves. She handed it to Aveline.

"And this will keep it away?" Aveline examined the curled, segmented leaves.

"It should. Just don't eat it."

Aveline tucked it into her belt. "I'm not in the habit of eating stuff you pull out of that cabinet." She turned toward the image of the inside of her home. "Do I just walk through?"

"Just go straight through. There might be a bit, just a bit, of resistance, like walking in a strong headwind, but it won't last long."

Striding forward, Aveline found Tasha's description apt. After a hint of pressure, she passed through and found herself home. She spun, expecting to find Tasha behind her, but saw only her own front door. "That's the damnedest thing I've ever done."

* * *

The portal reverted to inactive status as a door just after Aveline stepped through it. Sipping her tea, Tasha she closed her apothecary cabinet. She rummaged through her belongings, putting a fistful of talons and crowns in her pouch, then she picked up a sheet of parchment.

As she wrote a list of items she wanted to buy and didn't want to forget to ask about at the Arcane University, Korbin and Revan landed on the windowsill.

"Caw, caw!"

"I'm glad you're here. We're going to Muncifer." Tasha still didn't know if the birds understood her. She sprinkled some sand on the wet ink, counted to ten, and then blew off the sand. After rolling the parchment, she gestured for the birds to come with her. They flew into the hut to land on her shoulder.

Upon approaching the back door, it shimmered, revealing a winding cobblestone street between stonework buildings. Upon stepping through, she found herself outdoors in the middle of a city thoroughfare.

"Hey, watch it!"

Barely in time, Tasha moved out of the path of an oncoming minotaur. Glaring at her, he pushed his cart of potatoes past.

"Sorry. It's my first time here. It's a little overwhelming." Korbin and Revan flew away as Tasha bowed to the scowling minotaur.

"Next time, just look before you dart out into the street, all right?" The minotaur snorted before continuing on his way.

Muncifer's mountain air felt cooler to Tasha, although she trusted the mantle would keep her comfortable. Scores of people hurried up and down the street. As she turned in circles to gain her bearings, she realized viewing the city through the basin did not teach her the layout.

She was lost.

With the sun still making its way toward its zenith, Tasha figured she had time, so she followed the crowd on her side of the thoroughfare. The sound of cart wheels clattered over stone. In the distance, a bell tolled. Neighbors shouted across the street at each other, struggling to be heard over the echoes of an untold number of shoes scraping on the cobbles. Behind her, she heard the clip-clop of an approaching horse. She stepped to the side to let it pass, hoping it belonged to the city guard.

A woman wearing a heavy burgundy gown rode sidesaddle. Despite all indications pointing to her obviously not belonging to the constabulary, Tasha raised her hand, trying to gain the woman's attention. Passing Tasha, she sneered, sticking her nose in the air, "Out of the way, vagabond."

Slumping, Tasha dropped her hand. She glanced at her clothes, sighing, and admitted her handkerchief-hem skirt and feathered cloak probably appeared quite rustic in this cosmopolitan setting. Catching sight of the potato-cart-pushing minotaur ahead, she rushed to catch up to him. Passing the snobby rider, she ignored the woman's insults.

"Pardon me, sir? Potato... minotaur? Excuse me!" Tasha ran behind him, her feet already aching from running on the unyielding stone.

He raised an eyebrow. "Want to buy potatoes now? Can't you wait until I get to the market?"

"No, sorry. I'm looking for the Arcane University."

Ogling her up and down, he snorted. "You're certainly wearing the garb." He jerked his head to the side. "It's that way, six streets over. See that red lantern up ahead?"

Tasha strained to see over the crowd. "Yes."

"Turn left at the next street after that. It'll take you right to the gate."

"Thank you!" Tasha waved to him as she headed for the red lantern. "I'll come see you in the market before I leave and buy some potatoes."

The noise of the city crowd drowned out his reply. Passing the building with the red lantern, she ventured a glance inside through its open door. The scantily clad people within confirmed the nature of their business. She hurried to the end of the building and turned left. Ahead in the distance, she recognized the spires of the Arcane University.

Calling Korbin and Revan to her, she slowed her pace, giving her feet a chance to acclimate to the hard surface of the cobblestones. The birds followed along, flying from rooftop to rooftop on either side of the street. The nearer she drew to the Arcane University, the thinner the crowds became.

When she finally arrived at her destination, she found the gate open but guarded by two armored men wielding halberds. They crossed them in front of her as she approached.

"The university grounds aren't for looking. Keep moving, bumpkin."

Tasha drew her cloak around her. "I am Tasha Galperin of Curton, graduate of the Arcane University in Maritropa and Crow Queen. I have business here."

As she spoke, the cloak grew warm, and she felt as though she towered over the men. After pulling back their halberds, they gestured for her to enter.

"Sorry about that. Got to keep the riffraff away."

Tasha strode past them onto the university campus. Several buildings surrounded the main open area. To one side, students utilized a practice range for their destructive evocation spells. Other students sat around a large tree, chatting. Nearby, she smelled roasting meat from a building filled with the sound of laughter. Central to the whole compound stood the main building, a massive, multi-spired stone structure Tasha knew could only be the Court of Wizardry.

Revan landed on her shoulder, while Korbin perched on one of the branches of the lone oak tree at the center of the compound. She stroked Revan's head. "Well, let's pay our respects to the archmage."

Chapter 45

Aveline rushed through her morning rounds in Old Town, eager to compensate for the time she'd spent with Tasha. As she wandered the streets, keeping a watchful eye for ne'er-do-wells, she tried to keep her mind off how exciting it would be to travel the world with Tasha in the Crow Queen's hut. *I wonder if she needs a bodyguard.*

Long ago, the prestige of serving the crown faded, even before her guardian died, abandoned by those who charged him with keeping watch over the southeastern realm. She continued performing her duty because the people of Curton needed her. In addition, she liked transforming the city watch into a respected organization, despite Koloman's efforts to use the constables for his own purposes.

The idea of running off with her friend to see the world carried with it a special appeal. *I wonder how much Vlorey has changed since we left. I barely remember it. Sun, water, and palms.* She had not thought about the city of her birth in years. Curton had been home to her for as long as she could remember.

She stopped at the center of Caravan Bridge, listening to the rushing of the Copper Run while she contemplated a future in Curton with her best friend absent doing Crow Queen things. She feared she'd see much less of Tasha now.

"Remember when I fell off this bridge as a boy?"

Aveline started at the sound of Lieutenant Valon's voice. He apologized for startling her.

"I remember." Aveline smirked. "Old Agnar and I had just finished moving all our junk from Dawnwatch."

"You didn't hesitate. You just jumped right in after me. You didn't even know how to swim."

Aveline laughed. "They fished us out down by Fairstone Mill. I've never seen a man as angry as Agnar was that day. Angry I'd be so foolish but proud at the same time that I didn't think about it before trying to save someone's life."

"You were the first northerner I'd ever seen. When they pulled us out, I thought you were covered with mud."

Aveline chuckled, holding up her hand to examine it. "Come on now, my skin looks nothing like the muck they pull out of Copper Run. But I was covered with mud. That river is nasty."

"What are we going to do about Koloman, Lady Aveline?" Regarding the river, Valon leaned on the capstones of the parapet. "Alik says he only sleeps when he passes out from exhaustion, and he's talking to the walls. Maxim is demanding you speak to him; Alik turned him away repeatedly."

"Tasha's in Muncifer now, at the Arcane University, searching through their books and whatnot to see what can be done about Koloman's dreams." *At least, I hope that's what she's doing.* "I expect she'll be back by tomorrow with a solution. Or at least a sleeping draught that'll put him into a dreamless sleep for a while. Maxim can go soak his head. I'm still annoyed he showed up and started making demands."

"The Crow Queen." Valon chuckled. "Folks are already planning to make the Dusk of Autumn Festival and High Harvest bigger than they've been for years."

"I'd caution them about that. Tasha hasn't been Crow Queen long enough to make the crops extra bountiful this year. It'd be awful if they didn't have enough for the winter because they got excited. Besides, I think if someone just made her an apple pie for each of the feasts, she'd be perfectly content."

Valon laughed. "I'll pass that along. The apple crop looks like it's going to be really good this year."

"If the rock apples are any indicator, I think you're right." Aveline stretched. "Back to my rounds. Anything going on by Mudders' Gate?"

Valon shook his head. "Nothing important. I've already been through Drakton if you want to take Hillside. I can placate Maxim for a couple more days."

"Hillside it is."

* * *

Tasha strode into the antechamber of the Court of Wizardry with Revan perched on her shoulder. An elderly man stood at an unadorned podium in front of a set of ornately carved doors, wisps of white hair crowning his head.

He raised caterpillar-like eyebrows at Tasha's approach. "You're not a student here."

Glancing at her surroundings, she approached him. Glowing crystals in wall sconces illuminated the celestial mural on the ceiling featuring the symbol of the goddess of magic. Tasha paused to examine the image more closely. The Eye of Selene, composed of the twin moons of Calliome when the Queen eclipsed the King, occurred rarely. The alignment could only occur when both moons simultaneously displayed their full lunar faces and their orbits placed the King in the shadow of the Queen. The last such alignment Tasha recalled had occurred when she was a child.

"Excuse me." The seneschal rapped his knuckles against the podium. "What business do you have in the Court of Wizardry?"

Tasha bowed her head. "My apologies, this is my first time here, and I was admiring the mural. I am Tasha Galperin. I've recently become Crow Queen, and I wish to pay my respects to the archmage."

Frowning, the old man's eyebrows met in a collision of fuzz. "You're the Crow Queen?" He noticed Revan on her shoulder, seemingly for the first time. "You're younger than I last saw you. Been bathing in the blood of virgins?"

Tasha grimaced. "Annika is dead. I'm her successor."

He laughed. "Yes, we were aware of her demise some time ago. It was thought the line of succession was broken. I shall make a note you stopped by; however, the archmage is indisposed."

Forcing herself not to slump in disappointment, Tasha looked on as the man opened a ledger and recorded her name. "Is there someone else I can speak to? I need a… consultation, or access to the library, at least. Also, I believe I probably owe dues going back several years."

The seneschal pointed with his quill at the door behind her. "You'll need to speak to the bursar about that. Go left around the building. There's a side entrance near the compound wall. The archmage has altered how dues are handled."

"After that, you'll direct me to someone I can speak to?"

"I suggest you go to the library around the right side of the court." The seneschal closed his ledger. "Anyone who could help you should be there. Otherwise, they're working with their students. Do not disturb them."

"I wouldn't dream of it." Frowning, Tasha left the seneschal to guard his podium.

Outside, a crowd of students gathered in front of the oak tree to watch two older students toss alternating balls of fire and lightning to each other. Tasha studied the juggling for a moment, then she proceeded around the building to the bursar's office.

In the office, little more than a dimly lit cubicle, a rotund woman with grey hair tied into a bun sat behind a massive oak desk that occupied the majority of the space. With a haze clouding one eye, the woman glanced up as Tasha entered. "You don't look like a student. Are you sure you're in the right place?"

"I'm here to pay Mage's Guild dues." Tasha shut the door behind her and approached the desk. She noticed a tray of pastries shoved to one side. "I probably owe for several years."

Grunting, the woman withdrew a ledger from the lowest desk drawer. "No, you don't. The archmage granted amnesty for everyone owing back dues as one of her first acts when she took over last year. Name?"

"Tasha Galperin…"

The woman held up her hand, tapping a quill against the book. It flipped open, displaying a page filled with writing. "Continue."

"That was nice of the archmage. I'd heard some changes were made."

Scanning the lines on the page, the bursar grunted acknowledgment, then scribbled a few words next to Tasha's name. "Says here you attended the university in Maritropa."

"That's right. I live in Curton now."

Setting down her quill, the bursar examined Tasha, scrutinizing her with her healthy eye. "Curton? Why? Village witch?"

"When I moved there, they needed an apothecary. I now serve them and others as Crow Queen."

The woman recorded another note. "Finally. It's been too long since the last Crow Queen disappeared. It's an honor. When I was a lass, she made our fields fertile again after a bad blight. We were starving when she showed up."

She offered the Crow Queen her hand. Tasha clasped it, noting the woman's iron grip squeezed her fingers. "I'm Adina, by the way, Crow Queen. It's an honor to have you visit our city."

Tasha felt her cheeks grow hot. "Thank you. How much… how much are dues now?"

"Fifty crowns, a one-time payment for lifetime membership in the Mage's Guild."

Patting her pouch, Tasha swallowed. "Fifty? That seems…"

"Far less than paying five crowns a year for your entire adult life." Adina offered her a smile. "Pay what you can now and the rest the next time you're here. There are no penalties for late payments, and the archmage has rededicated the Slayers. They no longer hunt renegades, at least, not the ones who are only delinquent in paying their dues." Chuckling, the bursar shook her head. "The archmage is a reformer, there's no mistake about that. Manless would have had us subjugating half the city if he'd had his way."

Tasha counted out ten crowns, two-thirds of the gold she'd brought with her. She hoped the coin she had left would be enough for the mead she wanted to take home for Aveline. "I haven't heard any details of what happened, just that a new archmage took over. I guess I don't go to the right tavern to hear all the gossip from folks passing through Curton."

"She challenged him to the Rite of Combat. Took him outside the city, then impaled him on a spike of rock as big as my old master's tower. Never seen anything like it. She used elemental magic everyone here thought was lost." Adina made some more notations in the ledger, tapped the page with the quill, and shut the book. "Now, your records are updated. You can pay more at any Arcane University."

"I tried to get a meeting with her to pay my respects." Tasha wondered if Adina possessed more influence than the seneschal. "The old man at the court said she was indisposed."

"She has kin in town. I hear she does research in their home, to cloister herself from all the people demanding her attention here. I guess she finds her brother's family less of a distraction than the high wizards." Adina slid the tray of pastries toward Tasha. "Care for one? My husband runs a shop down the street."

Tasha selected a glazed sweet roll featuring some sort of berry jelly in a well in the center. "Thank you so much for your help, Adina. Is there anyone here who can answer a few questions about oneiromancy?"

"Dream magic?" Adina chose a cinnamon-and-sugar-crusted breadstick. "Hm, divination has never been popular around these parts. Although, I think that silly girl Katka has been studying up on it. Great enchantress, head in the clouds." Adina waved her half-eaten breadstick. "She's the archmage's apprentice. You can find her running around town at all hours doing errands. I can get a message to her to meet you here, if you like."

"That would be wonderful. I'd like to go to the library." Tasha bit into the pastry. The dough, both flaky and buttery, practically melted in her mouth, and the rich raspberry jelly in the center provided a splash of sweetness. "Can she meet me there?"

"I'll let her know." Adina gobbled the rest of the breadstick before invoking a messenger and sending the request to Katka. "Finish the pastry and clean your sticky fingers before getting to the library. The librarians get testy, you know."

"I will, thank you."

Tasha left Adina to her books and baked goods. Conversing with the older woman almost made her feel like a student again, except for the adulation she received for being Crow Queen. She finished her sweet roll as she made her way to the library, licking the sugary jam off her fingers when she finished. She anticipated perusing the stacks while she waited for the archmage's apprentice.

Chapter 46

Aveline's patrol through Hillside took her past many of the town's most opulent homes. At least, they were lavish when Curton's mine still produced a bounty of precious metals. Now, they decayed, still owned by the same families in many cases, the money for upkeep all but exhausted. Many of those families turned to trades or services like tailoring and laundry or gardening. A few remained solvent enough to maintain a relatively high standard of living despite Curton's slow economy.

She continued her patrol next in the market, perusing a vendor's booth offering a variety of sausages, both cured and fresh. She selected several of the cured, dried sausages for her larder, and a rope of fresh ones for that night. Recognizing the vendor as one of butcher Myasnik's nieces, Aveline paid while the girl tied the package. As she left the market, she noticed a furry arm waving at her.

Ra-Jareez trotted up to her. "Ah, our esteemed Lady Aveline. Do you need a fine copper skillet in which to cook your fresh meats?"

Aveline put her hand on her hip. "You're not even at your booth. Are you seriously trying to sell me something from several rows away?"

"No, but I knew it would annoy you." Crossing his arms, Raj tapped his foot. "We heard the Crow Queen returned, yet you did not tell us. Now her hut is gone."

She bit back a retort when she realized the faelix spoke the truth. "You're right. I'm sorry. There was some excitement around her return, and I forgot."

"Then tell me where she is. My sister and I still have questions about her old house."

Aveline noticed several people in the market paying close attention to her conversation with the faelix, no doubt listening to learn the location of the Crow Queen's hut. "She went to Muncifer."

"Where is that? Is it far?"

Aveline waited until the eavesdroppers moved on, discouraged by the news. Taking Raj by the arm, she lowered her voice. "She's planning to be back tonight. If you come by my house, I'll tell you where the hut is, then you can go out there tomorrow first thing."

"Very well." Raj narrowed his eyes, wagging his finger at Aveline. "But if you are not home, I will sit on your steps until you return. I would not want you to forget again."

"I'm headed that way now, and I don't intend to go out again." Aveline hurried away before the faelix made additional demands. She got as far as Caravan Bridge before having to stop, this time for a textile-filled wagon whose wheel had fallen off.

People crowded around the cart, straining to keep the broken side elevated while the driver slid the wheel onto the axle. A tall, dark-haired man, a southerner by the look of him, helped the driver struggling with the unwieldy circle. Aveline spotted a pin used to hold wheels in place rolling away. It had been kicked by one of the numerous helpers shuffling in the area. Lunging for it, she trapped it under her foot.

When she returned with the peg, the group had wrangled the wheel into place. After handing the pin to the driver, Aveline noticed the southerner staring at her.

"Is there something you need?"

Shaking his head, he helped lower the wagon. "You're Lady Aveline, aren't you, the city watch commander?"

"So they tell me." Aveline pushed past the crowd to continue on her way home.

"I am Torben. I understand you're a close friend of Tasha, the apothecary."

Aveline gritted her teeth, in no mood to deal with folk pestering her about the Crow Queen's whereabouts. "Her shop is closed now. The flood destroyed it."

"Yes, I know." He increased his pace, proceeding alongside her. "I was hoping you could tell me where to find her. I have something for her."

Aveline moved out of the center of the street, stopping at the corner by a candlemaker's shop. "She's gone to Muncifer. I'm not sure when she'll return."

"I see." Torben removed his pack from his shoulder, then opened it. "Then perhaps you'd be so kind?" From the pack, he withdrew a package wrapped in a dark cloth. He pulled back the fabric, revealing a larger-than-life crow statue carved from a single piece of weathered lumber. "I made this using a piece of wood I found while helping the draks clean up after the flood. It broke off from her shop, I think. When I saw it, I immediately saw the crow within the wood. I would really like her to have it."

Examining the statue, Aveline sucked in her breath at the exquisite detailing. The textures of the feathers, the scales on the legs, down to holes for the nostrils, they all pointed to the work of a master wood-carver. "It's beautiful, touched by the hand of Adranus himself."

"That's kind of you. My father told me wood carving was a waste of time, a pointless affectation."

Aveline wrapped the figure with the cloth. "I can't think of anyone in town who could rival this." She held it out for him. "Would you mind carrying this to my house for me? I like to keep at least one hand free." She patted the hilt of her mace with one hand while she hefted the package of sausages with the other.

"Of course."

She led him through the winding streets of the shortcut to her house. "What inspired you to carve a crow for Tasha? How do you know her?"

"I only just met her, as a customer in her shop. But I confess, I was smitten from the moment I first saw her."

She glanced at him as they traveled, noting his cheeks burned red. "I know it sounds stupid, like something a child would say, but I haven't been able to stop thinking about her."

"Hm." Aveline thought little of concepts such as love at first sight. In her experience, men who claimed to be smitten so early and strongly tended to want one thing from women. Once they had it, they were usually off to the next town.

"I know what you must think of me. I've tried to steal glances of her, when I can, to just look upon her once more." He laughed. "I failed at that. I only saw her twice again, and I was able to speak to her only once."

Aveline's free hand dropped to her mace. "You've been following her?"

"No!" Torben shook his head. "Pacha's balls, no. I would never do such a thing. I've been spending too much time in the market, hoping to catch her as she shopped. After the flood, I busied myself helping the draks clean and rebuild. They told me she was a good friend to their community, so I helped as much as I could, hoping to see her there."

"I'm sure the draks were appreciative of your help, even if you had an ulterior motive."

Torben grunted. "Judge me harshly, if you like. The draks needed help, so I saw an opportunity to accomplish two things at once."

"All right, fine." Aveline wondered if the man was sincere in his intentions. He seemed more well-spoken than most of the Watchfolk who came through Curton, and most would just as soon spit on a drak than help them clean up and rebuild after a flood.

"Where are you staying?" Aveline changed the subject.

"The Bristled Boar, for now."

"It's a good establishment. I'm surprised you're not flopping at Danica's Den. It's much less expensive."

"Too loud. Fine if you want gambling or wenching and don't mind sleeping listening to others pay for that, but I prefer quiet when I sleep."

Aveline stopped a few houses away from her own when she saw the furry form of Ra-Jareez sitting on her front step. "All right, this is close enough. I'll give it to Tasha when I see her next, and I'll tell her where you're staying. How long will you be in town?"

Torben handed the wrapped carving to Aveline. "I have no plans to leave before the harvest. I've agreed to help pick apples at some of the orchards."

Well, at least he's not a vagabond. "Fine. I'll let her know. You know"—Aveline chewed her lip—"if you're still in a carving mood, I could use an owl of Anetha. I'd pay of course."

"I'll keep my eyes open for a suitable piece of wood. See if inspiration strikes."

"Thank you."

Torben, bowing his head, left. Tucking the carving under her arm, Aveline approached Ra-Jareez. "I didn't expect you this early. I didn't even see you pass me."

"You know the short route. I ran the longer route faster." Raj bared his teeth in a pointy smile. "I did not want to miss you."

"Fine, hold these." She shoved the sausages and the carving into Raj's arms so she could unlock her door. Once inside, she directed the faelix to set them on top of the dresser while she searched for a piece of parchment. She drew him a crude map with directions to the hut.

"The hill overlooks the town. It's probably half a day away or more, so don't plan on just running out there and back before the market opens."

"Do you know when she'll be closer?" He rolled the map.

"I'm not her keeper. If you can wait a few more days, she'll probably move closer to town again."

"Bah, and you'll forget to tell us when that happens, no doubt."

Aveline pointed outside. "Don't push it. She's terribly busy now, and so am I."

Grumbling, he left. Aveline pushed the door shut with her foot. She turned her attention to removing her armor and eating as she waited for Tasha to return.

* * *

As Tasha pulled the door to the library open, a young woman with braided, raven hair charged out, crashing into her. The blow, knocking both women off their feet, sent them sprawling.

"Oh, I'm so sorry. I got a message I'm supposed to meet the Crow Queen here, and I was already here, so I ran down from the upper stacks. I didn't want to miss her, because we haven't had a Crow Queen in so long and my parents always told me about her, but I never thought I'd get a chance to meet her—"

Tasha held up her hand as she sat upright. "I'm the Crow Queen."

Holding her hands to her mouth, the young woman gasped. "I have Dolios's worst luck lately. I'm so, so sorry. Please don't turn me into a newt or make my nose disappear or something terrible. Hey... you're pretty young. My parents always described her as, well, not old exactly, but not as young as you."

Groaning, Tasha picked herself up, smoothing her clothes. "I'm not that young." She helped the young woman to her feet. "You must be Katka, the archmage's apprentice."

Nodding, Katka brushed dirt off her black skirt. She wore her robes open, revealing a dark blue tunic underneath. "I got a messenger from Adina. She said you needed help with oneiromancy?"

"I do, indeed. I sent my own messengers from Curton about a week ago, but I guess they haven't arrived yet. The university still doesn't teach divination?"

Katka held the door open for Tasha. "The masters think divination is for fortune-tellers, grifters, and village witches. Not for real wizards like us. Wait"—she thrust her arm across Tasha's path—"you sent the messengers a week ago and you beat them here? From Curton?"

"I sent them before I learned how to travel with the hut." Tasha gently pushed Katka's arm aside. "The archmage can ignore them when they arrive."

"You brought the hut? The one on chicken legs?" Katka bounced up and down. "Please, I want to see it so bad. My parents used to tell me stories about how it would dance around on chicken's feet."

"They're crow's feet." Tasha tried not to laugh at the young woman's exuberance. "And I used the portal in the hut to come here; it's still in the hills overlooking Curton."

"Oh." A gloom passed over Katka's face. Suddenly, she stared at Tasha again, her eyes widening. "A portal? You used portal magic? The archmage is researching teleportation. She got the moon gates working again, at least, the ones that weren't wrecked in The Sundering."

Katka pressed her hands to her mouth. "Oops. I'm not supposed to talk about that." She glanced at the library entrance. No one paid them any mind. She lowered her voice. "But you're the Crow Queen, so I think it's all right."

Tasha took Katka's hands. "Can you show me where the oneiromancy books are? Our Lord Mayor's having nightmares so terrible he's afraid to sleep. I need to help him."

"They're over here." Pointing to a poorly lit, deserted nook at the far side of the library, Katka led Tasha to it. "Since they kicked me out of alchemy for melting too many cauldrons, and the enchantment master is running out of things for me to do, I've been making up the time here. My little brother used to wake up screaming at night, terrified out of his mind, so I've been learning some oneiromancy to try to help him out."

"I had trouble with alchemy too. Did you help your brother?"

"He kept dreaming about spiders, centipedes, and other nasty bugs crawling all over him, getting in his mouth and ears. Poor kid." She scanned a shelf, running her finger along the spines of the books until she reached a thin tome with covers that appeared to be stiffened, tanned sheep's hide. "I found something in here that helped him take control of his dreams. He dreamed one night where he stomped all the bugs into goo, and he sleeps like a rock now. Mother and Father can barely get him up in the morning for his chores."

Tasha strained to decipher the remains of the title on the worn cover. Too few letters of the text remained to be legible. Katka handed her another book. "This one has the basics. How's your scrying?"

"Not bad. The hut has a basin I can use for that."

Katka flipped her braid over her shoulder. "Like a washbasin?"

"It's multipurpose, in the center of a stump."

"Huh... I want to try a crystal ball someday. They're expensive, though."

Tasha thumbed through the books. At first glance, they appeared they might be useful. "Can I sit somewhere and read?"

"Any of the chairs here are available for that." Katka gestured toward the main hall of the library. "No one will bother you. They're strict about that. Tyrannical, almost."

"While I'm doing that, there is something I forgot."

Katka raised her eyebrows. "What can I do?"

"There's a chaos rift near Curton I need to seal. I don't know the ritual, and I would appreciate some help with that."

"I'll talk to the archmage about it. She closed one last year, and she has a minotaur friend who has closed a couple. I think he's up in Vlorey now, deputy headmaster and master of alchemy at that university, I think she said."

"Vlorey?" Tasha smiled. "I have a friend from Vlorey. She hasn't been there since she was a child, though."

"I'll see what the archmage has to say while you're reading. Need anything else?"

"No, thank you, Apprentice Katka. You've been quite helpful." Tasha opened the book containing oneiromancy basics as Katka curtsied. "Wait, I could use parchment and a quill and ink. I should take notes."

Katka rushed off, soon returning with the supplies from the centrally located librarian's desk. "If you need more, just ask one of the librarians. If you need a drink or get hungry, you'll have to go outside." Leaning down, Katka lowered her voice. "They get really tetchy if you bring food or drink in here. I got away with it once, but only because the librarians were distracted by my friend Conner's candle. They thought he was going to burn the place down." Only enchanted lights were permitted in the university library--open flames tended to be bad ideas around old books and stacks of dry papers.

A glowing blue boggin leapt onto the arm of Tasha's chair. She recoiled with a shriek, drawing glares of disapproval from all within earshot.

"Sorry."

The boggin turned to Katka. "Apprentice Katka, Archmage Delilah needs you. Please come to Kale's shop immediately."

"Gotta run, Crow Queen. I'll ask Deli... Archmage Delilah what we can do to help with your chaos rift while I'm there."

Those can't be the same draks I met in Drak-Anor, can they? Probably coincidence. Surely they aren't the only draks named Kale and Delilah. "I appreciate it." Tasha dove into the book as Katka responded to the archmage's summons, hopeful the answer to Koloman's troubles lay within.

Chapter 47

Aveline awoke with a start to someone pounding on her door. Rubbing her eyes, she pushed herself out of the chair in which she'd fallen asleep. After checking to make sure she was wearing more than just her smallclothes, she pulled the door open.

Tasha held a sheaf of papers. "I think I have it."

Yawning, Aveline beckoned her forward. "It's late. Why didn't you just appear inside?"

"That'd be rude."

Snorting, Aveline cleared the table. She stoked the fire to a full burn, then lit more candles. "Hey, do you know a Watchman named Torben?"

"Torben? I wouldn't say I know him. Why?"

Aveline gestured toward the package on top of the dresser. "He gave me something to give to you. He seems to be sweet on you."

Tasha eyed the parcel. "He is? What is it?"

Aveline brought the carving to Tasha. "Go ahead and open it."

The Crow Queen unwrapped the package, gasping as she admired the carving's workmanship. "It's beautiful. Where did he get it?"

Aveline retrieved two goblets from a cupboard to pour some mead. "He said he made it. He carved it from a piece of wood that broke off your shop during the flood." She slid one of the goblets toward Tasha. "Supposedly."

"It's amazingly detailed." She turned the wooden bird in her hands, examining its precision. "Oh Aveline, I don't have time for this sort of thing anymore. I'm the Crow Queen."

Aveline sat opposite Tasha, then sipped her mead. "That's a cart of cow plop, and you know it. The only reason the mantle came to you is because the previous Crow Queen had no children to pass it to. You're supposed to serve Cybele, goddess of fertility, among others. You think she wants you to take a vow of celibacy?"

"And you think this Torben is my perfect mate?" Tasha scoffed, running her fingers along the edge of the carving.

"I didn't say that. I just don't think you should give up things you want because you're the Crow Queen now. So, obviously, you made it to Muncifer and back."

"I did." Tasha shuffled through the stack of parchment she brought with her. "I spent so much time reading and taking notes in the library I didn't have time to buy you mead, though, sorry."

Aveline dismissed Tasha's concern with a wave of her hand. "I'm not out. I appreciate the thought, though."

Cracking in the hearth, a popping log spat sparks across the floor. Aveline kicked an ember into the fire.

"So, I read up on the basic techniques of oneiromancy, took some notes, then read about how to get someone to take control of their dreams." Tasha pointed to one of the pages of her notes. "They can then basically fight whatever is terrorizing them to banish it from their mind."

"Are you going to do it tonight?" Aveline didn't fancy heading over to Koloman's house at this late hour.

"No, I want you to go with me tomorrow. I'll bring the hut to his house, since I'll need the basin. You can bring him inside, we'll get him to sleep, and I'll deal with it then." Tasha picked up the goblet, draining it.

"More?" Aveline poured while Tasha held the drinking vessel.

"I didn't get to talk to the archmage about the chaos rift, but I spoke to her apprentice. She said they'll send someone out as soon as they can to help." Tasha held up another piece of paper. "She wrote down the ritual for me in case the situation becomes dire, but they said if we can wait, it's easier with more than one person doing it. And safer."

Aveline deferred to Tasha's judgment where the chaos rift was concerned. "Whatever you say. As long as the draks don't go poking around down there, it should stay buried for years, right?"

"You'd think." Tasha folded the papers, then stuffed them in her pouch. "It is a chaos rift, though. I'm not sure what to expect. I'll go out there in a couple of days to make sure nothing unusual is going on."

Upon finishing her second goblet of mead, she picked up the carving. "I'll let you get back to sleep. Meet me at Koloman's in the morning?"

Aveline clicked her fingers to gain Tasha's attention before she teleported to the hut. "Oh, one more thing. Ra-Jareez is looking for you. I told him where you'd be tomorrow, at least, before you decided to move the hut again."

"Thanks, I'll send a message to him when I get back to the hut. Have him come to Koloman's estate in the afternoon to see me. Do you know what he wants?"

Aveline stoppered the bottle of mead. "He and his sister want to know what you're going to do with the old shop. They think they could fix it up and live there, turn it into a shop for whatever it is they think they're going to sell."

"Hm. I haven't given it any thought." Tasha hugged Aveline. "I'll see you tomorrow."

With a snap of her cloak, Tasha vanished. Aveline snuffed the candles she'd lit, stripped out of her wrinkled clothes, and crawled into bed.

* * *

After breaking her fast at dawn, Tasha conjured a messenger to send to Ra-Jareez. "I would be more than happy to talk to you about my old shop. I will come and see you once I have finished with the Lord Mayor." The glowing, emerald bird fluttered through the window in search of the faelix.

Tasha then assumed her position above the basin, moving the hut to the Lord Mayor's compound. Clusters of houses surrounding the perimeter of the estate made finding a location in which to stop difficult, so she directed the hut to hop over the wall. Delighted by the hut's agility, Tasha settled it in the courtyard.

Moving to the window, she watched for Aveline. The watch captain came up the lane, followed by a small line of townsfolk. Discouraging them from loitering as she entered Koloman's estate, the knight-captain shut the gate behind her and shouted for Alik to bring his gate key.

Tasha descended from her hut. "Our Lord Mayor is terribly ill, good people. Please, let me…"

"Good!"

"Aita take him, he's a thief."

"Maris take him first, with her bloody spear. Over and over and over!"

Aveline raked her shield against the bars of the gate. The crowd receded, quieting. "Enough of that. We're duty-bound to try to help him"—she eyed Tasha—"regardless of our personal feelings."

Tasha turned to her friend. "Are you going to get him, or shall I?"

Alik sped down the path from the house, jangling keys in his hand. The crowd shouted insults at him as he locked the gate. "Can't you do something about this rabble?"

"It seems Koloman's popularity is waning." Aveline gestured for the Crow Queen to follow her. "We'll get him together, Tasha."

"Excuse me, I demand to know what you're doing here, Lady Aveline." Alik seized the knight-captain's arm. "The Lord Mayor is not taking visitors at this time."

Tasha stepped between them, noticing Aveline clenching her fist. "I am here to put a stop to his nightmares, as he requested. I need Lady Aveline's help, Alik. If you object to our presence, you can bring him out and into my hut. Otherwise, stay out of our way."

Alik glanced at the hut, taking a step backward. "How did you get that in here?"

"I am the Crow Queen." Turning her back on him, she dismissed Alik's demands for answers. Inspired by the warming mantle, she proceeded into Koloman's house.

"I think Alik was born grouchy." Aveline chuckled, following her.

"If you had to work for Koloman, wouldn't *you* be angry all the time?" Tasha paused at the door to the study; the last place she'd seen Koloman. It stood to reason if he suffered from sleep deprivation and refused to see anyone, he'd sequester himself in the room in which he felt safest.

"If I had to work for him, I'd probably kill myself. If I didn't kill him first." Aveline gripped the door handle. "Let me go first."

Tasha stepped aside, allowing Aveline to open the door. The knight-captain unfastened the latch. Readying her mace and shield, she pushed the door open with her foot. The acrid tang of stale urine assaulted them as they entered the room. Cloaked in darkness, the only light in Koloman's study came from glowing embers in the hearth.

"Damn you, Alik, I told you I was not to be disturbed." Tasha barely understood Koloman's slurred words.

"It's Tasha and Aveline. I can fix your dreams, make the nightmares stop."

He peeked around the side of the chair in which he slumped. Light from the hallway illuminated his face, revealing dark circles under his bloodshot eyes. His hair, tangled and matted, appeared as though it had not been washed in ages.

"The dark man says you'll kill me. Boil my bones into stew." Growling, he fell out of his chair, then pointed at Tasha. "Arrest her, Captain. She'll kill us all!"

Aveline glanced at Tasha. Even in the dim light of Koloman's study, Tasha noticed her friend biting her cheek to stifle her first, impulsive retort.

"I'll take you somewhere where you'll be safe from her." Aveline secured her mace before lifting him under the arm. "Oof, you stink. Come on, then. I'll take you to my magical room where you can sleep, then we'll go to the baths."

He tried to push Aveline away. "Unhand me, woman. I'll not…" He stumbled, catching himself on the knight-captain's arm. "I… he… coming…"

Koloman blubbered as Aveline pulled him out of the room. Tasha closed the door behind her before racing ahead to intercept Alik. Putting her hands on his chest, she kept him from interfering while Aveline dragged the Lord Mayor out of his house.

"Draw a hot bath for him, then start cleaning that study, Alik."

"I demand to know where—"

"The hut isn't going anywhere. We're going to stop his nightmares. You'd do well to keep things quiet out here." Feeling the cloak growing warm around her, Tasha left Alik sputtering on the path. Upon confirming Alik had not followed her, she shut the door.

Tossing and turning on the Crow Queen's bed where Lady Aveline laid him, Koloman muttered. Tasha's blankets lay in a pile by the footboard.

"You may want to burn the bed when we're finished." She examined her mail where Koloman touched her. "I think he corroded my armor."

Tasha ignored the jibe, concentrating on utilizing the basin to enter Koloman's mind. "Pull the curtains, then shut the door and snuff the candles, would you please, Aveline?"

As Aveline did so, Koloman's restlessness diminished. Soon, he lay still. Tasha focused on viewing the moments between waking and sleeping, as the tome instructed.

According to the text, entering dreams was easiest if one connected to the subject's mind prior to them entering a deep sleep.

Unlike Aveline's, Koloman's sleeping mind lay wide open to Tasha. Moving into it felt like slipping into a pool of black slime. Anger, fear, and hatred coated her, laying claim to her limbs with a clinging chill. She felt the cloak grow warmer and warmer still, staving off the cold that enveloped her.

Surrounded by inky blackness, Koloman sat in his armchair, naked, emaciated, a hollow shell of the man Tasha knew. A tall robed figure leaned over the chair behind him.

"Yes, show me the object of your desires, Koloman." Its voice, posture, and thin frame seemed familiar to Tasha, although she could not place it.

"Show me, and they can be yours." The robed figure pointed at Tasha with a slender, almost skeletal, finger. "Is this one of the wenches you lust after? What do you want to do to her? Show me. Unclothe her and show me your deepest desires."

Koloman pushed himself out of the chair with shaking arms.

"No, Koloman. It is not your master." Tasha strode forward. "It is a dark figment of your mind. Cast it out, and you can sleep freely once more."

Hissing, the robed figure grabbed Koloman by the head, pulling him downward and into the chair. His fingers framed Koloman's face. "How are you in his mind?" The Lord Mayor's eyes appeared lifeless.

This is no figment of his mind... this is... I don't know what this is. She peered into the depths of the creature's hood. The resources she had found in the Arcane University library contained no instructions for combating an actual entity as the source of the nightmares.

"Fight it, Koloman. Cast it out. It has taken control of you. You are Koloman, Lord Mayor of Curton, not this creature's thrall."

"Tired... need sleep." Koloman's voice became a mere raspy whisper.

"Sleep when it is gone." Tasha gripped her amulet. "*Fos.*" It flared with brilliant, verdant light. She willed the light to grow brighter, holding her amulet before her like a beacon. "Leave this man, creature. Begone! You are not welcome here. Cast it out, Koloman. Take back your dreams, your mind."

"My dreams... I don't like my dreams."

"You have no power here, woman." The creature recoiled from Tasha's light, hissing.

"Cast it out, Koloman. It has invaded your home, your mind, and your dreams. It is an unwelcome guest."

"You are... unwel—"

"Koloman"—the creature leaned its head next to Koloman's ear, keeping a tight grip on his head—"I will give you the power to take all you desire. This woman, any woman in town, all the women in the world, if you so choose. They will do your bidding. They will service you willingly and lustfully."

"Koloman!" Tasha lunged forward, thrusting the blazing amulet into the creature's hood. For a brief moment, the blinding light illuminated the features of a man whose face appeared half-melted. Shrinking from the light, he screamed in agony.

Tasha thought about the forest, trees, and vines. The darkness retreated, replaced by an ancient forest. The vines sped toward the creature. "I am the Crow Queen. You are not welcome here, abomination. You are an affront to Gaia. Begone!"

Wrapping around the creature's arms and legs, the vines pulled them spread-eagle. Hissing, he thrashed in the vines.

"Tell him, Koloman. Tell him he is unwelcome. Cast him out."

"You are... unwelcome here."

Screaming, the creature flailed. Tasha retracted the vines, straining against the creature's strength. Shredding its robes, the vines pulled the creature apart. With a final shriek, the entity fell to the ground, melting into the dark landscape of Koloman's dreams.

The Lord Mayor collapsed, fading from Tasha's mind. Upon opening her eyes, she found Aveline viewing the scenery, unconcerned.

"Aveline?" Tasha found her knees weak, holding onto the stump to remain upright.

"What do you need?" Aveline turned, sunlight glinting off her polished armor.

"It's done. It's over."

Chapter 48

"What? That's it?" Aveline examined Koloman sleeping soundly on the bed. "I expected something… I don't know… more flashy."

Tasha rubbed her eyes, stifling a yawn. "How long did it take? I'm exhausted."

"Just a few minutes. Alik just entered the house."

Gazing at her bed, Tasha suppressed another yawn. "I feel like I need a nap."

"I suppose I could carry him down to the house. Let Alik deal with him." Aveline lifted Koloman's arm, then let it drop. He did not stir. "How much do you think he weighs?"

Regarding the Lord Mayor, Tasha crossed her arms. "A dozen stones at most, probably less. He doesn't look like he's been eating much lately."

"Too bad this place doesn't have a second bedroom." Aveline slung her shield around, bending to hoist Koloman over her shoulder.

"I could use a second bedroom, perhaps a little den so I can just sit with my friends and talk without"—Tasha gestured around the room—"all this clutter."

Shuddering, the hut sprouted a curved wooden handle on the back door. Aveline stepped away from Koloman. "What was that?"

Tasha shook her head. "I don't know, but this isn't the first time I've expressed a wish, and the hut responded." Upon approaching the back door, she tried the handle. The door swung open, revealing a room beyond.

"Aveline, it's another bedroom!" Tasha passed through the doorway. Aveline stuck her head through the opening. Made from tree branches and vines, the room resembled a sylvan cave more than a proper room in a house. A chandelier made of twisted branches hung down in the center of the room. From each branch sprouted several short vines with glimmering ends. The chandelier cast a warm glow over the entire space.

The bed, much like the one in the main room, grew from the floor, a rectangular mass of branches and vines with a mattress of fronds and moss. Through another doorway on the far side of the room, Aveline viewed an alcove containing its own hearth, a hammock, and several armchairs.

"You should be careful what you wish for in this place. You could bring everything down around you with a stray thought." Upon entering the room, Aveline half expected the door to slam behind her.

Tasha sat on the edge of the bed, testing the mattress. "I don't think it would do anything to harm me. It seems to know my intentions."

"You sleep here, and I'll keep an eye on Koloman out there." Aveline turned to leave her friend to rest.

"You don't have to stay, Aveline. I can handle Koloman on my own. He's probably going to sleep the rest of the day." Tasha covered her mouth, yawning.

"Nonsense, I'd feel better not leaving you alone with that man, no matter what you can do to him now." Aveline paused before closing the door. "Rest well. Mind if I raid the larder? I haven't eaten anything yet."

"Help yourself. Most of it replenishes itself."

That's handy. Aveline shut the door, heading for the larder. She delighted to find fresh cream, berries, and a variety of small sweet cakes. After pulling a chair near the window, she ate with her feet propped on the sill. Feeling twinges of guilt for babysitting Koloman instead of patrolling the city, she admitted that, as a citizen, he deserved her protection inasmuch as any of the people who reviled him. At any rate, the city council supported his rule for the time being, and Koloman kept to himself most days. The common folk on the street might despise him, but they could not say he affected their day-to-day lives in a significant fashion.

The sun streamed in through the window as the morning progressed, and Aveline found herself dozing. She awoke to Alik's calls for her from the courtyard. Shielding her eyes from the sun, she leaned out the window.

"Is he cured, Lady Aveline?"

"Tasha thinks so." She glanced at Koloman, still motionless on the bed. "He's sleeping now."

"The study is cleaned. I've drawn a bath, but it's getting cold."

"I'll see if I can rouse him." Aveline considered how best to do that as she approached the bed. Gripping him by the shoulders, she shook him. "Wake up, Koloman. Wake up!"

Groaning, he pushed her away before draping his arm over his eyes. "Away with you, woman. Can't a dying man have peace?"

"You're not dying, Tasha fixed your dreams, and you need a bath."

Koloman rolled over, cracking an eye to regard her. "Why are you in my house? And who opened those damned curtains?"

Clutching his arm, Aveline pulled him upright. "You're in the Crow Queen's hut befouling her bed with your unwashed body. Alik's drawn a bath. Time to get up. You can sleep again in your own bed after you bathe."

"Maris take you." He swung his legs off the bed. "Where am I?"

"I told you—the Crow Queen's hut."

Scowling, Koloman peered around the room. "You brought me to some peasant witch's hovel?"

"Don't make us regret saving your life." Aveline held the front door open for him. "Mind the step and consider showing some gratitude. You would have starved to death eventually had she not intervened."

"I doubt that." Koloman sniffed as he passed her. Pausing, he moved to put an arm around her. "Come, bathe me."

Aveline caught him by the wrist. "Touch me, and I'll throw you out. It's a long way down."

He peeked out the door, his eyes widening. "What sorcery is this? Where in Maris's domain have you brought me?"

Twisting his arm behind his back, Aveline marched him down the steps. She ignored his protests. "There are many who think I should have sent you to Maris's domain. I told you already, the Crow Queen's hut. Try listening for once." When they reached the bottom, she turned him toward his front door. "There. Your house."

She shoved him forward, releasing him. "Go inside, take a bath, and think of a way to thank the Crow Queen for saving your life."

Before Koloman responded, Aveline climbed the steps and entered the hut, shutting the door behind her. "Ungrateful bastard."

* * *

Tasha rolled out of bed, refreshed. She returned to the main room of the hut. Koloman and Aveline were gone, as was the bed. In its place sat a bench with an array of alchemical equipment. A scrap of parchment sat under the edge of the crow carving. Tasha recognized Aveline's handwriting on it.

Tasha,

As soon as I got Koloman up and out, the hut started rearranging itself. I decided to leave before it rearranged me. Hopefully, it doesn't forget you're in that other room and seal you up. I'll be home after dark if you want to talk.

Aveline

She returned the note to the table, then examined the alchemy equipment. Although she knew the names and uses of all the tools, bottles, and other accoutrements, alchemy remained a skill for which she possessed little talent.

"Are you trying to tell me something?" Tasha stared at the ceiling, as if the hut could answer.

Receiving no reply, Tasha climbed into place above the basin and walked the hut out of Koloman's compound. She headed north along the city wall toward the Copper Run River. While the hut ran over relatively level terrain, she tweaked the interior layout a bit by moving the alchemy equipment and apothecary cabinet to an alcove near her bedroom and returning the smaller, secondary bed to the central room. Gathering speed as she approached the banks, she leapt across, clearing the water with room to spare. She chose a spot near the edge of the forest just north of Mudders' Gate and settled in.

Thunder rumbled in the distance. From the top of the steps, Tasha noticed storm clouds on the horizon. The light breeze indicated rain coming this way would not arrive before dark. Calling her birds to her, she headed toward town.

People bowed, genuflecting as she passed. Stopping to discourage such activity caused more people to bombard her with requests and demands. Instructing Revan and Korbin to fly away, keeping them safe, she raised her arms to gain people's attention.

"Please, I have business in town. I'm not the apothecary anymore, nor am I soothsayer. Everything you want from me you can get in the market."

"You heard the Crow Queen." Torben's voice rose above the clamor of the crowd. He banged the heads of his axes together. "Give her space, for the love of Cybele."

Towering over the crowd, Torben intimidated most people to disperse. Tasha curtsied as he approached. "That's the second time you've parted the crowds for me."

"It's the second time I've been fortunate enough to pass through here at the same time you've been arriving." Torben returned his axes to his belt before bowing deeply to Tasha.

"Thank you for the carving. It's wonderful."

His cheeks growing rosy, he brushed his braids over his shoulders as he turned his gaze to her. "Think nothing of it. I was inspired."

Tasha caught herself staring into his grey-blue eyes, feeling warmth rise in her cheeks. Giggling, she averted her gaze. "I'm grateful for your help. The attention is a little overwhelming."

"W-w-would you…" He stared at his feet.

"Yes?" Tasha lifted his head. Torben's cheeks blazed red.

"I wondered if you would care to walk with me, tonight. Just out of town, there is an orchard. They have a wonderful garden growing there, benches, and…"

"I know where you mean." Tasha took his hand. "I have some business to attend to, but I will try to meet you there shortly before dusk, if that would be all right."

The Watchman bowed again. "I would be honored, Lady."

"Just Tasha, Torben."

"I would be honored, Tasha." He brought her hand to his lips.

Tasha felt a flutter in her stomach. "I should go. I need to go to the market before it closes."

"May you be unhindered by crowds, Crow Queen."

Tasha released his hand, then hurried down the street. *What are you doing? You're not a schoolgirl.* Smiling, she giggled again. *On the other hand, he is very handsome and polite too.*

She found if she kept moving and did not slow or stop to discourage people from bowing or kneeling as she passed, no crowd gathered around her. It pained her when people treated her with the same reverence they reserved for royalty. She entered the Church of Cybele to have a word with Mother Anya about it. The matriarch assured her she would instruct her congregation during services not to exhibit such subservience, although many people in town did not attend weekly rites.

After her brief chat with the matriarch, Tasha sought out Ra-Jareez in the market. As expected, she found him and his sister working in Imrus's stall.

"Ah, friend Crow Queen." Ra-Jareez bowed to Tasha.

Jazeera scoffed. "Will you next lick her feet clean while you're down there?"

Tasha ignored the sibling's snipe. "I understand you're interested in my old home and shop?"

"Yes, indeed." Raj nodded as he eyed his sister. "We think it would make an excellent trading post for exotic goods from all over the world. Jazeera has already been gathering inventory and capital."

"There was a time when I would question where you found the means to do so"—Tasha crossed her arms—"however, it seems a waste to let the building fall to pieces. I'm inclined to just let you have it. You may find it's in such dire shape you'll wish you'd gone back to Nakambe."

"Now that"—Jazeera gestured to Tasha—"we do not have the means to accomplish."

"If you want to go"—Tasha watched a child on the next row steal a loaf of bread, but the vendor caught and scolded him before sending the urchin on his way with it—"I can send you home. It's as easy as walking through a door."

"We came here to trade, sister." Raj stroked Jazeera's hand. "Let us not lose sight of that."

"We lost everything else." Upon withdrawing her hand, Jazeera turned away from her brother. "People here stare at us like we're freaks."

Tasha glanced around the market. For the most part, townsfolk browsing the stalls ignored the siblings unless

Raj spoke directly to them. "I think you might be mistaking curiosity for judgment. You should ask Aveline about that. She was the first northerner many people had ever seen."

"Do you really wish to abandon this, sister?" Raj put his hand on his sister's shoulder. "I will go back to Shak-Hayla with you, if that is what you desire."

"You can't go back. I will stay with you here; that was the agreement."

Tasha raised an eyebrow. "Why can't you go back? Family trouble?"

Chuckling, Raj waved his hand in dismissal. "Ah, trouble with law bringers. Certain magistrates disagreed with the way I did business. They are easily avoided."

"But if you are caught"—Jazeera spun on her brother—"they will dismember you."

"Yes, well, that is why I would prefer to stay here. No one wants to dismember me here, and the watch captain has been exceedingly kind to us."

Shaking her head, Tasha covered her eyes with her hand. "Aveline will come down hard on you if you swindle people. I'd stay on her good side."

"I will make sure he does." Jazeera yanked her brother's ear tuft. "I left several promising suitors behind to sail to Vornstaad."

Raj wriggled his ear out of his sister's grip, chuckling as she left in a huff. "We will be upstanding citizens, honest merchants. You have my word. We are most grateful for your generosity, even if Jazeera is too rude to acknowledge it."

"I'll leave a note of the change of ownership at the Hall of Records." Tasha decided to combine the trip with a visit to the citadel to check in with Aveline.

"You are most kind. Please forgive my sister. She has been feeling lonely lately. As she said, she enjoyed the attention of several suitors. Now that we are no longer fighting for our lives, the relative peace of idleness brings her boredom and loneliness into focus."

Tasha fished in her pouch for money. "I want one of those copper skillets you tout so effectively. The hut provides me with much, but I find myself wanting for different cooking vessels."

Beaming, Raj selected a medium-sized skillet from the stock. "I think this one will work best for you. Not too large, I think. A mere five crowns."

"Five? You sold that man a set for six just a few days ago." Tasha disliked this negotiation game.

"Did I? Well, for a good friend such as you, I will sell this for four, then."

Tasha counted out three crowns, then pressed them into his hand. "I think three will suffice, don't you, in light of my previous generosity?"

"Ah, yes. Of course. Shall I wrap it for you?"

Tasha took the skillet from him. "No, thank you. I'm going back to my hut soon. Be well."

Raj saw another potential customer, bowing his head to Tasha before approaching the matron. "Good woman, are you in need of a superior stew pot? We have the finest copper wares in town."

"I need a chamber pot."

Leaving Raj to his customer, Tasha proceeded toward the Hall of Records and the citadel. Updating ownership of her old shop took most of the rest of the afternoon, owing to poor record keeping and disorganization of the clerks. After completing her business, she stopped at the citadel, only to find Aveline had not been there yet. Upon leaving a note for her friend, she returned home to freshen up and change before going to the orchard to meet Torben.

Chapter 49

Although she managed to avoid Maxim while dealing with Koloman, as dusk approached, Aveline's luck ran out. He cornered her in the larder while she was taking inventory.

"You knew the Lord Mayor was indisposed, and you deliberately wasted my time sending me to see him!" His finger quivered as he shook it in dangerous proximity to her face.

She slapped away his hand. "I didn't know he was that far gone. We've solved his issue now, so he should be back to normal in a day or two. If it'll make you shut up, I'll authorize a temporary expenditure from the watch funds to hire workers for you to take to Dawnwatch, provided you sign a note saying you'll repay the money with interest and you send those other requests to Almeria."

Aveline hated drawing money from the Watch funds for any purpose apart from payroll and stocking the larder, but Maxim's presence irritated her to the point she would be willing to pay out of her own pocket to make him go away.

"You could have done that days ago." Lowering his hand, Maxim stepped backward.

"Even now, I do not want to." Pushing him aside, Aveline exited the larder. "I would be well within my rights to ignore your demands until we receive a response from Almeria."

"That could take months."

"Exactly." Upon returning to her desk, she sat in her chair, then propped up her feet.

"I understand your friend is someone the people here are calling 'Crow Queen.' According to local legends, she can travel great distances swiftly." He placed his hands on his hips. "Is there any truth to these stories?"

Upon pushing herself away from her desk, she stood. "I'm not going to ask her to run errands for us." She poked his breastplate. "She's a servant of the gods, supposedly, not a page and not your squire."

Maxim smirked. "Supposedly? You don't believe her?"

Sighing, Aveline approached the vault. "I only know what she believes. I never had much faith myself, but it seems clear to me Tasha's purpose is greater than delivering letters."

She shut the door to the vault behind her, cutting off Maxim's reply. She opened a leather pouch, counting a number of coins into it before returning to Maxim. She thrust the pouch into his hand. "There's a hundred crowns. Use it wisely. When you get the money from Almeria, I expect half-again as much back."

"A hundred and fifty?" Maxim's mustache quivered. "That's usury!"

"That"—Aveline pointed toward the bulging pouch—"is a loan from funds not intended for the Dawnwatch garrison. Agree to my terms or return it now. It's a drop in the bucket compared to what the princess should be sending you."

Snapping his mouth shut, Maxim growled. "Very well. I shall depart for Dawnwatch first thing in the morning."

Aveline retrieved her mace and shield from the rack. "Fine. I expect regular updates. Get those letters sent before you leave."

"Yes, m'lady."

She turned her back to him. Maxim bowed before stomping out of the citadel. *Aita take him and Princess Valene. Everything was running smoothly without the crown involved.* She made her way to the Drunken Horse, intent on washing the distaste from her mouth with several mugs of mead.

* * *

Viewing the orchard from the portal in her hut, Tasha's conflicting emotions collided. *I'd hoped that, by now, you'd have moved on.* Lorelei's words echoed in her mind.

Korbin flew into the hut. When he landed on her shoulder, she stroked the crow's head. "She's been gone from this world for over a decade. He's no elf, Korbin, but then again, few are. He is more to my liking than any of the men I've met in Curton, though. They're good folk, just… I've seen so much compared to them."

Steeling herself, Tasha stepped through the doorway. The sun, low in the sky, cast an orange glow across the orchard. Korbin flew away, darting among the trees as she made her way to the path leading toward town. She hoped to meet Torben before he entered the orchard.

To her satisfaction, she found him within minutes, just outside the orchard gate.

"Have you been waiting for me here?" He glanced over his shoulder toward town and then at her, tilting his head.

"I've only just arrived." She came up beside him, crooking her arm in his.

Torben cocked his head. "I… I… I am surprised I did not see you. H-how did you arrive here from town without passing me?"

Tasha smiled. "I'm the Crow Queen. My ways are varied and mysterious."

"Ah, yes, of course." He bowed his head. "I meant no offense."

She laughed. "There's a portal in my hut that can send me wherever I wish to go."

His eyes widened. "Truly? That is wondrous. How does it work?"

"How? That's beyond me. I just know it does. I could use it to send you back to the Four Watches, if you wish, although you'd have to take the long way back here. I don't know of a way to bring someone with me, or to send them and bring them back." Tasha suspected such feats were beyond the magic of the mantle, and she harbored little desire to experiment. She doubted the gods made the portal for townsfolk to use willy-nilly.

Torben extracted his arm from hers. "I'm sorry, this is wrong of me… you must have more important things to do than indulge—"

Tasha took his hand. "Nonsense. I'm not a goddess, a high priestess under a vow of celibacy, or a princess with a dozen royal suitors. This"—she lifted the edge of her feath-ered cloak—"makes me no less or more of a person than you. Right now, right here, for you, I'm just Tasha. Can I just be Tasha, Torben, please?"

"Yes, of course."

They passed under the arched, wrought-iron gate of the orchard. The rough, partially rusted metal depicted the leaves of an apple tree bearing fruit.

"What brought you to Curton?" Tasha paused to admire a cluster of sweet alyssum flowers growing around a grove of apple trees. The tiny white flowers resembled a splash of snow against the verdant grass of the orchard.

"I wanted to see more of the world than just snow and ice." Torben led Tasha down the winding path between the trees. "I sailed up to Vlorey, worked as a caravan guard en route to Celtangate, then traveled to Maritropa to see the magical, flying city."

The powerful arcane means that kept the city afloat, attracted Tasha to the Arcane University in Maritropa instead of the one in Muncifer. "And now you're heading home through here?"

"That was my intention." Torben glanced down at Tasha. "Once I arrived here, I found I didn't want to cross the mountains again. It's not that I fell in love with the town—it has few attractions—I just… there's little for me to go home to. And you? I hear you're an outsider, as well."

"Yes. I came here a little over ten years ago." Tasha watched a butterfly flit within a cluster of wildflowers. Curton had not changed much since she arrived, and she connected with only one person in all that time. "I was running, and I kept running until, well"—she chuckled—"I guess I didn't want to cross the mountains, either."

"What were you running from?"

"Facing my grief. At the time, I thought my lover died in payment for our past indiscretions." She patted his hand upon seeing his furrowed brow. "We were involved with a group that believed some pretty terrible things about draks and their place in the world. We were wrong. In the end, Lorelei died helping others—draks, minotaurs—achieve something noble. Something good."

"I'm sorry."

Squeezing his hand, Tasha smiled. "She was an elf. Only her mortal body died. Her spirit returned to Gaia's side, and she can again roam the Fae Realm. My time with her was wonderful, but I realize now we should make the best with what we're given, rather than constantly focusing on what we can't have."

Torben sighed, stopping under the boughs of an old, gnarled apple tree. The low-hanging green fruit, beginning to ripen, promised a bountiful harvest within a few weeks. "You and Lady Aveline…"

"Are just friends. That's what you're wondering, right?" Tasha released his hand, turning away before lowering her head. "It's what everyone wonders. I've been here over ten years, turning down every suitor, but spending so much time in Aveline's company at taverns or just sitting in our homes talking. Too many people assume we're lovers. Some don't care, others…"

"Are jealous they can't be happy in their own relationships." Torben moved behind her, placing a hand on her shoulder. "Among the Watchfolk, people are expected to get married and have children. Pacha's Pox, they call those who take lovers with whom they can't have children."

Pacha, the god of wine, madness, and passion, always caught the blame for what certain folk considered debauchery or perverted behavior, although in Tasha's experience, those truly guilty of heinous behavior toward others they didn't approve of rarely felt any passion, only hatred and fear. Loving another person was a blessing by Aurora, in Tasha's view.

She took Torben's hand. "I don't know why I feel comfortable around you, Torben. I barely know you. I'm still figuring out what it means to be Crow Queen."

"Helping the people in town clean up after the flood, I heard a lot of things. They regard you highly. Lady Aveline too. It's not my place to offer advice, but I would say don't be afraid to rely on your friend for guidance."

Tasha hoped she could. She didn't want to burden Aveline with her problems, though. Bringing Torben's hand down off her shoulder, she resumed walking. "This got maudlin. I thought we were supposed to talk about frivolities."

"We Watchfolk don't often have the luxury for frivolities." Torben chuckled. "I suppose, if you were of a mind, you could give me your blessing as Crow Queen for my hunt in a few days."

"I'm not up on my blessings for things that fall under Artume's purview, yet." Tasha made a mental note to add teachings about the goddess of the hunt to her reading list. "Though I suppose if you treat your prey with respect and are not wasteful with your kill, then the goddess will have no objection."

"It won't go to waste. I promised the folk here I would bring them a couple of boars for their larder."

Tasha frowned. "Which folk?" Boars were notoriously difficult to hunt. They tended to fight aggressively, unlike deer or mountain sheep who only sought to flee their hunters.

"Florin and Alina Maranu here at the orchard." He gestured toward the house at the crest of the nearby hill. "I've been helping them get ready for the harvest."

"Take care, Torben. I saw a werewolf in the forest south of town. I think I frightened it off, but there could be more."

He patted the ornate dagger at his hip. "Silver. We Watchfolk are no strangers to brothers and sisters of the moon. But I appreciate the warning."

As the sun sank beneath the horizon, fireflies joined the crickets, providing visual accompaniment to their evening songs. They continued wandering the paths of the orchard until the King and then the Queen started their journeys across the sky, chasing after the now-departed sun in their perpetual cosmic dance.

"Shall I walk you back to town, Torben? The paths grow dark, and I fear the light from the moons won't be enough to safely illuminate them for you." The Mantle of the Crow Queen afforded Tasha the ability to see clearly in low-light conditions, however, Torben enjoyed no such boon.

"No need." He pointed toward the house on the hill, illuminated from within by candles and its central hearth, like a beacon in the distance. "I've moved to a room in the orchard house. They're letting me stay for free in exchange for my labor, and they're paying me, too. It's not far, and I know these grounds well now. What of you?"

"I can return home in an instant." Tasha giggled. "I almost feel like being dramatic and telling you the power of the Crow Queen will usher me away safely. I don't know that it will be all that impressive in the dark."

Torben scratched his head. "I don't understand what you mean."

Smiling, Tasha stepped backward. "Then I'll demonstrate." Holding the edges of her cloak, she extended her arms at her sides, like wings. "Good night, Torben, perhaps we can do this again soon." Snapping the cloak shut around her, she returned to the comfort of her hut in an instant.

Chapter 50

The next several days of peace and quiet almost made Aveline think normalcy had returned to Curton. Then, she arrived at the citadel one morning to find Lord Mayor Koloman waiting for her. He continued to allow his beard to grow, now neatly trimmed, and his velvet doublet and dark leather breeches pointed to a man recovered from his ordeal.

"Ah, Lady Aveline"—he bowed, sweeping his arm before him—"a pleasure to see your beauty on this fine morning."

Behind the Lord Mayor, Lieutenant Valon raised his eyebrows, and the corners of his mouth turned slightly upward. "The Lord Mayor has graced us with his presence while waiting for you to arrive this morning, Lady Aveline."

"I'm flattered. What do you want?" Ignoring his attempts to kiss her hand, she stowed her shield and mace before sitting behind her desk.

"Only to thank the woman who allowed me to sleep soundly once again. My dreams, of you"—he winked at Aveline—"are lascivious and pleasant once more."

Aveline hunted for paperwork in which to immerse herself, but she found none. "Tasha's not here. You need to thank her. At least you bathed."

"Indeed, though, I was saddened to learn you were unable to help me with that." Koloman sat on the edge of her desk, leaning closer toward her. "I insist you join me for dinner at my estate tonight. As the only proper lady in town, it's high time you were married to someone befitting your high stature."

Lowering her brow, she glared. "That won't be happening. I have no desire to dine with you, or to entertain talk of marriage."

"Oh, come now"—he cupped her chin in his hand—"I could bring you such pleasure tonight."

Slapping his hand away, she jumped out of her chair.

Lieutenant Valon cleared his throat. "Lady Aveline, I need your help with a prisoner. Kettlegut's gotten rowdy again."

She turned her glare on Valon. He gestured toward the cellblock. She returned her gaze to Koloman. "I must attend to my duties. Don't let me keep you from the rest of your day."

Aveline turned her back to Koloman, picking up her mace before following Lieutenant Valon. She shut every door between the front vestibule and the cellblock as they passed through. Upon reaching the deserted cellblock, a quick glance confirmed her suspicions.

"I didn't think we had anyone here. Who in Tinian's name is Kettlegut? What's your game, Valon?"

"Apologies, Lady Aveline." Pressing his hands together, Valon bowed. "I merely wanted to get you away from the Lord Mayor before you assaulted him. He's been… in a mood."

She couldn't fault Valon for protecting her from herself. "Evidently. What's going on?"

"I know not. He addressed me by name. I didn't even know he knew my name. Inquired about my home life. He smiled. He joked." Valon pointed toward the front room. "That man is not Koloman."

Aveline flung open a cell door, then sat on a bench. "Maybe whatever Tasha cleansed from Koloman had been in there for years. It doesn't matter. He's still a letch."

"What did she do to him?" Valon sat next to Aveline.

"Something in his dreams. I don't understand it myself. Have there been any strange reports from the mudders or hunters lately? Something else Tasha mentioned."

"There's talk of more wolves about lately, but it could be a migration." He scratched his chin. "No one seems concerned. Why?"

She patted his leg. "Probably nothing to worry about. Can you check if he's gone? If not, bring me a set of shackles and tell him I'll be a while."

Valon laughed. "I see, sacrifice me." He bowed. "Very well, m'lady."

He returned after a few minutes to report Koloman had left. Taking a break, she ate with Valon and a few of the other guards in the citadel. Mailed boots stomping into the vestibule interrupted their gossip of goings-on in town.

"Lady Aveline? Constables?"

One of the sergeants leapt up, intercepting him.

"Maxim. Both in one day." Aveline rubbed her temples. "I must have angered Dolios to have luck this poor." She refilled her mug with mead.

Mug in hand, Aveline entered the room, observing Maxim wringing his hands while he spoke. Inhaling deeply, he nodded to the sergeant.

"Back so soon, Maxim?"

"There's a problem at Dawnwatch. The lads I hired are ill-equipped to deal with it, and I'm afraid… well, it's something I've not dealt with before."

Aveline pinched the bridge of her nose. "What is it?"

"A haunting. I believe there's a ghost in Dawnwatch."

* * *

Over the next several days, Tasha returned to Muncifer to browse the Arcane University library for more texts on Artume, lycanthropes, and chaos rifts. She filled several pages with notes. Each time she sought either Apprentice Katka or the archmage, both were indisposed and unable to give her further assistance.

Still, the trips proved fruitful. In combination with studying in the library, moving the hut with each dawn, and visiting the draks at the mine, she barely realized how many days sped past. Unwilling to risk another week-long absence, she altered the hut once again to include a bathing vessel. To her delight, it filled with hot water whenever she entered the room; however, it did not serve to relax her as well as the pool in the sylvan glade.

Each day, she sent Korbin or Revan to check in with Aveline. On the fifth day, one returned with a note from her friend requesting assistance with a problem a man called Maxim struggled with. She conjured a messenger, sending it ahead to Aveline, letting her know she'd meet her at the citadel shortly.

Tasha changed into fresh clothes, then held out her arm for Revan to join her. He landed on her shoulder. Upon summoning an image of the citadel vestibule in the back door, she observed Aveline conversing with an armored man. Stepping through the portal, Tasha raised her hand in greeting.

"You must be Maxim. I am Tasha, Crow Queen."

Maxim recoiled. "Tinian's lance! What sorcery is this?"

"What? They don't tell stories about the Crow Queen in Almeria?" Laughing, Aveline hugged her friend. "Surely you've heard people talking around town."

"No one talks about a feathered woman appearing out of thin air."

"What's the problem?" Tasha drew her cloak around her, keeping her distance from the agitated man. Revan hopped off her shoulder to perch on Aveline's desk.

Stammering, Maxim eyed Tasha with suspicion. Aveline sighed. "He thinks Dawnwatch is haunted. There's a ghost or something in the ruins."

Tasha regarded her friend. "Why call me?"

Putting her hand on Tasha's shoulder, Aveline walked her away from Maxim. "You were a sorceress before becoming Crow Queen. I need to get him out of my hair, and we don't have time to track down a priest of Aita, that Bonelord who came through here last year, or request help from the Mage's Guild. Can you see if you can help him for me, please?"

Tasha squeezed Aveline's arm. "I was simply curious. You know I wouldn't say no if I thought I could help." She turned to Maxim. "Tell me what you've seen. What makes you think it's a haunting? Have you actually seen a spirit?"

"I have not. There is a tree growing up through one of the buildings. It has destroyed the roof. When we tried to chop it down, it shook and roared. We were assaulted by stones flung at us with unseen hands, hounded by wailing and screaming as we retreated." Maxim's hands trembled as he related the tale. "Oroqs, boggins, goblins, I could fight. But this? How do you fight something you cannot see?"

"The disturbances started only when you tried to chop the tree down?" Nibbling on the end of her finger, Tasha furrowed her brow.

"Before that, some of the men with me reported seeing a fleeting motion out of the corners of their eyes. I dismissed it. Old places play tricks on the senses. Some of the folk here have an abundance of superstition." Maxim clenched his jaw. "I cannot believe I allowed myself to become so fearful over spooky noises."

"If it is an angry spirit, they are capable of much worse than just scary noises and throwing stones." Tasha faced Aveline. "I'll go out to Dawnwatch and see what I can do."

She tapped Maxim on the arm. "Come with me. You'll have to leave your horse here, but I expect the next group of helpers that go out there can bring her along."

Tasha held out her arm for Revan. The bird flew over to her, first landing on her hand, then hopping up her arm to her shoulder.

Sniffing, Maxim followed her out of the citadel. "I ride a stallion. By what means are we traveling?"

"I will take you to my hut, just outside of town, and we will go directly to Dawnwatch from there." She glanced over her shoulder at him. "That is, if you can stomach more sorcery. Otherwise, you're free to take the long way."

"I apologize for my outburst. I assure you, I have no anxiety of magic."

Resisting the urge, Tasha chose not to base her impression of Maxim on Aveline's obvious distaste for the man. "Good, because you've never experienced what I'm going to show you. Follow me, please."

She led him through the city streets to Mudders' Gate, then down the lane leading to the orchard where she had enjoyed her walk with Torben. She'd hoped to talk with him again when he returned from his hunt. However, waiting to see him until after she dealt with whatever caused the disturbances at Dawnwatch seemed the responsible choice.

Only a few people waited for her at the hut when she arrived. Staring at it, Maxim rubbed his chin. He seemingly puzzled over the logistics of a hut perched atop crow's legs on a hill overlooking the orchard. Flying from her shoulder, Revan landed on the edge of the roof overhanging the door.

The assembled people clamored for her attention. Tasha stopped before them, holding up her hands. "Please, one at a time. I have to leave for Dawnwatch, so be brief."

A young couple approached her. "Please, Crow Queen. We are just married and afflicted with a rash. It's…" Their eyes darted to Maxim and the crowd before they averted their gazes and stared at their feet.

"I'm sure what you have can be cured with a salve available in the market. I suggest speaking to Natalia. She usually has such herbs." *She's also a decent alchemist if that fails.* Tasha ushered them away, addressing the next man in line.

A stout, balding man with what little hair remained protruding outward from his head like a halo of fury scowled. "This is my orchard. Why are you here, Crow Queen?"

"You're Florin Maranu?"

"Yes, have you come to curse my crop?" Pointing at her, his accusing finger trembled.

"I was hoping to speak with one of your assistants when he returned from his hunt. Torben, the man from the Four Watches?" Tasha understood the orchard owner's concern. Upon rising one morning to view a hut from legend overlooking their livelihood, a person might feel intimidated.

"What's he done?" His scowl deepened. "He's a good lad."

"Yes, I agree." Tasha smiled. "I want to see him again. I like him very much."

"But why? What has he..." The man's eyes at first narrowed, but then they widened as a smile grew across his face. "Oh. You wish to *see* him." Florin cackled. "Oh, that dog." He rubbed his hands as, laughing, he strode away.

Tasha felt her cheeks grow hot.

"Is all this necessary?" Huffing, Maxim's armor clanked as he crossed his arms.

"Calm yourself." Tasha shot him a glare. "As I said, if my way is not to your liking, you can take the long way. If so, I'll see you there sometime tomorrow."

A group of people, farmers by the look of their attire, were the last waiting for the Crow Queen. One of the men, the son perhaps, knelt. An older man pulled him to his feet. "We saw your hut here, Crow Queen, and want your blessing. We'd normally go see Mother Anya, but since you're so close and such..."

"What is it, exactly, that you need?"

"Our farm used to be fed by runoff from the Copper Run, one of the little streams coming off it. Some beavers have built a dam, and now we get nothing. If we don't get our water back, most of our crops will die. I fear we won't have enough food at harvest for the winter."

"Cybele's tits, why are you farming on such arid land, then?" Maxim circled the group of farmers, sneering.

"Surely there are more suitable locations."

"The Lord Mayor took the rest of our land for debts he said we owed." The farmer rubbed the back of his neck. "We've made do the last several years, but please, Crow Queen, can we have your blessing to destroy those dams, maybe hunt the beavers?"

"For the love of… you don't need her permission for that."

Tasha glared at Maxim. The farmer fought to keep from scowling. "Begging your pardon, Sir Knight, but my family has always been given to seeking blessings for taking what's not ours. Gaia, Cybele, and Artume provide for us, but they don't provide those beavers."

The farmer lowered his eyes. "Back when our family was nobles, the beaver was on our crest. It seems wrong to be killing them for doing what they do."

"What family?" Maxim stopped in front of the man.

"Maxim." Tasha cleared her throat.

"Sir Maxim, if you don't mind."

"I do, in fact." Tasha interposed herself between Maxim and the farmer, placed a hand on the knight's breastplate, and pushed him aside. "Leave me to my business and stop interfering, or I will let you deal with your ghost on your own."

She returned her attention to the farmer. "What is your name?"

"Mircea Castor."

"Mircea Castor, the goddesses appreciate your devotion and your humble request." The mantle grew warm around her shoulders. "Try to drive away the beavers before destroying their dams. If you fail, you may hunt them, but do not let them go to waste. Instead, make an offering to Artume for their gift if you're forced to destroy them. Take care of your farm and your family."

"Thank you, Crow Queen. We won't forget your kindness."

"Be well, and may your harvest be fruitful." Approaching the hut, Tasha left the farmer and his family. Upon the door opening of its own accord, stairs erupted from the earth. She began her ascent even though they had not yet reached the open doorway.

"Come along, Maxim. The stairs go away when I close the door."

His clanking followed her up the steps. While waiting for him to reach the top, she conjured an image of Dawn-watch, a location with which she was unfamiliar. The scene in the back-door portal revealed a crumbling wall alongside a building that had a large chestnut tree protruding from the roof. The canopy of the tree stretched over half the court-yard. Revan and Korbin swooped through the back door.

"What sorcery—"

Tasha held up her hand. "Do they teach you skepticism in knight school? You cannot be this ignorant of magic."

"I beg your—"

"Stop. Walk through the door. You were extremely rude to those farmers, and I will not abide such behavior, particularly from one for whom I am performing a favor." Although Tasha knew her height had not changed, she felt as if she now towered over the nobleman.

Clearing his throat, Maxim approached the image. "How do I…"

"Just walk through. I'm right behind you." Tasha closed the front door. Upon crossing the room, she passed through the portal behind Maxim.

Chapter 51

"Lady Aveline!" A watch sergeant burst into the vestibule of the citadel, catching her with a butter-laden slice of bread halfway to her mouth. "You're needed at Danica's Den."

Reaching for her mace and shield, she tore into the bread. "Care to elaborate?"

"We were patrolling and heard screaming within. People started fleeing. Brana and Jolan are trying to maintain order, and I came to get you."

"Come on, Valon." Aveline stuffed the rest of the bread in her mouth, trusting Valon to lock the door of the citadel on his way out. One of the disadvantages of having a small constabulary was often not having enough people to keep the building open at all hours.

Just up River Road from the citadel, a crowd of patrons and onlookers surrounded Danica's Den. Folk wanting to get to their houses cursed, forced to wade through the mass of gawkers. Aveline pushed her way through until she reached the front steps. Physically blocking the entrance with his arms crossed, a barrel-chested, bearded man barred the doorway, glaring at anyone in the crowd who appeared as though they intended to gain a closer look.

Glancing at Aveline and the constables accompanying her, he stepped aside. Inside, the gloomy floor of the gambling den glittered with fallen gambling paraphernalia.

Danica circled the tables, muttering. She glanced upward, noticing Aveline's entrance. "There's nothing you can do unless you brought a mop."

"What happened?" Grinding coins and tokens into the wooden floor under her boots, Aveline could not avoid stepping on debris.

"The Lord Mayor was entertaining a woman upstairs, people were gambling, everything was going well. I was making a killing today on dumb mudders trying to take down Yun." Danica plopped into a chair. Her frazzled hair drooped over her face. "It was the most awful scream, and then something oozed between the floorboards. There." She pointed to a puddle on the floor.

"Where's Koloman? Why in Tinian's name was he here instead of home? He doesn't like to mingle with the common folk." Aveline approached the puddle. One whiff told her she did not wish to draw closer to it. The stench reminded her of the pile of bodies in the mine combined with rotten onions.

"I was as surprised to see our esteemed Lord Mayor." Danica scoffed. "Naturally, he was the first one out the door. Kept screaming, 'It wasn't me. It wasn't me.'"

Aveline peered at the ceiling above the puddle. Goo dripped between the floorboards, trailing strings of viscous liquid.

"Where's the woman he was with? Who was she?" Valon offered Danica a clean rag to wipe her nose.

Danica pointed at the puddle near Aveline. "I think that was her. I didn't know her. Not one of my girls, anyway. She came to town with a group of traders, I think."

Aveline's lip curled in disgust. "Maris's bloody spear."

She approached the back of the gambling hall.

Valon called to her as she climbed the stairs, "Want someone to come with you?"

"Not yet. Keep everyone out of here." Aveline readied her mace and shield as she neared the landing for the second floor. Upon entering the hallway leading to the private rooms, she found faint footprints leading toward her. The footprints grew darker as she proceeded, and it became apparent whoever made them trod in the dripping goo.

Following the footprints to their terminus, she came upon a closed door. Raising her shield, Aveline pushed it open with her foot. The stench of decaying flesh and rotten onion assaulted her, causing bile to rise in her throat.

Featuring only a bed and a small table with a basin and wash pitcher, the austere room was used for hired liaisons. Blankets strewn about the floor were soaked, and the mattress showed similar evidence of the substance currently dripping through the floorboards.

Koloman's clothes, what he left behind, lay at the foot of the bed. A sheer dressing gown, such as those the comfort women at Danica's often wore, rested on top. Upon approaching the bed, Aveline viewed a pile of bones, stained and discolored by the goo, lying near the edge of the soggy mattress.

Gagging, overwhelmed by the stench, Aveline backed out of the room. Fighting to keep her breathing slow and steady, she returned to the first floor. She hurried to a bottle of whisky on the bar, fumbling to open it.

Valon came up beside her. "Are you all right? What did you see?"

"I can't be sure." She drank from the bottle, only to find it empty. "It looked like the flesh melted off her bones."

Upon setting the bottle on the bar, she headed over to Danica. "You said Koloman ran away screaming? Did he say anything else?"

Shaking her head, the proprietor slumped in her chair. "That poor woman didn't deserve that. I told her not to go with him, but you know how he can be."

"I'll find out what happened." Aveline put her hand on Danica's shoulder. "She'll have justice. You have my word."

* * *

The midday sun flooded Dawnwatch with warmth and light. Tasha squinted until her eyes adjusted to the glare. A light breeze carried the scent of wildflowers through the courtyard, and she almost wished she had come alone. Clanking, Maxim's armor rattled in cacophonous contrast to the rustling of the wind in the leaves of the massive chestnut tree that had taken over the barracks and part of the outer wall.

"You see? Look at the damage that tree has caused." Maxim pointed at the thick trunk protruding from the convergence of the bailey curtain wall and the rear of the barracks. Several axes lay strewn about under the tree. Broken blocks of masonry also littered the area, evidence of the so-called ghost's attack on Maxim and his men.

"Where are the others?" Despite the interior spaces of the keep and ancillary buildings being hidden from the location where they stood, Tasha saw no one else in the courtyard.

"They set up a camp just down the hill. I assume they're still there." He darted forward, seizing an ax, then dashed again to Tasha's side.

The limbs of the chestnut tree shook as a deep wail filled the air.

"You see? You see?"

She slapped the ax out of his hands. "Don't provoke it. Stand behind me and remain silent."

Smoothing her skirt and cloak as she lowered herself onto the dirt, she knelt.

"What are you—"

"Do you not understand what silence means?" Tasha glared at him over her shoulder. "Remain silent or go away."

Exhaling, she opened her mind to the Earth Mother. She sensed the worms in the dirt, the grass, Maxim standing too closely behind her, and the tree.

A familiar sensation washed over her like the warm air of the sylvan glade. The loamy scent of earth filled her nostrils. She sensed another presence nearby.

The tree.

Opening her eyes, Tasha regarded the trunk. A face formed on it, matching the coloration, pattern, and texture of the tree bark. Eyes the color of chestnut leaves in spring blinked. A head, arms, and shoulders belonging to the face pulled themselves free from the tree, examining its surroundings.

The dryad glanced around the courtyard before focusing on Tasha. A wild mane of mossy hair brushed her shoulders. "I know you. Why are you with that biter, Crow Queen?"

Fully extracting herself from the tree, she regarded them, placing her hands on her hips. Her feet anchored themselves in the dirt with tiny roots. "They come with axes and fire, gnawing, biting, slashing, burning. This is my home now!"

"What is that?" Maxim drew his sword, holding it at the ready.

Tasha forced his arm down. "This is the dryad who moved in after the garrison abandoned Dawnwatch." She turned toward the tree-like fae. "What is your name?"

"Gwilvanwen. Send these biters away, Crow Queen." Stepping forward, the dryad smiled. Seductively, she ran her hands over her body. "Unless you mean to give him to me. A fitting payment for trying to kill me."

"I beg your pardon?" Maxim pushed Tasha away, brandishing his sword. His slack-jawed stare contrasted with his aggressive stance.

"Revan and Korbin screeched.

Maxim!" Tasha spun on him. "Put that away. I will not allow you to harm Gwilvanwen. And she will not attack you further as long as you don't come at her with an ax."

Tasha glanced over her shoulder at the dryad. "Right?"

"Or fire."

Maxim sheathed his sword, his eyes lingering on Gwilvanwen. "This creature cannot stay here. This keep is the property of the crown. I demand it vacate at once."

The Crow Queen stepped backward, surveying the dryad and Maxim. "I can tell you she can't do that. I will not allow you to harm her or her tree, so you have a choice. Talk with us about this, or you can leave this keep abandoned and allow the land to reclaim it." Tasha gestured at Gwilvanwen. "Would you be willing to share with them? They have claim to this structure from before that seed sprouted."

"Then why'd they let it fall to rot for more summers than I can count? Mother provided this for me. This is my home now." She ran her hands through her hair, tossing her head.

"Maxim, consider the advantages to having a dryad live here at Dawnwatch with you."

"I haven't said they could stay." Gwilvanwen stomped her foot.

Tasha held up her hand, eyeing the dryad. "And they have agreed to nothing. You said you know me. Do you trust I will allow no harm to come to you?"

Lowering her gaze, Gwilvanwen pursed her lips. "Of course I do, Crow Queen."

"I cannot imagine what use this creature could be. Almeria will not abandon Dawnwatch. Again." Staring at the preening dryad, Maxim's furrowed brow relaxed.

"Perhaps you could imagine more freely if you accept that she has a name and is not a mere *creature.*" Tasha dug her feet into the soft earth of the bailey. She felt grass sprouting beneath her feet and growing all around them.

Maxim crossed his arms, jerking his head at the ruined wall of the barracks. "Well, what about that? We can't just leave a great giant hole in the wall."

"Fae, like dryads, are connected to the land at all times. It doesn't matter what the weather is like. In spring, summer, and autumn, she'll be able to warn you of travelers or trouble long before any lookouts you have would spot them." Tasha glanced at Gwilvanwen. "Isn't that right?"

"I could, but why should I?" Gwilvanwen held out her arm. Revan and Korbin alighted on her.

Sighing, Tasha lowered herself to the ground. "Both of you, sit. We are going to learn how you can live together if it takes all night." *Or longer.*

Chapter 52

Several townsfolk related to Aveline and Valon that they witnessed a half-naked man running toward Old Town. No one confirmed his identity, however, as no one believed their elusive and snobbish Lord Mayor would ever allow himself to be seen in such a light.

Aveline had Valon gather several constables as backup and meet her at Koloman's estate. Both the gate and the front door lay ajar. Once the guards assembled outside, she laid out the plan.

"Valon and I will enter the house. Anton, you watch the front gate. Lock it after we enter, then allow no one to pass. Understand?"

Nodding, the young man straightened his helmet. "Yes, m'lady."

"Fania." Aveline addressed a stocky woman carrying an ax. "You and Jolan search around the back of the house. Lazlo can stand watch at the front door after we enter."

Upon securing her shield on her arm, she readied her mace. "This is the Lord Mayor of Curton, so fight to subdue, not kill, unless you're absolutely certain your life is in danger, understand? He's probably frightened, and he's not himself. He may not even put up a fight. We don't know what's going on, so"—Aveline loathed using a statement her guardian had used on many occasions—"expect the unexpected. Try not to be too surprised if something strange happens."

Creeping toward the open door, the knight-captain and Valon advanced. Drawn curtains on the first floor darkened the interior, making it impossible to see clearly past the foyer. Taking the lead, Aveline entered the house, pushing the door open fully. She monitored the stairway to the second floor as well as the left and right hallways.

Having been in his house only a few times, she tried to recall the layout. She found visiting the Lord Mayor's home an unpleasant task at best, and she had pushed it onto other people whenever possible. Hearing no evidence of movement, she gestured for Valon to follow her down the hall toward Koloman's study.

"We'll clear the first floor, then check upstairs."

The door leading to the study stood closed at the end of the hall. She tried the handle. Upon unlatching, the door swung open. A fire blazed in the hearth, but the chairs normally arranged in front of it lay overturned with Alik lying between them.

She pointed toward the curtains. While Valon moved to open them, Aveline examined the old man. Deep scratches, such as those left by fingernails, marred his face. Blood pooled around his head, and shards of a crystal bottle lay scattered about. The tang of blood mixed with the aroma of alcohol.

Sunlight streamed inside upon Valon opening the curtains. The area in which the struggle had occurred seemed confined to the front of the hearth.

Valon regarded Alik. "Poor old man, looks like someone staved his head in. Koloman?"

Aveline rose to her feet. "Possibly. Let's check the dining room and kitchen."

Crossing the foyer, they proceeded to the other side of the house. A glance revealed an uneaten meal in the kitchen. Otherwise, there was no sign of a disturbance.

Valon examined the food. "Koloman's you think?"

"Probably Alik's. Koloman wouldn't take his meals in the kitchen. That old man did everything for him." Aveline inspected the embers in the hearth; the fire there had not been stoked as recently as the one in the study. Valon opened the door to the larder occupying the space under the stairs. Satisfied there was nothing amiss with the potatoes and dried meat, he shut the door.

"Damn shame. Alik was a curmudgeon to be sure, but he didn't deserve that." Valon then entered the dining room, crossing the hall to open the curtains.

After checking in with Lazlo, Aveline led Valon to the second floor. Stairs creaking with each step, she noticed splits in the wood beneath the runners. At the top of the stairs, a hallway ran the width of the house. The knight-captain went left while the lieutenant checked the bathing room.

Aveline opened the door before her. Inside, Alik's bedroom served as a model of fastidiousness. Not a knick-knack, accessory, or piece of furniture was out of place or dusty. Aveline supposed the old man viewed his bedroom as the one thing he could control while serving an impulsive narcissist like Koloman. Unlike in the rest of the house, Alik's opened curtains allowed sunlight to fill the room.

"Koloman's bedchamber must be the other one." Valon crouched to peer under the bed.

"Does this place have a root cellar?" Aveline retreated to the hallway.

"I think so, but the only entrance is outside, around back."

Upon proceeding across the hall, she opened Koloman's door. In spite of the darkness, she noticed discarded clothes strewn about. The wardrobe doors hung open, its contents scattered. They poked through the clothes on the floor and in the wardrobe.

"No Koloman, and no sign of who killed Alik." Aveline dropped to the floor to peer under the bed.

"Are we assuming Koloman did not kill his manservant?" Valon threw open the curtains, ushering daylight into the room.

"I'm not assuming that, but it's possible whatever happened at Danica's Den and Alik's death are not connected." Aveline gestured for him to follow her downstairs.

Lazlo poked his head into the foyer. "There's some folk here who say they saw Koloman come and go earlier."

"What folk? Where?" Stepping outside, Aveline peered toward the front gate, using her hand to shield her eyes from the glare of the sun. Several people waited on the other side of the locked gate, likely Koloman's neighbors.

"Just there." Lazlo pointed toward the street. "Anton's been keeping them out."

"Valon, take Lazlo and check the root cellar, just in case. I'll go talk to these people."

After saluting, the two men jogged toward the back of the house while Aveline approached the gate. "Open up. Let me out."

Anton pulled the gate open just enough for Aveline to join the crowd outside. Everyone spoke at once until Aveline shushed them.

"One at a time. What did you see?" Aveline addressed an older couple.

The woman pulled her shawl closed around her shoulders. "I thought he was naked at first, but after a good look, he wasn't. He had a wild look in his eyes."

"Mmm." Her husband nodded, chewing on the end of his pipe.

"He ran into the house. Since he left the gate open, I walked up to the porch." The old woman thrust her nose upward. "Out of concern, of course. I heard shouting, screaming, and breaking glass. That's when I came back out. I didn't want no part of anything going on in there."

"Mmm." The old man pointed the stem of his pipe at Koloman's house. "Always been a high-strung sort."

"At least he had the sense to put clothes on before he ran out again." A younger man wearing a black velvet doublet leaned against the stone wall.

"Which way did he go?" Aveline hoped they agreed on that detail.

After glancing about for a moment, the three pointed toward the east.

"I don't suppose any of you followed him?" Aveline gazed in the direction they indicated. The road led toward some large estates in Old Town, ending at the outskirts where there was nothing to stop Koloman from escaping into the wilderness.

"None of our business what the Lord Mayor gets up to." The old woman sniffed. Her husband and the younger man grunted their agreement.

"Did you see anyone else come or go?"

After confirming no one saw anyone except Koloman, Aveline dismissed the crowd. Valon trotted up the path.

"There's nothing suspicious in the root cellar."

"Fine." Aveline secured her mace on her belt. "Take care of everything here. I'm going after Koloman."

"Do you want anyone to go with you?" Valon gestured for Lazlo to come forward.

Aveline shook her head. "I can handle him, and I'm only going to the outskirts. Maybe someone else saw him."

Leaving Valon to take care of Alik's body and secure Koloman's estate, she followed the lane out of town.

* * *

Tasha rubbed her temples. The back-and-forth bickering between Maxim and the dryad grew knots in her shoulders and caused a throbbing in her head. Letting them argue, she tried to think of a way that would allow them to coexist peacefully.

"Maxim"—Tasha turned her gaze upon the knight—"what if you repaired the interior of the barracks and the roof around the tree? In Maritropa, there's an inn with a tree growing through the hearth room and up through the roof. Everyone considers it good luck."

"Then they are very stupid. There'd be nothing keeping the rain out with a tree poking through the top of the building."

"Then build a wall to block off the interior of the barracks from the tree. You can do that."

Gwilvanwen sneered. "My home isn't occupying that much space in your nasty rock-and-mud building."

"We'd lose several bunks, at least."

Tasha crossed her arms. "How many people do you have staffing this garrison right now?"

"There will be more…"

"But how many right now? And how many will the princess send?"

"Well, one." Maxim clenched his jaw. "I imagine they'll expect me to recruit a new garrison from locals, but they may send one or two other knights."

"Then between the beds in the keep and the barracks, you can surely spare the space. I suggest you simply recruit fewer people to accommodate losing a couple of bunks. And you"—Tasha turned toward Gwilvanwen—"if he makes this accommodation to you, what can you give the garrison in return? Will you watch the land for them?"

Flicking her hair, Gwilvanwen fluttered her light green eyes at Maxim. "I suppose I could do that, even though I am letting them share my home."

"I thought your home was the tree?" Maxim gestured toward the towering chestnut. "What use have you for the keep? And the forge, the stables, and the kitchens?"

"It would all be mine, in time." The dryad averted her eyes.

"But for now, I'm not hearing any reason why you can't share this space. Surely you can find a way to live with the land, Maxim, rather than tearing everything down."

"Perhaps." Grunting, he stepped over to the chestnut tree and peered into the building through the crumbled wall. He turned to the dryad. "Can you keep your roots from further destroying the floor if we wall off the rest of the barracks from the space you've already claimed?"

Gwilvanwen raised an eyebrow. "Perhaps."

"As long as she has no objection to us using wood from elsewhere for certain repairs, perhaps we could come to an agreement."

Tasha raised her hand to silence the dryad's objections. "Bring the wood from what is available from Curton. She has too close a connection to any of the trees around here."

"What? Even those over yonder?" He pointed to a mixed grove of maples and pines in the distance."

"They are my friends." Gwilvanwen leapt to her feet and charged Maxim, stopping with a finger in his face. "You cannot have them."

"What are we to do for warmth in the winter?" Maxim, sidestepping the dryad, addressed Tasha. "We cannot burn rocks."

"Sleep as I do." Leaning against her tree, Gwilvanwen fluffed her hair.

"Deadfall only, Maxim." Tasha clasped her hands behind her back. "Any hedge wizard should be able to help you with lighting and extending the supply so what you forage is sufficient. The right hedge wizard may even be able to use magic to warm your stoves."

"As a general rule"—Maxim crossed his arms—"Knights of the Order of the Shield of Etrunia do not employ sorcery."

"Times change. You can be a pioneer in helping a garrison live with the land instead of despoiling it." Tasha shrugged. "Or we're back to you abandoning this keep for good and the Earth Mother reclaiming it."

"You cannot expect me to abandon my duties."

She spun on him. "I will not abandon mine." Upon her cloak warming, Tasha approached him. "I can guarantee you swift reprisal if any harm comes to Gwilvanwen."

"The crown will—"

"Will what?" Tasha's cloak spread behind her like a great pair of black wings.

Gwilvanwen came up behind Maxim, stroking his ear with a twig-like finger. "It's two against one. Three, if you count the Earth Mother."

The knight lowered his head. "The crown will respect Gaia. Of course. We… I will learn how to accommodate your"—he glanced over his shoulder at Gwilvanwen—"her needs, and I will respect the land. Now, if you'll excuse me."

Ducking away from the dryad and the Crow Queen, Maxim headed out of the bailey toward the makeshift camp on the hill.

Once he was out of earshot, Gwilvanwen giggled. "If you'd put the fear of the Earth Mother in him at the beginning, we would have wasted so much less time. It doesn't matter to me, of course, but you humans live for such a frightfully short time."

Sighing, Tasha slumped, letting go of the tension in her shoulders. "I hoped he would see reason. Strong-arming someone like that can lead to unintended consequences."

Upon circling the Crow Queen, the dryad wrapped her arms around her from behind. She rested her hand on Tasha's shoulder. "He desires me. I will have him eating my nuts within days."

Tasha disentangled herself from the dryad's embrace. "You are not to take him or his men for your tree. If you harm any of them, I will not be able to stop them coming with axes and fire."

Laughing, Gwilvanwen waved her hand in dismissal. "I won't promise not to seek comfort, but you have my word I will not harm anyone as long as they don't hurt my tree or my friends."

"Then I will leave the two of you to get acquainted. When he returns, tell him I've gone home to Curton."

"Yes, eventually, I will." Winking, Gwilvanwen sank into her tree until no evidence of the dryad remained. Tasha hoped whatever peace they built here today lasted. Snapping her cloak closed around her, she thought of her hut.

Chapter 53

Aveline reached the edge of town without having seen any sign of Koloman. A few people she encountered on the way mentioned they saw him flee into the wilderness. Leaning against the wall of an old abandoned estate, she stared into the forest.

What's out there? Hills. Trees. The river is the other way. Old mines.

Frowning, she turned toward town. A tracker like Brana probably could follow his trail. Koloman's exposure to the wilderness, as far as Aveline knew, remained limited to snubbing foresters and mudders as he passed them on his brief forays to the market. She suspected she could follow his trail, but she didn't fancy going into the untamed forest alone and unprepared.

By the time she made her way through town and returned to the citadel, the sun hung low in the afternoon sky. After a brief conference with Valon and some of the other constables, she ordered Valon to send Brana and Jolan to pick up the Lord Mayor's trail and return with him unharmed, if possible.

"I'm surprised you're not heading the search party yourself." In the doorway, Valon faced Aveline.

"I'm no good in the forest. I'd just get in the way. Brana and Jolan will move faster without me. Besides, I'm going to have to put Alik's affairs in order and talk to the magistrate about Koloman. He may be Lord Mayor, but even he will have to stand trial for murder."

Valon chuckled. "As I said, I'm surprised you're not going with them." He pulled the door shut when he left. Aveline plucked a cured sausage from the larder, eating it while she walked home. She purchased a few hand pies from a vendor in the market, as well.

Aveline found Tasha sitting on her front porch, talking to some of the neighborhood children.

Rising, she gestured to the knight-captain. "Story time is over, children. I have important business with Lady Aveline."

The children said their goodbyes to the Crow Queen. Upon unlocking her door, Aveline let Tasha in. "I didn't expect to see you tonight. I guess I'm just not used to how quickly you can travel to places like Dawnwatch now. How's Maxim's ghost?"

Tasha lowered herself into the armchair. "Maxim's ghost is a dryad, and they've agreed to share Dawnwatch. The dryad gets to keep her tree, and Maxim will work around it. I think they'll learn to like each other in time, as long as Maxim keeps his head out of his arse."

Aveline laughed. "Yes, well, miracles can happen, I suppose." She cut one of the meat hand pies, then handed half to Tasha. "See? I was right sending you to deal with the problem. A guild mage couldn't have dealt with a dryad like that, right? What exactly is a dryad anyway?"

Tasha smiled as she chewed. "One of the fae. They make their homes in trees. They have a reputation for seducing people, dragging them into their trees to become nourishment for the roots. The average dryad doesn't want that, though—not usually. They get lonely. They can't venture far from their trees."

"No one talks much of the fae around here." Aveline sat on a nearby stool, enjoying her meal with her friend.

"I learned a lot during my brief visit to the Fae Realm. Also, in Muncifer's library."

For a moment, Aveline considered asking Tasha to scry and find Koloman, but she decided against it since she had already sent out trackers. She didn't want to become overly reliant on her friend's new abilities and resources in order to do her job.

"Anything exciting happen around town?" Tasha brushed crumbs off her chest.

"Oh, where to begin?" Aveline related the story about Koloman, starting with the dead woman at Danica's Den, Koloman's flight, Alik's death, and Koloman's disappearance into the forest.

Furrowing her brow, Tasha leaned forward. "He killed a woman at Danica's Den and Alik?"

Aveline held up her hands, shrugging. "Presumably. We must find him before we can ascertain what really happened. I have my best trackers out there looking for him."

"How did he kill the woman? You were vague on that."

"I don't honestly know." Aveline pondered how best to describe what she saw. "I don't think it's possible, but it looked like she liquefied and melted off her bones. It was... vile."

"Melted..." Tasha stared into the distance.

Leaning forward, Aveline touched her friend's leg. "What?"

"The wizard at the chaos rift, his face looked like a melted candle. The thing in Koloman's dreams melted away when I defeated it. Now this... there's probably a dozen ways to describe each of those things. I don't know. I have a feeling..."

"Wait"—Aveline shook her finger at Tasha—"you think what happened at the mine and Koloman's bad dreams and subsequent madness are all related?"

Tasha shrugged. "I don't have proof, just a hunch. It could be. Or it could be coincidence." She adjusted her cloak. "I'm going to see if I can figure it out." She hugged Aveline. "I'll let you know if I learn anything, and I'll stay at the orchard just outside Mudders' Gate for now. In case you need me."

Before Aveline said another word, Tasha returned to her hut with a snap of her cloak. Aveline sighed, glancing at the uneaten fruit pie on her table. "Well, it's just you and me tonight."

Once in her hut, Tasha scried for Koloman. Within minutes, she traced Aveline's route in Old Town to the edge of Curton. From there, she found the two trackers searching for the Lord Mayor. They crept forward through the underbrush, following broken branches and trampled shrubs. Their quarry made no effort to conceal his path.

She concentrated on finding Koloman. Her familiarity with him from being in his dreams made him easy to locate. Relentlessly, he drove forward, ignoring wounds caused by branches and brambles. While watching him flee, she witnessed trackers from the city watch overtake him, although she didn't know their names.

The male tracker circled ahead, while the woman approached Koloman from behind.

"Lord Mayor! Lady Aveline sent us to help you. You must come back to Curton with us." Distracting him, the woman's pleas kept Koloman from noticing the man creeping up behind and, ultimately, tackling him.

Thrashing, Koloman wailed, "I must go. You don't understand! He's coming! The melted man is coming!"

After a brief struggle, Koloman collapsed. The two trackers fashioned a makeshift litter before beginning the arduous task of carrying him back to the city. Tasha used the relative calm of Koloman's unconscious repose to focus on his mind.

The visions she saw reminded Tasha of why she loathed speaking with Koloman in person. He dreamt of wine, women, and writhing, naked bodies. He fantasized of the powerful women he desired, but found out of reach, such as herself and Aveline.

Frowning, Tasha broke the connection. His unconscious mind did not seem unusual, not for Koloman at any rate. She sent a messenger to Aveline letting her know the trackers found Koloman, were returning with him, and she planned to move her hut into the forest south of town.

Meditating on what she learned brought no new insights. Koloman's ranting about a melted man, however, convinced Tasha his new madness was, in some way, related to the wizard they defeated at the chaos rift. After a frustrating and fruitless hour of seeking answers within, she moved the hut before retiring for the night.

Perhaps answers can be found at the Arcane University.

Using the portal the next morning, Tasha traveled to Muncifer once again after breaking her fast. Having visited several times now, she stepped through into the street just adjacent to the gate of the Arcane University. The librarian, accustomed to seeing her, greeted her as she entered. In the dim, far corner of the library, she saw a familiar face.

"Good morning, Apprentice Katka."

The young sorceress, glancing up from her book, recognized Tasha. Upon stumbling out of her chair, she curtsied. "Crow Queen, what an honor to see you again. I mean, that you even remember me. I've been reading up on you."

Tasha smirked. "On me personally, or on the previous Crow Queens?"

"Oh, uh"—Katka glanced at her book—"the previous Crow Queens, I guess."

"Don't let me interrupt. I came to research chaos rifts. I don't suppose you know where books on those are located?"

"Should be in the section covering primal magic." Pointing toward a nearby set of shelves, she took her seat. "Having trouble with that one you mentioned?"

"Not as such, but I think someone who fell into the rift is causing trouble. I'm hoping to learn what happens when someone enters one."

"Oh, the archmage's brother fell into a chaos rift a couple of years ago."

Tasha seated herself in a chair across the table from the apprentice. "Oh, what happened to him?"

"He was just a regular drak before. Now he has wings and can breathe fire, like a dragon."

Blinking, Tasha recalled from her studies that drak were dragon kin. "It made him more dragon-like?"

"Mm-hm." Katka nodded. "The archmage says he's lucky. He could have come out with two heads or tentacle arms and legs. Imagine walking around on those. What happened to the guy you know who fell in?"

"I'm not sure. We assumed he died, but if he didn't…"

"There's no telling what he came out as. Chaos is… well, unpredictable."

Tasha chuckled. "Hence, the name." She chewed her bottom lip for a moment. "I don't suppose it would be possible to meet with the archmage today? Or someone who knows about chaos magic?"

"The archmage has gone to Vlorey." Katka frowned. "She left me behind again. I think she's afraid if I go up there, I'll like it better than here. It's warm and sunny, and there's water everywhere. So I hear."

"That's what I hear too." Tasha raised an eyebrow. "Didn't you say that wizard who closed several chaos rifts was in Vlorey at the Arcane University? Maybe I should go up there and see both of them."

Katka's cheeks flushed red. She covered her mouth with her hands. "I wasn't supposed to say where she went. She took her brother and his family up there for a wedding. If you just show up, she'll be really angry with me."

Leaning forward, the apprentice took Tasha's hands. "Please, please, please don't go up there. I promise I'll tell her you have an urgent need as soon as she gets back, but she swore me to secrecy, and I'm really bad at keeping secrets."

Tasha laughed. "All right, all right. Why the secrecy?"

"The Council of Wizards has been a pain in her arse lately, and she just wants them to leave her alone for a few days so she can spend time at the wedding with her brother, his mate, and their baby. They've been pestering her about petty stuff every day for weeks. She gets irritable."

"I understand." Tasha rubbed her head. "It's inconvenient, but I understand. I suppose I'll read up on these chaos rifts on my own. See what I can learn."

Chapter 54

Brana and Jolan carried Koloman down the hall toward the cellblock. Often, Aveline had fantasized about imprisoning the Lord Mayor in the cold stone walls of the jail with spiders and the iron bars as his only companions; however, she never imagined she'd ever have a valid reason to do it.

Lieutenant Valon approached from behind. "The magistrate left for Cliffport yesterday."

She slumped against the wall. "What? For how long?"

Jolan supported Koloman's limp form as Brana opened the cell. She helped him maneuver the Lord Mayor through the doorway, then settled him on the cot.

"A couple of weeks at least."

Shaking her head, Aveline covered her eyes with her hand. "What excellent timing he has." The magistrate officially lived in Cliffport, but he visited Curton regularly to preside over trials. Most of the time, the cases were simple civil disputes, which could usually wait until he made himself available.

"The one time I need him for an important tribunal."

"If Koloman confesses"—Valon peered down the hallway while Jolan and Brana returned from the cell —"you could dispense summary judgment, like with the smith, Piotr."

"I really don't believe that will happen." Aveline narrowed her eyes. "Do you?"

"He was ranting about a melted man when we caught up to him, m'lady." Brana handed the cell keys to Valon.

"Didn't put up much of a fight, either." Jolan regarded his captured quarry. "Passed out right in the middle of it."

Aveline accompanied them to the vestibule. "Hopefully, he won't be a raving madman the entire time after he wakes up."

"So, what do we do?" Valon threw another log on the fire in the stove.

"Our duty is clear: unless he confesses to one or both murders, we hold him until the magistrate returns and convenes a tribunal." Aveline sighed. "In the meantime, I need to inform the city council."

Upon retrieving her mace and shield from the rack, the knight-captain left Valon to finish with Brana and Jolan. The city council met in a private room reserved for them at the Bristled Boar, despite her suggestions they make use of available space in the citadel. Most members felt their duties did not require such formality since Koloman possessed the power to overrule them and Aveline kept the peace well enough without their interference.

Skirting the edges of the market shortened her trip, and she observed even the least desirable market stalls facing the river enjoyed bustling business this day. Stopping on Caravan Bridge, she watched a couple of children feeding ducks near the water's edge. When the children ran out of morsels and became bored, she resumed her trek to the inn.

This early in the morning, few people patronized the Bristled Boar. Members of the city council, however, spent much of their time in the private dining room of the establishment. In fact, some came to the tavern daily. On this morning, Aveline found five members of the seven-member council seated around a table playing cards as they discussed city business.

Valentina, the head of the city council, frowned when Aveline entered. After placing her cards on the table, the tall, slender woman, wearing her salt-and-pepper hair arranged in a tight bun, steepled her hands in front of her. "This cannot be good."

The other members of the council likewise set down their cards. Grigori, the youngest and a bricklayer by trade, pursed his thin lips, huffing. "What is the meaning of this, Captain? Can't you see we're terribly busy?"

Josef, the former head of the council and the eldest, wiped his bald pate with a rag. "Yes, Grigori, I'm certain Lady Aveline can see she interrupted our card game."

Aveline informed them of recent events concerning Koloman, including his involvement with the dead woman at Danica's Den. "Now, we have no eyewitnesses who can confirm Koloman killed either the woman or Alik, but he was at both scenes just prior to their deaths. For that reason, I am holding him until the magistrate returns from Cliffport."

One of a handful of humans who lived in Drakton, Alik's cousin Yuri, slumped in his seat. "Poor Alik. We were supposed to meet tomorrow."

Nikolai, a man of considerable girth and jowls, tapped sausage-like fingers against the table. "What has Koloman to say for himself? Has he offered any defense?"

Aveline shook her head. "He seems afflicted by some sort of madness. When captured, he was ranting about a melted man, but he spends so much time unconscious I haven't had a chance to properly question him."

"A melted man? What does that mean?" Valentina nodded across the table to Josef.

"He's gone mad." Grigori clapped his hands. "This is an excellent opportunity to replace him with someone more amenable to the citizenry."

Nikolia scowled. "Like you?"

"Well"—Grigori put his hand on his chest—"I would not turn down such an honor."

Valentina rapped her knuckles on the table. "The town charter is clear on the order of succession. In the event the Lord Mayor is unable to serve, the council leads the city until the Lord Mayor is no longer incapacitated. If he is unable to reclaim his office, then we appoint a provisional replacement or continue to serve in that capacity ourselves until such time that the crown says otherwise."

"Neither of which involve me." Aveline rested her hand on the hilt of her mace. "In the meantime, I will continue to ascertain the truth, and I will keep Koloman safe until justice can be dispensed. Councilor Yuri, does Alik have any other kin in Curton?"

Running his hand through his thinning hair, he shook his head. "I was the only kin he had here. We have kin in Almeria, but we haven't seen them since we were children."

"Very well. When you're ready, come to the citadel. One of my people can take you to Koloman's estate to collect Alik's possessions." Aveline left the council to their card game.

* * *

After spending most of the day reading every book in the Arcane University library on the topic of chaos rifts, Tasha understood little more than when she started. Each author presented different ideas, some more outlandish than others, and no two agreed on the exact effects of chaos energy. She voiced her complaints to Katka as the apprentice returned with a lumpy package concealed under a blanket. She placed it on the table next to Tasha.

"The mead you wanted." Katka winked, whispering, "That's the whole point about chaos, though, isn't it? It's unpredictable. If it weren't, it wouldn't be chaos."

"Obviously. I just kept hoping some bit of insight would help me understand." Tasha buried her face in her hands. Thus far, she felt as if her time conducting research had been a waste. "Infinite possibilities where literally anything can happen. But the gods made everything out of primal chaos."

"And they say everything eventually falls back into chaos." Katka picked at a knot on the table. "I mean, think about it. You build a house, you must keep maintaining it or it falls apart and the land eventually reclaims it. Within decades, you can't even tell it was there, right? Unless it was stone, then it just lasts longer."

"Yes." Tasha met Katka's gaze. "Yes. Gaia reclaims it. And that"—she scowled, slumping—"and that doesn't help me at all. Chaos energy could cause someone's flesh to melt off their bones, right?"

Curling her lip, Katka recoiled. "It can do anything. You can't predict what or when or how."

"But how did Koloman do it?" Tasha slammed shut the book in front of her. "Assuming he was even involved. He's not a wizard. He doesn't even know enough about magic to know I couldn't turn him into a frog until I told him I couldn't."

"You said there was someone in his dreams?" Katka tapped her finger against her chin. "He could be possessed. Maybe the dream man did it through Kolormen's body."

Tasha leaned back in her chair until her view of the library behind her appeared upside down. "I suppose that's possible. How do I prove it?"

"Why do you need to prove it? If your theory fits the facts, it's enough to act on. You're trying to figure out how to fix something, not defend someone in front of a tribunal, right?"

Leaning forward, Tasha righted herself. "You're right. So, a wizard falls into a chaos rift. He survives, yet somehow possesses Koloman? Haunts his dreams until I go in and defeat him, only he melted away in the dream—melted into Koloman—and can now bring the power of the chaos rift through him? Does that even work?"

"Anything is possible." Katka waved in greeting to a passing student.

"But why Koloman?" Tasha leaned on the table. "Why not me or Aveline? Or any of the others who fought him at the rift?"

Katka shrugged. "Some people are more susceptible to certain effects. I've tried enchantments that just fizzle on some people and are wildly successful on others. I don't change the spell, just the person. Maybe Kalormon was the first person your melted wizard found he could actually attach himself to."

"Koloman. Perhaps." Tasha contemplated the apprentice's words. "I couldn't get into Aveline's dreams. She even felt me scrying on her. I slipped easily into Koloman's mind both times I tried. I thought it was just because Aveline was my first attempt ever, but she's pretty strong-willed. Koloman is a man ruled by his vices, and the creature in his dreams was appealing to his base desires."

"See? Makes enough sense to me." Smiling, Katka laced her hands behind her head. "I wish I could go with you to this chaos rift to see it."

"Maybe you and the archmage can come out and help me when she returns."

"Unless you can give us a lift, it'll take weeks to get there from here. We can't all zip around like you."

Tasha chuckled. "I have to admit, it beats walking or riding a horse."

"I really want to see your walking hut."

"When all this is over"—Tasha leaned toward Katka—"I promise I'll bring it here."

The pledge brought a grin to Katka's face. "I'll bet Delilah would love to see it and learn about that portal you have."

"As long as she doesn't expect me to explain how it works." Tasha chewed on her finger. "What do you suppose happens if we close the rift? Will the thing controlling Koloman die?"

Throwing up her hands, Katka shrugged. "I'm the wrong person to ask. Probably can't hurt, but it might not change anything about Koloman."

"Looks like I have to wait for the guild to send a mage to help with that rift. I'll try to figure out how to get it unburied in the meantime." Upon gathering up the tomes she had read, Tasha took them to the shelving cart.

The librarian glared. "You should restrict yourself to one at a time. Other students might need these books."

Tasha apologized before returning to Katka. "I'm going back to Curton now. I'll check in every couple of days. Maybe you can signal me or something when the archmage can meet or has someone who can help with the rift."

"Right." Katka scratched her head. "How?"

Tasha frowned. "A colored lantern or something in a tower window?"

"I know!"

"Hush!" A nearby librarian hissed.

Katka lowered her voice. "I can enchant a candle to sparkle and glitter, and I'll put it in the archmage's tower window. If you see it, come immediately. I'll make sure she knows to stick around if I light it."

"And she'll listen to you?" Tasha raised an eyebrow.

"We were friends before she became archmage. It'll work. Trust me."

Picking up the bundle, Tasha took her leave of Katka and returned to Curton. Although night had fallen already, she only took a few moments inside her hut to freshen up before calling up the image of Aveline's house in the back door. She collected her notes and chose a bottle of mead from the package Katka had brought to her in the library.

"Caw! Caw!" Korbin's cries stopped her just before she stepped through the portal. She glanced over her shoulder. He hopped along the windowsill, flapping and squawking. Revan joined him. First setting down the papers and mead, Tasha went to comfort them.

"What's wrong? What's got you so upset?" She peered through the window. Lying on the forest floor below her hut, in an expanding pool of blood staining the grass, a man reached toward her before he collapsed.

Tasha flung open the door, running down the steps as fast as they formed. Dropping to her knees at the man's side before turning him over, she cradled his head in her arms.

Torben's eyes fluttered open. A deep laceration marred the side of his face, and a half-dozen gouges shredded his tunic. Soaking what remained of his clothes, blood flowed in bright crimson rivulets down his chest. White streaks gleaming in several of the gouges, exposed his ribs. He reached toward her with a trembling, blood-covered hand before falling unconscious.

Chapter 55

After leaving the city council, Aveline returned home to fill a pack with clean clothes so she could stay at the citadel while Koloman remained unconscious or incoherent. After locking her home, she notified her neighbors so they could keep an eye on her house and inform the Crow Queen should she come calling.

Once settled in quarters at the citadel, Aveline paid Koloman a visit down in the cellblock. The guard, Niko, leapt to his feet, saluting as she entered.

"Has he woken yet?" From the doorway, she could not see the interior of Koloman's cell.

Smoothing his mustache, the guard shook his head. "The last time I looked, he was still sleeping. Shall I wake him?"

"No, but if he wakes, I want to be notified. I'm staying here tonight. Probably tomorrow too."

"As you say, m'lady."

Aveline gestured for Niko to return to his seat while she proceeded toward Koloman's cell. The other cells currently sat vacant with their doors hanging open. Koloman slept sprawled on the cot. Even from the door, Aveline saw the chamber pot remained unused. Gripping the bars, she studied him.

Did you finally go mad or is this something else? What have you gotten into?

After a few minutes, he stirred. Groaning, Koloman squirmed on the bed until his feet hung over the side. Sitting up, his eyes rolled back in his head. Then, he fell forward until his head hung between his legs. Aveline reached for her keys in case he collapsed.

Panting, Koloman forced himself to his feet. He lurched around the cramped cell, grunting. Holding out his hands, he felt for the walls.

"Koloman? Can you see? Do you know where you are?"

At the sound of Aveline's voice, Koloman snapped his head toward her and seemed to stare directly at her. A cloudy film cleared from his eyes. "Ah, the Lady Knight. We meet again."

Again? "Who are you? What have you done with Lord Mayor Koloman?"

Leaning his head to the side, he popped the bones of his neck, smiling. "I am Koloman. The Lord Mayor. Release me."

Drool dribbled from the corner of his mouth. He wiped it away with his sleeve, licking his lips. Extending his arms in the knight-captain's direction, he lurched toward the cell door.

Aveline stepped backward, beyond his reach. "You killed two people. You must stand trial."

He scoffed, gagging. "They were unimportant. Impure. Unworthy." He swallowed.

"One was your manservant, Alik." Despite his affirmation, Aveline remained unconvinced she spoke to Koloman. "Do you remember him?"

"Stodgy old bastard." Koloman grinned. "He won't trouble you any longer."

"What did you do to the woman at Danica's Den?"

Koloman's eyes darted back and forth. "Ah, yes. A magnificent, though unfortunate, side effect of my manifestation." Gasping, he covered his mouth with his hands. "Oh, but I'm giving it away too soon. I still have a finger or two left of my hands."

Shuddering, he lurched away from the cell door, then sped into the wall. He fell backward, collapsing on the floor. Aveline approached the door, crouching to get a better look. Upon rolling over, Koloman pushed himself to his hands and knees and retched.

"This is not my bed chamber. Where am I?"

"You're in jail, at the citadel."

Turning, he glared. "What is the meaning of this? I demand you release me at once."

"You bashed in Alik's head with a crystal decanter, and you killed a woman at Danica's Den. You're staying here until the magistrate returns from Cliffport."

"What?" Koloman held onto the wall to steady himself. "I did no such thing. Release me now, and I'll consider not having you stripped of your rank and titles."

Aveline raised an eyebrow. Koloman possessed no such authority over her, although he could pressure the city council into punishing her in such a manner. "We have witnesses."

"Release me!" He lunged forward, grabbing the bars. Aveline again stepped backward.

"If you're going to be belligerent and rude, I'll just leave you alone. I'll send a guard down with food—if you can remain conscious that long."

"How dare you!" Koloman trembled in fury.

Aveline turned her back on him. The Lord Mayor ranted, swearing as she exited. She paused when she reached Niko at the door. "If he keeps this up, feel free to move to the other side of the door and keep it shut. No one needs to hear all that. Feed him on a regular schedule. I'll check the roster to see who's scheduled to relieve you in the morning, then let you know."

Niko saluted. "Yes, m'lady."

Even at her desk in the vestibule, Aveline heard Koloman screaming to be released. Despite her annoyance, his perseverance impressed her, but she hoped his voice would give out before long. Fortunately, several floors of archives and abandoned city offices dampened the sound between the cellblock and her quarters. She returned to her quarters confident Niko could handle things downstairs.

Her cot in the citadel proved less comfortable than her bed at home. Sleep came first in short, fitful visitations before exhaustion set in and she finally succumbed for the night.

* * *

After only one attempt, Tasha knew she would never get Torben into the safety of her hut alone. She dug her toes into the mossy earth. Closing her eyes, she opened her mind to Gaia. His life-force faded as his blood soaked the dirt. She focused on the flora, the forest floor, and the surrounding trees.

Vines pushed upward underneath Torben, wrapping around him and carrying him into the air as they grew. She moved forward, keeping him in her mind as she ascended the stairs. The vines took Torben through the doorway. Tasha directed them to withdraw after they placed him on her bed. By the time she reached the entrance to her hut, the vines had retracted. Torben flailed, groaning. Catching his arms, she held fast.

"It's all right, Torben. It's Tasha. It's going to be all right."

Upon unbuckling his belt, she noticed both of his axes, as well as the ornate dagger and sword, were missing. She removed his shirt, then tore what remained into strips for bandages. The gouges in his chest welled with blood, and several clusters of puncture wounds marred his upper arms. Blood also covered his breeches, although they appeared intact. After unbuttoning and removing them, she tossed them aside.

Apart from minor bruises, his legs appeared uninjured. Tasha pressed the makeshift bandages into the worst of his wounds. After, she rinsed her hands in the basin and searched through the apothecary cabinet for something to staunch the bleeding. She found some yarrow, then mashed it into a poultice. Upon choosing a plain linen shift from her wardrobe from which she would make additional dressings, she approached the bed.

When she finished, Torben's upper torso resembled that of one wrapped for burial. She draped a blanket over his legs, then moved a chair so she could sit at his bedside. His body burned with fever; Tasha didn't need to touch his skin to feel how hot it had become since she began ministering to his wounds.

She glanced at Revan and Korbin, who had not moved from their perch in the window since the excitement began. Huddling together, they slept. Choosing not to disturb them, she stood over the basin. The blood had cleared away through some power of the hut; she had neglected to consider how she'd clean it when she first washed her hands.

Using the basin, she viewed the forest, starting with the spot below the hut where Torben collapsed. She followed the trail of blood, the inherent power of life contained within it beaconing her way.

Tasha found one axe, bloodied, near a bramble bush. She located the other embedded in a tree nearby. Of the ornate dagger, she saw no sign. Finding more blood and entrails in an area with trampled vegetation, she determined it as the site of a struggle. She followed the clear trail of blood and offal leading away from the site until she came to a carcass. It might have been a deer, but, because it lay in such a dismembered state, she couldn't be certain.

A groan from her bed broke her connection. She returned to Torben's side. Fluttering open, his eyes darted around the room without focusing.

Tasha took his hand. "Torben, can you hear me? You're safe now. You're in my home. Torben?"

"When I saw your hut, I thought I was dreaming." He leaned back. "I did not dare to hope it was real."

"It's real. I've bandaged your wounds." She squeezed his hand. "I need to know what attacked you, Torben. Was it a bear?"

He shook his head, licking his lips. "No, no." He croaked unformed words, his body wracked by coughing.

Tasha released his hand to retrieve a goblet from the cupboard. Upon filling it from the basin, she held it for him to drink. "Take it easy."

"It was… the biggest wolf I ever saw. It was feeding. I should have run, but it was so fast."

"A wolf did this?" Tasha glanced toward the window. Although she viewed neither of the moons from this angle, she surmised, based on the amount of illumination, the Queen was full. "Are you sure it was just a wolf?"

Torben swallowed, opening his eyes. "I think… it was not just a wolf. A werewo…"

He lapsed into unconsciousness. Tasha cursed. Since there'd been no recent reports of disturbances, she'd hoped she had driven away the werewolf she encountered a few weeks earlier.

Picking through the drawers of the apothecary cabinet, she made several tea sachets. If Torben awoke again, and he had, indeed, been attacked by a werewolf, he faced two choices: attempt to control the beast within with Tasha's help or die, whether by his own hand or another's. She understood herb lore enough to know which ones would help him gain control of his beast. By her reckoning, the next full moon, a full King, would come in eight days, the day after Remembrance.

After making the tea sachets, she assembled the ingredients for another concoction, a wolfsbane poison. Torben had eight days to decide what he would do, but she did not intend to allow the werewolf that attacked him to run free that long.

When she finished, she locked away the poison in her cabinet. Torben slept curled up on one side of the bed. He lay trembling, soft whimpers escaping between ragged breaths. Tasha slid into bed alongside him, pulling up the covers. Draping an arm over him, she stroked his hair, reassuring him until he quieted. She dozed off and on until, finally, sleep came for her as well.

Chapter 56

"I don't suppose you have any suggestions for what to do about Koloman?" Aveline sat at her desk, oiling her chainmail.

Lieutenant Valon stoked the fire in the stove. He shook his head. "No idea. He's gone mad."

While awake, Koloman spent half his time taunting whoever could hear him in the calm voice of one who expected to exact revenge and the other raving like an inconvenienced noble. So it went throughout the night, according to Niko. Anton now guarded the cellblock, taking advantage of a period when Koloman lay quiet to switch out the chamber pot in his cell and remove the tray of half-eaten food.

"I think it's more than that." Aveline hoped Tasha would deign to come by soon. The knight-captain disliked not being able to stop by her shop when she wanted to talk, a disadvantage that accompanied her friend's new status.

Remaining members of the city watch, checking in, stopped by before beginning their daily duties. Aveline addressed them before they resumed their patrols. "Valon, make a shift rotation for cellblock duty. I don't want anyone spending more than a few hours in there with him. We'll do fewer patrols around town if we have to."

One of the constables grimaced. "I was hoping for gate duty today. Another dwarf caravan is coming."

Aveline glanced up. "From Dwegerthon?"

"Aye, supposed to arrive this morning."

She collected her armor. "I'll go to the gate myself. Valon, you can handle things here, yes?"

"Of course, m'lady. There'll be no trouble."

Aveline ducked into the armory to don her armor. She adjusted her tunic over it before returning to the vestibule to retrieve her mace and shield. Yelling from within the cellblock informed everyone Koloman had awakened.

Aveline wished them luck before leaving the citadel. She hoped Dwennon led the caravan from Dwegerthon. So much happened since the last time her dwarf friend visited, and she wanted an update on goings-on in the mountains.

She reached Miners' Gate ahead of the caravan. Fluffy clouds cast shadows, moving over the mountains to the south. Aveline busied herself with an inspection of the gatehouse. She whiled away the morning, engaging in small talk and helping the constables check over incoming travelers to Curton. As the sun moved across the sky, the light morning breeze gave way to a stiff wind, bringing with it scattered clouds. Near midday, the caravan finally appeared around the bend at the far end of the road. She recognized the Stonehelm banner before she could identify individual dwarves, but she saw her friend Dwennon leading the column.

Raising her hand in greeting, Aveline strode to meet him. The dwarf spread his arm, noticing her approach. "Ah, lass! Always nice to receive a personal greeting when coming to town."

Dwennon wrapped his arms around her before she had a chance to kneel, digging the front of his helmet into her stomach. Grunting, she appreciated the protection of her armor.

"Give me some good news, Dwennon." She directed him to step to the side of the road so the caravan could pass. "The mud's gotten deeper around here, and I'm floundering."

"Well, lass, lots of news. Nothing that concerns Curton, though."

Aveline fought the frown threatening to replace her smile. "I notice you didn't say it was good news."

He ran his fingers through his beard. "Oh, here's something. We scouted a few empty oroq villages while traveling east along the mountains before crossing the pass. Not bodies, just nothing. It was like they all packed up and moved."

"I hear they're heading west, a great crusade to find Ankor."

"For them to empty out entire villages, they must really think they found it this time." Removing his helmet, Dwennon plopped on a nearby boulder. "I suppose I should be thankful they left without harassing our surface villages."

Aveline crossed her arms, smirking at Dwennon. "You almost sound sad they left."

"Well, we like a good fight, don't we? Oroqs put up a good one."

"Well, we've got a new drak clan taking up one of our mines, the Icescale clan from the south, no less. We collapsed part of that same mine on top of a chaos rift too. The Lord Mayor has lost his mind—it may not be related to what happened in the mine. My best friend is the new Crow Queen. Princess Valene has finally sent someone from Almeria to take over Dawnwatch, which is now inhabited by a dryad, by the way." She rubbed her temples. "I'm sure I'm leaving something out."

Disappearing beneath his shaggy hair, Dwennon's eyebrows rose. "I'm surprised you have time to come out here to talk. We're just here to trade, lass."

"I'm sorry, Dwennon." Slumping, Aveline sighed. "My burdens are not yours. I'm just coming up short on sources of wisdom right now. Know anything about the Crow Queen or chaos rifts?"

He shook his head. "Sorry, lass, nothing about those. You said those draks had white scales, eh? Might be the refugees we saw last time we came up here. How have they been?"

"I assumed they were. They've been keeping to themselves, mostly. I haven't heard anything since I returned from the mine."

Dwennon tugged on his beard. "Do you reckon they'd be up for some trading? I could send a couple of carts out that way."

"I don't see why not. Honestly, I expected them to visit Curton by now for supplies. There's not much out there." Aveline described the best route to the mine.

When she finished, he stood. "Thanks, lass. I'd better catch up with them before they make some bad deal. See you tonight at Hon's Hearth?"

"If I can get away, I'll be there." Upon bidding her friend a good day, Aveline crossed town to check on the goings-on at Mudders' Gate. Upon confirming all was well, she embarked on a patrol around town, hoping Tasha would make contact by the end of the day.

* * *

Tasha awoke to a bright summer morning. Sunlight streamed through the windows of the hut, bathing the interior with a warm glow. Beside her, Torben still slumbered, although he no longer shivered. She changed his soiled bandages, cleansing his wounds, before going outside.

A symphony of nature greeted her as she strolled through the clearing, sounds of the forest filling the air around the hut. The mossy earth, still in the shade, felt cool beneath her feet. Connecting physically with the world each day helped center her; yet, finding the time to actually do it seemed a challenge of late.

Flying past her, Revan landed near the base of a tree and pecked the area, searching for something to eat. Korbin dove from the canopy into the clearing, circling her head before alighting on her shoulder. She stroked the crow's breast before sending him to the window of the hut to keep an eye on Torben. Uninterrupted rest would do the man good, but Tasha hoped he hadn't lost too much blood. If he had indeed contracted lycanthropy from his unfortunate encounter, the affliction might be the only reason he survived the night.

Tasha noticed a silence descend upon the forest. Not even the buzzing of insects could be heard. Through her connection with Gaia, Tasha felt a familiar presence entering the clearing a moment before she heard the rustling of branches. Steeling herself, she turned.

A woman wearing loose animal skins strode into the clearing. Her hair hung in a tangled mass of knots. She carried a bow in her hand with a quiver slung over her shoulder. Stopping in a shaft of sunlight, she regarded Tasha with honey-colored eyes.

"Know I am not your enemy, Crow Queen. My name is Vasilisa."

Tasha remembered the name from her conversation with Mother Anya. "The huntress. You know who I am, but we have never met. Yet, you seem familiar to me."

"You have seen me"—her eyes scanned the forest, seemingly searching for prey—"by the river." She swayed. "Hunting. Feeding."

Tasha stepped toward the stairs leading to her hut, careful to keep Vasilisa in front of her. "You're the werewolf I've seen. Did you attack Torben?"

"I am. Your friend stumbled upon me while I was feeding. I stay away from Curton so that doesn't happen. I control the beast, but when I feed"—glancing over her shoulder, she stared at Revan sitting on a nearby branch—"well, wild animals defend their kills, do they not?"

Tasha wished for the poison locked in her apothecary cabinet, even though she possessed no way to administer it. "What do you want?"

"Did he die?" Turning her head, she stared at Tasha with unblinking eyes.

"No, but he lost a lot of blood." She pulled her cloak closed around herself. "He may not make it through the day."

"He will." Vasilisa squatted, placing her bow on the grass. "And he will change at the next full moon. Spare him the curse. I can end his suffering before it begins."

Tasha clenched her jaw. "You're responsible for his condition."

Vasilisa lowered her head. "I am. It was not intentional. Do you require assistance killing him now?"

"I have no intention of killing him."

"Then you will let him be at the mercy of his beast?" She raised her head just enough to meet Tasha's gaze. "That is unwise."

"I will let him choose his own fate. I know a brew that will help him maintain control of the beast."

The huntress nodded. "I am familiar with such draughts. You lack a necessary component, hair from the blood-sire. My fur."

Tasha held out her hand. "Then you will provide me with some, and I'll consider it the start of an apology."

"Caw, caw." Korbin's cry startled Tasha. Despite her efforts to intimidate the werewolf before her, she recoiled.

"Wait here. I shall return shortly." Tasha ascended the steps to her hut. She glanced at Korbin as she moved. "Let me know if she tries to come up or leave."

"Caw!"

Tasha found Torben struggling to sit up. She helped him into a seated position, propping him up with pillows. His skin felt warm, but it did not seem as feverish as the previous night. He coughed. Groaning, he held his stomach.

"Would that I had died."

The words pained Tasha. She took his hand. "I think you're going to live, Torben."

"Live?" Closing his eyes, he swallowed. "I know what happens to sons and daughters of the moons."

"You can control it. I can help you learn." She brushed his cheek with her hand. "I know it can be done, and you're strong enough to succeed."

"And if I don't want that life? Do you have a silver blade to thrust into my heart?" Cracking his eyes open, he met her gaze. "I lost mine."

"I've made a wolfsbane poison. For you or for your blood-sire if it becomes necessary."

"How will we ever find the exact werewolf that did this to me?" Torben shook his head. "I should have run as soon as I heard it feeding. I thought it was a normal wolf. I… was foolish."

"She is here right now." Tasha glanced toward the doorway. Fluttering on the windowsill, Korbin maintained his vigil of the clearing below. "I think she came to apologize."

He laughed until coughs wracked his body. Holding his stomach until the spasms stopped, he leaned on the pillows, panting. "Then let her up to apologize, for that is a sight I would like to see before I die."

"If she tries anything, I may not be fast enough to stop her." Tasha squeezed his hand.

"I believe I am safe in the hut of the Crow Queen." He pressed her hand, although his grip remained weak. "Even from a werewolf."

"Very well." Tasha returned to the doorway. She gazed upon Vasilisa, who still squatted where Tasha left her. "He's awake and will see you if you wish to face your victim."

Vasilisa rose, striding forward with fluid motion like a predator stalking her prey. She ascended two steps at a time. Tasha moved aside to let her pass. Upon entering the hut, Vasilisa's eyes widened, examining the interior until her gaze finally rested upon Torben.

"I will kill you, if you do not wish to become like me."

So much for an apology. Tasha stepped between Torben and Vasilisa. "Not in here you won't."

"No." Vasilisa glanced around the room again. "Never in a divine sanctuary such as this." Cocking her head, she arched her back. "I can feel the presence of the goddesses. They cow my beast. I could live here free from it."

"If Torben chooses life, will you give your hair so I can make him the draught to help tame his beast?"

Slumping, Vasilisa faced Tasha. "I will bring you some fur, if he chooses life."

Chapter 57

By the time Aveline finished her patrol, clouds covered most of the sky, and the sun neared the horizon. Apart from encountering minor troublemakers and some young men fighting over petty grievances, she found the day refreshingly uneventful. Returning to the citadel, she regarded its imposing stone edifice, dreading entering to check on Koloman.

Passersby greeted her as they went about their business. Clenching her jaw, she tried to summon compassion for Koloman and his struggle, if he were even aware of it. However, she felt only contempt for him. Years of his casual abuse and lecherous behavior eroded any sympathy she might have for his plight.

I guess I'm just not that good. Climbing the steps, she gritted her teeth. Two guards she recognized from her morning at Miners' Gate chatted near the door to the larder. They snapped to attention upon noticing her.

She returned their salute. "Kolya, Galina. Anything going on here? How's our guest?"

Glancing at her comrade, Galina, a freckle-faced mudder's daughter with auburn hair, shook her head. "He's been ranting off and on for most of the afternoon. Brana's watching him now. He's said the most horrible things to her."

"Then, in the blink of an eye"—Kolya clicked his fingers—"he'll turn on the charm and be sweet and seductive, promising you the moon and stars if only you'll let him out."

"I was hoping he'd settle down." Aveline stowed her mace and shield in the rack.

"M'lady?" Galina, frowning, approached Aveline. "What's wrong with him? Has he really gone mad?"

"Mad, possessed." Aveline shook her head. "I can't say for certain. I only hope when the Crow Queen returns, she has some answers for us."

Kolya chuckled. "Insane nobles... I'll bet the Crow Queen wishes for a nice simple drought or cow plague right now."

Aveline nodded. "You're right. She'd have those fixed in no time."

The door to the hallways leading to the cellblock opened. Brana stuck her head through the opening. "Oh, Lady Aveline. You'd better come down here. Something has changed with the Lord Mayor."

The knight-captain and Galina followed Brana down the hallway with Kolya bringing up the rear. "What's changed, exactly?"

"He's carrying on a conversation with himself, but it's like there's at least three people in there with him." The young woman held the cellblock door open. Aveline heard Koloman whispering in a raspy tone, but she couldn't determine what he said. When she reached his cell, she found him squatting in the corner, his head darting to the left and right.

"What is this place, Master?"

"Who are you?" Aveline rattled the door to gain Koloman's attention. "Who is your master?"

Koloman ignored her. "It's strange in this place. Too soft. Too weak."

The Lord Mayor clutched his head. "No, no! Not another one. Go away. In my dreams, in my head, in my bed, in my... no, no, no!"

"Who's in your head, Koloman?" Aveline considered entering his cell, but the Lord Mayor leapt across the chamber and onto the door, clinging to the bars with his hands and feet.

"Ah, the Lady Knight returns." Dangling from the bars with one hand, he dropped to the floor. Smoothing his loose clothing, he rose in front of her. "You keep us locked up. Why? You despise this man. He knows. All the guards know it. This whole mudhole of a town knows it."

"You will stand trial for the murder of Alik and the woman at Danica's Den."

Scoffing, Koloman waved his hand in dismissal. "Worthless lives. They meant nothing." He leapt upon his cot. "They weren't important, and no one will even remember their names in a few years." Spinning, he pointed at her. "You don't even know the woman's name, do you?"

"She was from out of town. I never met her, and no one at Danica's Den knew who she was. Except maybe you." Aveline clasped her hands behind her back. "So, why don't you tell me who she is."

"A lonely woman from Muncifer. Her husband, a minor noble, left her for a younger lass. Estranged from her children, she left to travel to Cliffport. From there, she was to take a ship to Vlorey, seeking a new life. I am young and handsome, and she desperately wanted to feel loved again." Smiling, he laughed. "I never learned her name. Why? I gave her pleasure in her last moments. Now, she's with, well, whatever god she fancies. Maybe Maris took her. I don't care."

Aveline's lip curled at his callous disregard for the woman's life. "You're not that young."

Upon stepping off the bed, he approached the cell door. "Release me. I'll leave Curton and never trouble you again."

"I have a better idea."

"Oh?" Koloman grinned. "What's that?"

"Sit in there and keep quiet. We'll keep feeding you until your trial. When you're found guilty and I'm ordered to execute you, I'll try not to enjoy it."

"Pfft. Weak widow. You couldn't even keep your husband alive." Pressing his face against the bars, he licked at her. "I'll torment your dreams before the end."

She cocked her fist, preparing to drive it into his face. Brana seized her arm before she could strike.

"He's not worth it, m'lady."

Koloman sneered at Brana. "Come in here with me, sweet. I'll show you what I'm worth." His hand dropped to his crotch. Aveline spun Brana, marching her out of the cellblock.

"No one goes in there with him. Open up the second cellblock if we need to jail anyone else." Aveline slammed the door, locking it. She felt her blood boiling. "Bring him food and water twice a day, but just slide it in. Make him stand at the back of the cell first."

"What about his chamber pot?" Kolya grimaced at the thought.

"Replace it when he goes to sleep but only when he sleeps. If you're not sure, let him stew in it." Partway to the vestibule, Aveline faced them, pointing at the cellblock. "And no one goes in there alone. I want two of you at all times, armed, whenever anyone goes in there with him, and do not engage him in conversation. Understand?"

Brana and Kolya answered in unison. "Yes, m'lady."

* * *

Shortly after Vasilisa left, Torben fell into a fitful slumber. Tasha slumped in her chair, wracked with indecision about the huntress. She fought at the side of a werewolf years ago, a young woman named Aeryn, so she understood they could be responsible citizens, despite the need to hunt and kill. Tasha had never heard anyone in Curton mention werewolves to be a danger to the town, and Mother Anya had vouched for her.

Perhaps it was just an accident. Tasha wanted to check on Aveline, but she did not want to risk leaving Torben alone just yet. She used the basin to locate her friend instead, finding her at Miners' Gate talking with some of the guards there. Not wanting to eavesdrop, she severed the connection.

While she waited for Torben to awaken, she sliced some cured meat from her larder, preparing a plate with cheese and bread before putting on a pot of tea. Sipping from her cup, she sat by the window overlooking the forest clearing. She'd placed the hut in a remote part of the foothills east of town, only a few hours walk from Curton.

Korbin and Revan nestled close to her as she rested her arm on the windowsill. They preened the edge of her cloak. Torben stirred. He sat up on his own, looking around in confusion for only a moment before noticing Tasha and smiling.

"There's food." Tasha pointed at the plate sitting on the edge of the stump. "You should eat. How do you feel?"

"Better." He glanced at his bandaged chest, flexing his muscles. "Better than I should, I think."

"You'll heal faster now, unless the wounds are caused by silver." Letting Revan and Korbin hop away, Tasha put a kettle of fresh water on the hearth, selecting one of the sachets she had made earlier. "I have a tea you'll need to drink. I don't have the last ingredient, but it'll help a bit even without it. Once I have it, it should allow you to maintain control at all times."

She glanced over her shoulder at him. "That is, if you want it."

He threw the covers aside, but upon realizing bandages were all he wore, he quickly pulled them over himself again. "I feel a great deal of despair right now. If I were to harm an innocent…"

"It's not a decision you have to make immediately. You won't change for several days still." Tasha dropped the sachet in the kettle. "But the longer you drink the tea, the easier it'll go for you, should you choose life."

Torben nodded. "I understand. Um, if it's all the same to you, though, I'd like to go outside for a bit first."

Tasha narrowed her eyes. "Why?"

"I slept for what? Almost a day? Plus, I ate before I went hunting… I feel as though I may burst."

She suddenly understood, feeling her cheeks redden. "Yes, of course. Be careful and shout if you need anything."

"Do you need help getting down the stairs?" She turned her back to afford Torben privacy.

Groaning, he hobbled toward the door. "I think I can manage. I'll just take it slow."

As he descended, Tasha kept watch out the window with furtive glances to make sure he didn't need help. When he returned, she waited until he was covered up in bed again before bringing him a plate of meat and cheese.

Accepting it with thanks, he ate a bit before meeting her gaze. "I don't suppose I could get some clothes?"

"What you had was pretty shredded. If you promise to lie here, rest, and not die on me, I can go out to get some for you." She offered him a smile. "Unless you want one of my skirts?"

He laughed. Wincing, he pressed his arms against his sides. "As lovely as they are, I don't think they're quite my style."

"Do you have a preferred tailor in town?" From the now-screaming kettle, Tasha poured a cup of the bitter brew. She handed him the steaming cup.

Upon sipping it, he grimaced. "I suppose if it tasted good, it wouldn't be good for me."

"Oh, you know how medicine works. I'm impressed."

"Would there be any harm in adding some honey to this?"

Tasha tidied the apothecary cabinet while considering his request. "It has some healing properties, so I think it would be all right, at least until we get Vasilisa's fur to add to the brew."

"Fur? I'm going to have to drink something with fur in it?"

After shutting the cabinet door, she brought a chair to his bedside. "It will help you gain control over the beast."

"I believe you." He sipped from the cup again, wincing. "You can pick up a set of clothes for me from the orchard house. No need to buy anything new."

"All right." Tasha opened a portal to the orchard. "Stay here. Promise?"

"I will not move from this spot." He gawked at the image of the orchard house displayed in the back door. "How is that possible?"

"I don't fully understand the portal magic. It does work, however. I'll return shortly." She stepped through the doorway. In an instant, she found herself outside the orchard house. From the outside, it resembled Koloman's home, albeit in worse repair.

She approached, knocking on the door. From inside, Tasha heard Florin complaining. Fumbling with the door handle, he cracked the door open, greeting her with a scowl.

"No stories ever said anything about you calling on folk."

"Times change." Tasha clasped her hands together in front of herself. "Torben's been injured. I'm here to pick up some of his clothes."

"Injured? How?" Narrowing his eyes, he glared, as if blaming her for Torben's condition.

"An animal attack." At this point, Tasha saw no advantage to giving more information to the suspicious orchardist.

"Bah, I told him going after a boar alone was foolish. Can't tell those Watchfolk anything." He pulled the door open. "Is he dying?"

Tasha followed Florin to Torben's room. "No, but his clothes were torn to shreds. He can't very well run around naked, can he?"

Grinning, he held open the door to Torben's room. "You wouldn't mind that though, eh?"

"Oh yes, binding his wounds to keep his guts from spilling on my floor was so romantic I swooned." It took most of Tasha's resolve to keep from slapping Florin as she passed him. She opened the wardrobe, gathering as many of Torben's clothes as she could carry in one arm. "He'll come back for the rest of this himself. He just needs a few days to recover."

"If he's not back by the end of the season, I'm tossing it out."

"Your generosity is unparalleled." Tasha glared at the man before using her free arm to snap her cloak around her. She heard his gasp of alarm as she vanished. Appearing in her hut, Torben recoiled at her sudden arrival, groaning in pain as he clutched his sides.

"Sorry about that." Tasha dropped the clothes on the bed. "I'm going to head into town for some supplies and catch up with Aveline. Try not to reopen any of those wounds."

Torben picked through the clothes she'd brought back. "Is there any way you can warn me before you just appear like that again?"

She took a honey pot out of her apothecary cabinet, along with another tea sachet, and set them on the stump. "I'll send Korbin or Revan to warn you."

"Who?"

Tasha gestured to her birds in the windowsill. "The crows. If one kicks up a fuss, and you don't see anyone outside, expect me back momentarily. Make another pot of tea, the water in the basin is fine to use. And feel free to add honey to your taste. Is there anything I can pick up for you in town?"

Torben held up a pale blue tunic, shaking his head. "No, thank you. Your generosity is overwhelming. I owe you my life."

Tasha summoned an image of Curton's marketplace in the back door, then, smiling, looked over her shoulder at Torben. "You're welcome."

Chapter 58

Aveline selected a bottle of ale from the larder, drinking half before returning to the vestibule. Upon plopping into the chair, she leaned back, propping her legs on her desk. "Maris take him. All two or three of him. I need this like a fish needs fur."

Considering she should have done so before giving voice to her frustrations, she checked to ensure none of the guards stood within earshot. *The magistrate cannot return soon enough, although I daresay this new Koloman would hardly let him get a word in edgewise.*

Banging at the citadel door interrupted her musings. She glanced over her shoulder to see if anyone else heard the sound before answering the door herself. Upon opening it, she met Tasha laden with a plethora of goods from the market, various foodstuffs, by the look of it.

"You shouldn't have." Aveline held open the door, allowing her friend to enter.

"I'm taking this back with me. I just wanted to check in with you before I turned in for the night."

Aveline shut the door as Tasha set her bundles on the desk. "I rather expected you sooner than now. We need a better way of communicating with each other now that you're so important."

"Rather a lot has happened." Tasha sought a place to sit.

"Sorry, I have extra people in watching our esteemed Lord Mayor." Aveline offered Tasha her chair, but the Crow Queen declined.

Tasha sat on the edge of Aveline's desk. "How is he?"

Groaning, Aveline buried her head in her hands. "It's like there's at least three people in his body. It's quite disturbing. I don't recommend you go in there right now." She rubbed her eyes. "I don't suppose you learned anything useful?"

Tasha slumped, crossing her arms. "If it's in any way related to the chaos rift, then it could explain everything, because with chaos magic, anything is possible. If it has nothing to do with the rift, then I can explain nothing."

Aveline furrowed her brow. "Anything is possible?" She leaned back, covering her face again. "That is spectacularly unhelpful. Or is it?"

"Thinking about it gives me a headache, Aveline. Infinite possibilities. Everything or nothing. Something in between."

Aveline felt Tasha's hand on her shoulder. She studied her friend's eyes.

"I believe what's happened to Koloman is connected to the rift and that wizard. There are similarities that are just too coincidental to be unrelated."

"The melted man?"

Tasha nodded. "Remember what the wizard at the rift looked like? His flesh hung off his bones in places."

Aveline swigged her ale. "So, what do we do about it?"

"We have to dig out the rift, and I have to seal it."

"Dig it out? That could take weeks." Aveline pinched the bridge of her nose. "Anyone who knows how to do that kind of excavation is too old now. None of the mines around here have been active in twenty years." Sighing, the knight-captain shook her head. "Anetha give me strength. So, what's been keeping you so busy? Were you studying chaos magic all this time?"

Chuckling, Tasha raised her eyebrows. "No, I came back that same day. I was coming to see you, but I came across Torben."

"Oh really? You two, um…" Smirking, Aveline nudged Tasha's knee.

"He'd been mauled by a werewolf."

Aveline closed her eyes, cursing. "I'm sorry."

Tasha took Aveline's hand. "It's fine. He's alive. I'm helping him. Hopefully, he's going to try to tame the beast."

"You're joking." Aveline pulled her hand away from Tasha's. "You're going to let him run around wolfed out? That's crazy. I'm not going to have a werewolf in my town, Tasha. I don't care if you are the Crow Queen."

"He actually hasn't decided if he's going to try to keep control or if he'll just"—Tasha licked her lips, averting her eyes—"kill himself before the next full moon."

"Does he need help?"

Tasha covered her mouth, stifling a sob. Aveline felt her heart drop into the pit of her stomach. She pulled her friend into a hug. "I'm sorry. I didn't know you…"

"I didn't either." Tasha squeezed Aveline, then pulled away. With her red-rimmed eyes, she met Aveline's gaze. "I like him, Aveline. He's kind and polite. He's interested in me. *Me*. Not what I can do or what I look like. I'm not sure if things would have gone anywhere, but I don't want him to die. He's scared, and I fear for him. He's been a good friend."

"All right." Aveline crossed her arms. "So… help him. I just worry about this town if we let a werewolf run around unfettered."

"There's already one. The huntress, Vasilisa."

The name was unfamiliar to Aveline. "I don't know her."

"She only comes to town for festivals. She lives in the wild, keeps to the forests and hills east of town."

Aveline recalled hearing stories of a wild woman out that way, but since drunken men always seemed to be the sources of the stories, she'd dismissed them. "Did she attack Torben?"

"Yes." Tasha nodded. "She's apologetic; it was an accident."

"An accident?" It sounded like an excuse if Aveline ever heard one. "If she was in control, how did she accidentally attack him?"

"He stumbled upon her feeding. They startled each other, and, like any predator, she lashed out when she feared her meal was threatened."

Aveline found her head in her hands again. "There are days when I don't want to listen to you, you know." She peeked through her fingers at Tasha. "But you've yet to steer me wrong."

* * *

"I'm sorry to add to your stress." Tasha put her hand on Aveline's shoulder. The cold steel of the knight-captain's pauldron did not convey to Tasha the tension her friend felt.

Aveline patted Tasha's hand. "Don't worry about it. I trust you'll make the right decisions. Do you happen to have anything we can slip into Koloman's food or drink to make him sleep more? He's really disruptive."

Tasha frowned. "Are you sure we should do that?"

"He's getting physical. I'm concerned he might become injured if he continues throwing himself against the walls or bars. I'd rather not have to put him in shackles." Aveline rubbed her chin. "Though that might be an option. We have some. Somewhere."

"I'll see what I can find." Tasha glanced toward the hallway leading to the cellblocks. She heard guards talking softly among themselves. "I may have to go to Muncifer. Again."

Aveline approached the door leading to the cellblock and pressed her ear against it. "I'm surprised you haven't gone to more places. Can't you go pretty much anywhere in the world in an instant?"

"I could go running off to Hoseki or Nakambe." Of course, Tasha spoke none of the languages in use on the northern continent. "Leave you to deal with all of this all on your own."

Aveline returned Tasha's smile. "I know you'd never do that."

"We need a plan, Aveline." Tasha's smile faded. "We can't let things get out of control. Can the city council help? What about Maxim?"

Aveline returned to her chair, leaned back, and stared at the ceiling. "The council is doing their thing, running the city and not interfering with how I handle the guard. Which is good. Maxim has no obligation to help here, and, even if he agreed to help, what would I have him do? Guard Koloman? He'd be up my ass constantly. No, it's better if he stays at Dawnwatch."

"How long until the magistrate returns for the tribunal?"

"Too damned long." Aveline shook her head. "How much time do you need for Torben? How long until the next full moon?"

Tasha counted on her fingers. "Seven days, the night after Remembrance."

"Oh great." Aveline pinched the bridge of her nose. "The draks will be out in force that night."

"It's an important observation for them. They're not usually trouble, are they?"

"No, it's the other people being afraid that's trouble." Upon pushing her chair back, Aveline rose and began pacing the room. "You don't think those White-scale draks will come to town to join in the celebration, do you?"

"The Icescale clan?" Tasha crossed her arms, eyeing Aveline. "I doubt they'll even come to town. I probably should go out there and check on them."

"Take care of Torben, and try to encourage the draks, all of them, the Icescales and the clans here in town, to keep things subdued this year. I have to manage Koloman and whomever they pick to succeed him."

Tasha grimaced. "The city forces them to live in squalor, and now you want me to tell them to keep things quiet when they observe their most sacred holiday? It's not right, Aveline."

"I don't mean it like that. Guarding Koloman around the clock is stretching us thin. I just…" Aveline rubbed her forehead. "I just want things to be calm."

"The draks don't want trouble, but they don't want the people who keep them from improving their station telling them to keep their observances quiet." Tasha put her hand on Aveline's shoulder. "Maybe stop by the celebration? Convince a councilor or two, maybe the one who lives in Drakton, to attend? Show the people they've nothing to fear. I'll go to Muncifer first thing tomorrow if I can't find a sleep aid for Koloman. That should take some of the pressure off. I'm not an alchemist, so what I can do is somewhat limited."

"Thank you, Tasha." Aveline pulled her friend into a hug. "I'm glad I have you to count on. I'll see if I can find some folks to go to Drakton during Remembrance and take part in the observances."

"You can always count on me, Aveline." Tasha held her friend a little longer than usual. "I'll find a way to make it easier for you to contact me. There must be a way."

Aveline pulled away. "We'll figure it out." She glanced at the pile of food on her desk. "Do you want a pack for all that? I'm sure we can find one you can borrow."

Tasha gathered it all in the crook of her arm, placing each item in a specific location in the stack. "I got it, thanks. I'll try to come by here tomorrow, earlier rather than later, if that's all right."

Aveline regarded the door to the cellblock. "That'd be great."

The Crow Queen closed her eyes, focusing her thoughts on Revan. She found him circling above the forest, then shifted her attention to Korbin. He sat on the windowsill, twitching with nervous energy, ready to go hunting but unwilling to abandon his post. She informed him she was about to return, requesting he notify Torben. As Korbin flew into the window, squawking at the Watchman, she used her free hand to snap her cloak shut while thinking of the hut.

Torben started when she appeared. He still lay in the bed. Korbin cawed a greeting before flying through the window to hunt his dinner.

"Damn. I thought expecting it would help."

Tasha dumped all the food and goods she purchased on the table. "Sorry. In the future, I'll arrive outside and use the door."

"You've gone to too much trouble on my account already." He fiddled with his hands while eyeing his bandages. Tasha went over to him to examine his wounds. The healing progression of such grievous injuries was far ahead of where a normal human's would be at this point.

She tugged at one of the looser dressings. "We can change these tonight, probably for the last time. There's a bathing vessel in the other room. Would you like to bathe?"

Lifting his arm, he peeked under it. "Don't I just have to lick myself clean now?"

Tasha chuckled. "You're not a dog." She pulled off his covers. "Go on, it's through that door. It should fill itself when you enter the room."

His eyes widened. "That's amazing."

He swung his legs off the edge of the bed, using the headboard to steady himself as he stood. Torben took a deep breath in before releasing it. Once steady on his own feet, he stretched. "I feel… pretty good, actually. Perhaps I'll stretch my legs outside a moment before bathing."

Torben opened the door and disappeared down the stairs into the twilight. Tasha took the opportunity to add the food she bought to the already-full larder and tidy the rest of the main room. Then she took the remaining packages she'd brought with her from the market into the bedroom and laid them on the bed. After unwrapping them, she put her new tunics and skirts in the wardrobe.

When she returned to the main room, she heard a cry from the forest floor.

"Crow Queen!"

Rushing down the stairs, she observed Torben holding himself statue-still before a great wolf. A wolf with honey-colored eyes.

"Get behind me." Tasha held out her hand, moving between the wolf and her injured guest. Rearing on its hind legs, its bones cracked, shifting as it transformed into a human-wolf hybrid form.

"Fear not, Crow Queen. Do you not recognize me in this form now?"

"Vasilisa." Tasha clenched her jaw, unimpressed with the werewolf's timing and theatrics.

The huntress crept forward. "He's healing well." Sniffing, her nose twitched. "He will be strong." Her canid lips and tongue formed the words with difficulty.

Tasha glanced over her shoulder at Torben, noticing a tremble in his step as he backed away from his assailant. She took his hand to reassure him. "What do you want, Vasilisa?"

The werewolf turned her gaze on Tasha, holding out her paw. "To keep my promise. Take what you need."

Korbin and Revan cawed from the branches above. The moons, still low in the sky, provided little light, but it was enough for Tasha to see with the aid of the mantle. She removed a knife from her pouch, then sliced off a clump of fur from Vasilisa's forearm.

The werewolf licked the nearly shaved spot. "When his time comes, I will come for him. He can decide then to hunt with me or die."

Torben's breathing quickened. Tasha reached toward him again. "Perhaps it would be useful if the two of you spoke during the day before that happens."

"I have nothing to say to her."

The metal tinged odor of fresh blood wafted from Vasilisa's maw. She snarled. "Perhaps not, but there is much you will need to hear if you choose life."

"Go now." Tasha pointed toward the forest. "He needs rest."

Vasilisa raised her head. Tasha winced at the ear-splitting howl. Upon witnessing Torben cowering from the werewolf, her heart ached. Several answering howls drifted through the night before Vasilisa dropped to all fours, loping into the darkness.

When they were again in the safety of the hut, Tasha shut the door. Torben slumped on the edge of the bed. He buried his face in trembling hands. "Look at me. She's reduced me to a simpering coward."

Sitting alongside the Watchman, Tasha put her arm around him. "The howl of a werewolf can make even the most hardened warrior's blood run cold. Plus, she *did* just try to eat you a couple of nights ago. You have nothing to be ashamed of."

"I ran because I was afraid. I should have stayed. I should have let her kill me."

"Torben"—Tasha turned his head, studying his eyes, their grey-blue color now replaced with the amber indicative of lycanthropy—"I'm glad you're going to live. I want you to live, although I'll support whatever decision you make. But, please know, I am glad you're alive."

A single tear ran down his cheek. Shuddering, he averted his eyes.

"Take a bath. I'll make you some more tea, proper wolfsbane tea this time. We'll get your bandages changed, and you'll feel better." She told herself it wasn't just an empty promise.

Chapter 59

The next morning, groaning, Aveline rolled out of her cot, barely getting her feet under her before standing. After Tasha left, the night generally remained quiet, even though Koloman ranted and raved well into the middle of the night.

After pulling on her clothes from the night before, she stuffed a change of clothes in her pack. Tossing it over her shoulder, Aveline went downstairs to check on their guest. Fania sat in a chair abutting against the door leading to the cellblock. Her hair, greying at the temples, cascaded around her shoulders. Whistling a tune, she sharpened her axe. The steel blade sang as she ran the edge across the sharpening stone.

"M'lady." The constable moved to stand, but Aveline gestured for her to remain seated.

"How are things?"

"Been quiet since I took over." She thrust her thumb over her shoulder toward the door. "Jolan left some food for him before leaving. I don't think the Right Honorable Lord Mayor is awake right now."

"That suits me." Aveline hefted her pack onto her shoulder. "I'm off to the baths, then I'll relieve you. Hopefully, things will be calm while I'm away."

"I've noticed he rants less when there's no audience."

"Good, then we won't give him one." Poking her head into the larder, Aveline glanced at the inventory. "Is there anything we need that you know of?"

"No, m'lady."

Aveline headed for the public baths. The streets of Curton bustled with the flow of people going about their day without a care for what transpired with their Lord Mayor. Small windows in the cloud cover allowed blue sky to peek upon the town. After finishing with her ablutions, she returned to the citadel, stopping at a bakery to purchase a bundle of sweet rolls. She tossed them on her desk when she entered. "Help yourself. We may as well get some reward for our suffering, right?"

Fania hopped up to select a pastry. Aveline pulled the chair away from the door, then peeked down the hallway leading to the cellblock. So far, everything seemed quiet. She shut the door. Just then, Tasha entered through the front door of the vestibule.

The Crow Queen held up a basket full of vials. "Enough sleeping draughts to last far beyond the magistrate's next visit."

She placed them on Aveline's desk, eyeing the sweet rolls. "Go easy on them. If you give him too much, he'll never wake up."

Fania raised her eyebrows. "Really? How much is that?"

Aveline slid the basket toward Tasha, glaring at Fania. "We're just giving him enough to suppress the ranting and violent outbursts."

Tasha chose a roll with a central well of berry jelly. "They've been divided so one will make him groggy all day. He'll still be able to eat and whatnot, but he'll feel sleepy all the time."

"Thanks, Tasha." Aveline pulled the basket toward her, then removed one vial to put on her desk. "I'll lock these up, so no one is tempted to accidentally spill more than one into his gruel."

"Aveline, I'm going to move the hut to Mudders' Gate. I don't have any other way of keeping myself accessible to you right now."

"Is that safe?" The thought of having a werewolf that close to the city made Aveline's stomach clench into a knot, despite Tasha's assurances.

"I'll be mobbed day in and day out by people wanting me to cure their bunions."

Fania talked around the bit of sweet roll in her mouth. "They should just rub it with oil until it goes away. If that doesn't work, whack it with a hammer."

Tasha covered her eyes with her hand. Turning her around, Aveline walked her to the door. "We'll be all right here. Let me know if you need help with anything."

"I'll see you soon."

Aveline shut the door behind Tasha. Picking up the vial on her desk, she left Fania to watch the vestibule, and she entered the cellblock. She crept toward Koloman's cell, listening as she approached to see if she could tell whether he slept.

Stopping short of his cell door, she peeked around the corner. On his back, Koloman lay on his cot, his chest rising and falling in a steady rhythm. The tray with food still sat on the floor by the slot at the bottom of the door. Pulling the stopper out of the vial with her teeth, she reached through the bars. Stretching, she held it over the top of the bottle of ale.

I don't know why we're not just giving him muddy river water. She chastised herself for the stray thought. All their prisoners received clean food and drink at her orders. No less. She tipped over the vial, spilling its contents into the ale before withdrawing her arm. Thus far, he had not stirred. Cupping the vial in her hand, she rattled the bars of the cage.

"Better eat up. If the rats get your food, you're not getting anything else until tonight."

Koloman stirred. Sitting up, his eyes narrowed as he saw her, but Aveline left before he began ranting. She tuned out his demands for release, making a point of slamming the door to the cellblock as she exited.

Meanwhile, in the vestibule, Fania had finished her first sweet roll and started on a second. Admonishing her because she had brought only one for each constable, Aveline took a seat behind her desk. It promised to be a long, boring day.

By the time Tasha returned home after delivering the sleeping draught to Aveline and purchasing meat from the butcher for Torben, she found the Watchman awake, sitting upright in bed. Tasha set a skillet in the hearth, then tossed in some sausages.

"How are you feeling today?" After starting another kettle of tea for him, She approached to check his dressings.

"I feel well." He tugged at a bandage on his chest until it fell away, revealing bright pink lines across his chest where gouges once exposed his ribs. "It disturbs me how quickly these healed."

Tasha examined him with wide eyes, tracing one of the new, already-fading scars with her fingers. Realizing her hands had lingered, she snatched them away from his chest. "That's rather amazing."

She turned away, feeling blood rise to her cheeks, and devoted her energy to cooking. While the sausages sizzled, she told Torben of her plan to move the hut for Aveline, then check on the draks and their Remembrance celebration.

"That's something to do with The Sundering, yes?"

"Yes, a celebration of Rannos Dragonsire, the father of all dragon kin, including draks. His death triggered The Sundering." She moved the skillet to a cooler part of the hearth while she prepared Torben's tea.

He came up behind her. She felt her heartbeat quicken at his proximity.

"I appreciate everything you've done for me."

Glancing over her shoulder, her eyes met his beard. Tasha adjusted her view upward. "I'm happy you've recovered so quickly. Have you come to a decision yet?"

His hand hovered near her shoulder. Holding her breath, she anticipated his touch. Torben lowered his hand, turning away. "No. I'm going to speak to the werewolf before I decide."

"I think that's wise." She poured the tea into a cup, then handed it to him. "Even though you're healed, you'll still need to drink this daily. I'll bundle enough of the sachets to last you until the next full moon."

He thanked her, taking a seat on the end of the bed, then sipped the tea. She served the sausages along with some bread from the larder. They ate in somber silence. Once they had finished, she moved the hut to its new location just outside Mudders' Gate. Within minutes, people exited the city to gawk at the crow-footed hut. Most did not linger. It pained her to ignore those who did, but entertaining their petitions would distract her from the tasks she needed to accomplish.

As Tasha prepared to visit the draks at the mine, Torben packed his things. "It'd probably be best if I go back to the orchard for now. Working will help me come to terms with what I must do."

"If you need a safe haven, you're welcome here." Tasha hugged him, then opened the door.

"Thank you, Crow Qu… Tasha." He smiled, stroking her cheek. He descended the stairs. Tasha tuned out the cries of the people below. From the requests she heard, her intervention in their lives was not needed. Once Torben reached the bottom of the steps, she shut the door.

With reluctance, she summoned the mine in the back door. The image displayed in the portal showed the mine entrance as well as the edge of the graveyard. She stepped through into an overcast day. The rhythmic tapping of metal on stone filled the air as sculptors chiseled the monument and headstones. The air smelled of earth and embers as smoke rose up the chimneys of the small earth-and-wood huts the draks had erected outside the mine.

After greeting the workers and paying her respects at Vasco's grave, Tasha sought out Klatt. She found the drak elder in one of the larger huts. He sat on the ground, whittling a piece of wood. The thatched ceiling sat low, forcing Tasha to crouch upon entering. Wood, bone, and feathered totems hung from the walls, and a small fire burned near the back.

Glancing up when she entered, he returned to his work. "I wondered when you'd pay us a visit."

"I see you've settled in nicely. Are things well?"

"Well enough." He pointed in the direction of the mine with his half-carved wood. "There is slumbering evil in there."

"The chaos rift." Tasha lowered herself to sit cross-legged in front of the drak elder. "We collapsed the cavern around it."

"Something else." His lips curled away from his teeth. "The rift is leaking into the mine. Even now, we've had to close off some of the lower chambers."

The weight of the mantle pressed down on her shoulders. "It's growing. I'm sorry. We thought it was contained. I have the ritual to close it, but I'm waiting on help from the Arcane University. We'll also need to find people to help us dig it out."

"It is deep, yet it changes the world around it." Upon setting down his knife and sculpture, he folded his hands in his lap. The popping fire behind him showered the air with a swirling cloud of sparks. "We will help to protect our new home."

Tasha described the collapsed cave in the hills that led directly to the chamber containing the chaos rift. Klatt fiddled with his knife. "That may be a safer approach. I will have my scouts look for and evaluate it."

"Thank you, Elder Klatt. May I ask you about Remembrance?"

He bowed his head. "What do you wish to know?"

"Are any of your people planning to join the draks in town for their celebration?"

"No. We have had no contact with our brethren in town."

"Perhaps that will have changed by next year. The people in town don't understand the celebration, they even fear the draks a bit, but the townsfolk could make an effort to learn about drak culture."

Klatt nodded. "Thank you. Know that our brethren and any townspeople who are interested are welcome here at our celebration."

Tasha's heart soared at the prospect. "Thank you. I will let them know. I don't know how many will want to travel two days out of town for it, but I think you can expect a few families."

The drak elder spread his arms. "We will welcome them. We are all children of Rannos Dragonsire. You are welcome that night, as well. We would be honored to include you, Crow Queen."

"The honor would be mine, Elder Klatt." Tasha bowed to the drak. "If I am able, I will be here. For now, I must return to Curton. I will pass on your invitation to the draks there."

After taking her leave of Elder Klatt, she returned to the graveyard. Row upon row of wooden stakes marked each grave; dotted among them stood stone markers for the victims whose identities were known. At the center of the graveyard, stoneworkers chiseled a boulder that formed the base of the memorial honoring all the wizard's victims. She thanked them for their hard work before returning once more to her hut.

Korbin greeted her from his perch in the window. She stroked his back while she checked on the crowd, careful to remain hidden from view. Save for a few individuals she recognized from their repeated attempts to inquire about their futures, the earlier crowd had dispersed. Nevertheless, she decided to use the hut's portal to go directly to Drakton. Once there, Tasha sought out Zadok and relayed the Elder Klatt's invitation.

"It pleases me to hear more of our brethren have arrived. We planned a rather nice celebration this year, although, it would be nice to celebrate with other draks for once." He rubbed his hands together, his light grey scales even duller than usual in the diffuse overcast light.

"There's been trouble in town, and Lady Aveline is unable to commit the guards she needs to keep order if mudders show up and get rowdy."

"Trouble?" He glanced at the draks milling about, teaching their children, hammering away at buildings still in need of repair, or just loitering. "Things are pretty much back to normal after the flood."

Tasha shook her head. "It's nothing to do with you. It's the Lord Mayor. His situation has unsettled a great number of people."

Zadok scratched his chin, nodding. "I'll see if any of the families want to visit the Icescale clan then. Perhaps we will find lost kin among them."

"Elder Klatt has extended an invitation to the towns-people, as well, Zadok. It would be good to see you there."

Tasha shared Klatt's invitation with Aveline before returning home. She spent the rest of the afternoon tending the folk who came to her hut seeking assistance, most of whom she referred to fortune-tellers or other herbalists in Curton. At night, she scried on Muncifer on the lookout for Katka's sparkling candles. She dared not venture near the Arcane University, fearing the barrier might knock her out again. The apex of the archmage's tower rose above the rest of the university compound, however, making it visible from the center of the city.

Over the next several days, her routine remained much the same: check in with Aveline, tend to townsfolk with serious concerns, and check the Arcane University. On the eve of Remembrance, she finally saw the promised sparks and glitter cascading down the side of the tower.

The time had come to meet the archmage at last.

Chapter 60

Strolling through the marketplace, Aveline adjusted the shield slung across her back. Tasha's sleeping draughts made life guarding Koloman at the citadel immeasurably easier. For the past several days, the knight-captain felt almost relaxed. She stopped to examine a stall selling hand-woven blankets when she heard the clanking approach of someone clad in armor.

"Lady Aveline, how fortunate to run into you here." Maxim crossed his chest with his closed fist in salute, stopping alongside her.

Aveline scanned the marketplace. "Strange, this does not seem like Dawnwatch."

Maxim forced a smile. "You jest, but know I am here only to procure more supplies."

"That's good, I suppose."

"I enjoyed a great deal of success recruiting people from Cliffport to garrison the fort." He pulled off a glove to feel the fabric of one of the blankets. "Even a trader or two to set up a waystation there for folks moving inland from the port."

Despite her desire to hold Maxim in contempt, Aveline clapped him on the shoulder. "That does sound like good news. Well done, you."

She held up a woolen blanket dyed green and blue. "How much for this one?"

"Three talons, m'lady." The weaver, a young woman from Vlorey with her tight curly hair trimmed short, took the blanket from Aveline, then tied it into a bundle with paper and string while the knight-captain counted the coins from her pouch.

After accepting the package, Aveline headed toward Caravan Bridge. "How's your dryad?"

"She is…"

Aveline noted a flush blooming on Maxim's cheeks. "Yes?"

"Immodest. She enjoys teasing me, I think. However, we have come to an understanding. I believe she will be a great asset to Dawnwatch. Plus, we'll never want for nuts."

Aveline laughed. "Well, be careful. Those fae will steal your heart away."

"So I hear." Maxim cleared his throat, stopping at the top of the bridge. "Anyway, I have brought you payment in full for the loan."

"How?" Aveline narrowed her eyes. "You cannot possibly have heard from Almeria yet."

Clearing his throat a second time, Maxim swung his pack around to rest on the bridge's parapet. "Indeed not. However, with Gwilvanwen's help, we located a sealed vault behind a bricked-up room in the keep's dungeon. It contained a treasure trove of antique weapons as well as several chests containing gold crowns."

He withdrew a small, bulging sack from the pack, then handed it to Aveline. It jingled with the weight of many coins. She set her blanket on the parapet to peek into the sack. The glint of gold caught the sunlight. She plucked one coin from the pouch, examining it. It bore the seal and likeness of Princess Gabrielle the Macabre.

"These are old. I always wondered why that wall was bricked up." Aveline returned the coin to the sack, then stowed it in her pack. "I remember hearing about Prince Gavril's grandmother when I was a little girl. Everyone believed she was a necromancer, but the princess was so kind and willing to socialize with anyone in the city and she remained popular her entire life. I haven't heard much about Princess Valene since she assumed the throne after Prince Gavril's death."

"She certainly held eccentric tastes, but you can find no one with an unkind word about Princess Gabrielle. Too bad her grandson Gavril was such a small, petty, and cruel man." Maxim held out his hand. "I must be off. Do come visit us. I'll be in town from time to time."

Aveline clasped his hand. "You've done well. I'm sorry things were difficult at first, but you have proven your mettle."

"I've heard about the difficulties you've been having here, and I am sorry for contributing to your anxieties. It's an honor to serve with you, Lady Aveline." Maxim saluted once more before turning on his heels and returning to the marketplace.

* * *

Gathering her records, along with a book she'd prepared in case she needed to take more notes, Tasha opened a portal to Muncifer and strode through. Weak light from oil lamps and candles spilled onto the streets from nearby windows. Though few clouds obscured the night sky, only one moon, the waxing King, provided light. However, most buildings on either side of the street blocked it until just before it reached its zenith.

Tasha approached the gate of the Arcane University, where two minotaur guards held halberds large enough to split her in half. Towering over her, they didn't bother lowering their weapons to block her path; they just flared their nostrils, sneering upon the comparatively diminutive human.

Rare visitors to Curton, Tasha had not interacted with minotaurs in years. Still, she stood her ground. "The archmage is expecting me."

"At this late hour?" The bigger of the two guards, his muzzle tinged with grey fur, snorted.

She pointed toward the sparkles and glitter falling from the tower window. "Apprentice Katka set alight that candle to let me know the archmage is waiting for me. Imagine how upset she'll be if she learns you refused a guild mage entry."

The other guard glanced over his shoulder toward the tower. "That sounds like something Katka would do." He nudged the older, taller minotaur. "Better let her in. You don't want to end up on the archmage's bad side."

"No. No, I do not." He withdrew a key from his pouch. After unlocking the gate, he held it open. "Enter then, but don't expect to get out before morning. It's not permitted."

Tasha didn't bother telling him she had other means of egress. She hurried across the campus toward the archmage's tower. A pair of young wizards held hands, chatting under the blood oak. Caught up in their own world, the young men paid no mind to the feather-cloaked woman rushing past. Tasha chuckled to herself upon remembering how, like plague rats, she had avoided dalliances while attending the Arcane University in Maritropa, shunning unnecessary distractions from her studies.

Upon reaching the archmage's tower, she found herself wondering about Torben. Tasha had not heard from him since he returned to the orchard. She hoped he'd made peace with his new existence. Climbing the stairs, she admitted she would welcome his distraction.

She paused at the ironbound oak door to the archmage's private chambers. Little news about the goings-on at the Arcane University made it as far as Curton, so all she knew about this new archmage was she was a drak named Delilah. *I've only ever met one person named Delilah, and it was a long time ago.* She shook off her misgivings.

Tasha knocked on the door. The muffled sounds of swearing preceded the shuffling of feet. The door swung open. She found herself gazing upon a striped drak with crimson and ebony scales and golden silk ribbons tied to her horns. Behind her, Katka waved.

"What do you want?" The drak glared at Tasha. "Don't you know what time it is?"

Tasha felt her knees go weak. Squeezing her eyes shut, she drew on the power of the mantle to give herself strength enough to remain upright. The memory hit her like a charging minotaur, transporting her back to that fateful battle over a decade in the past.

Drak-Anor. The day of Lorelei's death.

She felt a clawed hand on her arm. "Are you all right?"

Tasha waved her away. "I'm sorry. This is a shock. We have already met, Archmage. At Drak-Anor. Many years ago."

Clapping her hands together, Delilah hooted. "I knew it! Katka's been telling me all about you. You're that sorceress who tried to kill me! Come in, come in."

Katka, her mouth agape, turned toward Delilah. "This is her? The one with that stupid knight who wanted to kill all draks?"

Blinking back tears, Tasha entered the room. Delilah closed the door.

"I'm not that person anymore." Swallowing the lump in her throat, Tasha wiped her eyes. "I have spent my whole life since then trying to atone for what we did." Composing herself, she curtsied. "Archmage? Your apprentice signaled you were in. I have urgent business. I'm the Crow Queen."

Delilah glanced over her shoulder. "You lit those damned candles?"

"You said you were free!" Katka's defense came as a high-pitched protest.

The archmage bared her teeth. "I thanked Dolios for a free evening. It's not the same thing. She's been pestering me for weeks to meet with you, regardless of my schedule."

Books and fetishes covered a round table shoved to one side of the circular chamber. A stairway led to the higher levels of the tower. Near the window where a candle spewed sparks outside, stood a smaller table with a bottle of wine, goblets, and dirty plates.

"Katka, open another bottle of wine." Delilah waved her hand, returning to her seat. "Your slate has been clear since you helped us fight the oroqs. And now you're the Crow Queen? I guess we've both moved up in the world."

She pointed toward the stool Katka vacated. "Sit, please. Drink with us."

Katka brought another goblet to Tasha, then filled all three before dragging another stool over.

"She told you about me?" Tasha sipped the wine. It burst with berry flavor, possessing a subtle floral nose. "Did she tell you about the chaos rift? My research into chaos magic?"

Delilah shook her head. "No, but she did tell me some very interesting things about how you get around. I've gotten some moon gates working again, and I've been using them to figure out proper teleportation magic."

When she first studied at the Arcane University, Tasha learned about artifacts believed lost during The Sundering, including the moon gates. Much like the back door in her hut, moon gates allowed instant transport from one to another.

"Being able to teleport around Calliome would make a great number of things easier." Tasha certainly found the convenience of the hut's portal addictive.

"I want to study your hut." Delilah gestured toward Tasha. "I'll come help with the chaos rift. In exchange, you let me study that portal you use."

As soon as Delilah made the offer, a chill ran down Tasha's spine. She pulled her feathered cloak tight around her shoulders. "I don't think the goddesses approve of that exchange."

Lowering her brow, the archmage narrowed her eyes. "Excuse me?"

"The hut is the domain of Cybele, Gaia, and Artume." Confirming the cloak as the source, Tasha focused on the chilly sensation covering her back. "I have a very strong sense they're not keen on you examining the magic involved."

"I see." Delilah snapped her mouth shut, clicking her teeth together. "So, you come asking for favors and are willing to grant none in exchange?"

"I have come as a guild mage asking for assistance closing a chaos rift."

"I received your messenger." Archmage Delilah faced the window. "I only know of two wizards besides myself with experience in that area. One is in Vlorey, and the other Frost Rime."

Vlorey lay several months away by overland travel, and even by sea. Tasha guessed that Frost Rime was equally distant, but she did not know how to get there. Indeed, the last she'd heard, it had been abandoned and lay decrepit. Still, she did not intend to yield so easily. "Then the obvious solution is for you to come to Curton yourself. It's becoming a danger to Curton and to the Icescale clan of draks that have recently settled in the area."

Tasha noticed the archmage clench her jaw at the mention of draks in danger, but she waved her hand in dismissal. "That'll take weeks."

"If you leave now"—Tasha set her goblet on the table— "we'll have it dug out by the time you arrive. I can get you home instantly once we've finished."

The archmage sat in silence for a moment before facing Tasha. She sighed, slumping. "I want to be petty and say I won't help you without examining your portal, but I can't. I have a duty. But neither can I just leave the Arcane University for weeks at a time. Not right now."

"Deli..." Katka reached across the table toward the archmage.

Archmage Delilah held up her hand, silencing her apprentice. "Katka, you will take those siblings from Vlorey, Hayden and Jordan, and leave for Curton in the morning. Ride as hard as you can."

The color drained from the apprentice's face. Then she bowed her head. "Yes, Archmage. I should go tell them now."

Katka slid off her stool, curtsied to the archmage and the Crow Queen, then left them alone.

"Hayden and Jordan have been studying chaos since they joined the Arcane University." Delilah drank from her goblet, draining the wine. "They'll be able to help you with the rift. The four of you should be able to make short work of it and any nasty beasties that come out."

Tasha bowed her head. "Thank you, Archmage."

"Take care of them. I expect them to return home—all whole and unmutated."

"I swear to you"—Tasha placed her hand over her heart—"I will guard them with my life."

Chapter 61

"Ah, Lady Aveline." Lieutenant Valon entered the vestibule. Aveline glanced up from the pay ledger. Valon helped himself to a sweet roll from the plate on her desk. "A runner arrived from Cliffport."

"Cliffport?" Aveline closed the ledger. "Regarding what?"

"The magistrate has left and will be here the day after tomorrow. He's been apprised of the situation, and he says he looks forward to any tribunal where he can sit in judgment over Koloman."

Aveline leaned against the back of her chair. "That's good news. I didn't realize he had such a grudge against Koloman."

"Yes, well, don't forget how Koloman became Lord Mayor in the first place." Sitting on the edge of Aveline's desk, Valon chewed the sweet roll.

"I remember he sent a sizable coffer of gold to Prince Gavril." Aveline shook her head. "He demanded Sir Agnar accompany the bribe personally, leaving me alone in Curton for the first time since my parents died."

"Thus securing his position from Grigori the Stern."

"Right." Recalling the incident, Aveline realized why Grigori's son, Grigori the Younger, seemed so keen on assuming Koloman's place. She assumed his desire was born of arrogance. She understood now it was more than that. "I wonder what happens to Koloman's estate if he's put in prison or I'm ordered to execute him? He inherited it, right? He has no heirs anyone knows of."

Valon thought about this for a moment. "I suppose it would revert to the city council to decide its fate."

Aveline chuckled. "It'd make a lovely orphanage. Mother Anya has been wanting to set one up for ages."

"That's justice." Valon laughed. "An excellent use for his ill-gotten fortune."

"Let's not get ahead of ourselves. Koloman's been quiet, so I'm going on patrol." Aveline returned the ledger to the vault before retrieving her mace and shield. Hearing Valon conversing with the guards in the cellblock, she left them to it as she headed into the city.

Most of Curton only paid lip service to Remembrance, with mudders needing to be reminded of who they were supposed to honor or remember. Were it not for the draks in town, Aveline doubted anyone would observe the day. She started her patrol upriver toward Danica's Den. Surprisingly, the gambling house bustled with business, despite the horror of what recently occurred there. Part of her wanted to inquire how the cleanup went, but she decided not to endure the crowded, smoky environment just to satisfy her own curiosity.

Across the river, she saw Ra-Jareez and Jazeera working on the exterior of Tasha's old house. From where she stood, their progress seemed slow, although Aveline assumed they'd spent much of their time working on the ruined interior. Unwilling to linger, she turned the corner, moving away from the river, before doubling back through Drakton.

Every building occupied by draks presented some sort of visual recognition of the day. Some families honored the sacred day by painting their doors with a blazing silver dragon head, while others hung faded pennants passed down through the generations. Like the calm before a storm, few draks wandered the streets, and those who did appeared to be traveling with purpose. Aveline knew the scene would be quite different once the celebration was underway. She hoped her invitation to the town councilors on behalf of the Crow Queen did not go ignored.

She checked in at Mudders' Gate before making the arduous trek through the streets of Hillside. She spent the rest of the morning circling the area near the market before crossing Caravan Bridge and heading into Old Town. By the time she approached her home by the city wall west of Miners' Gate, the sun had sunk low in the sky, casting long shadows over the streets. She didn't like leaving her home unoccupied, but she felt obliged to sleep at the citadel for as long as Koloman remained imprisoned there.

By the time she returned, Valon had been relieved by Brana. Aveline shared a meal with the young woman before turning in for the night. She prepared to spend much of the following day in a similar fashion.

* * *

Tempted as she was to burn her blood-soaked tunic and dung-covered skirt, Tasha lowered herself into the mill pond. Fed by a tributary of the Copper Run, the water felt as brisk as the snow from which it came, chilling away lingering fatigue from a late night of thinking about Torben.

Every knowledgeable farmhand told Yana and Dinara their cow's pregnancy, an accident resulting in a mid-summer calving, should be written off in light of the calf's breech position. The two women, distraught at the thought of losing their only milk cow, pled with the Crow Queen to intervene.

Delighted to deal with a problem more serious than a wart or boil, Tasha called upon the mantle to aid her and the cow. The task proved messy, although the magic of the mantle kept the cloak clean. As she rubbed her arms in the cool water to loosen dried blood, she contemplated whether to feel honored for having a calf named after her.

Once the pond water had chilled her to the bone, Tasha waded up the bank, balancing on the stones near the edge. Her heart skipped a beat as she spotted a man approaching.

Torben.

Crouching, he offered her a hand. He pulled her up and out of the water, chuckling. "I don't believe I've ever come across a fully clothed bathing beauty before."

Shivering, Tasha plucked the mantle from the branch where she left it for safekeeping. "Lucky for you. It's frowned upon to come across unclothed bathing beauties."

Throwing the cloak over her shoulder, she drew it closed. It warmed her. With the summer sun still high in the sky, she knew it would not be long before she felt comfortable, if not dry. "I'm happy you stopped by. I was hoping to see you again before…"

"Yes… before." Torben sat on a nearby fallen tree.

Tasha joined him. "Have you been drinking your tea?"

"Yes." Torben rested his hands on his legs, studying the sky. "And I have come to a decision."

Forcing herself to maintain steady breathing, Tasha faced the southerner. Dark circles under his eyes told of recent sleepless nights, although he remained well groomed. He wore none of his usual gear, just a pair of breeches and boots, his tunic, a fur-lined vest, and a pouch on his belt. His clothes, all neutral shades of brown, seemed old.

Torben met her gaze, furrowing his brow. "I have chosen life."

Unable to contain her joy, Tasha threw her arms around him. She held him for several minutes, fighting back tears. Putting an arm around her, he rested his head on top of hers.

"Vasilisa is a difficult woman, but she taught me much. She will be with me when I change, and she will guide me tonight. Keep me away from any temptations."

Tasha finally released him. "I'm glad to hear that. I know you'll be strong."

"Without you here"—Torben held Tasha's hand—"I would not have made the same choice."

Leaning close, she pressed her lips to his. His spine stiffened at first, but then he relaxed, pulling her close. Tasha let the passion of the moment flow through her, warming her from head to toe as she kissed him.

At last, he pushed her away. "Things will be different after tonight. I'm sorry we didn't have more time."

Tasha pursed her lips. "I'm the Crow Queen. I will not fear you. In fact, I expect a full report tomorrow. I want to know how my tea worked, if nothing else. My hut will be in the hills outside of Miners' Gate."

Chuckling, he averted his eyes. "Very well." Torben moved to leave. "I'm going to say my goodbyes to Florin and his family. I won't be staying with them anymore."

She held onto his hand as he moved to leave, finally releasing it when he reached arm's length. "Promise me you'll seek me out, Torben."

"I will. I don't know where I'll be when the hunt is done, but I will return to find you as soon as I can." He squeezed her hand, releasing it as he withdrew. "I promise."

Tasha watched him leave before returning to the hut. Since her clothes still dripped with water, despite feeling warmer, she changed into one of the new skirts and tunics she'd recently purchased. She called Korbin and Revan to her. With both perched on her shoulder, she used the back door to return to the mine and join the draks in their Remembrance celebration.

Though the festivities had not yet begun, Tasha observed workers from the cemetery mingling with draks, setting up the bonfire. Several of the stoneworkers erected the long tables at which they would later feast. Already, hogs rotated on spits; their dripping fat sent fire dancing into the sky. The aroma of roasting pork mingled on the breeze with the fragrance of wildflowers.

She greeted a group of draks she recognized from Curton, their dusty blue, green, and grey scales conspicuous among their brethren Icescales. It warmed her heart to see draks from different clans, as well as humans, all coming together to remember the fallen and celebrate that which survived.

While she waited for the festivities to begin, she paid her respects to Vasco. Mounds of churned, muddy earth covered the graves, outlining where each of the bodies lay. Sparse grass covered the area, most of it worn away from constant foot traffic over the past few weeks. Tasha knelt before Vasco's grave marker. For now, a wooden stick with the initials of "VD" replaced the simple marker Aveline had placed there. Soon, the stoneworkers would install a permanent granite marker to commemorate their companion's sacrifice.

She sank her hands in the mud, closing her eyes. Through her connection with Gaia, she felt each body, as well as the host of terrors visited upon each one. Even though the spirits had moved on to the next realm, the evil they experienced lingered. At the edge of her perception, Tasha felt the chaos rift deep under the hills. Pushing it away, she concentrated on the life all around her.

Despite the barren appearance of the graveyard, the earth teemed with life. From the worms and beetles feasting upon the interred dead, to the seeds waiting to erupt from the churned earth, they all flourished under the bosom of the Earth Mother.

Tasha drew from that power—energy of the land itself held in the earth and in the deep roots of ancient trees. Spreading outward from where she knelt and encompassing the entirety of the graveyard, grasses and flowers pushed their way through the dirt, covering the land in a blanket of green accented with splotches of red, yellow, blue, and white. At each corner of the rectangular graveyard Aveline so painstakingly plotted, a tree burst from the dirt, punching its way toward the sky, unfurling branches and leaves like fingers reaching for the gods above.

The trees—cherry, apple, plum, and pear—would bring life. Shuddering, she opened her eyes, forcing herself to take each breath slowly until her limbs stopped shaking. Tasha noticed the crowd had gathered around her. Wide-eyed in awe, they stared at the Crow Queen's creation—a verdant field of grasses and flowers, a living monument to the dead. The first stars of night sparkled in the sky, and the nearly full King began its journey from east to west.

She brushed soil off her skirt, rubbing her hands to remove as much dirt as possible as she approached the crowd. They fell to their knees, prostrating themselves before her.

"Please, no, don't do that. I just wanted to do something nice for all our kin who died." Reaching downward, she urged one of the workers to his feet. "I need to wash this mud off my hands before the festivities begin."

One drak from the Icescale clan, still kneeling, pointed over his shoulder with a trembling claw. "There's a rain barrel you can use, over by the mine." He averted his eyes once he saw her heading in the correct direction. Tasha hurried through the crowd, hoping they would resume their activities once she was out of sight.

She found the barrel. While she washed up, a familiar grey-scaled drak approached her. He pounded his chest. "You know that onion honey did the trick."

Tasha laughed. "I'm happy to hear it. I'm surprised you came all this way for Remembrance."

Tilting his head, Toviah scratched under his chin. "I heard the Icescale clan was here, and I couldn't pass up the opportunity. I used to visit them in my traveling days. You know, I knew Klatt when he was a young drak before his tail stiffened and made him grouchy."

"I'm happy to see you here." Tasha put her hand on the drak's shoulder. "And I'm happy both the Firetender and Ashenscale clans sent draks out this way."

He bowed his head. "It is we who are honored. You're the Crow Queen. I had no idea. You've done so much for us, all three of our clans now. I truly feel as though Rannos Dragonsire himself is working through his beloved Earth Mother on this day."

"Now, you can help me, Toviah."

He studied her with teary eyes. "Yes, anything."

"Tell your people not to bow to me."

Blinking, he frowned.

Tasha knelt. She took his hand. "I'm serious. I don't want people bowing to me like I'm some sort of ruler or goddess. I'm just Tasha. Well, I am the Crow Queen, but I'm here to help, not be worshipped. Understand?"

"I think so, yes." The old drak chewed on his lip.

"Now then." Tasha rose. "Let's see what they have in store for us, shall we? It looks very elaborate."

When they returned to the area prepared for the party, Elder Klatt stood before the bonfire. With a clap of his hands, the pile of wood ignited. Upon raising his arms, flames shot upward, swirling high into the air. They coalesced into the shape of a great fiery dragon before turning toward the crowd. The draks first gasped, then cheered. The human attendees, ready to flee, brightened when they realized the draks were unafraid. While the dragon swooped overhead, wheeling to circle the bonfire below, they held their ground.

"On this night, we mourn the death of Rannos Dragons-ire, struck down by men seeking the doom of all—power." Klatt, with the help of draks from his own clan, climbed onto a nearby table. "On this night, we celebrate those who persevered through The Sundering, all those who did not give in to despair in the wake of a god's death and the break-ing of the world, but, instead, who chose life. They fought, they died, and they lived. They healed the world. In so doing, they brought together not only the broken pieces of Gaia, but also people. Draks and dwarves, minotaurs and men, even oroqs, and all the forgotten peoples abandoned by the fae during their exodus: the faelixes, the cathar, and the caprikin."

Elder Klatt paced the length of the table. "Our world is not the world of the Age of Legends, but we have not forgotten it. All of us here, draks and humans alike, come from folk who lived in that faraway world, folk who endured the horror of The Sundering, who chose life, bore children, and lived to see the world healed. Tonight, we remember them and our father, Rannos Dragonsire."

The draks cheered in unison. A few humans joined in. They seemed unsure exactly what they cheered for. Elder Klatt, moving to hop off the table, accepted assistance at the last moment from a crimson-scaled drak and climbed down. Once both of his clawed feet touched the ground, he clapped his hands again, and the feast commenced.

Chapter 62

Aveline spent the morning touring Drakton and Hillside before returning to the citadel to sit her shift guarding Koloman. The morning after Remembrance usually involved a prodigious effort to clear the streets of trash and drunks still too besotted to make it home on their own. This morning proved no different, so she tasked her constables with the job.

Upon checking on Koloman, she found a half-eaten plate of food. It occurred to her that they could no longer give the Lord Mayor the sleeping draught. With the magistrate en route, Koloman needed to be fully awake and lucid for the tribunal. With each day that passed, the Lord Mayor's appearance worsened. His unkempt hair and beard would do him no favors, but Aveline dared not provide him with a razor and a basin.

When she returned to the vestibule, Aveline found Tasha waiting for her. The Crow Queen's eyes appeared slightly bloodshot with dark circles under them. Stifling a yawn, she greeted the knight-captain.

"What happened to you?" Aveline took a seat in a chair by the door to the cellblock.

"Late night. A good one, but late." Tasha helped herself to a free chair near Aveline's desk. "How's Koloman?"

"Enjoying his last day of good sleep. We have to stop the sleeping draughts before the magistrate arrives."

"Good idea." Tasha arched her back, stretching. "The magistrate needs to see how far gone he is."

Aveline leaned forward. "I'm dreading it. He's so unhinged. I'm beginning to wish I'd taken over Dawnwatch with Maxim. I'm only half serious." Venting her frustrations made them seem less severe.

"We'll get through it. Help is coming from the Arcane University. Once the rift is closed, everything will return to normal."

Tasha's smile did little to boost Aveline's confidence. She harbored no doubts the magistrate would be fair and make the right decisions. Instead, she worried about Koloman's behavior. "Do you think a week of those sleeping draughts will calm him or make his ravings worse?"

"Interesting question." Tasha bit her lip. "If he's possessed, it's possible the entity grew bored with him sleeping so much and left. Or maybe it will release pent-up energy once he's fully awake again. It's hard to say."

"And if he's not possessed?" Aveline stared into space. Wringing her hands, she questioned herself almost as much as she did Tasha. "If it's all Koloman in there?"

"I don't have any definite answers for you, Aveline."

Sighing, the knight-captain regarded her friend. "I guess it doesn't matter. We'll just have to be ready for whatever happens. I want you here when the magistrate arrives, just in case. That is, if the Crow Queen can be bothered…"

"Bothered?" Tasha raised an eyebrow, and she put her hand on her chest. "You're my friend. I would never be bothered by helping you."

Aveline pinched the bridge of her nose. "That's not what I meant. I just… oh, I just want this to be over. I want to go home. Sleep in my own bed."

Tasha moved closer to Aveline, hugging her. "I know. It'll be all right. You'll get through this. You're the strongest person I know."

Aveline returned the embrace, forgetting for a moment she was knight-captain of Curton's city watch. Pulling away, she regarded Tasha. "Thanks. Now tell me about this party you attended last night."

Aveline welcomed the distraction of her friend's tale of the Remembrance celebration out by the mine. She checked the fire in the stove, preparing for a lengthy regalement of the previous night's events.

"Elder Klatt gave a nice speech, we had a lot of food, draks from three different clans mingled with humans, and everyone got along. It was nice."

Aveline faced her friend. "That's it? It was nice? You look like you haven't slept, and it was just *nice*?"

Tasha dropped her eyes to the floor. "I paid my respects to Vasco, and I may have caused a field of flowers and some trees to grow around all the graves. Everyone was pretty impressed by that."

"How exactly did you do that?" Aveline caught herself just before leaning on the hot stove with her bare hand.

"I'm the Crow Queen." Tasha's cheeks flushed red. "Power of the Earth Mother."

"That's impressive." Aveline returned to her seat by the cellblock door. "Any news about the chaos rift?"

Tasha's expression fell. "I felt it. It's growing. We'll have to act soon."

"We'll make it our priority after we deal with Koloman. I hope a few more days won't make a big difference."

"If we start digging out the cave after the tribunal"— Tasha clasped her hands in her lap—"we should have the rift exposed by the time help from Muncifer arrives. The draks also said they'd help."

"Excellent." Aveline sighed, feeling unexpectedly relieved at the offer of help. "Now we just have to get through the tribunal."

* * *

Tasha left the citadel to return to her hut. As before, people gathered seeking aid from, or the blessings of, the Crow Queen. She spent the rest of the day and most of the next morning indulging them. Turning away no one, no matter how insignificant their need, kept her mind off Torben, for a full moon came the night after Remembrance.

Now, the following day, she hoped to see him, but she did not want to focus on that.

And so, she taught people remedies for their rashes and boils and pretended to prognosticate the futures of their babies and loved ones. All the while, she took care to remind fortune-seekers that divination was not an exact art and they'd do just as well with any number of soothsayers in town.

Finally, as the sun set, she sent the last of the townsfolk home satisfied. Breathing a sigh of relief, she found a large, flat rock upon which to sit and watch the moons rise. Fireflies flashed in nearby bushes, and crickets began their evening songs. Interrupting the nocturnal symphony, Korbin alerted the Crow Queen to another approaching supplicant.

"It's getting late." Tasha didn't bother to face whoever approached. "Go home. I'll still be here in the morning, and I want to rest now."

"It is a long way home"—Torben's voice quickened her heart—"and I would never leave without saying goodbye."

She leapt to her feet, racing to meet him, but she stopped moving after a few steps. The southerner walked with a slouch, and his hair, once so neatly groomed, stuck out at odd angles, as though he'd slept in a typhoon.

"How are you feeling? Did it work?"

"Yes." Watching her from the sides of his eyes, he approached, keeping his movements slow and deliberate. "I have spoken with the beast within, and it with me, thanks to Vasilisa. We have an understanding now."

Tasha reached for him. Recoiling, Torben shook his head. "I have feasted on flesh and blood, and I enjoyed it. I am... unworthy of your touch, Crow Queen."

"That's nonsense." Tasha held her hand toward him.

Torben fell to his knees, prostrating himself before her. "I have no home. My kin will never accept the beast I am. I don't know what I expected, but it wasn't this... these feelings of hunger, a primal need to hunt. I should have asked you to help me end it."

Tasha took his arm, encouraging Torben to rise. "I would not have done that if I could save your life instead."

He resisted her efforts to pull him to his feet. "I have faced down frost wyrms in the ice, and spent the night surrounded by ravenous wolves with only a meager fire to protect me. But this? This is beyond my ability to endure."

A flurry of emotions flooded Tasha. Pity for the pain the once-proud man felt. Disappointment he needed her to take responsibility for his condition. Clenching her jaw, she turned away just as their eyes met, crossing her arms in front of her. "Your fate is not my responsibility. I saved your life. Would you have preferred I let you bleed out in front of my hut? Left you for the carrion eaters?"

"I would have chosen death were it not for you." Torben choked back a sob.

"I am glad you chose life, Torben. Now you have to live with that choice." She glanced over her shoulder. Tears ran down his face.

Sighing, Tasha rubbed her eyes. She knelt before him, taking his hands in hers. "I don't think you're a monster. But I wonder where the proud, strong Watchman went. You are not the same man I kissed a few days ago. I know that man is still here."

"I told him not to come so soon."

Tasha faced Vasilisa. The other werewolf approached. She tilted her head, regarding Torben. "Look at this mewling pup. His beast has thoroughly cowed him. He needs to take control, embrace it but not fear it. Only then will the Torben you remember return."

"Can you help him? He said he had an understanding with his beast."

Torben's eyes darted to her, then to Vasilisa and back. He cowered like a chastised puppy.

"Obviously, he decided to submit to his beast. To be frightened of it, rather than take hold of it and control it." Vasilisa cupped Torben's chin in her hand, peering into his eyes. "If he does not take charge, eventually the beast will take complete control and he will become a monster, fit only to be hunted down and destroyed."

Tasha clenched her jaw. "I thought spending time with you before the full moon would prevent this."

"Men can be stubborn and foolish." Releasing Torben, she turned her attention to Tasha. "I told him all he needed to know, yet he did not listen."

A tear rolled down Tasha's cheek. Wiping it away, she bit her lip. "I need you to succeed, Torben. I want your help. We must go back to the mine; I want your help there. I want you with me. But you're no good to me like this." She nodded at Vasilisa. "What can we do?"

Circling Torben, the elder werewolf stared at him with unblinking honey eyes. "He has to want to change. He will need to force the beast to obey his desires. Once he does this"—gesturing toward him, she shook her head— "weakness will fade. It will be like night and day. Otherwise, fear will consume him, and, at the next full moon, the beast will take control."

"Then there's no time like the present." Tasha clasped her hands behind her back. "I will move deeper into the forest. There's a clearing to the south, not far from here, but far enough away no one from town should wander by at this time of night. Meet me there, and we'll deal with this tonight. If I don't see you by the time the moons fully rise, well, then I'll know what his decision is."

She ascended the stairs to her hut, shutting the door behind her. Wiping the tears from her eyes again before climbing onto the stump, Tasha took her place above the basin. She guided the hut out of the clearing in which it sat, moving it farther away from the city. As the hut climbed the hills, she saw Vasilisa transform, chasing after her. Torben followed. Outpacing both, she slowed the hut, allowing them to pass her and run together. By the time she settled into the new location, Vasilisa waited for her.

Tasha joined the werewolf, now in her hybrid form, as they waited for Torben to catch up. "You're sure this will work?"

Growling, Vasilisa arched her back. "Yes. This is normal. The last pup I helped had it far worse." Baring her teeth, the werewolf leaned in close to Tasha. "Don't tell him. He's done well. If he can force the change now, the beast will never control him."

In the distance, Tasha heard wolves howling. Bristling at the sound, the werewolf caught herself, then relaxed. Picking at her teeth, she squatted next to Tasha. "He spoke of you. Often. If he can seize control of his beast, he would make a good mate."

"Really?" Tasha tried to keep her tone flat. In the darkness, she hoped Vasilisa could not see her blush.

Torben stumbled out of the woods. Lacerations caused by branches that had slashed his face during the run healed before Tasha's eyes. Doubling over to catch his breath, he panted. Vasilisa lunged at him, grabbing him by the throat. He clawed at her paw, gasping.

"Take control, Torben. Change. Force the beast to submit to your will." She brought his face close to her slavering maw.

Tasha pulled the cloak close around her shoulders, fighting to keep her distance. Concentrating on the life around her, she flexed her toes. In the formidable presence of the two werewolves, the connection with Gaia calmed her. Vasilisa's aura glowed as a beacon of fury; yet, her force of will and her devotion to Artume, goddess of the hunt, controlled the beast within her. Torben's energy, in contrast, felt simultaneously passionate and apologetic like a battle between uncontrolled rage and fear. The storm of conflict threatened to tear him apart in an instant.

"I… can…" Through the massive paw wrapped around his neck, Torben choked on the words. "I cannot. Not in front of—"

"Yes! In front of her." Vasilisa pushed her nose into Torben's. "I smell your desire. Does she not deserve to know what you are?"

Through her connection to the land, she, too, felt Torben's desire, trembling at Vasilisa's ferocity. "What are you, Torben? Show me. I am not afraid." She said the words to convince herself as much as to motivate Torben.

"No, no." Torben pried Vasilisa's fingers away from this throat. Snarling, she threw him to the ground. Clearing his throat, he pushed himself to his hands and knees.

Tasha closed her eyes. Appearing like an unkempt wolf, Torben's beast stalked the Watchman cowering on the forest floor. Reaching out with her mind, she caressed Torben's hand. *You're strong, Watchman. I know you are stronger than that beast. You are Torben, of the Four Watches, and I believe you control this beast. Show me. Don't be scared. Don't be ashamed. I'm here with you.*

Torben screamed.

Tasha's eyes snapped open, meeting with his for an instant before he thrashed on the ground. Fur sprouted from his skin as his limbs, popping sinew and cracking bones, stretched. His screams continued as bulging muscles tore through his clothes. Crackling and deforming, his face grew longer. Teeth became fangs, whiskers punched through his cheeks, and a tail thrashed as fur grew to cover it in a shaggy coat.

Tasha forced her eyes to remain open, despite fear seizing every muscle in her body. She wanted to turn and flee to the safety of her hut, but she remained and witnessed his transformation. He stood on all fours, panting. Tasha knelt, holding her hand out to him. The newly transformed werewolf sniffed the air before padding toward her. From the periphery of her vision, Tasha saw Vasilisa drop to all fours before disappearing into the darkness.

Covered head to toe in black, bristly fur, Torben's werewolf form stood half again as tall as the largest dog Tasha had ever encountered. Sniffing her hand, he licked it. He then sat on his haunches, gazing at her with soulful amber eyes.

"Can you understand me, Torben?"

The werewolf bowed his head. With a trembling hand, she scratched between his ears. He crept forward, then sat at her side, leaning against her. Tasha folded her legs beneath her, wrapping her arm around him. Glancing up at her, he laid his head in her lap and closed his eyes.

Chapter 63

Aveline descended the stairs after a night of fitful sleep. Without the effects of the sleeping draught, Koloman's ranting and raving returned full force, almost as if he made up for lost time. He cajoled, threatened, and pleaded for freedom in between offering foreboding predictions and random non-sequiturs.

In the vestibule, Valon and Brana offered their captain casual salutes as she entered, yawning. She returned their hails. "Is there any good food, or just what's in the larder?"

"Meat and veg hand pies from the bakery." Valon gestured toward a covered tray on Aveline's desk. "Plus, I have good news."

"That's a switch." Aveline reached under the towel, helping herself to a pie. It still felt warm. Bits of flaky crust fell to the floor as she bit into it.

"The magistrate arrived late last night, and he said he'd be here after breaking his fast."

Aveline shoved the food to the side of her mouth. "Finally. Has anyone seen Tasha yet today?"

Valon shook his head. "We've reports that her hut moved last night."

The news made Aveline's heart skip a beat, but she forced herself to remain calm. *Tasha won't abandon you. She'll be here.* "Probably nothing to worry about."

"There was a lot of howling going on in the forest last night." Brana unsheathed her sword, then sat in the chair by the cellblock door. She ran the blade along the whetstone.

Full moon last night. I hope everything went all right with her. "A wolf pack on the hunt, most likely. Did anyone report any disturbances?"

"Nothing out of the ordinary. Certainly nothing related to the wolves." Valon hooked his thumbs into his belt. "Just noise."

Just then, the door opened. Tasha entered the vestibule. She greeted everyone. "Am I late? Is the magistrate here?"

Swallowing, Aveline shook her head. "Not yet. He's in town, and he'll be here after eating."

"Oh good. I was worried." Tasha slid the tray of meat pies to the side, taking a seat on the edge of Aveline's desk. "Another late night?"

"Is everything all right?" Aveline kept her query vague in the presence of Valon and Brana.

"Yes." Smiling, Tasha nodded. "Everything is fine. I'm looking forward to ending this business with Koloman."

"So say we all." Aveline flipped back the cloth on the tray. "Hungry?"

"No, thank you. I already ate."

"By the grace of Anetha"—Brana polished the hilt of her sword—"we'll be done dealing with that raving madman today. Honestly, Captain, his ranting is getting to me."

Aveline sympathized. Despite almost a weeklong respite, the previous night's harangue ignited all her anxieties. "It'll be over soon." *I hope.*

Valon moved to answer a pounding at the door. The magistrate, a middle-aged silver-haired man who wore a formal silver-trimmed blue tunic over black breeches pushed his way past the lieutenant. "Knight-Captain Aveline, care to bring me up to speed?"

Aveline summarized the events leading to Koloman's arrest. "Now, we have no direct evidence he caused either death, but we have witnesses placing him with both victims just prior to their deaths and saying he fled both scenes."

"Some sort of madness?" The magistrate's gaze settled on Tasha. "Who is this? Why is this… witch here?"

"Tasha is the Crow Queen." Aveline gestured toward her friend as Tasha slid off the edge of Aveline's desk. "She may be of help if Koloman becomes uncontrollable."

The magistrate raised an eyebrow at Tasha. "I thought the Crow Queen was dead. Or, at least, she left decades ago to never return."

"Crow Queen Annika died. I succeeded her." Tasha bowed her head toward the magistrate. "Aveline is my friend, and I'm ready to help in whatever way I can."

"Fine. Let's see what Koloman has to say for himself first, eh?" The magistrate gestured toward the cellblock. Brana hopped off her chair, sheathing her sword, and pulled open the door. Aveline led the way down the hall toward the cellblock.

She glanced over her shoulder at the magistrate. "Be aware, he's quite agitated and volatile."

They arrived at Koloman's cell to find the Lord Mayor pacing, conversing aloud with himself. When he noticed his audience, he lunged, leaping onto the bars. Sneering, he pressed his face in the spaces between them. "Ah, Magistrate. It's about time someone came to release me. Throw this woman in here, instead." His face contorted.

His voice raised in pitch, becoming shrill. "Oh, no, it's nice in here." He shook his head. "We get free food. It's warm, and there's no mud."

Koloman snarled. "Silence. The lady knight will be ours, perhaps the servant of the goddess too. Ooh, her power will taste sweet." He smacked his lips.

The Lord Mayor's expression changed again, and his eyes widened. "You see? She has me locked up in here with these creatures. I'm the Lord Mayor of this town. I am above the law, no matter what this bitch says."

The magistrate leaned toward Aveline. "Yes, I see what you mean."

"Lies!" Koloman rattled the bars of his cell door. "It's all filthy lies!"

Tasha crossed her arms. "Something plagued his dreams a few weeks ago. I don't know if this is a manifestation…"

Snarling, Koloman stuck out his tongue. He jumped off the bars and fell to the ground. "Time to end this." He gurgled. Grabbing at his throat, he gagged between screams. "Do... do something. Help me!"

Aveline and Tasha restrained the magistrate as he lunged toward the Lord Mayor. "Let me go."

"No, stay back." Aveline strained. Despite the magistrate's age, he remained a strong fellow. "It's not safe."

The Lord Mayor, thrashing on the floor, writhed in pain. "It burns!"

His screams intensified into high-pitched wails. Continuous shrieks of agony assaulted their ears. They witnessed his skin churn, bubbling. It turned first blue, then green. Finally, it turned orange. His body swelled, bloating.

"By Hon's Hearth"—the magistrate clutched at Aveline's arm—"will you do nothing for him?"

"Like what?" Aveline pushed the magistrate farther away from the cell, interposing herself in front of him.

"Make it stop! I'll do anything! I'll give you any—" Koloman's cries garbled. The Lord Mayor's orange skin stretched, and his eyes bulged.

The magistrate stopped struggling, his jaw hung agape with horror.

Koloman burst.

Recoiling, Aveline suppressed a gag as ichor and blood sprayed like a fountain, splattering the walls of the cell. Skin and muscle sloughed off the Lord Mayor's bones until a ragged, blackened skeleton lay in a puddle of rainbow goo. Rattling and dripping, it rose. Flesh coalesced, swirling like a whirlpool, onto the skeleton. A high-pitched wail pierced the room as a reptilian head emerged from the torso and another head, a human one, sprouted at the top of the oozing mass of flesh.

The reptilian mouth opened in a groaning scream. Hair sprouted, grew, then sloughed off in clumps. Twisting, the torso hunched, and arms erupted from its side. The arms flailed until they cradled the snarling reptilian head.

"By the gods..." Tasha recoiled from the monstrosity, pulling the magistrate even farther away from the cell.

Aveline readied her mace. The creature lurched away from them. It spun. Quivering, it glared with four black eyes, two from a fully formed drak head and two from a fully formed human head. A grin appeared on the face of the human head.

"Time to go."

Aveline recognized the voice, a harsh rasp, as belonging to the wizard they encountered in the mine.

Shrieking, the magistrate fled the cellblock. Before either Aveline or Tasha acted, the fleshy creature liquefied, splashing a perfectly circular hole through the stone floor. Aveline fumbled with her key, unlocking the cell. She flung the door open. Gawking, she peered into a smooth-sided tunnel that descended straight before veering to the right.

Tasha came up beside her. "Before you ask, I have no idea what just happened."

"I wasn't going to ask." Swallowing, Aveline shuffled her feet. She pulled Tasha away from the creeping edge of the goo puddle leftover from the Lord Mayor's transformation.

Black smoke wafted from the hole. It grew thicker and more concentrated with each passing moment. Tasha seized Aveline's arm, intending to pull her away, but the knight-captain needed no encouragement. They fled the cellblock, urging all the guards into the vestibule. Aveline locked the door behind them.

To her relief, the smoke seemed confined to Koloman's cell. She slid her chair out from behind her desk with trembling hands and sat.

Tasha leaned on the knight-captain's desk. "We have to go back to the mine. We must seal that rift. Now."

Aveline tossed the key to Valon. "No one goes in there." He nodded as he attended the magistrate retching in the corner.

Brana stared at them. "That sounded horrible. What happened?"

Aveline glanced at Tasha.

The Crow Queen shrugged. "Koloman… well, I think he's dead. And whatever that was, it's gone now."

"But to where?" Aveline flung open the vestibule door to look both ways down the street. "I want everyone on alert. There's no telling what's going to happen now. Brana, go to Miners' Gate and tell them to watch out for… I don't know, some abomination with multiple heads. Valon, you take Mudders' Gate."

"Yes, m'lady." The two saluted her before rushing out of the citadel.

The magistrate stumbled into Brana's chair. "That was horrific. What did I just witness?"

"Tasha?" Shutting the door, Aveline glanced over her shoulder at the Crow Queen.

"I'm just guessing, but I believe it was the manifestation of some manner of chaos beast emerging into this realm through Koloman."

"I'm sorry I asked." The magistrate removed a cloth from his pocket to wipe his forehead.

"The good news is we no longer need a tribunal." Aveline entered the larder, soon returning with three bottles of ale. She offered one to the magistrate, who, nodding his gratitude, opened it. "Magistrate, can you inform the City Council they'll need to request an appointment for a new Lord Mayor from Almeria?"

After downing its contents in several gulps, he nodded. "That wasn't nearly strong enough. What are you going to do about this… creature?"

"We're going to find it and end it." Tasha refused the drink from Aveline. Instead, she took her friend's arm. "I'll find him. My hut is just north of town, in a clearing over the hill. The one that used to have that big oak before lightning hit it a few years back. Do you know it?"

"I do. I'll gather volunteers, horses, and supplies." Swigging her ale, Aveline rubbed her neck. "We'll be light on people. I don't want to leave the town unguarded, but I'll find some diggers. I hope."

Tasha shared her plan. "We'll go through the cave. We should be able to expose the rift more easily that way. Yun's a good fighter, if you don't want to bring too many of the city watch. We'll have Torben too."

Narrowing her eyes, Aveline lowered her voice. "Is he safe? With the rift and chaos and all that…"

"Yes." Tasha gave a curt nod. "I'd stake my life on it."

"Fine. I wish there were a way to get your wizard friends here quicker."

"Wizards? What wizards?" The magistrate raised his head.

Tasha held up her hand. "It's a long story. There's a problem at a nearby mine. It's related to what happened to Koloman. Aid is on the way from Muncifer, but they're still weeks away on horseback. We can no longer wait for them."

"Can you do it alone?" Taking Tasha by the shoulders, Aveline searched her eyes.

"I have no choice. If Annika could end a plague alone, then I can do this. I've studied the ritual. I have to try." The cost Annika incurred to end the plague wormed its way into Tasha's thoughts, but she pushed the concern aside. The people of Curton were worth more than her vitality.

Aveline clicked her fingers. "I have an idea. You can get to Dawnwatch and back by the time we're ready to go. Have Maxim get his best fighters together, then march on the mine. They should be able to get there about the same time as we do."

The magistrate rose from his chair. "I see you two ladies have things well in hand here. I'll speak to the council." He bowed. "Lady Aveline, I know you'll do as you have always done and see to the safety of Curton. Crow... Tasha... thank you for your help." He hurried away, leaving the knight-captain and Crow Queen alone in the vestibule.

"Aveline, I'm taking the hut. It won't take us long to get there. It will be much quicker than on horseback."

The knight-captain raised her eyebrow. "All the diggers, too, and their equipment? How much space do you have in there?"

"I can make it bigger."

"How taxing is that? I want you at full strength."

Tasha could not answer Aveline's question with any degree of certainty. "I didn't feel any different after making a proper bedroom and bathing room."

"No." Shaking her head, Aveline held up her hand. "You need to keep an eye on whatever that thing is that came out of Koloman. You'll have your hands full with that and moving the hut. Don't push yourself too far. I know you're still getting a handle on this whole Crow Queen thing."

Tasha forced herself to concede Aveline's point. "I'll get Yun and Torben and wait for you at my hut, then."

"If we're going to the mine, doesn't it make more sense to move the hut to outside of Miners' Gate, then?" Aveline filled a pack with food from the larder.

"That's also a good point."

Tasha bade her friend farewell, leaving Aveline to her preparations. She followed the road running along the Copper Run until she reached Danica's Den. From the outside, one would never guess what horrible events had transpired there. Inside, the smoky gaming house bustled with people intent on winning enough money to leave their life of mudding behind, despite most understanding the odds favored the house. She asked the doorman where she could find the caprikin. He directed her to the upstairs fighting ring.

Tasha found Yun sitting ringside, his arm in a sling. Intending to slip away without approaching him, she cursed when he spotted her, waving her over.

"Come to watch fight?" Yun raised his arm. "No fight for me today."

"I see that." Tasha frowned. "I was rather hoping to recruit you for a potential battle at the old mine."

"I fight where pay is good, but you saved me." Yun slapped his chest. "I fight one arm for you."

Tasha put her hand on his shoulder to dissuade him from rising. "No, it's too dangerous. I won't have you risking your life while you're injured. You can repay your debt later. Did you see what happened with the Lord Mayor and that woman?"

Yun shook his head, spitting on the floor. "Foul sorcery. I was… not here until after." He flexed his free arm. "Lonely woman wanted strong one. I helped her."

"That's… fine." She patted him on the shoulder. "I have to leave. Will you check in on Ra-Jareez and Jazeera? Make sure they're safe, will you, please?"

"Yes."

Tasha thought about asking the faelix siblings for their assistance, but she decided against doing so. It would be irresponsible to expose them to danger just because she didn't know what to expect. They were merchants, after all, not warriors. She left the smoke-filled gambling den behind and returned to her hut, ducking into a nearby alley to use her cloak hidden from passersby.

Korbin cawed at her when she appeared in the hut. He hopped about the windowsill until she approached, then dove into the forest. Peering out the window, she saw Torben on a stump whittling a stick with his carving knife. Tasha noticed he wore clean clothes once more as well as new axes, and he had groomed himself. She opened the door and joined him.

"Feeling better?"

He blew wood shavings off his carving, then held it up, examining it. "Yes. I can never repay you for what you've done."

"It's not necessary. I was helping a friend."

Gone was the slump in his shoulders. Strength filled his amber eyes as he gazed at her. "Though I spoke out of fear, I meant what I said." He slid off the stump and knelt before her, taking her hands in his. "I will guard your life with my own, for as long as I live. I pledge myself to the service of the Crow Queen."

"Torben, I appreciate the sentiment. I really do." Tasha pulled him to his feet. "But I don't need protection."

"Of course not." Holding her hands, he searched her eyes. "But neither does one need a plow; yet, farmers often find it makes their work easier. Since dominating my beast, I have a greater understanding of what it all means, how it ties together. Artume, Selene, the Earth Mother. I am unnatural now; yet, I am still part of this world. I want to continue helping people, but, obviously, I will not be welcomed into most communities."

Tasha knew of only one city, in fact, that had ever welcomed a werewolf: Drak-Anor. She heard stories about villages in the Four Watches on good terms with local lycanthropes, but she sensed Torben preferred not to return to a land of ice and snow.

"We'll have to talk about this later. There's a situation. If you want to help, if you're willing to fight alongside Aveline and myself, we need you."

"I will give my life if necessary." He bowed, bringing Tasha's hands to his forehead.

"I hope it won't be." She gestured toward the hut. "Let's go."

Chapter 64

After saying goodbye to Tasha, Aveline employed parchment and quill formalizing her request to Maxim for aid. She kept the letter short and to the point. As a fellow knight of Etrunia, Maxim would be obligated to lend assistance. Whether he could actually get to the mine in time, however, remained a different matter entirely. When finished, she retrieved her triangular seal bearing an image of the owl of Anetha from the payroll vault. She rummaged in her desk drawer for a stick of wax. Upon melting part of the candle she found, she authenticated the document.

After stowing the letter, she slung the bag over her shoulder, then took her shield and mace from the rack. Fingering the hilt of her sword, she decided against taking it. Just touching it reminded her of its last distasteful duty. Satisfied she had everything she needed, she exited the citadel.

The Mining Guild office, just down the street, remained open, despite years of mine inactivity. Aveline passed the building daily, but she rarely paid the crooked, weather-beaten structure any mind. She strained to pull the door hanging on rusty hinges open. Inside, an elderly man with a shock of snow-white hair snoozed behind a desk.

"Excuse me." Aveline cleared her throat. The man's snoring continued unabated. Even after tapping on the top of the desk, she noticed no change in consciousness. Finally, she kicked the desk with enough force to move it.

The man jerked his head, blinking several times before his eyes focused on the knight-captain. "Lady Aveline? Forgive me, I don't know why you're here."

"I need diggers." She leaned on the desk. "I need enough people to excavate a collapsed cave near the old copper mine east of town, and I need them now."

"There's Mikhail... no wait, he died last week." The old man leaned back in his chair, tapping his chin. "Alexei... is no longer fit enough to dig. Hm. I think Leonid is dead too. Anastas is bedridden. Kosta... no, he left for Cliffport years ago."

Aveline threw up her hands. "Why is there a Mining Guild if there are no miners?"

"People don't like change. We had money in our treasury after the last of the mines closed and nothing to spend it on, so we've stayed open." He wrenched a knife free from where it was stuck in the top of the desk, then picked at his teeth. "Hasn't been much to do. The mudders have their own shovels, but they don't know anything about excavating. I suppose you could ask old Kilment, but I doubt he wants to go out to an old mine. I've been thinking about closing down, to be honest, since I'm the only one who still comes to the guildhall."

Pinching the bridge of her nose, Aveline sighed. The town's diggers had grown old since the last of the mines closed. Apparently, the guildhall was a meeting place for old folk to sit and reminisce about the good old days and not much else. "What then, do you suggest?"

"You might be able to hire some folk from Cliffport if your need is desperate or dwarves from Dwegerthon."

Aveline thanked the old man for the information before heading for the stables. She found Lieutenant Valon waiting for her. His frown told her all she needed to know. "If we want anyone from town to go out there, we'll need to conscript people."

"I'm not forcing townsfolk to risk their lives for this." Aveline clenched her jaw. "You're in charge until I return. *If* I return. I just hope the draks are up to the task of excavating that cave."

Valon offered her his hand. "You'll come back, m'lady. I have faith in you and the Crow Queen."

She gripped his forearm. "Thank you, Valon."

Hefting her pack, Aveline headed out of town. Turning right just past the gatehouse, she followed the city wall until she found the Crow Queen's hut. Beyond it, she spotted what looked like a burned section of land stretching eastward from the city wall. Approaching the charred area, she determined it was rotted, not scorched. Blackened vegetation writhed, withering before her eyes, like a creeping finger stretching across the land toward the distant sea.

She returned to the hut, shouting for Tasha. Upon the door opening, stairs erupted from the ground. Aveline climbed them as they appeared, not bothering to wait for them to reach the top before beginning her ascent.

"There's something going on outside." Aveline leapt over the gap between the top of the still-growing stairs and the threshold. "Have you seen it?"

Tasha, levitating above the basin, nodded. "Yes. Whatever Koloman has become is corrupting the land as it passes."

Just then, Aveline noticed Torben sitting in a chair next to the door. Despite herself, she backed away. Torben crossed a closed fist over his chest. "My Crow Queen has told me what I need to know. I am honored to aid you, Lady Aveline."

Aveline nodded at Torben. "There aren't any diggers left in town, Tasha." The knight-captain shut the door, crossing her arms as she leaned against it. "They're all too old or too dead."

"That's unfortunate." With unfocused eyes, Tasha stared forward.

"I'll get Socks while you go to Dawnwatch." Reaching in her pouch for the letter she'd written to Maxim, she noticed the room gently swaying. Aveline glanced out the window. The hut moved away from the city, following the blighted trail.

"No need. We'll follow Koloman's trail as far as we can. I think I can outpace it, so I'll veer off for Dawnwatch before we head to the mine. We can carry Maxim and whatever soldiers he can spare. It'll be tight quarters, but I think I can go from the fort to the mine in under a day. I've sent word ahead for the draks to get started, if they can."

"Well, if you're sure." Aveline tucked the letter in her pack. Giving it to Maxim would be a mere formality now. "What if it gets there before us?" Aveline shivered at the thought of what Koloman had become, or what emerged from him. "Will the draks be in danger?"

"Almost certainly. I told them everything I could in my message. I emphasized they were to put their own safety above all else."

Aveline moved to a chair by the table and settled in. "I just hope we're not too late."

* * *

Tasha only partially listened to Aveline while she focused on guiding the hut. As her friend seemed uncomfortable around Torben now, the conversation quickly lulled. Soon, Aveline drifted off to sleep. Torben seemed content to observe the passing landscape from his seat by the window.

Following the blighted trail proved easy enough. Moving forward at the pace of a human running on foot, it shriveled all plant life in its way. More than a match for the entity that was once Koloman, Tasha soon guided the hut past the end point of the trail. Unable to directly detect the source of the blight, she observed only its relentless drive eastward through the wilderness. Soon, adjusting course, she veered toward the north and Dawnwatch.

While controlling the hut required near-total concentration, Tasha found traveling more or less in a straight line did little to fatigue her. She hoped when she finally stopped, her body would neither collapse nor force her to sleep to recover her strength. In the periphery of her vision, she regarded the waning King and waxing Queen glide overhead as the earth sped below her. She piloted the hut through the night until dawn broke.

Overhead, gathering clouds flushed pastel rose and blue as the sun began to peek over the eastern horizon. Dawnwatch appeared in her view. Through her connection with the Earth Mother, Tasha sensed the dryad.

I see you, Crow Queen. Why do you speed this way? The dryad's voice, unmistakably Gwilvanwen's, echoed in her thoughts.

Can you rouse Maxim? Tell him Lady Aveline requires his aid. Tasha slowed the hut as they drew closer to Dawnwatch, circling to locate the front gate.

I'm not your messenger. What's in it for me?

Somehow, Tasha managed an entirely mental sigh of exasperation. *We're en route to close a chaos rift and defeat some sort of chaos beast. It's already blighting the land between Curton and the mine. Imagine what it will do if it finds out you're here.*

I'll just wake Maxim then, Crow Queen.

Tasha stopped the hut a short distance from the front gate of the fort. Aveline still slept, slumping in the chair with her head tilted back . Torben opened the door.

"Aveline, we're here." Tasha shook her friend's knee.

Gasping, Aveline rubbed her neck. "Damn. This is going to ache for a while." She gazed at the bed.

Tasha gestured toward it. "You would have been welcome to that, or the one in the back. I'm sorry I didn't mention it. Controlling the hut takes effort."

Aveline stretched. "It's fine. It's no worse than sleeping on the ground. I'll take the bed in the other room on the trip to the mine, though. Away from Maxim and his people, if you don't mind."

"You're welcome to it." For her part, after moving the hut throughout the night, Tasha did not feel fatigue to the point of needing rest. She hoped she could maintain her energy until they completed their task.

Hearing shouts from within Dawnwatch, Aveline, Tasha, and Torben descended the steps. As they approached the gatehouse, the portcullis raised with the clanking of metal and wheels. Maxim, still in his dressing gown, met them at the entrance. Tasha noticed a single broad leaf stuck in his beard.

"Now, what's all this then?" Squinting, he looked past them at the hut. "How did that get there?"

Tasha spread her arms. "After all you've seen, you still doubt the power of the Crow Queen?"

Aveline snorted. "It's not really important right now, Sir Maxim. What's important is that we have a rampaging abomination headed for the old copper mine and we need to stop it and close a chaos rift."

The knight-captain handed him the letter she'd written. "I'm formally requesting your aid."

Upon examining the seal, Maxim broke it, then read the letter. "Ah, yes. Well, in that case, I shall muster as many as I can. I'm sorry to say it won't be more than a few. I cannot leave Dawnwatch unoccupied."

Gwilvanwen slunk around the corner, placing her arms around Maxim's neck. "It wouldn't be unoccupied. I would still be here." Running a finger through his hair, she kissed his ear. His face flushing bright red, Tasha deduced how he acquired a leaf in his beard.

"Yes, well, I can spare myself and two others." Maxim extracted himself from Gwilvanwen's embrace. "Will that be sufficient, Lady Aveline?"

"It'll do." Aveline turned to Tasha as Maxim retreated into the keep to dress himself and rally his soldiers. "I hope it's enough."

Tasha nodded. "I believe it will be. If all goes well, I will need you only to keep the abomination busy while I close the rift. It will take all my concentration. Closing the rift might destroy it outright, but, even if it doesn't, it should weaken the creature considerably."

She stifled a yawn. Despite feeling the warmth of the sun on her face, or, perhaps, because of it, Tasha felt a wave of fatigue overtake her. "While we're waiting, I'm going to rest."

Aveline followed Maxim into Dawnwatch to assist in preparing the soldiers, while Torben followed Tasha up the stairs. "I will ensure no one disturbs you."

"That's not necessary." She clasped his arm. "I want to leave as soon as they're ready to go. Will you be all right out here by yourself?"

"Naturally." Torben withdrew the carving he'd been working on from his pack, then held it before Tasha. "Besides, I'm not alone. Your birds will keep me company."

Revan and Korbin flew in at that moment, circling the interior before landing on the windowsill. "Very well. Wake me when we're ready to leave."

She retired to the bedroom, collapsing into the bed. Falling asleep soon after her head hit the pillow, she dreamt of endless forest glades and bountiful harvests. In her heart, Tasha knew the goddesses would guide her, no matter what transpired at the mine.

Chapter 65

A gate guard, Gwilvanwen, and Aveline were the only people stirring in the early hours at Dawnwatch, and Maxim, of course, in his chambers. Whistling, the knight-captain viewed the renovations that Maxim and his recruits completed to restore the command post. Based on Tasha's descriptions, she had expected the task to be almost insurmountable.

One of the guards roused by Maxim exited. With his mail jangling, he crossed the yard. She surmised from his dark complexion he hailed from the north. Obviously, he was one of the recruits Maxim enlisted from Cliffport. Aveline waved him over.

"Where are you headed?"

He offered a sloppy salute to Aveline. "Sir Maxim says we are to make for the old copper mine east of Curton at once. I go to ready the horses."

She took his arm to keep him from running off. "That won't be necessary. The Crow Queen is taking all of us. What"—she pulled her hand away from his arm, her fingers covered with oil—"what in Anetha's name have you done to this armor? What is your name?"

"Oliver, son of Sebastian the Coopersmith of Port-of-Dogs. The armor we've had to clean and oil. We weren't quite finished."

"I'm Lady Aveline, Knight-Captain of the Order of the Shield, Watch Captain of Curton. It is appropriate for you to refer to me as 'm'lady' or 'Captain Aveline.'"

Chastened, he bowed. "Yes, m'lady. Sorry, m'lady."

She turned him to face the barracks. "Return to the armory and take off that armor. Change into clean clothes. When you come out next time, have the armor and what you need to finish cleaning it. I'll not have you enter into battle dripping like you fell into a vat of butter."

As he trotted off, she shouted after him. "And tell whoever else is coming the same."

"My, aren't you a stern one?" Gwilvanwen appeared alongside Aveline, as though from nowhere, and ran a rough, bark-like finger under the knight-captain's chin.

Aveline slapped the dryad's hand away from her face. "These men haven't been properly trained yet."

"Oh, they're not all men. There are a few women here as well. But they don't have fun like Maxy and me."

Raising her eyebrow, Aveline turned. The dryad circled Aveline, strutting. "Frankly, I don't care what you and Maxim get up to, as long as you don't suck him down into your tree for all time."

Gwilvanwen pushed out her bottom lip. "I would never do that to my Maxy... he does like it in my tree, though. Says it feels like a warm hug that never ends. Oh, we do have such pleasures there."

Aveline held up her hand. "I do not need details." Closing her eyes, she tried to banish images of the dryad and Maxim from her mind. "I just need him to be able to perform his duties. Though, I'm impressed you were able to seduce him. I didn't think he was the type to fall for a fae."

"I can be very persuasive."

"Yeah, I'll bet." Aveline viewed another soldier exiting the barracks, a woman this time. Like Oliver before her, she had the warm ochre complexion of a northerner. She wore her hair shorn much closer to her head than Aveline's. The woman wore greaves and a breastplate that bore several dents and gouges; however, her they had been recently polished. She moved with seamless fluidity, as if her armor were skin.

Marching toward Aveline, the soldier slung her bow and quiver over her shoulder. "Lady Aveline." Resting one hand on the hilt of her sword, she saluted.

Aveline returned the hail. "And who might you be? Are you coming along on this little misadventure?" Upon uttering the words, Aveline regretted her flippant attitude about their upcoming fight.

"Abigail Stonewright. I didn't know any northern folk served Almeria. Follow the princess down, did you?"

Aveline bristled at the presumption she should answer such a question from a stranger. The wide-eyed glee in Gwilvanwen's eyes anticipating a verbal reprimand persuaded her to take a more diplomatic approach.

"No. My parents brought me down to Curton. They were traders. Sadly, they died over the winter, and Sir Agnar, the former commander of this garrison, took me in and made me his ward. I've been here ever since. That was before Valene married Gavril. Now, Stonewright, are you coming with us? What do you want from me?"

Abigail cleared her throat. "Right, sorry, m'lady. I got excited seeing another warrior from the north. Oliver's a bit of an idiot. He's staying here; I'm taking his place."

"I see." Aveline clasped her hands behind her back. She narrowed her eyes, glancing at the dryad, who still watched them, albeit with less glee. "Is that what Sir Maxim ordered?"

"Not originally, m'lady. He intended Oliver and Lukas to accompany you. Lukas is fairly competent, but Oliver can barely hold his sword straight. Sir Maxim thought it would be a good training opportunity for him."

Aveline saw the logic in Maxim's thinking. "You disagreed?"

"Yes, m'lady." Abigail glanced over her shoulder at the barracks. "For one, Maxim doesn't think women should be doing any fighting. Two, I'm the best he has. And finally, I've heard enough talk about the Crow Queen from the faerie there that I know you wouldn't be asking for assistance if an untrained kid could help."

"Well, you got that right." Aveline observed Gwilvanwen slink across the yard and sink into her tree. "How many folk from up north are down here, anyway? I hardly see any of you in Curton."

"With due respect, m'lady, there's not much reason for us to go to Curton. There's a fair number of us in Cliffport. Oliver was pressed into a sailing crew, but they found out he's a lousy sailor, so he ended up working the docks. One of the trading companies paid me well to be a guard for them down in Cliffport at their warehouses. That's where I found him."

"Nice of you to take him under your wing like that."

"Yeah, well, he owes me money. I didn't want to let him out of my sight."

Typical mercenary attitude. "And Maxim's paying you more than that trading company?"

"Hardly. But the warehouse burned down one night. He pays more than not working does."

Maxim emerged from the barracks followed by a stout, bearded man with a ruddy complexion and arms like tree trunks. The man carried a maul slung over his shoulder, and the mail he wore threatened to spill out his belly.

"That must be Lukas." Over Abigail's shoulder, Aveline watched the men approach.

Abigail glanced backward. "He's a bruiser."

"Ah, Lady Aveline." The men saluted. Aveline noticed Lukas wore a pack twice the size of the one she carried.

"Are you ready?"

"Yes. However, I hoped I could have a minute to rouse the rest of the men and give them instructions to follow until I return."

Aveline nodded. "Go ahead. I'll take Lukas and Abigail and get them settled."

"Settled, m'lady?" Abigail motioned for Lukas to fall in behind her. They followed Aveline past the stables and toward the gatehouse. "Won't we need horses?"

She led them through the gatehouse, gesturing at the rickety-looking hut standing on crow's legs. "Who needs horses? We have the Crow Queen's hut."

* * *

In the midst of a lovely dream with bunnies, sunshine, and quiet forest glades, Tasha found herself awakened by a rude banging at her bedroom door. Several expletives raced through her mind before she remembered her situation. She threw off the covers, leaving the warm comfort of her bed, and shuffled to the door, yawning. What little sleep she managed seemed insufficient payment for the effort of moving the hut throughout the previous night.

Opening the door, she revealed Aveline as the source of the banging. Catching a glimpse at Tasha, her friend shook her head. "You look terrible. Are you sure you're all right to keep going? You haven't slept all night."

"I'll be fine." She moved past Aveline, closing the door behind her. In the main room of the hut, she saw Torben by the window, Maxim by the door with his arms crossed, and two armored individuals she did not recognize. The knight-captain introduced them as Abigail and Lukas.

Greeting them, Tasha climbed into position above the stump. Ignoring the gasps of astonishment from the newcomers, she closed her eyes and focused on the hut itself. As she established her connection to the land once more and the hut stood ready to move, Tasha's fatigue faded.

While the hut traveled, she remained aware of conversation occurring around her, but she managed to keep it from distracting her as she guided the hut over hill and dale. She had a vague sense of where the mine lay in relation to Dawnwatch. However, using her connection to the land, she steered the hut to intercept the creeping corruption extending to the east from Curton.

As the morning dragged on and clouds overtook the sun, Aveline retired to Tasha's private bedroom, and the conversation in the main room lulled. Soon, the others in the hut drifted off to sleep, except for Torben, who maintained his vigil at the window. The next full moon, the Queen, rose the following night. She sensed his anticipation and anxiety at the upcoming event.

In control of his beast, Torben could change forms at will, but the urge would feel strongest during a full moon. She knew he'd be wise to not resist that change, else the next full moon could bring with it an involuntary one.

The clouds grew darker as the day progressed. She stopped a few times to allow her passengers the opportunity to relieve themselves and stretch their legs, but she encouraged them to keep delays to a minimum. Bad weather promised to make their task more difficult. From stories Tasha heard about previous Crow Queens, she understood she could wield some influence over local weather, but she feared doing so would overtax her in light of what they anticipated facing at the mine.

By the time Tasha and the hut overtook the corruption headed toward the mine, the sun neared the western horizon. She turned the hut to run parallel to the blight. Even though it felt to her like a thick ooze of death and decay, she noted the scourge seemed confined to a relatively narrow path, no wider, perhaps, than a horse-drawn cart. At its current pace, she estimated even if the blight continued moving through the night, it would not arrive at the mine until midday the following day.

Tasha increased the pace at which the hut traveled, passing the edge of the blight as she sped toward the mine. With luck, the draks had already begun excavating the cave. She hoped that, together, they could subdue the abomination long enough for them to expose the rift. In truth, Tasha did not know whether the ritual she studied could close it while it remained buried. She sensed there would be no time to explore that possibility.

With the sun gone and illumination from the King and Queen diminished by thick, rain-laden clouds, the glow from lanterns and fires in the new drak village provided the only indication they had arrived at the mine.

Tasha descended from her levitation spot. "We're here. We beat the blight and that abomination, so feel free to stretch your legs outside. I'm going to check on the scourge before I talk to the draks."

Aveline clapped her on the shoulder as she passed. "I'll take care of apprising the draks."

Torben stretched. "I'll get us some fresh meat."

"I'll go with you." Abigail stepped forward. "I'm handy with a bow."

Torben held up his hand. "I hunt alone. Stay with the others."

Ignoring her protests, he descended the stairs. Aveline led the others outside, and Tasha sat in front of the basin. She sought out the blight. As she suspected, its pace remained much slower than the hut. It had not yet reached the place where she, Aveline, and Vasco made camp the first time they ventured to the mine on horseback.

Scrying verified the creeping blight had not veered from its course; it headed straight for the mine, or, more properly, the chaos rift within the mine. Attempting to focus more closely on the blight filled her with unease. Its form, although unnatural, felt familiar. The world itself formed from raw chaos eons ago, and, as her research indicated, it would eventually return to chaos. The blight represented an acceleration of that decay; yet, it also possessed the familiar presence of both Koloman and the wizard she'd encountered in the mine. Merely approaching it via scrying caused her to feel as if it left an oily film coating her body that then consumed her skin.

After severing contact, the room spun around her. Fighting a wave of nausea, she clutched the sides of the stump. After steadying herself, she released her grip and went outside. The air, although cooler than it had been during the day, felt laden with the promise of rain.

The group had built a small fire a short distance away from the hut. Tasha saw no sign of either Torben or Aveline.

Maxim rose as she approached. "Ah, Crow Queen. I have to admit, that was a most remarkable journey."

"It was very taxing." The warmth of the fire made Tasha want to curl up in bed.

"I hope that Watchman returns with meat before it rains." Abigail sat near the fire, hammering a dent out of her breastplate.

"He shouldn't be long. The rain won't arrive until after midnight." Tasha paused, unsure of how she knew that.

"He has wicked eyes." Lukas frowned, accentuating his frightful jowls. "Like a hungry wolf."

"Torben is one of my closest friends, and I trust him with my life." Tasha hoped Aveline had not shared Torben's story with Maxim or his soldiers, and she expected her endorsement, though overstating the nature of their relationship a bit, settled the matter.

"That's good enough for me." Maxim glanced at Lukas.

The burly man shrugged. "If he fights with us, I don't care what he looks like."

"When Aveline returns, please have her come up to my room. The rest of you can sleep in the main room. I'm sorry there isn't more space; I don't have the energy to reconfigure the hut right now."

"Aren't you going to eat?" Abigail gestured at the fire. "You need your strength."

"There's food in the larder. Tell Aveline she can raid it to supplement whatever meat Torben returns with. I'm going to sleep now."

It took significant effort not to stumble up the stairs. Every step upward felt encumbered by a ball and chain. Her vision blurred as she forced her eyes to remain open. She shut the door to her room as soon as she passed through the doorway, falling into bed as exhaustion took her.

Chapter 66

Aveline returned from her meeting with the drak elders to find Maxim sitting with Lukas and Abigail on the opposite side of the fire from Torben. The haunch of an animal suspended above the fire, hissed, spitting fat as it roasted.

"Ah, Lady Aveline." Maxim gestured at the cooking meat. "Fresh mutton. It shan't be long now. Your friend here wouldn't tell us where the rest of the sheep went.

She glanced at Torben. The dancing firelight reflected in his amber eyes. "Hm, I wonder."

Torben met her gaze, then returned his attention to the fire.

Maxim cleared his throat. "The Crow Queen wants to see you in her room. She said to help yourself to the larder to supplement this fine meal."

"Fine. The draks have begun excavating, but they don't think they'll finish by tomorrow afternoon, even if they go all night, which they're reluctant to do." Aveline watched the flames dance under the haunch. The aroma of rendering mutton fat made her mouth water. "I'll be back shortly."

Aveline entered the hut. She knocked on the door to Tasha's room. Upon hearing no response, she cracked the door open. She found her sprawled across the bed. After closing the door behind her, Aveline sat on the edge of the bed.

She shook the Crow Queen's shoulder gently. "Tasha. You wanted to see me?"

Groaning, the Crow Queen opened one eye. "Oh good, you're back." She stifled a yawn, inciting Aveline to do the same.

"Torben brought back a mutton haunch. The others are puzzled about where the rest of the sheep is. I assume he ate it."

Tasha sat up, nodding. "Probably. Feel free to get more food from the larder. There's bread, cheese, fruit, even ale, I think."

"We will, thanks. Do you want me to bring you anything?"

"No." Shaking her head, Tasha yawned again. "I need sleep. That abomination will be here sometime tomorrow afternoon. I'd like you to stay here with me when you're finished eating. Make sure I'm up not too long after dawn. What's going on with the draks?"

Aveline rubbed the back of her neck. "They've started work, but it's slow going. It's going to be here before they've exposed the rift, I think."

"That's unfortunate. I'll see if there's something I can do in the morning. I'm just too tired right now, Aveline."

She put her hand on Tasha's shoulder. "You've done plenty for now. Sleep. I'll be in soon."

Leaving her friend to her well-earned rest, Aveline returned to the fireside with two loaves of bread, a handful of fruit, and bottles of ale for all. While they ate, Aveline told them about her previous experience at the mine. She included her capture at the hands of the wizard's minions, but she omitted the part about Therkla's aggression toward her.

Mutton juices streamed into Maxim's beard. After wiping his mouth, he waved a bone at Aveline. "What happened to this oroq woman? And the Watchman she was with? They seem like they would have been useful companions now."

"They returned south before I knew we needed to come here." Aveline remained uncertain she would have hired them to help, especially since Maxim regarded his assistance as a duty. "The woman, at least, joined the oroq expedition west, to find Ankor, I think. I don't know what became of Aerik."

"What about you?" Abigail nodded at Torben. "Do you know the Watchman's whereabouts?"

"How would I know?" Torben glowered. "Do you think we're all acquainted down in the Four Watches?"

Abigail looked away, licking her fingers. "I guess it was a foolish question."

"What more can you tell us of this abomination that's destroying the land?" Maxim tossed his bone into the fire before reaching for a nearby loaf of bread.

"I can't tell you what it is, exactly. Koloman swelled up, burst open, and the flesh melted off his bones. From the mess, this... thing rose. It grew two heads before it liquefied and ate through the stone floor of the jail cell. It was like nothing I've ever seen. Tasha says it's all related to the chaos rift. Anything can happen." Aveline shuddered at the memory.

"Can it spray acid on us? Or fire?" Lukas reclined against a stump, his fingers laced across his belly.

"Maybe. I don't know." Aveline sighed. "I can't tell you what the possibilities are when they are literally endless."

"It matters not." Maxim thrust out his chin. "We are two knights of Etrunia and three more accomplished warriors. Along with the Crow Queen, I'm confident we will be victorious."

Aveline hoped Maxim had not misplaced his confidence.

* * *

Tasha slept from utter exhaustion, never noticing when Aveline returned and crawled into bed next to her. She only became aware of the world again when her friend shook her gently the following morning. At once, she became conscious of the rain pounding on the roof of the hut.

She rolled out of bed on the opposite side from Aveline. "It's going to be a quagmire out there."

"We'll deal with it." Aveline pulled on her tunic and breeches. "You'll need your strength for the rift and that thing that's coming."

After freshening up a bit and dressing, Tasha and Aveline joined the others in the main room of the hut. Abigail, moving beside Torben at the window, gazed at the deluge.

"I don't suppose the rain will keep that thing away?" Aveline retrieved several cured sausages from the larder. After cutting each in half, she distributed the meat among the six of them.

"I doubt it." Tasha peered into the basin, focusing her mind on the abomination that was Koloman. After taking a moment to get her bearings, she noticed with dismay its proximity to the mine. "It looks like it kept moving all night, and it's awfully close now. Much closer than I expected."

She looked up from the basin. "We need to get busy."

They scrambled to finish their meal while Tasha moved the hut in front of the cave behind the mine. Once she settled the hut in position, they entered the downpour, joining the draks who excavated the entrance. Tasha observed their progress, but it was precious little. The air filled with the *clank-clank-clank* of draks attacking fallen rocks with pickaxes. Other draks collected small pieces, and, after loading them into baskets, they carried them away. Still others, using axes to shape deadfall, reinforced the tunnel extending into the hillside. The troupe of humans sheltered in the entrance, briefly escaping from the pelting precipitation.

"I hate fighting in the rain." Abigail scowled, making a rude gesture toward the sky.

"I love it." Lukas swung his maul in a practice arc. "Things go further in mud."

A drak approached them, his white scales glistening like ice in the rain. "I am Klatt the Younger, my sire put me in charge of the excavation. I'm sorry, Crow Queen, we've worked through the night, but we just can't move enough of these rocks. We'll be digging another week at least."

"I don't think that thing is going to wait a week, Tasha." Aveline held her shield over her head, allowing the rain to pour off it behind her.

Tasha felt the mud and grass squish between her toes. "I didn't want to try this because I've never done it, but perhaps the Earth Mother can help me move this debris out of the way. Klatt, please order all your people to a safe distance. Aveline, help them. Make sure they're not in the direct path of the blight, if you can. And be wary, other creatures may emerge from the rift; it's the only way chaos beasts can enter this world. They'll be drawn to it from the other side."

She wiggled her toes, digging them deeper into the muddy earth. Spreading her arms, she closed her eyes. Tasha warned her birds to stay as far away as possible. She visualized the collapsed cave before her. The life-force of the draks beaconed as they scurried away from the worksite. She waited until they joined Aveline and the others at the far side of the hut.

Besides earth and mud, piles of granite boulders the size of livestock blocked the rift. The fissure's ever-shifting presence thrummed in the foreground of her perception, as if beckoning her forward. She felt the abomination that was Koloman approaching. Not quite to the grove where she waited with the horses the first night, but close.

While unsure where to start at first, Tasha remembered two things capable of breaking rocks given time: water and roots. She could do nothing with water. Roots, however, pervaded the area. Trees in the forest surrounding the mine were old, and their roots ran deep. Grasses, shrubs, and bushes also bore roots which could aid her.

She visualized the roots as fingers, curling around the rocks and earth that blocked her way. Resisting her at first, the roots soon became accustomed to her touch and submitted to the power behind it. Roots of shrubs and young trees writhed their way deeper into the earth around her path. Roots of older trees surrounded the boulders.

A scream of primal rage filled her consciousness. Lights shimmered in her mind, like the play of colors on oil-slicked water. The abomination, too, felt her power. Understanding her purpose, it passed through the campsite where she and

Aveline had stayed during that first trip to the mine. Trees blackened and withered at the abomination's touch, transforming healthy, full-grown timbers into decaying stumps. Tasha felt the world itself howl in anguish.

Cresting the hill overlooking the mine, the abomination, tempted by the small village of draks, changed course. Tasha redoubled her efforts, reaching out to it.

That's not me. If you want to stop me, you have to come here. Straight here, not around the mountain.

Without knowing if it could hear her thoughts or even understand her, she continued taunting it. Just before making contact with the first hut, it veered off.

Suddenly, the earth shuddered as it split above the chaos rift.

The roots weren't deep or strong enough yet to fully excavate the land obscuring her objective. She urged them to work faster.

Mustering enough energy to interrupt her focus, Tasha shouted, "It's here!"

Chapter 67

"What is she doing?" Scowling, Abigail regarded Tasha standing motionless in the rain.

"Crow Queen stuff." Aveline trusted Tasha, but she'd be hard-pressed to explain Tasha's methods to anyone.

"Can you not feel it?" Torben gazed at Tasha. Water streamed down his face, dripping off his beard. "She calls upon the Earth Mother to rend the earth and expose the rift."

"I just hope she has enough left to close it when she's finished." Aveline glanced at the collapsed cave opening, searching for a sign of movement before returning her gaze to her friend.

From where they waited, the landscape appeared unaffected by Tasha's efforts, no matter how long they observed her. Water droplets pinged off Aveline's armor and shield, a constant high-pitched drumming accented by the occasional rumble of thunder.

Even through the din of falling rain, wind, and distant thunder, Aveline sensed an unnatural stillness. Tapping her arm, Torben pointed. Leaves on the trees atop the nearby ridge turned black and fell. The trunks withered, rotting before their eyes.

Tasha's voice rose above the gale. "It's here!"

Like shadowy fingers reaching down the hillside, the blight crept toward them at an alarming pace, destroying all it touched. The abomination that was Koloman burst from the earth, showering them with dirt and rotten vegetation. Its bulbous, pink form glistened in the rain. Snarling, the drak head snapped its teeth at the group, while the wizard's head sneered.

It pointed at them with a swollen hand. "You cannot fight the primal force from whence you came and to which you will return."

"Maris's bloody spear, what is that?" Abigail nocked an arrow, then drew back her bow. Streaking through the rain, the arrow sped toward their enemy. The drak head snapped at it, catching the arrow and biting it in half. Its arm shot forward, extending the distance between them. The appendage slapped Abigail away as though she were a fly.

Holding her shield before her, Aveline slammed her mace into the arm as it retracted past her. Her weapon bounced off its rubbery skin. Roaring, Lukas charged from behind her. Maxim approached from its flank, raising his sword, and Torben hurled one of his axes toward the abomination.

From the corner of her eye, Aveline saw Abigail land near the drak workers. The warrior slid through the mud, barreling over several of the diggers. Groaning, she slipped as she failed to regain her footing. A few of the draks assisted her up, while others raised their picks and charged forward.

Passing the knight-captain, Torben's axe spun end over end, finally embedding itself into the abomination's chest. The thing that once was Koloman plucked it out. The creature threw it toward Torben, the axe dripping ichor as it spun. The southerner slid under the spinning weapon.

Now I wish I'd brought my sword. Aveline continued her approach, holding her shield high as the abomination's arm shot toward her. Impacting the center of her shield, it drove her backward through the mud. She widened her stance to keep from falling. Using her shield for cover, she repeatedly bashed the rubbery appendage.

Hurry up, Tasha. Aveline lifted her weight off one foot, allowing the abomination's arm to push past her. She thrust down with her shield, leaping forward. Throwing her weight on it, she embedded the edge into the appendage. The rubbery tentacle proved too tough to sever, however, and she succeeded only in pinning it to the ground. Retracting, the arm dragged her toward its body.

One of the draks, with his pick raised above his head, ran past Aveline. He swung it in an arc toward the abomination's chest. The creature caught it, lifting the drak in front of its reptilian head. Upon opening its reptilian mouth, it spewed an inky black miasma all over the digger.

The drak screamed as his scales blackened. His flesh peeled away in sheets, revealing raw, twitching muscle underneath. As the abomination continued spewing oily mist on its victim, the drak's muscles withered. The tissues sloughed off, revealing the organs beneath. Then they, too, rotted away until only bones remained on the upper half of the drak's body.

Aveline pushed away from the creature's arm, slipping in the mud. She swung her mace wildly, catching the abomination's wizard head. With its jaw dangling from its face, it turned a baleful gaze on her. The creature drew back its arm, readying it to strike her.

Just then, Maxim dove forward, thrusting his sword into the abomination's side. Wheeling on Maxim, the beast knocked Aveline into the mud once more. The knight-captain backpedaled in the muck. Clinging to his sword, Maxim planted a boot on the abomination's torso. He ripped out his blade and fell, sprawling.

Aveline scrambled to reclaim her shield and regain her footing. Torben slid past, hacking with his remaining axe. Another arrow flew over her head, courtesy of Abigail, striking the abomination's chest. The beast snapped off the shaft. A third leg sprouted from its backside. After two tentacles erupted from its torso, they whipped at Aveline and Maxim.

Aveline glanced over at her friend. Seemingly unaware of and unmoved by the battle that raged nearby, Tasha stood near the cave entrance with her arms spread. *By the gods, Tasha, hurry!*

* * *

Working the earth with roots, a slow, arduous process, reminded Tasha of untangling a knotted ball of yarn. Each time she thought she'd made progress, she would find another knot, another complication. Exposing the rift took all her effort. However, at the edge of her perception, she felt the abomination destroy the drak. She also felt the efforts of her friends to keep the creature's attention fixed on themselves.

Proximity to the abomination, as it fought her companions, pained Tasha. Its existence, an unnatural fusion of two entities combined with elemental chaos, was an affront to the gods, who created order from that chaos.

Tasha redoubled her efforts. Thus far, she'd reserved energy to later deal with the abomination, but if they couldn't access the chaos rift, she supposed their plan would be rendered moot. Her perception of the world around her darkened. She felt the earth yield.

The hillside tore, splitting open like an overripe melon. A thundering crash surrounded her, the reverberation of thousands of tons of boulders and earth moving aside at her will. Trees cracked and shattered, falling away, as the ground which supported them catastrophically rearranged itself.

The shaking earth unbalanced her, and she slipped in the mud. Landing hard on her back, she lay gasping for breath. She rolled over, pushed to her knees, and regarded the cave entrance. The rift still lay concealed under layers of rock; yet, through the dust and driving rain, she detected faint flashes of kaleidoscopic light.

Rather than risk another fall, Tasha remained kneeling. She suppressed a flash of annoyance toward the mud covering her skirt as she splayed it, allowing her skin to make a physical connection to Calliome. She prepared again to move the earth.

Before she fully regained her connection to the Earth Mother, she noticed a flash of motion headed toward her.

Tasha ducked just as a fleshy tentacle whipped through the air where her head had been a mere second earlier.

She focused on the earth, willing the roots to obey her. Around where she knelt, vines erupted, reaching toward the sky. Enclosing her in a wooden dome, they hardened. The root shell shuddered as the tentacles beat against it, but spongy flesh, no matter its origin, proved no match for wood.

Kneeling, Tasha pressed her hands in the earth, focusing on the hillside covering the rift once more.

Chapter 68

Aveline and Abigail stood back to back, fending off thrashing tentacles and muscular arms. The abomination, extruding new appendages, engaged those protecting the Crow Queen and her work.

Thrusting her shield to block a meaty fist, Aveline risked a glance toward Tasha. She felt the earth rumble. The hillside split, showering them with earth and rocks. Lukas flew past her at the end of a tentacle, and she saw Tasha fall.

Resisting the urge to rush to her friend's aid, Aveline fought to maintain control and trust Tasha. Torben ran toward the Crow Queen. Just as Tasha ducked to avoid a tentacle rocketing in her direction, Torben launched himself at one of the other ones thrashing between them. He hacked at it with his axe until it severed. Another tentacle wrapped itself around him, then flung him beyond Aveline's sight.

Upon ducking under the fist pounding Aveline's shield, Maxim swung his sword upward, cutting through the fleshy appendage. Mixing with the pouring rain, blood and ichor drenched them.

The abomination lunged, bashing them with its body. Aveline landed on her back, then rolled to safety. Barreling forward, the beast trampled Abigail and Maxim.

Finding a patch of rough terrain, Aveline regained her footing. The abomination beat its fists against Maxim's back, denting his armor. It captured him with a tentacle, then lifted him in front of the drak head. Charging with a primal scream, Aveline brought her mace down on the reptilian cranium, driving the upper jaw downward and causing the beast to bite off its own tongue.

After tossing Maxim aside, the abomination turned its attention to the knight-captain. Raising her shield, Aveline backed away as it advanced. From the corner of her eye, she saw Abigail, who, still on the ground, thrust her sword into the abomination's leg. The creature screamed when the blade pierced its flesh. The drak head's bloody maw opened, spewing oily miasma toward Abigail. Scurrying away, she reached safety only after the greasy cloud enveloped her arm.

The warrior woman gritted her teeth, stifling her anguish, as the substance digested her hand and forearm. Upon summoning the last bit of strength remaining in her dominant arm, she tossed her sword to her left hand, retreating. The muscles sloughed off her right arm, exposing the bones and rendering it useless.

Seizing Maxim's sleeve, Aveline dragged him to safety before helping him up. Blood ran from the corner of his mouth, but he set his jaw in grim determination. Raising his sword, he charged the abomination. Gashing the blubber on its back, he brought his weapon down.

The creature spun on Maxim before melting into the earth. A black stain spread from where the abomination previously stood.

"Back! Get back! Stay away from it." Aveline snatched Maxim away from the stain. Abigail, holding her ruined arm close to her body, scrambled backward toward bare rocks.

With his left eye swollen shut, Lukas stumbled toward them. Maxim gestured for him to keep clear, but the burly man, squinting, shook his head. He limped in their direction.

"The ground, man, look at the ground." Maxim pointed toward the black circle of expanding rot. "Move away from it."

Holding his head, Lukas fixated on the area where Maxim pointed. Aveline could almost see the man's addled mind parse each word of Maxim's order.

She lunged toward him, but Maxim held her back. The blight reached Lukas's feet, then climbed his body. His eyes bulged. He shrieked as rotting flesh sloughed off his bones. Thrashing and screaming, he fell into the blight. Still alive, he decomposed, liquefying before their very eyes.

From the pool of rot and gore, the abomination—three legs, two muscular arms, and a multitude of tentacles—rose again. Both heads turned toward Tasha, still encased in a protective dome of wood.

Tentacles shot from its body, flinging Aveline and Maxim away. It charged the Crow Queen.

* * *

Mustering as much power as possible, Tasha called upon the land to part. She poured her very life-force into the roots and vines in the ground. She rent the cave entrance, as if it were silk. Unleashing a wave of chaos energy, the hillside gave way, exposing the rift.

The wooden dome around her shattered, showering her with sharp splinters. She moved just as the abomination reached her. The wizard and drak heads snarled. Both heads laughed as the creature brought its arms down on her.

The impact knocked her away, breaking her connection with the land. She slid through the mud, snatching hold of a root to arrest her motion. Blinking the water and mud out of her eyes, she noticed the land had split apart from the rift in a straight line, creating a deep crevasse.

Her feet barreled over the edge.

"Tasha!" Torben lunged toward her, diving into the mud. Arresting her fall, he dragged her away from the crevasse alongside him.

The Crow Queen's shoulder ached from being wrenched. A stabbing sensation accompanied her every breath.

Lifting her, Torben set Tasha on some newly exposed boulders, not yet covered with slick mud.

Roaring, the abomination charged, its tentacles flailing. Beside her, she heard a primal scream, but when she turned her head in the direction of the sound, she saw only shadows. Tasha wiped her eyes; yet, despite her efforts, the world remained a hazy blur. The rift illuminated the creature before her, however, like a lantern revealing a hidden horror.

Upon opening its mouth, the drak head spewed greasy, black smoke toward her. She pushed herself backward, attempting to avoid it. Someone else collided with the abomination. When Tasha drew her cloak around her, her vision cleared slightly. She viewed a great, shaggy wolf locking its jaws around the snout of the drak head.

Torben's claws scratched deep gouges in the abomination's flesh, spraying ichor through the air. He pushed, the muscles in his legs bulging, until the abomination slid backward. Torben continued pressing the creature of chaos toward the crevasse. Even though the creature's three legs provided it stability, they did little to prevent it from sliding in the mud as the werewolf proved its equal in strength.

Tasha stepped forward until her feet rested in earth once again. She felt electricity in the air. Summoning the power of Gaia coursing through her, she raised her arms above her head.

"Torben, let him go!" Her voice cut through the rain and cacophony of battle. To his credit, Torben shoved the abomination, allowing the momentum to hurl him backward. Tasha allowed the energy to intensify. The clouds above flashed.

A bolt of lightning impacted the mud just in front of the abomination. The earth exploded beneath it, thrusting the creature over the edge of the precipice and shooting steam into the air.

Through the Earth Mother, Tasha felt, more than saw, people approaching. Aveline, Maxim, Abigail, and a handful of draks caught up to her. Closing her eyes, she drew her cloak around her. A dim, hazy vision of the world provided her only insight into the action around her. The knight-captain peered over the edge.

She swore. "Tinian's sacred lance. Why won't you die!"

A tentacle shot into the air, whipping past her. She swatted at it with her mace. A dozen more tentacles sailed over the edge of the crevasse, finding purchase on trees and boulders to pull itself up.

Aveline turned to Tasha. "Close that rift. We'll keep this thing busy."

Each began to hack, bash, and gnaw the nearest tentacle. Tasha faced the rift. The kaleidoscopic colors seemed clear as day to her, cutting through the haze of her vision.

Gripping her amulet, she called upon her arcane knowledge as well as her connection to the Earth Mother. *I hope it's enough.* "*Stenee pyealee. Stenee pyealee.*" Tasha repeated the phrase over and over, pouring as much arcane energy as she could muster into the rift. With each repetition, she felt the rift grow smaller, bit by minuscule bit.

Her shoulder ached, her ribs throbbed, and her legs trembled with fatigue. She forced herself to focus only on the rift. Tasha compelled herself to press onward. "*Stenee pyealee.*"

Chapter 69

Beating tentacles into a bloody pulp frustrated Aveline, and she again lamented the absence of her sword. Despite pummeling the rubbery flesh with her mace, the tentacles did not loosen their grip.

Thus far, the abomination remained unable to pull itself out of the crevasse. Maxim sliced and hacked through tentacles with his blade, as did Abigail, despite her horrific injury. For each limb they severed, another writhed its way toward a tree.

Draks, armed only with picks, attacked the tentacles as though they were rocks to be busted apart. It took a team of draks several strikes to completely sever a tentacle; however, they remained more efficient than Aveline and her mace.

Torben bounded to her, then gnawed on the appendage she'd been bashing until it tore apart. Ichor dripped from his jaws as he locked eyes with her. Staring into the slavering maw of the werewolf, her heart skipped a beat, but, behind his amber eyes, Aveline recognized Torben's humanity.

In a flash, he attacked another tentacle. Aveline observed Tasha holding her amulet aloft. Sapphire wisps of aether swirled around her in a whirlwind of arcane energy before pouring into the rift.

She detected motion in the breach. Reflecting the light from the fissure in a rainbow of sparkles, a giant creature covered in crystals lumbered forward, freeing itself from the chaos.

Unleashing a roar like the sound of grinding gravel, the crystal creature raised a boulder-like fist, preparing to pound Tasha into the mud.

Aveline screamed, charging forward. She deflected the creature's first blow with her shield, leaping in front of the Crow Queen. Forcing her to her knees, the impact reverberated through her shield and into her arm.

"No. You can't have her!" Aveline swung her mace, slamming it into the creature's fist as it swung at Tasha a second time. Shattering upon impact, crystal shards exploded from the creature's hand.

The crystal creature focused its attention on the warrior who injured it, swinging wildly at Aveline. She deftly dodged the blows until one caught her on the shoulder.

The impact, as strong as a charging horse, spun her. She pitched forward, gasping. Raising her shield at the last second, she landed face first in it instead of on the ragged rocks. Rolling away from the boulders, she noticed a rocky fist sailing toward her head. She swung her mace, batting it away.

Avoiding another strike, Aveline used the momentum to tuck her feet under herself. Pushing off a nearby boulder, she leapt to her feet. After catching another blow with her shield, she returned the creature's punch with one of her own.

Roaring, the crystal creature swung its arm in a wide arc, catching the head of her mace and ripping it from her hands. From behind her, she heard another roar. Risking a glance, she observed the abomination that once was Koloman hauling itself out of the crevasse. It slipped as picks, swords, and sharp teeth assaulted three more tentacles.

"Hurry it up, Tasha." Another blow from the crystal creature caught Aveline's flank. She twisted in agony, feeling her ribs snap. Grimacing from the pain, she rushed the creature, holding her shield in front of her. Slamming into it, she pushed it toward the rift. She noticed the scintillating field of color seemed smaller. As she drew close to the fissure, its energy set her hair on end.

Tasha's voice rose to a crescendo. "*Stenee pyealee. Stenee pyealee!*"

Grunting, Aveline shoved the creature backward just as the rift glimmered. Light from the rift extinguished, plung-

530

ing them into darkness. A flash of lightning reflected off the remaining crystals as the creature wobbled, then disintegrated into a pile of rubble.

"Great work, Tasha." Aveline turned, witnessing her collapse. Racing to her side, she fell to her knees alongside her fallen friend. She pulled Tasha into her lap, ensuring the Crow Queen still breathed before noticing the abomination still fighting the others.

"Damn it." She set Tasha down. "Don't you die on me."

Aveline rose to her feet, spotting her mace nearby. Scooping it up, she rejoined the battle.

The abomination hauled itself over the edge of the crevasse, resting its bulk on the jagged rocks and rent earth. Wrapping the tentacle upon which Torben chewed around the werewolf, it lifted him before the drak maw. Torben snapped at it, writhing helplessly.

As the fraying tentacle they attacked fractured, the draks cheered. Likewise, Maxim hacked through another. Abigail severed the final tentacle with a furious screech. The abomination slipped, teetering on the edge of the fissure. Thunder rumbled through the sky.

The beast's drak head spewed its oily miasma on Torben, washing it over his chest and abdomen before the weight of its body falling over the edge jerked it away. Abigail dove, slicing her sword through the tentacle holding the werewolf. Slamming into the mud, she slid toward the precipice. Charging, the assembled draks intercepted her. Together, they prevented her descent.

Torben fell, whimpering. Dropping her mace and shield, Aveline raced to him. She observed pink tissue twitching behind a window of parallel bones. The fur and flesh of his stomach excoriated, and ropy coils of viscera spilled onto the ground. He yelped like a wounded puppy.

Aveline searched his eyes, holding his hand. "Torben, can you understand me?"

The werewolf nodded. "Tasha..."

"She's alive." Aveline dared not convey she didn't know the extent of her friend's injuries.

Torben's voice became a guttural rasp. "Tell her... I..." His eyes fluttered closed. Behind the bare bones, the twitching ceased. Reverting to his human form, his body shrank, his fur shed in clumps, and his snout shortened. As he lay motionless and naked in the rain, Aveline witnessed his wounds closing. Finally, he drew a ragged breath.

Abigail stood above Aveline and Torben, shivering, as she cradled her arm. "Damn, they're hard to kill. I'm glad he's on our side."

Grateful for the rain concealing her tears as they fell, Aveline studied the woman. "What about the wizard-Koloman beast?"

"No idea. Can't see anything down there."

Aveline approached the crevasse, then peered over the edge into the darkness. In the distance behind the hills, she saw the boundary of the weather front, beyond which followed lighter skies. She determined by the force of the wind they still had a while to wait.

A flash of distant lightning answered Aveline's question. A severed, shattered body lay hundreds of feet below. Rivers of blood and ichor splattered the rocks at the bottom. "I think it's dead."

"Thank the gods for that." Maxim limped over, joining the two warriors. "Perhaps when the rain stops, we can burn what's left."

"Agreed. In the meantime, let's get Tasha and Torben to the hut. Abigail, go on ahead of us. We'll take care of that arm as soon as we bring them in."

The woman scowled at the skeletal hand dangling lifeless from her arm. "Damn it. That was my favorite arm."

* * *

Tasha floated above the land. Calliome's sun shone bright. Only a few clouds dotted the sky, creating soft shadows that sailed over the hills and trees. Below her, she viewed the drak village at the mine. The industrious, diminutive people worked to repair the damage caused by the abomination's attack.

A little way to the east, around the side of one of the hills, she found the hut, standing amidst a field of rubble. A new gorge spread east and slightly north from the sight of the collapsed cave, a gouge in the earth leading away from the now-closed chaos rift. At the bottom, she saw what remained of the beast that Koloman became, a bloated mass of rotting flesh. Sunlight glinting off sparkling jewels drew her eye to the mouth of the collapsed cave. She viewed the crumbled form of the crystal chaos creature that tried to prevent her from closing the rift.

Already, she felt new life sprouting in the churned land surrounding the gorge. Seeds took root, feeding on the blood spilled that night and returning to the earth what remained behind. From the destruction, the cycle of life continued. Even the carcass of the abomination nourished carrion and fungus, a creature born of chaos feeding the order of life.

Tasha searched for her friends, but she saw no sign of them. It made sense they would have moved away from the scene of the battle to care for the wounded, and she thought perhaps they had returned to the hut.

Her eyes fluttered open. A foggy light filled her vision. Although she saw only the diffuse haze around her, she felt the comfort of her bed. Someone had undressed her before laying her under the covers. Nevertheless, she sat up and felt around her.

"Oh good, you're awake." Aveline's voice sounded nearby. Tasha turned toward the source.

"Where are you?"

"I'm here." Aveline took her hand.

Tasha turned toward her friend. "Aveline, I can't see you."

The knight-captain gasped. "Your eyes… they're…"

Tasha felt her face. Her eyes still resided in their sockets, but they saw nothing except light and dark. "My cloak. Where's the Mantle of the Crow Queen?"

"It's here." Aveline released her hand. Tasha heard her take a few steps before returning. She put the cloak around Tasha's shoulders. "We took it off to dry. I stripped everything else off you too. You wouldn't believe how much mud and gore there was on everything except the mantle, of course. I wish my clothes stayed clean like that. I washed you up as best I could last night."

"Thank you." Tasha pulled the cloak around her. Shapes appeared out of the haze. Aveline came into focus, peering into Tasha's eyes.

"They're solid black, Tasha. What happened?"

"I think it's the price I paid for what I did yesterday. Curing the plague for the whole town cost Annika her youth and vitality. Ripping open the earth to expose the rift cost me my sight. A small price to pay, all things considered."

Tasha glanced around the room. Close objects seemed clear, although they appeared in shades of muted violet. Distant objects appeared fuzzier, but they were recognizable. "The cloak lets me see after a fashion. Though not in the way you see."

Aveline handed her a skirt and tunic. Tasha shrugged off her cloak before pulling the tunic over her head. She winced at the throbbing in her ribs as she bent to put on the skirt. "How are the others?"

"Maxim and I got banged up, but we'll be all right." Aveline glanced toward the door to the main room. "Torben, well, if he weren't a werewolf, he'd be dead. He's sleeping in the other bed."

"Last night was a full moon." Tasha wanted to go to him, but she felt it would be inappropriate to tell everyone else to leave. "He'll need food when he awakens, a lot of it."

"Lukas... the abomination killed him. Abigail lost her arm, well, most of it. It's pretty awful to look at. She needs a healer; they're going to need to remove it below the elbow, I think." Aveline chuckled. "She seems more annoyed by it than anything. I tell you... I may try to steal her from Maxim."

"I should go see them. The abomination that was Koloman is dead. I saw it... while I was sleeping."

Aveline raised her eyebrow. "I don't understand how that's possible, but after everything I've seen the last few days, I'll take your word for it."

Tasha and Aveline entered the main room. Curled up on the bed, Torben lay in a deep sleep with his chest rising and falling. Maxim sat in the chair by the window. Abigail sat in the other chair, cradling her injured arm in her lap. A blanket covered it. She nodded at Tasha and Aveline.

"May I see?" Tasha gestured toward the warrior's arm.

"If you really want to. Sorry about the blanket, but it was all I could find." Abigail revealed the skeletal arm protruding from a stump of gangrenous flesh.

Wincing, Tasha lifted the hand. "Are you in much pain?"

"You'd think so, wouldn't you?" Abigail shook her head. "It doesn't actually hurt at all. If the stump didn't stink and I could move the fingers, I'd consider keeping it. Do you think that's too macabre?"

"Put a glove on and no one could tell." Tasha returned the arm to Abigail's lap before covering it. "Mother Anya has some good healers at Cybele's Church in Curton. They'll be able to remove it for you."

"Maxim?" Tasha approached the knight. "Are you ready to go back to Dawnwatch?"

"I am." The knight rose. "When I saw the skies were clear this morning, I returned to the gorge. What we fought is definitely dead. Carrion birds were already fattening themselves on its carcass." He patted his pouch. "I took the liberty of taking some of the stones from that rock creature Lady Aveline defeated, as well. Along with the treasury we discovered at Dawnwatch, they'll go a long way to funding the garrison until we receive our supplies from Almeria. I hope that's all right."

Tasha smiled, nodding. "I'm happy someone is gaining use of it."

"You know, Curton needs an orphanage. A donation from the Dawnwatch Garrison would build goodwill." Smirking, Aveline crossed her arms.

Turning to the back door, Tasha summoned an image of Dawnwatch's gatehouse. Abigail's eyes widened at the sight.

Maxim approached Abigail. "Obviously, your injury is grievous enough that you're released from your obligation to me. However, there's still a place for you at Dawnwatch, if you feel up to it. After you heal, of course."

"I appreciate that, sir." Rising, Abigail saluted him with her left hand. "I'll consider it."

"Lady Aveline." Maxim fished through his pouch of gems, then placed several large ones on the edge of the basin before saluting. He nodded at Tasha before striding through the back door. As soon as he passed through, Tasha changed the scene to the alley next to Cybele's Church in Curton.

"Aveline? If you're ready, you could take Abigail through. I'll come back to town in a few days. I want to rest some more."

Aveline scooped up the gems, putting them in her pouch before hugging her friend. "Take all the time you need. I think life will be good and boring for a long while now."

"One can hope."

After Abigail and Aveline stepped through the doorway to Curton, Tasha closed the portal behind them. She grazed in the larder until she heard Torben stirring. She piled cured meat, cheese, and bread upon a plate for him.

"Hungry?" She entered the main room, holding the meal before her.

Bleary eyed, he sat up, the covers sliding off his bare chest. He ran his hands along his chest and stomach. The flesh, although pink, showed no other sign of injury. "Mm. That beast tasted awful. I'm famished and, frankly, amazed to be here."

Tasha sat on the edge of the bed. "I'm certainly happy you're here."

Gasping, he studied her eyes. "Your…"

"There was a price to pay for what I did last night. I'll explain later, but I'm fine." She handed him the plate, kissing his cheek. "Help yourself to what's in the larder if you're still hungry. I'm going to have a nice, hot bath."

Tasha left him to eat, passing through her bedroom to the bath. Steam permeated the room as the bathing vessel filled itself with fragrant water. She slipped out of her clothes, feeling for the edge of the vessel. She swung one leg over the edge at a time before lowering herself into the water. Gritting her teeth, she slowly grew accustomed to the temperature, and she let it soothe her aches and dissolve her stress.

Chapter 70

After delivering Maxim's donation to Mother Anya and escorting Abigail to Mother Anya's healers, Aveline headed straight for the baths in Old Town. She envied Tasha her private, self-filling bathing vessel, but she knew the temptation to fall asleep in the tub would be irresistible.

Aveline resisted another temptation—the desire to return straight home and sleep the rest of the day. First checking in at the citadel, she then sought out the city council to inform them of their success.

True to her prediction, the next several days proved uneventful, mercifully boring, in fact. She returned to her patrols with a fresh spring in her step, finding joy with each report of nothing unusual.

Tasha returned to Curton a few days later, and they enjoyed several quiet evenings together reviewing the events that occurred.

"How's Abigail?" Sitting before the hearth in Aveline's home, Tasha sipped her mug of mead.

"Mending well. I've offered her a job on the city watch. Like you said, I need to employ more women. I think she's tempted. And Torben?"

His name brought a smile to Tasha's lips. "He's been helpful. I can see with the cloak, but I miss seeing colors. Flowers are different and brilliant, but I'm having to rely on him to tell me what they actually look like. I'm having to learn how things look with the cloak. He's… I…"

Tasha's cheeks flushed.

"You like him, don't you?"

The Crow Queen nodded. "More than that. He's so kind, very devoted. I just have to break him of thinking he must serve me now. I haven't felt this way about someone, especially a man, in many years."

"Before the elf woman, yes?" They didn't talk about past loves often. Life seemed too short to spend reliving painful memories.

"Lorelei." Tasha regarded the ceiling. "You know, were it not for her, this all would have turned out very differently. I wouldn't have been inspired to follow a mystic's path. I wouldn't be Crow Queen."

"Funny. Someone over a decade ago set you on the path that let you close that rift and defeat the Kolbomination." Aveline raised her cup to Lorelei.

"The what?" Tasha laughed.

"Koloman the abomination. Kolbomination." Aveline giggled. "Something Abigail came up with when I told her about how it all happened."

Tasha drained her mug. "I should go home. I want to tell Torben how I feel. I want to... well, you probably don't want the details."

Aveline clucked her tongue. "Not right now, I don't. Be careful, though, all right? I don't trust him not to wolf out on you."

"I will, and I do trust him. He's earned it." Tasha hugged Aveline before snapping her cloak and disappearing in a cloud of crows.

* * *

When Tasha returned home, she found Torben sitting outside the hut, carving a hunk of walnut. A pair of rabbits, skinned and dressed, hung from a nearby branch. He pointed at them with his knife. "I resisted the urge to gorge myself. I'd hoped we could dine together tonight."

"That would be wonderful." Tasha led Torben inside, then prepared a pot with vegetables and wine. She submerged the rabbits in the concoction, covered it, and slid it into the hearth.

"I'm glad you're here tonight, Torben. I've been wanting you… to talk to you." Tasha bit her lip at the slip.

He did not seem to notice. "I hope nothing is wrong. I've tried to be attentive and helpful."

She stroked his cheek. "Nothing is wrong." Through her crow sight, she no longer saw his amber eyes. "I've grown to care about you very much, Torben. More so than I ever expected."

"I am your devoted…"

She put her finger on his lips. "Is that all I am? Someone to be served? That's not what I want." Tasha took Torben by the hands, leading him to the bed. "It'll be a few hours before the food is ready."

"Tasha… what I am…"

"I cannot think of anyone I would rather be with right now." She put her hands on his face.

Torben leaned toward her. When their lips joined, her heart soared. Warmth engulfed her. His arms slid around her waist, and she drew him back before lying on the bed and pulling him alongside her.

When at last their passion was spent, Tasha smelled the aroma of the finished stew while they lay entwined in each other's arms under the covers. Straddling Torben, she kissed his chest and then his chin before finding his lips with a giggle. She slid off him, fumbling for her cloak.

Upon Torben wrapping it over her shoulders, her crow sight returned. He lifted the pot off the hearth while she retrieved bowls and bottles of ale from the larder. Watching him eat, she smiled. "You know, one day, I'll learn where your lips are. It's easy enough with the cloak on, but it tends to slip off when all the other clothes come off."

"I don't mind if you leave it on, even if the feathers tickle a bit." He chuckled.

They returned to the bed after eating, not bothering to tidy their dishes. The next morning, Tasha decided the extra cleanup was worth their night of passion. She relished the next few days, just her and Torben alone in the woods, getting to know each other in ways she once feared she'd never know someone again.

The next day, Tasha and Torben went to Curton to walk the city market and visit Aveline. Ra-Jareez and his sister worked from Tasha's old apothecary full-time now, selling trinkets and bric-a-brac the faelix siblings acquired from traveling traders. They decided to browse Raj's shop, after explaining all that had happened recently.

"You should sell your carvings here, Torben." Arm in arm, Tasha and he browsed the shop.

"Ah, yes, we would make you a most excellent deal, friend of the Crow Queen." Raj bared his fangs in a smile.

"Split the sale? You take half, and I'll take half?" Torben held his hand out to Raj. Behind the counter, Jazeera crossed her arms, nodding to her brother when he glanced at her for approval.

"Fair enough for us."

They shook on the deal. Later, as Tasha and Torben paused to discuss buying sweets from the baker, they overheard a crier at the nearby intersection.

"Hear ye, hear ye! The city council has appointed a provisional replacement for our deceased Lord Mayor Koloman. Pending approval by the crown, effective immediately, Lady Aveline Durant will serve as Lady Mayor of Curton." The crier, a young man with unruly sandy hair, rolled up the proclamation and trotted to the next location from which to make his announcement.

Tasha stared after him, her jaw agape. Torben gently closed her mouth before putting his arm around her shoulders. "The town is in good hands."

"We're going to have a lot to celebrate at the Dusk of Autumn Festival." Tasha hugged him. They found Aveline at the citadel, sharing a drink with Lieutenant Valon.

"Join us!" Aveline waved them in. Valon brought over two mugs into which Aveline poured mead. Abigail raised her mug in greeting.

"Good to see you all." Tasha hugged her friend. "We just heard from a crier. That's so wonderful, Aveline."

Swigging her mead, the knight-captain swayed slightly. "I'm still not convinced, but I get to stay on as knight-captain of the city watch until the official appointment comes through from Almeria. I got them to turn over Koloman's estate to Mother Anya for her orphanage as well." She turned, pointing at Abigail. "Want a job? The Lady Mayor needs a bodyguard."

"You do?" Abigail raised her stump. "You're drunk."

"Maybe." Grinning, Aveline winked. "But I'll bet you could take on an angry mudder with only one hand and not even break a sweat. It's just for show, anyway. I can handle myself, but as Lady Mayor, it looks bad if it seems I'm spoiling for a fight."

Tasha regarded Abigail. "You seem to be doing well. Apparently, Mother Anya and her acolytes did a superb job."

"You should have seen the look on their faces when I told them I wanted to keep the arm." Abigail laughed. "I thought that poor old woman was going to keel over."

Torben scratched his head. "You kept the arm?"

"It was my favorite arm." Abigail raised her mug. "I have the good sense not to leave it just laying on tables and such. I suppose I'll need a place to stay if I'm going to be your bodyguard, Lady Mayor."

Aveline clapped her on the shoulder. "You can bunk here until we get it all sorted."

Tasha took Torben aside while Aveline, Valon, and Abigail discussed their futures. "I'm going to return to the hut to move it to the hill between Mudders' Gate and the orchard. Meet me there later?"

"Yes. I want to visit the smithy and replace my lost sword." Torben kissed her to the cheering of their friends. Tasha said her goodbyes and snapped her cloak around her, returning to the hut in a flutter of crows.

Tasha scried on the mine and cave. The Icescale clan seemed to be settling in, and she detected no lingering effects from the chaos rift. By the time she relocated the hut, she found Torben waiting for her as he practiced with his new blade. The sun, already low in the sky, cast a red-and-orange glow across the wispy clouds. She took him inside for another evening of passion, and, when they remembered, nourishment.

They emerged the next morning to shouts from outside, calling for the Crow Queen. Tasha pulled on her clothes and cloak. "Time to get back to work, I suppose."

"Perhaps I'll have a hunt today. Fancy some venison?" Torben pulled on his boots, sitting on the edge of Tasha's bed.

"That'd be nice." Tasha glanced over her shoulder at him. "I'll be outside."

She entered the main room, greeted by Revan and Korbin. After she opened the door, she descended the steps. To her surprise, Katka and two other wizards, the siblings Hayden and Jorden, she assumed, were the people shouting for her. Katka's once-stylish robes were now covered in dirt from weeks of travel. The two wizards from Vlorey dressed alike, but with only her crow sight, Tasha couldn't determine the color of their simple light-trimmed robes.

"We're here to close the rift." Katka spread her arms with a grin. "We made excellent time. Dolios was with us on the journey."

Tasha laughed. "You're too late. I had to go it alone."

She invited them in, then related the story of Koloman's demise, the rise of Kolbomination, and how they feared if they didn't close the rift then and there, it would spell doom for the town and surrounding area. Continuing, she told them of the price she paid for calling upon the power of the Crow Queen to split the earth and expose the rift.

"A steep price." Furrowing her brow, Katka studied Tasha's eyes. "You can't see anything without the mantle?"

"Just light and dark. But it's an acceptable price to have saved the town." She sighed. "You can bring your horses through the hut one at a time to use the portal to go back to Muncifer. Tell the archmage I'll be happy to help her with her teleportation research. I understand the constraints much better now."

Since sacrificing her sight during her connection with the land that night, Tasha felt more confident about the limits of her power and how it related to the world. She planned to add to Annika's journals and document as much as she could about being Crow Queen, just in case she, too, bore no heirs.

It occurred to her, as she sent the apprentices home, that the end of summer drew close. The Dusk of Autumn festival, and the equinox, a mere week away, heralded the coming harvest, and she knew the people of Curton wanted their Crow Queen there.

The role she once feared now felt right. With Torben and her friend Aveline to aid her, Tasha no longer felt uncertain about her destiny or her past. Although she could not foresee the future, she felt confident events would unfold as they should.

The Crow Queen looked forward to the journey.

Heraldy of Andelosia

Free City of Celtangate

Free City of Ironkrag

Principality of Etrunia

Heraldy of Andelosia

Duchy of Muncifer

Free City of Vlorey

Arcane University

Hans Cummings
Author/Publisher

Author of the fantasy duology: The Foundation of Drak-Anor: *Wings of Twilight* and *Iron Fist of the Oroqs* as well as the Zack Jackson science fiction series, Hans Cummings published his first novel in 2011. Two of his short stories appear in Fear the Boot's Sojourn speculative fiction anthologies. He was Nuvo's Best of Indy—Best Local Author Honoree for 2014 - 2016 and maintains a gaming blog http://doctorstrangeroll.wordpress.com in addition to his writing blog http://vffpublishing.com.

Hans earned a Bachelor of Arts degree in English from Indiana University in 2006. He grew up in Indiana, Germany, and Virginia and returned to Indiana when he was 21. He currently lives in Indianapolis with his wife. Hans's hobbies include tabletop and computer gaming, cooking and smoking meat, and igniting young people's curiosity and passion for science and exploration.

Learn more about this and other works by the author at:
http://vffpublishing.com/

Use Twitter? Follow the author @hccummings

www.ingramcontent.com/pod-product-compliance
Lightning Source LLC
Chambersburg PA
CBHW050839030726
47503CB00007BA/2239